Praise for John Freeman Gill's

THE GARGOYLE HUNTERS

"Marvelously evocative. . . . Exuberant. . . . Eye-opening. . . . [An] urban Indiana Jones–like escapade." —*The New York Times*

"In the spirit of Jonathan Lethem and J. D. Salinger, John Freeman Gill strips the mask off New York City in this poignant, incisive, irreverent novel about fatherhood, art, obsession, creation, and destruction. This is a wonderful, compelling debut."
—Colum McCann, National Book Award–winning
author of *Let the Great World Spin*

"[An] unabashedly charming story. . . . What fantastic adventures these two have while creeping around and up New York buildings in the middle of the night, liberating ornaments that might fall by the wrecking ball tomorrow—or *someday*. There's no job too risky that Watts won't send his son tiptoeing on a crumbling ledge or crawling across a sagging board, or even dangling from a fraying rope to rescue an endangered gargoyle fifty stories off the ground. Looking back, Griffin realizes these were not 'reasonable things for a grown man to ask of a thirteen-year-old boy who wanted only to get close to him,' but at the time, he was thrilled. And frankly, so are we."
—Ron Charles, *The Washington Post Book World*

"*The Gargoyle Hunters* is wonderful, strong, funny, with yards and yards of beautiful writing. Its pages are full of reading pleasures. . . . Extraordinary." —Annie Proulx,
Pulitzer Prize– and National Book Award–winning
author of *The Shipping News* and "Brokeback Mountain"

"John Freeman Gill is a wonderful writer. . . . The novel's going to make you laugh, you'll cry a little bit, and you'll root for this thirteen-year-old, who is one of the great characters."

—Joan Hamburg, WABC Radio, New York City

"A brilliant evocation of many things: the world of a thirteen-year-old boy, with its mixture of thoughtless destructiveness and wrenching emotion; a son's relationship with a charismatic, architecture-loving, thieving father; the endless changes to timeless Manhattan during the crumbling, tumultuous 1970s. Funny, heartbreaking, elegiac, unforgettable—David Mitchell's *Black Swan Green* meets E. B. White's *Here Is New York*."   —Gretchen Rubin, #1 *New York Times* bestselling author of *The Happiness Project*

"Seventies New York comes alive in *The Gargoyle Hunters*. . . . An ambitious, elegiac tale that gazes up at the greats. . . . Wholly original. . . . There's more than enough page-turning action here for any reader to envision the movie adaptation, but back to the central virtue of this buzz-worthy book: the sentences. The screen can't capture those. . . . As Gill writes in the book's final chapter: 'Any New Yorker who's paying attention will tell you that the city is a living, breathing organism at war with itself.' Why do we stay? For stories like this."   —*The Village Voice*

"A stellar debut. . . . Gill, who is a noted expert on historical architecture, brings a DeLillo-like eye for detail to his descriptions of the city while also perfectly capturing the father-son relationship in all its warmth, hero-worship, and, ultimately, disappointment. A bildungsroman rich with symbolism, wistful memory, and unabashed longing, this is a remarkably tender love letter to a city and historical fiction par excellence. For fans of Donna Tartt and Colum McCann."   —*Booklist* (starred review)

"Zounds. *The Gargoyle Hunters* is one amazing novel."

—Caroline Leavitt, *New York Times* bestselling author of *Is This Tomorrow*

"Extravagantly satisfying. . . . It held me, delighted me, and left me enthralled. And it reads, like all the best novels do, as both the encapsulation of private, urgent experience and a radical, inscrutable transformation of the same."

—*The Los Angeles Review of Books*

"Fans of Richard Russo will appreciate the complex dynamic between needy, young Griffin and his father, whose breezy affability masks profound, even abusive, flaws. . . . *The Gargoyle Hunters* is an absorbing family tale and a wise meditation on aging."

—*BookPage*

"*The Gargoyle Hunters* is that rarest of all animals—a beautifully written literary novel that also just happens to be a rollicking, cinematic, ripsnortingly funny tale with action sequences as exciting as those of Hollywood's best films."

—Doug Liman,
director of *The Bourne Identity*,
Mr. & Mrs. Smith, and *Edge of Tomorrow*

"Funny and touching. . . . In much the same way that Donna Tartt and J. D. Salinger capture the city in their stories, Gill has made New York City one of his most vivid main characters. In mordant prose, he has taken a wrecking ball as much to the human heart as he has to the priceless gems of the city's past."

—Mary Morris,
author of *The Jazz Palace*

"A must-read book."

—*New York Post*

"Erudite, irreverent. . . . With a fresh, wry narrative voice, Gill presents a vividly imagined slice of New York history, a quirky portrait of the 1970s and a tender father-son story."

—*Shelf Awareness*

"For those who treasure the dappled beauty of New York's early modern buildings, the plight to protect each cornice and filigree from the scourge of redevelopment is a rather high-stakes drama. It is simple, then, to grasp why *The Gargoyle Hunters* has been received with such delight."

—*The New Criterion*

JOHN FREEMAN GILL

THE GARGOYLE HUNTERS

John Freeman Gill is a native New Yorker and former reporter for the *New York Times* City section. His work has been anthologized in *The New York Times Book of New York* and *More New York Stories: The Best of the City Section of* The New York Times. His writing has appeared in *The Atlantic*, *The New York Times Magazine*, *The New York Observer*, *New York* magazine, *Premiere*, *Avenue*, *Guernica*, *Literary Hub*, *The Washington Post Book World*, *The New York Times Book Review*, and elsewhere. A summa cum laude graduate of Yale University, where he won two prizes and was elected to Phi Beta Kappa, he received an MFA in writing from Sarah Lawrence College. He lives in New York City with his wife, three children, and a smattering of gargoyles.

johnfreemangill.com
facebook.com/johnfreemangillauthor/

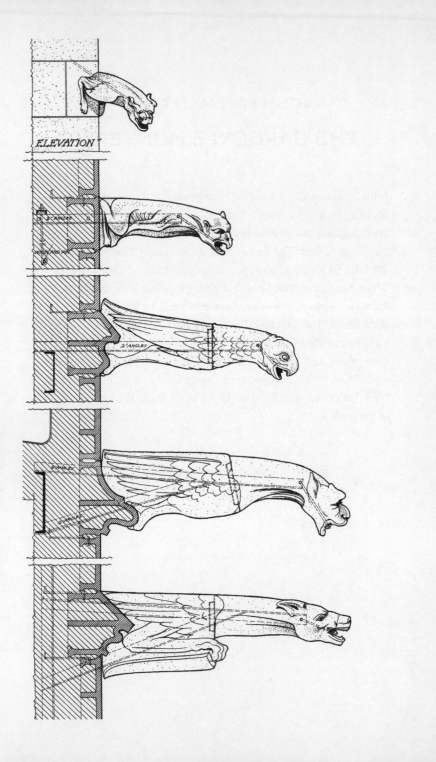

ELEVATION

2" ANGLES
2" ANGLES

2" ANGLES

2" ANGLES

THE GARGOYLE HUNTERS

A Novel

JOHN FREEMAN GILL

Vintage Contemporaries
Vintage Books
A Division of Penguin Random House LLC
New York

For Julina, who believed

FIRST VINTAGE CONTEMPORARIES EDITION, FEBRUARY 2018

Copyright © 2017 by John Freeman Gill

All rights reserved. Published in the United States by Vintage Books, a division of
Penguin Random House LLC, New York, and distributed in Canada by Random House
of Canada, a division of Penguin Random House Canada Limited, Toronto. Originally
published in hardcover in the United States by Alfred A. Knopf, a division of Penguin
Random House LLC, New York, in 2017.

Vintage is a registered trademark and Vintage Contemporaries and colophon are
trademarks of Penguin Random House LLC.

Grateful acknowledgment is made to Hal Leonard LLC for permission
to reprint an excerpt from "Any Major Dude Will Tell You,"
words and music by Walter Becker and Donald Fagen. Copyright © 1974
by Universal Music Corp. and copyright renewed. All rights reserved.
"Gargoyles and Grotesques" images courtesy of Dover Publications.
"Antique Woman Mask" image courtesy of Shutterstock.

The Library of Congress has cataloged the Knopf edition as follows:
Names: Gill, John Freeman, author.
Title: The gargoyle hunters / by John Freeman Gill.
Description: New York: Alfred A. Knopf, 2017.
Identifiers: LCCN 2016012828
Subjects: LCSH: Fathers and sons—Fiction. | Gargoyles—Fiction. |
Decoration and ornament, Architectural—Fiction. | Business enterprises—
Corrupt practices—Fiction. | Self-actualization (Psychology) in adolescence—Fiction. |
New York (N. Y.)—Fiction. | Psychological fiction. | Domestic fiction.
Classification: LCC PS3606.R44547 G37 2017 | DDC 813/.6—dc23
LC record available at https://lccn.loc.gov/2016012828

Vintage Books Trade Paperback ISBN: 978-1-101-97090-4
eBook ISBN: 978-1-101-94689-3

Book design by M. Kristen Bearse

www.vintagebooks.com

Printed in the United States of America
10 9 8 7 6 5 4 3 2 1

New York, thy name is irreverence and hyperbole. And grandeur.

—Ada Louise Huxtable

It'll be a great place if they ever finish it.

—O. Henry

CONTENTS

THE GARGOYLE HUNTERS

PROLOGUE

WHY DO WE STAY? Why do we members of this oddball tribe known as native New Yorkers stick around, decade upon decade, as so much of the city we love, the city that shaped us in all of our wiseacre, top-of-the-heap eccentricity, is razed and made unrecognizable around us?

We are inured to so much bedlam here, so many exotic daily distractions, yet are somehow inexplicably surprised and pained every time a new wound opens up in the streetscape. We barely notice the shrieking ambulance whizzing past or the man in the octopus suit struggling to get all his arms through the turnstile, but let them tear down the Times Square Howard Johnson's or the Cedar Tavern or Rizzoli, let them shutter H&H Bagels or CBGB or the Ziegfeld, and we wince as if our own limb has been severed.

"Every block, it's just one goddamn ghost after another," my big sister, Quigley, told me last year when she'd finally had enough and decided to move away for good. "I'm tired of being homesick in my own hometown."

So why do I, whose ghosts are at least as obstreperous as hers, stay on? Why is this maddening, heartbreaking, self-cannibalizing city the only place where I feel like I'm me?

And what about you? If you've lived in New York long enough to resent some gleaming new condo that pulled a *Godzilla vs. Bambi* on a favorite restaurant or deli or bookstore, then this is your city, too, teeming with your own bespoke ghosts.

As for me and mine, most of the things I need to tell you about happened in the seventies. But it was in late 1965, when I was about to turn five, that I first sensed what it is to love a city that never quite loves you back.

We were not even in New York at the time. We were in our VW Bug, taking a predawn road trip to a mystery destination my father refused to reveal. It was the sharp left turn at the slaughterhouse that awakened me, the momentum burrowing my head deeper into the ribbed warmth of his corduroy armpit. Out the window of our little car, in a now-you-see-it-now-you-don't pocket of yellow light, men in blood-smeared smocks hosed down the pavement, clouds of steam rising into the night. On a wide brick wall, our headlights gliding across it, the faded image of a grinning cartoon cow, its speech bubble saying, "Pleased to Meet You! Meat to Please You!"

We drove on another few minutes, the world still more dark than light. Mom and Quigley murmured groggily in the backseat. When we reached an enchanted point along the highway that looked exactly the same to me as every other part of the highway, Dad pulled off decisively and parked in a marshy softness. Another few cars, three or four, followed his lead, but Dad headed off on foot without hailing or waiting for the others. He preferred to make people keep up with him.

The marsh grasses were just the right height to keep hitting me in the face as we walked, and I didn't much like the way the soggy ground sucked at my Keds. So Dad hoisted me up and let me doze on his shoulder, slobbering contentedly on the rise of muscle beneath his shirt. I was part of him, my whole limp body lifting and subsiding with his breaths. When I opened my eyes again, the darkness had thinned and we were moving through a shadow landscape strewn with hulking oblong shapes. They loomed all around us, tilting this way and that, one across the other like gargantuan pick-up sticks. The ground crunched beneath Dad's feet as he picked his way carefully over the treacherous terrain, his broad hand flat against my back. The air smelled burnt.

Daylight was seeping into the sky now from the marsh's edge, faster every moment, until at last the colossal tilted shadows around us resolved themselves into the grand ruined forms of classical columns, dozens of them, toppled and smashed and abandoned here in an empire of rubble. Dad put me down. We were standing amid the wreckage of some magnificent lost civilization—even I, the runt of the party, could see that. And we were going to have a picnic.

Dad set a wicker basket on the ground, and Mom pulled out a red-and-white-checked tablecloth, which she spread on a broken cylinder of stone, a column section only a bit higher than our round kitchen table back in the city. Their friends, the rest of our extended clan, were beginning to straggle up now, picking their way across the majestic junkyard, huge goofy smiles on their faces as they took in their surroundings.

There was a lot to see, crushed bricks and tortured iron railings and enormous fragments of pink-white stone carved in the shapes of leaves and scrolls. Here and there, the place was smoldering, ribbons of smoke curling skyward from the debris. Poking diagonally from a rubble pile, not far from Mom's makeshift picnic table, was a woman's white, intricately veined stone arm, its middle and ring fingers snapped off at the second knuckle.

It was a terrific party. Quig and a couple of other big kids ran around and hopped from column to column, their arms outstretched for balance. A lanky bearded guy plucked at a guitar with silver claws. Mom, dark-eyed and grinning, wearing a short white sweater-dress cinched at the waist with a yellow scarf, handed round mismatched cups—some old freebie Mets glasses from the Polo Grounds and a bunch of those little mugs her favorite mustard came in. At the center of it all was Dad, the unmistakable leader of the expedition, pouring out the red wine, slicing hunks of chorizo, tossing people astonishingly sweet figs he'd found in Little Italy.

It was really something being his little guy. I was the smallest one here by far, but I was the princeling, sitting right beside him, basking in his reflected glow and helping him open wine bottles with a corkscrew that looked like a man doing jumping jacks. Everyone looked our way, vied for his attention. People ruffled my hair.

Something important had been left behind in one of the cars, a casserole or a cooler. Mom headed back to get it. The silver-claw guy put down his guitar to go help. Someone started tossing around a Frisbee.

The grown-ups had a lot to talk about. They wandered among the ruins in groups of two or three, prodding half-buried objects with their shoe tips and venturing opinions. Dad was the only one who'd been here before. He led me and a married couple with matching curly hair along a road rutted with truck tracks, left and then right and then left, until he found what he was looking for: the biggest clockface I'd ever seen, jutting slantwise from a rubble heap like a crash-landed flying saucer. It was a great white disc with elegant black metal letters around its edge in the places the numbers should have been: the letter *I* mostly, with a few *V*s and *X*s mixed in. It had no hands.

Dad climbed up the rubble slope to the clock and took from his back pocket a vise grip, a pair of shiny locking pliers whose teeth always suggested to me the polished grin of an alligator. He adjusted its bite by turning a knob on one of the handles, then locked its teeth onto a letter *I*: the only one all by itself.

"See if you can't snap that off to give to your mother," he told me. "I can drill a hole in the top to run a chain through as a necklace." Mom's name was Ivy.

Half-buried along the flank of the rubble pile was what appeared to be the feathered stone wing of an eagle. Using its slant surface as a ramp, I clambered onto the clock, which was about twice my height. The clock had two black metal rings, one inside the other, running around the periphery of its face like a circular toy-train track. Suspended between these two tracks were the letters. They were cold and a little sharp in my palms, but they made pretty good handholds, so I climbed cautiously up the clock's curved edge to the letter *I* on which Dad had clamped the vise grip. Up close, I could see that this *I* had been attached to the metal rings at top and bottom, until someone—Dad, surely, when he'd been here before—had sawed it loose at the top. All that was left to do was to wiggle the vise grip back and forth until the *I* snapped free at the bottom.

Holding the tool with both hands, I rotated my wrists, left-right, left-right, while Dad explained to the curly-haired couple just how tricky it had been to find this dumping ground here on the other side of the Hudson: something about how the railroad's Jersey-based wreckers—"Lipsett's guys," he called them—were keeping the location on the down-low, for safety reasons. My wrists were starting to get awfully sore, and after a while I complained to Dad, who excused himself to come help me.

My hands inside his, Dad took hold of the vise grip and worked it vigorously back and forth, then pretended to get tired out so I could give it the triumphant final twist all by myself. Off popped that stubborn letter *I*, right into my palm. It was cool along most of its length but hot where it had just broken loose. I couldn't wait to give it to Mom. I knew she'd love it.

Together Dad and I started making our way back, taking care not to trip over a felled black post marked TRACK 3. But we'd gone so far, and everything was so wildly disordered here, that I wasn't sure how we would find the right route. One junk pile looked like another, and the truck roads running every which way all looked alike, too, and all the heaped debris and stone columns made it hard to see more than ten or fifteen feet in front of us. Still, Dad looked as handsome and as sure of himself as ever, and I loved roaming this broken landscape with him, no one around but us, the world's two greatest living explorers conquering the unknown side by side.

Snatches of sound came to us now and then, the squawking of seagulls and the distant rumble of machinery layered upon the crunch of our footfalls. Dad kept up a steady pace, his usual certainty of gait, until an unfamiliar hesitation in his step, somewhere between a hitch and a stumble, caused me to stop and look up at him, at his face, where I saw at once that something had changed. He wore a look of weakness, of panic almost, that I'd never seen before. I followed his gaze, stared at the same debris he was staring at, but saw nothing, nothing but a hill of scarred rubble and several long, shiny marble rectangles—the shoe-burnished steps of a grand staircase, maybe.

Then I saw it. Amid a contortion of brass that might once have been a banister, Mom's yellow scarf had wrapped itself around a bent post.

From somewhere behind it, how far away I couldn't tell, I thought I heard her laughter, a gasping stifled giggle. It was a joyous sound, but self-strangled somehow, shushed. I watched a long moment, hoping to spot something I could understand, but saw only my mother's scarf wavering in the breeze, delicate and almost see-through now that it was no longer bunched at her waist.

When I looked up, to learn from my father's face how to feel, I discovered something new. My father was no longer beside me.

PART ONE

THE CITY WE HAVE LOST

1

E VERY NEW YORKER HAS his own idiosyncratic system of
cartography, his personal method of charting the points of cor-
respondence between the external city and the landmarks of his interior streetscape. No surveyor's equipment is necessary, just a wry
acceptance of the ephemeral. For many of us, the resulting map is
a distorted but truthful rendering of New York in which vanished
buildings and storefronts are as present as surviving ones, often more
so. Glance at your own homemade map as you walk around town
and you'll be struck by all the uncelebrated places—a rent-controlled
walk-up you lived in before you knew yourself very well, or the site
of a long-gone bar where you used to meet a close friend who's since
drifted away—that pop out of the mad eternal rush hour and demand
your attention. But only yours. Everyone else on that street hurries
past with places to go, dry cleaning to pick up, important artisanal
cheese to purchase. They are oblivious to that crucial landmark of
that earlier you. They have their own landmarks.

Me, too. The sacked capitol of my New York will always be the
Queen Anne row house on Eighty-Ninth Street between Lex and
Third where my family lived in the late 1960s and '70s. A brick-and-
brownstone confection enlivened with ironwork, a pedimented dor-
mer, an oriel, and even a mansard roof, it was something of a grandly
tricked-out imp, just twelve feet wide, squashed in the middle of a
jostling troupe of six.

You can still go see it. Along with the rest of the row, built in 1887 by descendants of sugar baron William Rhinelander, it appears in most city architectural guidebooks (though it's notably absent from the three I've written, as well as from all my magazine columns). And in one of New York's colossal ironies, my childhood brownstone will outlive us all. After everything was over, after all the intricate destruction, the city went and designated the row of houses as historic landmarks, throwing a too-little-too-late bubble of protection over them.

If you have a taste for good architecture, you may appreciate the look of my family's old house, may even stop a moment to take in its quirkish elegance as you pass by. But it won't shimmer with meaning for you as it does for me, just as I can walk right by that old coffee shop—the one where you had those eggs before that big job interview all those years ago, or where that exasperating lover with the beautiful neck told you it was over—without the slightest inkling that this is the capitol of *your* New York.

Every few years, I climb the chipped steps of our old brownstone when I'm pretty sure nobody's home. I lean over the ornate wrought-iron stoop railing, cup my hands around my eyes like horse blinders, and peer through the stained-glass window.

To me, it's always 1974 in there. At that time—the year of being thirteen, the year before President Ford took one look at our vividly crumbling city and told us all to DROP DEAD—that brownstone started getting mighty crowded. My mother, you see, had adopted another stray, her fifth since my father had left us a few months earlier. This one's name was Mr. Price, and he was going to share the third floor with me, which meant half my medicine cabinet, all of my toilet seat, and probably even my loofah.

I just hoped to hell he wasn't one of those really *hairy* guys. It was bad enough waiting for some boarder to finish toweling off his privates before you could get in to use your own shower, but if he was one of those molting oldsters who were always leaving hair on the soap, well, that's when I felt like stomping down to Mom's room and telling her enough was enough.

I spied through the spindles of the second-floor banister while Mom blathered with Mr. Price on the first-floor landing. She was holding his wrist, gripping it with her fingers like a nurse who doubted his pulse, and lying cheerfully about how glad Quigley and I were that he was joining "our little jury-rigged family." He had on a rumpled gray suit with a magnificently pressed hankie, two white peaks rising from his jacket pocket flat and perfect as postcard Alps. He bowed his balding head a lot and called my mother Mrs. Watts in a fussy English accent.

I wondered what was wrong with him. He seemed reasonably civilized—not too hairy, either—but I didn't trust this impression, because all of Mom's boarders were misfits. So after Mr. Price had spent some quality time in my bathroom and had begun puttering around in his new bedroom down the hall, I locked myself in the crapper and started going through all his stuff. Foreign guys like Mr. Price always had these hoity-toity toilet kits made of buttery leather and filled with swanky things like eau de cologne.

"*Griffin!*" My mother was banging on the bathroom door. "You *in* there?"

I turned on the faucet so she wouldn't hear Mr. Price's personal effects jostling around in their case. When I didn't answer her, Mom gave a couple of follow-up knocks, less confident than before. Her knuckles sounded soft and fleshy, the way the chicken breasts always had when Dad pounded them before dinner with a meat tenderizer shaped like a gavel.

"Listen, Griffin," she said through the door, "I've made up my mind about the ruin—and it involves *you*. So as soon as you're done in there, maybe you could come downstairs and give Mr. Price a little privacy."

"Yeah, all right," I answered. "I understand."

That was what I always said when I planned to ignore her. I'd gotten so good at it that I could say, "Yeah, all right, I understand"—in sincere, good-son tones—all while paying so little attention to my mother that the noises she made with her mouth never once registered in my mind as words.

"You're not even *listen*ing to me, are you?" She sounded pretty irritated.

"Sure I am. Sure I'm listening." I quickly replayed in my head our last thirty seconds of conversation. Some people have photographic memory; I've always had *phono*graphic memory.

I cleared my throat. "You've . . . made up your mind about the ruin," I repeated, "and the thing is, it involves me. So . . . when I'm finished in here and all, you were sort of thinking that I could come downstairs and maybe give Mr. Price some privacy." I took a deep breath. "See, I *was* listening."

"That doesn't count! I used to do that *exact* regurgitation trick when *I* was thirteen. Just because you can repeat what I say word for word doesn't mean you're *listen*ing. You hear what I'm saying?"

"Well, I'm not sure, but it sounded to me, Mom, like you were basically saying that you used to do that *exact* regurgitation trick when *you* were thirteen, and just because I can repeat what you say word for word doesn't mean I'm *listen*ing."

"Jesus, you're exasperating. Just come down to my room when you're done."

"Yeah, all right," I said. "I understand."

After taking pains to put Mr. Price's things back in order, I turned off the running water. But I didn't go downstairs right away. There was this lump inside my corduroys that I wanted to handle first.

Just before Mr. Price had shown up, I'd come across another of those nasty notes my father was always leaving for my mother. I'd been quick to stuff it in my pocket, because I couldn't stand how upset Dad's letters made her. Her eyes would get this awful down-in-the-dumps look before she'd read even a sentence or two, and then her whole face would get all twisted and gargoyley from the effort of trying not to cry. It was more than you wanted to see, really, and you pretty much had to get the hell out of the room or risk getting all gargoyley yourself.

I pulled the crumpled ball of paper from my pocket, sat down on the toilet, and flattened it on my knee. It was maybe the ninth or tenth furious Dad-note I'd intercepted since he'd moved out. He was our landlord now ("landlord of all he surveys," Mom called him), and he was constantly stopping by for surprise inspections my mother could never pass. Over time, his visits had come to resemble an endless series of pop quizzes given by an unfulfilled teacher who wants only to watch you fail so he can feel hurt about how you've let him down. Half the times Dad came by, he'd discover something that infuriated him, and when that happened, he would whip out his pen and leave Mom an embittered note in the very spot where he'd been jumped by his anger.

I spent a certain amount of my free time scouring the house in search of these little cow pies of disgruntlement, hoping to scoop them up before Mom stumbled on them. At one time or another I'd found irate notes from Dad in every one of our boarders' rooms, as well as in Mom's underwear drawer, in her closet, and in her artist's palette, jammed scrollwise into the thumbhole and sealed with a hardened white tadpole of paint.

The note now resting on my leg, however, had been sitting right by the kitchen phone. Dad's rage was becoming respectable, a commonplace notation alongside messages from Quig's theater friends and Mom's framer:

Ivy—

Some unctuous Brit called while I was here checking the stove for gas leaks. He said his name was Price and that he was moving in here this week. I hope you're at least getting some rent from this one. I asked him what he did for a living, and he just kept saying he was "in newspapers."

That last bit, I learned later, was one of Mr. Price's little jokes on himself. With a pointed vagueness that made listeners suspect he was the lost heir of William Randolph Hearst, Mr. Price was forever telling people he was "in newspapers." He took private glee in saying so, as he often slept on a park bench with sections of the *Daily News* stuffed up his pant legs for warmth.

The rest of the note was scrawled at full tilt, ending with a rant: "At the rate you keep bringing these men under my roof, you're sure to be too busy giving them all head to raise my kids right."

"*Griffin!*" My mother was hollering again, this time from down-stairs. "*No one* takes that long to go to the bathroom!"

Memory is a slippery thing, and whenever Quigley and I compare notes about those years growing up in the brownstone, there are inevitably a bunch of little details we disagree on. But one thing we remember the same way is the yelling: everybody was always yelling in that house. This was partly because we were eternally pissed at each other and partly because it was a big old five-story brownstone and the person you wanted to talk to never seemed to be on the same floor as you. We were all experts at escalating a squabble, too. If you pitched your voice down the stairs with just the right amount of put-upon forbearance, you could make it pretty clear that you considered the distance between yourself and your listener not just an inconvenience but a symptom of some hideous flaw in her character.

I opened the door a crack. "All *right* already! I'll be right *down!*"

I shut the door and toed the toilet seat upright with one of my red Puma Clydes. Then I ripped Dad's letter in half and in half and in half until his hostility toward my mom was torn into thirty-two manage-able fragments. These I scattered into the toilet bowl, letting them settle on the blue Sani-Flush water no more than a few seconds before I unzipped my fly and whizzed all over them. It felt good: I was a Pee-51 fighter pilot above the Pacific Basin, raining destruction upon the enemy flotilla. Death from above.

Mom's room, as usual, was bathed in shadows. Some months earlier she'd painted the ceiling black and the walls a dusky brick red, which gave the room, at all hours, an air of incipient nightfall. Her curtains, decorated with engravings of timeworn Italian towers, jagged bites chomped from their corners, were always tugged closed. She didn't want the folks in the tenements behind the brownstone to look in her window.

"Just thinking about it makes me feel violated," she said.

Losing her view of our backyard garden didn't bother her a bit, though. She was a city girl, a native New Yorker, and I think she found the natural world almost hokey, a lowbrow entertainment for rural folk like my dad.

This afternoon, astonishingly enough, Mom was not sitting on her bed, the spot where she spent most of her waking hours reading, chatting on the phone, or carving woodcuts on a blue gingham picnic blanket. So I nearly jumped out of my tube socks when I heard her voice from the other side of the room: "Mr. Price's toiletries in order?"

She was standing near the window, wearing a brick-red turtleneck that blended her into the wall. A breeze came up, parting the curtains slightly and opening a thin fissure of light in the belly of an Italian rampart.

"Any reason they shouldn't be?" I answered.

She didn't pursue it. "Listen," she said instead, "your father's still refusing to pay anyone to tear down the outhouse, so I was hoping you could take care of it for me." She picked at a scab on her thumb, worrying it with an elegant maroon fingernail. "I mean, it's *such* a wreck, and I'm really trying to get things straightened up around here."

She pulled back the Italian ruin to reveal the New York ruin behind it. The invading sunlight made me blink, but for a rare moment I saw what she saw.

That ruined outhouse had always been with us. At the edge of the yard it stood, shafts of light slicing through the rotten slats of its walls. Older than even the brownstone, it had supposedly been put up to serve the wood-frame cottage that originally stood on the spot the brownstone now occupied, in what was then the country village of Yorkville. Dad surmised that they'd left the outhouse up for the workers to use while they built the brownstone (which had indoor plumbing), and then for some reason—cost or maybe inertia—the old thing was never taken down.

After the brownstone was finished in 1887, the outhouse was abandoned, sealed shut, left alone. Nothing entered or exited. Except, that is, for a single stealthy tree, whose seed blew through the bars of the window and through the hole in the seat, fertilizing itself in the human waste. In time, the tree grew thick and coarse, shooting upward and heading back out the window in search of light. It was hard to guess how long its jailbreak had taken, but there was no missing the violence of its escape. The moment was preserved within the window frame, the tree thrusting through the thin iron bars, shoving them aside like a great knotted fist emerging from the abdomen of a guitar. A tree, unlike a person, cannot hide its past.

"Okay, I'll bust up the outhouse if you want," I said. "But you've gotta make me breakfast tomorrow in exchange—an omelet."

"An *omelet*?" Mom had been sleeping through breakfast for years, leaving Quig and me to fend for ourselves.

"I mean, if you know how. Jelly, maybe. Or whatever. I don't really care."

"No, I can do jelly. Jelly omelet it is."

"You want me to set an alarm for you?" I asked. "Or rent you a rooster or something?"

She gave me a grudging half smile. "And you'll cut down that tree branch, too, of course."

I knew the branch she meant. It was an uncontrolled outgrowth of the filth tree, a misshapen, veiny bark forearm that stretched across the garden, coming to rest a couple feet below her window.

Ever since Dad had taken off, Mom had been on a rampage of order. Cleaning, whitewashing, throwing things out. But since she was intimidated by any job involving machinery or tools, she'd been after me for months to cut down that limb. It had no leaves, never bloomed. It was ugly.

It irked me (that was my new favorite word) the way she always assumed I would do all the "man's jobs" that Dad refused to perform now that he was her landlord instead of her husband.

"What do you mean, *'of course'* I'll cut it down?" I gave my voice that edge. It was an old edge, but it had a new name: my *irked* edge.

"Well, you said you'd do the ruin, and they're connected, aren't they?"

"Lots of things are connected, Mom. My fingers and fingernails are connected, but that doesn't mean if you tell me to clip my nails I'm gonna go *ker-chunk*ing my thumb off with a pair of bolt cutters just to please you."

"Don't be fresh. I'm just asking you to saw off a branch."

"I'm not your gardener, Mom, so stop vexing me." (*Vex* meant *irk;* it sounded cooler, though, 'cause it had an *x* in it.) "I mean, you're really being vexatiously irksome."

She looked at me. Her face had a twinge of gargoyle in it. "You're a very unpleasant boy."

"Maybe, but I'm the boy who decides whether that tree gets pruned, because we both know you don't exactly have a bunch of extra cash lying around to hire someone to do it."

Mom went slack. Her neck, her shoulders, lost their shape, as if the picture wire that held up her self-possession had slipped from its hook. My money insult was a low blow. Mom was broke, and according to my parents' Separation Agreement, a document of near biblical force, Dad owned three-fourths of our house. She was lucky his lawyers let her have even that sliver, she said, because Dad's name alone had been on all their financial papers during their marriage. He'd always told her it was better for taxes.

After he moved out, Mom had found part-time work in the art department of *Life* magazine, the first job she'd had since her time as a gallery assistant in college. During the first couple of issue closings, she came home with hands all blotchy-red from doing battle with the hot wax machine they used for pasting up layouts. (The task was made no easier by her refusal to remove any of her twenty-seven rings.) Though she'd gotten the hang of the whole thing before long—an accomplishment I could see made her proud—the job was only two weeks a month and didn't seem to pay much.

I guess Mom and I had been arguing pretty loudly, because Mr. Price poked his head in the door, looking all fidgety and apologetic.

"Excuse me, folks," he said, with exaggerated chipperness. "I hope I'm not intruding, but if there's some household chore that needs performing, I'd be more than happy to be of assistance. I don't seem to have much scheduled today." He pronounced *scheduled* in that snooty English way: "*shed*-yuled."

I turned to Mom. "Look," I said, trying to sound like the most reasonable boy in the world. "Lemme tear down the ruin first. Then I'll see how I feel about that tree branch."

Mr. Price was still standing at the doorway in his wrinkled suit. He had the look of a baffled understudy, a *Masterpiece Theatre* butler who couldn't remember his lines.

"We don't need your help," I said, pushing past him.

Dad's toolshed had always been strictly off-limits—he was notoriously secretive about his stuff—so I took great pleasure in poking around inside it against his wishes. Amid the fertilizer bags and clay pots full of color-bled dead stalks was a motley collection of tools: a rusted spade, a trowel, some kind of wide-fingered claw implement. When I moved a bag of topsoil to free the crowbar it was hunched against, things shifted around and a board shook loose from the wall behind a box of bonemeal, revealing the corner of a concealed white plastic case. I freed the case from its hiding place and opened it. Inside, I found a set of three small surgical saws, each resting in an indentation precisely its shape. In the middle, also pressed into the plastic, was one of those medical shields with a pair of snakes twining themselves around a winged staff.

The gnarliest of the saws had a thin silver handle with an angry-toothed wheel on the end that looked like a morbid version of a pizza cutter. Its curved teeth were covered with a grainy white-gray powder that felt disgusting on my fingertips. I hastily wiped my hand on my jeans, closed the case again, and shoved it back into its hiding place. I couldn't say why, exactly, but the saws felt like contraband, or worse: objects you might catch something from.

What on earth my father needed surgical saws for was beyond me, but I tried not to dwell on it. It seemed best just to get to work with that crowbar.

Rotting and pointless, the ruin stood at the edge of our fenced-in yard, a gloomy gray crate surrounding the base of a big fat tree. Its doorknob had been removed forever ago and a chain looped through the remaining hole and back through a second hole drilled in the wall, fastening the door to its frame. There was no getting through that chain, so I jammed the crowbar into the ancient hinges, the bottom one first, which broke away in a spray of rust. When the top hinge split, the door swung out a foot or so. I pulled it all the way open.

There in the doorway stood the rough-skinned tree trunk, filling out the doorframe like a truculent fairy-tale troll awakened from a nap. Without meaning to, I found myself moving my hand over the trunk's harsh bark, my palm coming to rest on a lumpy, wart-like growth the size and shape of a face.

The ruin, it now turned out, was in even worse shape than it looked. Wherever I rammed the crowbar, the wood split instantly, and I began ferociously attacking the boards: swinging the crowbar like an ax, jamming it like a spear, kicking in the ruin's front wall while frightening the bejesus out of it with fierce karate cries: *kyaawoo-HAA!* When at last the roof caved in, sliding down the slanted trunk into the dirt, I jumped back and stood gawking at the odd sight I'd made.

The outhouse was now gone, a crosshatch of rot heaped haphazardly around the base of the great trunk. But the tree itself seemed to swell with renewed vigor, bursting out of the ground, lurching left toward the vanished window, and surging through the iron grate, wrenching apart its black bars, which now hung seven feet in the air, jealously guarding an absence. Inside was outside was inside.

It was pretty clear to me I wasn't going to be sawing any part of that tree, which I now realized could help me acquire biceps powerful enough to win the attention of Dani Gardner, a ninth-grade girl I had my eye on. Not far above the window grate, that deformed limb emerged from the tree trunk and twined its way grotesquely toward the second floor of our house. One section of it was almost horizontal, forming a natural crossbar, and it was here that I intended to make myself the most fearsome thirteen-year-old in all of New York City.

My plan was to do one-armed pull-ups, the way my annoyingly athletic best friend, Kyle, did. But I couldn't reach the limb without something to stand on, so I went back to the toolshed, where I remembered seeing a plastic cooler stenciled with the words DECARLO FUNERAL HOME & CREMATORY. I knew Tony DeCarlo. He was a bluff, thick-necked friend of Dad's who sometimes went to Mets games with us, one time even driving us out to Shea in a hearse. He and my father had a fond, ribbing sort of friendship. Dad always referred to Tony's Mulberry Street funeral parlor as "the body shop," and Tony liked to joke that the two of them got along so well because they were both in the antiques business. Kidding aside, though, my father got quite a few referrals from DeCarlo. Tony would give him an early heads-up whenever a widow or widower died so Dad could approach the grieving descendants to offer his services appraising and selling off the deceased's vintage furniture and heirlooms.

Why Dad had a cooler of DeCarlo's I didn't think to wonder. What mattered was that the cooler was just the right height to help me with my one-armed pull-ups. So I schlepped it across the yard to the spot beneath that horizontal limb, stepped onto it, and leapt up to grab the limb with both hands. I then let go with my left, hanging there help-lessly for no more than a nanosecond before I slipped off and landed on the cooler, sending a bunch of weird wrapped lumps spilling from its innards.

Man! I said to myself. *What a vexatious cooler!*

But it was more than vexatious; it was revolting. The stench of putrefying meat wafted from those wrapped lumps, making me retch violently. I nudged them back into the cooler with my sneaker—*sooo gross*—slammed the cover shut again, and dragged it across the gar-den to the toolshed. I heaved it back where I'd found it and got the hell out of there.

2

THERE WERE DEMONS LIVING in the furnace, furious hammer-handed creatures who subsisted on rust flakes and kept our family warm with their anger. When their tantrums were at their worst, you could hear them hissing and banging clear up to the top floor of our brownstone. That's what jolted me awake so rudely the next morning.

As man of the house, I was personally responsible for the care and feeding of these furnace dwellers, that much my father had made clear. He'd led me down to our clammy basement the night he left us and jabbed a beefy index finger at the tube of rust-brown water clinging to the furnace's flank.

"Whatever you do," he said, "don't ever let the water get below the horizontal line on that tube. Because if you do . . ."

Here he filled his cheeks with air like a blowfish and made a dramatic gesture with his hands that seemed to mean, roughly, *"Kaboom!"*

It was my job to turn the ancient blue knob and refill the tank with water every few days, but the clanging ruckus now echoing through the brownstone's pipes up in my third-floor bedroom made me realize I hadn't done it in weeks. On top of that, I'd overslept again.

I shoved on my moccasins and hurried down the darkened stairs in my canary-yellow pajamas, past the familiar sleeping lump of my mother in her second-floor bedroom. I should've known better than to trust her about that promised omelet. But before I could even pause to contemplate the full, disappointing majesty of her torpor, I was nearly knocked over by Quigley, who came sprinting upstairs two steps at a time, wearing a Unique Clothing version of the flowered robe Liza Minnelli wore in *Cabaret*. This was one of those mornings when Quig had even given her left cheekbone a showbizzy makeup mole like Liza's. But far more distressingly, she was clutching a quart of milk and what I happened to know was the last packet of Carnation Instant Breakfast.

"Good luck finding any eats, slow*poke!*" Quig crowed, poking me in the ribs for witty emphasis as she slipped past and ran up to her room.

On the first-floor landing below, I caught a glimpse of what I was up against as a gray-faced man emerged from the half bathroom at the foot of the stairs, took one look at me, and shuffled quickly into the dining room in his tattered espadrilles. It was Monsieur Claude, the boarder who lived on the fourth floor, scratching his butt and yawning.

Monsieur Claude was always scratching his butt and yawning. A bored Frenchman with scraggly shoulder-length hair and sunken pothole eyes, he was supposed to be some kind of utterly fascinating world traveler—"He's got *such* a talent for living," Mom said—but all I knew about him was that he always wore these droopy gray sweatpants that exposed the top of his butt crack, and his only talent I'd ever spotted was for exhaling Gauloise cigarette smoke and inhaling scrambled eggs at the same time.

Monsieur Claude's tendency to Hoover up every egg in sight instantly became my chief concern. Because as badly as the furnace demons needed my attention, the emptiness in my belly was even more pressing.

Stepping into the light of the dining room, I could see at once what a struggle it was going to be to get my hands on any food. A vanquished Count Chocula box lay sideways on the big round table, beside which sat Mathis, the blubberous Associated Press news clerk who slept on the second floor in what used to be our living room. He was hunched fleshily over a bowl in the posture of a semidomesticated manatee.

"Little Man!" he declared grandly when he saw me. "A very good morning to you!" And with that, he looked down again and quickened his pace, shoveling cereal puffs into his mouth so urgently that I was surprised the brown milk didn't leave little spatters on the round lenses of his eyeglasses.

I made my way tentatively through the dining room. In the kitchen behind Mathis, Monsieur Claude was already removing a pan from the stove and spooning a Matterhorn-size mountain of scrambled eggs onto one of my Hamburglar plates. He was singing a jaunty French song whose lyrics I imagined meant something like, "*Starve! Starve!* You late-sleeping, omelet-less little American fool, ha-*HAA!*"

At his left hand, one last sweating white egg remained in the carton. But as I sidled into the kitchen to claim it, Mr. Price, who had been standing over by the fridge where I couldn't see him, stepped forth in a shabby red velvet robe and plucked up the precious orb with his fingertips. In one deft move, he cracked it into a tall glass filled with some tomato-juice concoction, then seasoned this vile elixir with a few drops of dark sauce from a bottle wrapped in brown paper. His chin held high, he tipped the glass to his mouth and swallowed its contents with ostrichy gulps of his skinny, stubble-stippled throat. As the last of the drink disappeared, he gagged, recovered, then wiped his mouth on his velvet sleeve and sighed with relief.

"*Ahhhh,*" he exclaimed brightly, turning to gaze at me with eyes so bloodshot they hurt to look at. "The very thing!"

The brownstone's pipes gave an exclamatory rattle, reminding me to get a move on, so I edged past Mr. Price without saying anything and peered into the fridge. It was pretty barren in there: skinny bottles of capers and horseradish, two desiccated lemons, an assortment of cheese rinds.

But then something truly exciting caught my eye: resting atop the fridge for some reason, not far above my head, was a second egg carton, its top open a crack.

A late-rising boy has to make his own luck, so without looking around at my competition, I lunged for the carton—and immediately realized my blunder as a shower of tiny eggshell fragments spilled from inside it like jagged confetti, right into my face and all down my pajama front.

"What on earth?" cried Mr. Price, hurrying over and raising a hesitant hand to help brush the fragments off me. "What are these things? What are they for?"

"My mom collects them for her art," I said, trying to pick a pointy shell bit from the corner of my eye with my pinky tip. It hurt like a bastard.

"I don't understand."

"She smashes up different-colored eggshells and uses them to make mosaic landscapes and country scenes and stuff," I said. "Usually she keeps her eggshells in Baggies, but I guess she ran out."

I wriggled away from Mr. Price's help and headed out of the kitchen, snagging a rejected heel of Wonder bread from the counter as I went.

The basement door, set into the polished mahogany wall below the main staircase, was an olive-green eyesore, swollen with moisture and layers of old paint. It took me several tugs to loosen it from its frame. When the door finally opened, the basement exhaled mightily, and I stepped into a stale belch of moist heat.

The metallic clanging was louder in here, more dangerous-feeling. Fumbling around in the dark, I found the dangling overhead bulb and yanked its shoelace, spilling an oily mayonnaise light down the narrow stairwell tunnel.

With crabwise steps I crept down toward the source of the clamor, trying not to touch the filthy walls, whose sandplaster gapped and puckered, flowing into the lumpy ceiling. Though Mom had tried to make this slanted tunnel cheerier by painting it bumblebee yellow, the color only highlighted the thousands of tiny dust balls, one on each stucco barb.

At the bottom of the stairs, where the light was weaker and the air all clammy thick, I stopped and squinted through the darkness at the big rusty box of the furnace.

I didn't really get how it worked. Boiling coils of cable burrowed in and out of the ceiling above it before surging into a metal panel on its side. A chipping pipe rose from its top, made an abrupt turn, and plunged into the wall. And inside its tank thrashed the furnace demons, thirsty and scared, rattling the brownstone with their parched rage.

A funny thing happened then. The banging quieted as I drew close, changing to a kind of grinding supplication, as if the young rust creatures inside could feel I was there to care for them.

"All right, fellas, hang in there," I said, trying to sound sort of soothing. "Sorry I forgot about you. But I'm gonna give you a little something to drink here, some nice filthy rust water, just the way you like it." I didn't entirely believe there was anyone in the furnace to hear me, but it was more comforting than talking to myself.

The blue knob turned easily, sending a gurgling torrent of water into the furnace's innards. After about a minute, a little water sloshed up into the bottom of the empty glass tube, its level slowly rising until it passed that critical horizontal line.

It looked like everything was going to be okay, no explosion or anything. I filled the tube just shy of the top and listened as the tank's relieved inhabitants settled into their rusty bath and thanked me, muttering curse words of gratitude in their abrasive native tongue.

Turning to hightail it out of the basement, I did my usual little head tilt to avoid looking at the locked door of Dad's abandoned studio, which was only a few feet away on my left. Though I had years ago spirited away and hidden the antique skeleton key that could open any of our brownstone's old-fashioned locks—I sometimes used it to collect change from our boarders' trousers—I had never dared let myself into Dad's studio. He had rarely allowed me inside it over the years, and from what I recalled, it was a forbidding chamber of table vises and wood scraps, its floor strewn with screws and obscure antique hardware that could impale your foot right through your moccasins. Who needed *that*?

But today something felt different, as if a sharper, more intrusive quality of light was pushing its way through the frosted-glass transom above the door. Curious, I retrieved the skeleton key from inside the asbestos sleeve of a boiler pipe, and I unlocked the studio. It was a place of shadows, illuminated only by a murky blade of sunlight penetrating the room through the dirty little window at the top left of the back wall. For the first time in years, I stepped inside.

The studio looked like it had been left in a hurry. There was an old take-out coffee cup on the back counter, glass Taster's Choice jars full of eye hooks, even a couple of packets of gold leaf. Cautiously I ran my eyes along the back wall from right to left, across dirty outlines of vanished tools.

And then, startled, I felt my throat close up like a fist. On the window ledge high up on the back wall, tilted in the soil of a dead houseplant and swathed in grimy light, was half of a woman's face. Her forehead had been severed along the diagonal, across the shattered bridge of her nose, and her lone eye looked like it had given up.

Horrified but fascinated, I climbed up on the back counter to get a closer look. The face appeared to be a woman's death mask, or part of one. All of her features, from her eyebrow to her lips to her throat, were fashioned from the same unforgiving material, a hardened clay maybe, the blended color of melted scabs and orange rinds.

Behind her, in the dirty window, I half saw my own smudgy reflection frowning. And then my reflection shouted.

"GRIFFIN!" it boomed, scaring the living crap out of me. "What the hell do you think you're doing?" It was Dad, out in the backyard on his hands and knees, peering at me with enraged green eyes through the curtain of filth on the window.

I didn't stick around to find out what would happen next. I was a speedy little guy when I wanted to be, and I was out of that studio and up the staircase in seconds, not thinking of much at all, not even where I might be headed, until my forehead plowed right into Dad's lumpy belt buckle at the head of the stairs and I realized that I'd been running straight toward the thing I was running away from.

As I brought my hand up to rub my forehead, Dad closed his big fingers around my wrist and lifted me up to his level on the landing. He wasn't hurting me, not quite, but he sure wasn't letting me go.

"I want to talk to you," he said. "I'm very upset about something."

I didn't look up at him, only stared straight ahead at his chest, where sandy hair geysered from the top of his red flannel shirt. His odor crowded into my nostrils, a thick male smell of struggle.

"What is it?" My voice sounded very far away.

"Well, you're a peculiar kid," he said, "but you notice things, right? At least when you want to."

I nodded.

"Someone tore down the ruin. I specifically forbade your mother to do that, and now someone's gone and smashed the whole thing to pieces. Which one of her boarders did it?"

I looked up at him carefully, shaking my head. He had a nasty, freshly scabbed scratch arcing across his unshaven cheek from his right earlobe to his upper lip. His hair was a tumult. He looked like he'd been in a fight or had been up all night. Or both.

"You know what? Never mind, it doesn't even matter who did it." His eyes had a wild exhausted look, a fierce powerlessness that frightened me. "*She's* the one who put them up to it, anyway."

Just like that he was done with me. He let go of my wrist and started upstairs toward where Mom lay sleeping, his big work boots thumping on the steps.

"No, wait!" I called after him in a panicky voice that came out almost as a shriek. "*Don't go up there!*"

He stopped, his big hand gripping the newel post so hard the flesh of his knuckles turned pale. "Why not?" he asked. "Why *shouldn't* I go upstairs in my own house?"

I rubbed the sore spot on my wrist where he had gripped it.

"It was my idea," I said quietly. "*I* smashed up the outhouse. With your crowbar. *I* did it."

Dad craned his neck up the stairs toward Mom's bedroom, then looked back down at me.

"I don't believe you," he said. But he ungripped the newel post—let go of his intention—and came back down the stairs. "Prove to me you did it."

I was getting a little jumpy. I extended my hands, palms up, in a desperate, I-got-nothing sort of way, until suddenly I saw the answer right there in my own flesh.

"Here!" I said, thrusting my left hand at him. "*Here.*"

He closed his thick hand around mine and looked closely at my left palm, where a long dark splinter from the outhouse had pierced the meaty part below my thumb. It hurt. The splinter was ringed with red, an infection I'd nurtured by trying to gnaw it free in bed the night before.

Dad let my hand drop in disgust.

"Well, what possessed you to go and do such a destructive thing?" he asked angrily. "You know how I feel about preserving antiques. And I *own* that antique you destroyed—it's *mine*! How could you possibly think it was going to sit well with me if you just took it upon yourself to trash the goddamn thing?"

"I don't know. It was just such a wreck. I mean, it had been there for, like, *forever.*"

"But that's just the point!" he said. "The city had a rich, complex life long before you ever came along and started having your own personal little responses to it, Griffin. It's bigger than you."

"I know that."

"Well, you do but you don't. Otherwise you wouldn't treat a rare nineteenth-century structure like garbage."

You could see how frustrated he was to have to explain all this to me.

"Look," he said. "The lives lived by generations of New Yorkers in and around a historic building give it all kinds of layers of collective meaning—a patina of memory and grime and experience, really— that you can see, and even feel, if you open yourself to it."

I thought about all this a moment.

"The lives people lived in an old building?" I asked. "That's what gives the building meaning?"

"That's right, yes."

"*Dad,*" I said. I couldn't help myself. "It's an *outhouse!*"

Oh, did that piss him off. His face flushed, and he stepped forward and shackled my wrist in his big hand again. This time he didn't raise his voice or stomp around. He just eyed me with a ferocious blend of hurt and contempt. When he spoke, it was with a measured calm far more menacing than any of his yelling.

"I don't know how this happened to you," he said. "But you, son, are going to learn to look up. You are not going to be another one of those blinkered goddamn New Yorkers who walk around town staring at their shoes, or worse, have their eyes so fixed on whatever goal they're hurrying toward that they never see the city around them. You are not going to join that complacent army of blind men who went and let a civic cathedral like Penn Station get smashed to pieces right under our noses."

I had no clue what he was going on about. Penn Station was alive and well, and it was no cathedral. It was a chaotic, subterranean, fluorescent hellhole where bums peed in Rheingold cans and throngs of tacky Long Islanders waited beneath an enormous clickety board, watching its colorful horizontal stripes endlessly shuffle exotic names like Patchogue and Ronkonkoma. The clicking was as relentless as the passage of time, each town migrating jerkily up the board until it tumbled off the top and vanished like the Indian tribe that had named it.

"I want you at my downtown studio at three o'clock this afternoon," Dad said. "You're going to do a little work for a change. See if we can't teach you a little respect for old things."

"But I don't even know how to get there," I blurted. "And Mom wanted me to go to Finast after school to get her some coffee."

"Forget the coffee." He took a fat construction pencil from his shirt pocket and scribbled an address on the back of a receipt, which he shoved into my hands. "Three o'clock," he said. "Take your bike. Get to know your own city a little on the way down."

The conversation was over. He turned and strode out of the brownstone in what seemed like just two or three outsize strides, the wrinkled tail of his red flannel shirt riding the air behind him. Nestled under his left arm, I noticed for the first time, was the case of surgical saws. The sight of it almost made me gag, as if I were smelling that putrid meat stench from the cooler all over again. What was he up to?

I listened to the sudden silence. Upstairs, my mother slept on, all tucked into herself. The boarders, meanwhile, had apparently all slunk away when Dad appeared on the scene. But as I trudged upstairs to get ready for school, I came across Monsieur Claude, lounging in the paisley chair on the second-floor landing with my now empty Hamburglar plate on his lap.

"Your father. He is wrong, of course," Monsieur Claude said with a sniff. He wasn't even looking at me. He was lazily squeegeeing the last traces of scrambled egg from the plate with his index finger, which he carefully cleaned off between his pale lips.

Only then, when there was no evidence that any eggs had ever existed, did he look up.

"That building which you have killed," he told me. "It is valuable only now. Before that? A grand nothing."

A question began to form on my lips, but Monsieur Claude waved me off.

"It is always this way," he said. "Always. The only city worth saving is the city we have lost."

3

EVERYONE KNEW THAT NEW YORK was the most crime-ridden, unruly, and graffiti-blasted place in America. A lot of us were even a little proud of that distinction. But there was still an awful lot about my hometown that was obscure to me at the time. For starters, I had no idea that New York was going broke, that mayor after mayor had made outlandish commitments he couldn't possibly pay for, that every spring the city had to borrow vast sums just to keep the lights on and the cops in uniform. People don't tell you this sort of thing when you're a kid.

I had never heard the word that just a year later would be on everyone's lips: *default*. I didn't know what a municipal bond was, or a wildcat strike. It didn't occur to me that the city could be forced to fire tens of thousands of workers in a single day, or that when it did the streets could fill with thousands of irate policemen and tons of uncollected garbage.

But I picked up the tremors nonetheless. To me it was obvious the city was loosish. Not to be trusted.

The evidence was everywhere. Streets shuddered from tenement demolitions. A hansom cab horse, a huge beast with a wet brown marble of an eye, had been electrocuted right across from FAO Schwarz by a stray current in a manhole cover. Over on Third Avenue in the lower Nineties, where three monstrous redbrick towers were rising on the site of the old Ruppert Brewery, a workman's lunch box fell nineteen stories and just missed braining a delivery boy.

In the two weeks since this last mishap, I hadn't once left the house without wearing my scuffed blue Mets batting helmet for protection. It had an awkward adjustable plastic ring inside that dug into the tops of my ears, but wearing it made me feel just safe enough to stand up to the city's urge to harm me. That morning, for instance, I was pedaling up Ninetieth Street to school on my ten-speed, practically daring incoming lunch pails to target my plastic-encased noggin.

It was a relief to get out of that brownstone, let me tell you. My mind always wandered away from my problems when I got on that bike, which was why I loved it so much. It was a metallic-blue Panasonic my dad had given me after he moved out, and it had shiny toe clips I could tell Kyle was jealous of. I had even used the flat edge of my Kryptonite key to personalize my vehicle on one side of its diagonal tube, scraping off several of the block letters in the word PANASONIC so that I was now the proud owner of the only ten-speed ANAS in all of New York City.

Just in case anyone was watching as I approached school, I suavely dismounted by swooping my right leg over the bike seat and back wheel, gliding up to the entrance in that effortless way it had taken me so much effort to master in Carl Schurz Park one Saturday. Because I was late, though, no one was near the school's bike rack to witness this slick maneuver. So I hurried in to first-period algebra after locking my bike beside Dani Gardner's lipstick-red Raleigh—the one with the Pink Floyd stickers partly obscuring the remnants of Wacky Packages she'd scraped off the previous spring after finishing middle school.

Biking downtown to learn what kind of punishing work my father had in mind for me was about the last thing I wanted to do that afternoon, so after slipping out of fencing class early at two o'clock, Kyle and I just headed out into the streets as usual. We wandered up Madison together, scuffing the pavement with our sneakers, making fart noises with our armpits, angling the mirrors of parked cars in the hope that drivers would see their own eyeballs during crisis moments in Midtown traffic. At the twin phone booths outside Taso's Pizza, I had the idea to make a collect call from one pay phone to the other, inches away.

Kyle was magnificent. He let it ring twice before answering, and he didn't crack up when the operator told him that a "Mr. Julius Rosenberg wishes to reverse the charges."

"Why, yes, operator," Kyle said graciously, thrusting his chin against his down-jacket collar to try to deepen his prepubescent voice, "I'd be *more than happy* to pay for a call from my dear old dad. I've really been missing his electric personality."

We jabbered awhile on the phone company's dime, grinning at each other and saying unclever things like "Long time no see!" Talking this way was at once both intimate and remote enough that it felt almost possible to say something to Kyle about the rotting meat lumps and other creepy stuff I'd found in my dad's toolshed. But I didn't want to put my father at risk in case the operator was still listening in.

When nobody came along the street and got annoyed at us for tying up both phones, Kyle and I left the receivers dangling in their booths and went around the corner to Jolly Chan's, where I had a repellently greasy egg roll and Kyle chugged half a bottle of soy sauce just because.

On our way out, we ran into Lamar Schloss—the kid with the jumbo-size cranium who most of us called Fathead—shlumping along Madison in that Eeyorey way of his. You could tell by the hopeful look on his face that he'd been following us. He was always following us.

"Hey, guys," he said. "Is it okay if I hang out with you?" He was moving his hand around in the pocket of his big pea jacket, and I thought he was actually going to show us that stupid Liberty Head dollar of his again. His mother had given it to him not long before dying in an apartment fire the summer after sixth grade, and he was always taking the thing out and trying to get people to admire it.

"Sure, you can hang out with us," I now found myself telling him. It hadn't felt like Kyle and I'd been doing much of anything, but now it did.

"Can I get an egg roll first?" Lamar asked.

"Go ahead," Kyle told him. "We'll wait out here."

"Cool." He went into Jolly Chan's, the blinds clacking against the glass door behind him.

Kyle glanced at Lamar through the open slats of the blinds, then at me. He didn't have to say anything: the second the Chinese guy started taking Lamar's order, the two of us went tear-assing up the block, choking on our laughter and looking over our shoulders. When we got to Fifth, we hung a left around the corner and rested our butts against an apartment building, panting for breath with our hands on our knees. A graffiti-tagged green bus lumbered past, trailing a dirty pennant of smoke. A second bus followed immediately behind—they always traveled in convoys—this one with a grinning gaggle of black kids clinging to its back, their splayed sneakers balanced precariously on its rear bumper.

Kyle had to go home for a drum lesson, so I headed back toward school on my own. I was trying to figure out how else I could delay going to my father's studio, which was way downtown in a barren loft-and-warehouse district Dad said some people were starting to call TriBeCa, for "Triangle Below Canal."

I had no idea you could do tricks on a bike that didn't have a banana seat, so when a gangly Puerto Rican kid with a pubey mustache came tooling up Ninetieth Street toward the park popping a big old wheelie on a ten-speed, it brightened my mood quite a bit. The kid's eyes and mouth were wide-open in such childlike self-delight it was impossible not to share his euphoria, as if this were not just any old wheelie but a Universal Wheelie—a splendid gift intended by this beneficent stranger to enliven, for at least one exhilarating moment, the drab, wheelieless world the rest of us lived in.

The bike, I noticed as it sped past me, was a metallic-blue Panasonic like mine, made especially vivid by its unusual lipstick-red front wheel.

Things became even more vivid a moment later, when Dani Gardner saw me coming toward school. Her sweaty copper hair was back in a ponytail and her face was flushed, presumably from fencing class. She was seething in a way that made me glad she'd left her foil inside.

"What kind of a *bonehead* locks his bike by the quick-release front wheel instead of the frame, anyway?" she asked me. "What kind of a boneheaded *buffoon*?"

Holding her fingers together like a tomahawk blade, she hacked at the air in the direction of the school's bike rack, where my poor front wheel, now absent the rest of my bike, was locked beside her bike, absent its front wheel.

My boneheadedness was the complement of her own. That morning, apparently, she had slipped her U-shaped black Kryptonite lock through her bike frame and secured it to the rack the way you're supposed to. But she had neglected to take off her quick-release front wheel and lock it to the frame. The lucky thief had simply slipped her front wheel off her locked bike with a flip of his index finger, slipped my bike off its locked quick-release wheel in the same manner, mated the two to create a complete new bicycle, and pedaled off in wheelie-popping glee that the private-school world had produced two such well-matched dolts.

"I can't believe it," I said sadly. "I can't believe someone stole my ANAS."

I was in deep trouble. That bike had cost my dad two hundred bucks, and now all I had left was a lousy front wheel. I turned to Dani.

"Hey, mind if I borrow your bike?" I asked. "I mean, since you can't exactly ride it home now or anything?"

The look of withering disgust she turned on me was pretty impressive for a fourteen-year-old. It really was.

"You are *seriously* disinvited from my party next Saturday," she said, turning on her heel to head inside. "It's at seven."

4

I T WAS ALREADY TWENTY TO THREE, way too late for me to get to Dad's studio on time, and it was now looking pretty idiotic of me to have blown my last dollar on that horrendous egg roll. I needed cab fare fast.

I found Quigley where I knew she'd be, on the bridle path in the park, near the big gold bust of that old New York mayor who looked like Commissioner Gordon on *Batman*. She was smoking clove cigarettes with Valerie, the alligator-shirt-and-Tretorns girl she was always hanging out with. I hid in the bushes awhile and watched them.

Quig was wearing her rainbow-leather newsboy cap, along with a shiny silver jacket and her favorite denim bell-bottoms, the used ones from Canal Jeans that she'd embroidered along the hem with stars and comets. Beneath all that applied pizzazz, though, she was an ordinary-looking teenager with a round, freckled face and frizzy orange hair—something like a girl Danny Partridge with prettier eyes. She was wearing tangerine lipstick; she always applied it the moment she left school, where makeup wasn't allowed, because she hated the way her freckles encroached on her lips.

Valerie was supposed to be her new best friend this year, but Quig kept scratching the psoriasis on her elbows through that silver jacket, something she mostly did when she was nervous. From the scraps of conversation I could catch, it sounded like the girls were talking about acting. Quig was constantly running around town to auditions, but she'd only ever gotten one part: grinning dorkily while picking up trash from the curb on a "Give a Hoot, Don't Pollute" public service announcement. Valerie, on the other hand, almost never went on auditions. She didn't need to. Her father, who was some kind of big cheese at Grey Advertising, had gotten her a couple of Sunday-circular modeling gigs, one wearing white denim shorts for JCPenney. The rumor was that she'd even gotten a callback for *ZOOM*, that striped-rugby-shirt PBS show that everyone liked. Though she hadn't gotten the part, Valerie was a celebrity in our school just for getting close. When she parted her bee-stung lips to speak Ubbi Dubbi, *ZOOM*'s secret language, boys would swoon.

"Why *should* I?" Quig asked me, showing off for Valerie, when I approached and begged her to lend me her mug money for cab fare to Dad's studio. In those days, every New York kid with any sense carried mug money, the three or four bucks you kept in your pocket for muggers so they wouldn't beat the hell out of you.

"I'll get your next *cuppa* for you," I promised. "Your next *two* cuppas." *Cuppa* was Mom's annoyingly cutesy shorthand for the cup of instant coffee she asked us to go get her pretty much every time we passed her bedroom—as in, "Could you make me a cuppa, Griffin?"

"*Fine*," Quig said grudgingly, after waiting just long enough to make me sweat. "But you *better* pay me back!"

The farthest downtown I'd ever been by myself was FAO Schwarz on the south side of Fifty-Eighth Street, a bit past where the pigeons liked to crap on the tarnished head of General Sherman. So when the park dropped away on my right, I got to feeling pretty uncomfortable, and by the time we shot off the edge of the known world—the grid system—I was downright anxious.

To calm myself, I began to think up ways I might get my revenge on Dani for chewing me out about the stolen bike parts. The best plan, I decided, was to master the Malaysian Pincer Grip, a nifty martial arts technique that Kyle had read about in one of his ninja magazines. Known to initiates (or at least to Kyle and me) as the Beak of

Doom, the exercise involved picking up a juice jug about a million times using just your fingertips. You'd start with the jug empty and then add a little bit of sand every day (I would substitute kitty litter) until eventually your fingers became so very mighty that just by beaking your five fingertips together you could rip out chunks of people's skin at will.

That sounded pretty damn cool to me. Because it was awfully hard to imagine Dani, or any girl for that matter, giving me a hard time when they knew that at any moment the Beak of Doom might flutter out from my fingertips and extract chunks of smirking freckles from their cheeks. It was only because of my masterful falconry, my secret of holding back the savage fowl that quivered within my fingers, that their skin remained intact. They would know this, and respect me for it.

My cabbie was clearly lost, the downtown street names rushing past us as foreign to him as the nearly vowel-less last name on his hack license was to me. The meter clicked up toward three dollars, ten cents at a time, and just as I became absolutely certain we'd never find the studio, I caught a glimpse down a potholed side street of a figure as familiar to me as my own reflection.

"Stop!" I yelled at the cabbie.

The driver disgorged me midblock with my orphaned bike wheel and fled back uptown as fast as he could, leaving me to pick my way on foot past the piles of splintered crates and leaky trash bags that lined the curb outside the sealed-up warehouses. At the corner, I peered around the edge of a building and saw my father standing alone in a street called Worth, squinting up at a fifth-floor window through binoculars.

There was more than a whiff of disrepute about whatever he was up to, although I suppose that might just have been the mingled stench of trash juice and chemical disinfectant given off by the liquid stagnating in the cobble cracks.

It wasn't hard to figure out what had so captured Dad's attention. The big window he was scoping out across the street had a graceful arc at the top, giving it the shape of one of those little stairwell niches Italian families stuck their saints in. Every so often a woman in a white T-shirt would appear in profile within its frame, holding something that might have been a paintbrush. It was too far away to be sure with the naked eye, but it seemed like she had some fairly significant knockers going on under that shirt.

Dad couldn't take his eyes off her. He seemed so consumed with mastering her every detail, her every nuance of movement, that he never put the binoculars down.

Dad was a peeping Tom! The realization coursed through me with a thrilling shame. I'd never understood, even before he moved out, what exactly Dad did downtown when he wasn't home. He was an antiques dealer with a big old restoration studio on the margins of the city (by appointment only). That much everyone agreed on. He had a woodshop there, and a metalworking shop, too. He was good with his hands. But Mom always intimated that there was more to it than that. "Oh, that's where Nick stashes all his *women*," I'd once heard her say scornfully to her friend Nadine.

I watched Dad watch the woman. There was an animal refinement about his fixation as he tracked her, an intensity somehow both reverent and predatory, as if he felt that the act of unbroken observation, of appreciating a thing of beauty more fully than the next fellow, could somehow bring it under your control, make it yours.

And then his gaze, his need, did seem to command her. Dad glanced at his watch, nodded, and looked up expectantly at the woman's window with his arms crossed, binoculars dangling from his neck. Within seconds, as though heeding his unspoken directive, she disappeared from the window and her room went dark. Dad seemed to know what would happen next. Taking his time, he crouched behind a car and watched as the woman emerged a minute later, a zippered bag over her shoulder, from the building's battered metal front door. She had wavy, dirty-blond hair. He made no move to follow her, just watched as she clicked down the block away from us in her knee-high Naugahyde boots, hugging a denim minidress tightly around her body. Turns out I'd been right about those knockers.

5

DAD'S BUILDING WAS A FORTRESS with its eyes closed. A run-down redbrick warehouse built in the style of a medieval castle, it had a notched roofline like a battlement and four rows of tall arched windows, each one sealed shut with a pair of massive iron shutters. You kind of got the feeling that if you hung around out front too long, a couple of workmen in flannel shirts and chain-mail overalls would peer out from the roof and pour boiling oil on you.

The warehouse, flanked by grubby loft buildings, sat midblock on an asphalt-patched cobblestone street with no sign of human activity other than the parked hearse up the block. I'd followed Dad here from his little curbside reconnaissance mission, watching from a safe distance while he let himself in. Though I wasn't in any hurry to get into an enclosed space with his unpredictable temper, I was certainly curious about what lay behind his building's imposing street wall. I'd never been inside, and had glimpsed the outside just once before, the day three years earlier when Dad dragged me down to this area to watch the metal face of a decrepit antique building get peeled away, piece by piece. I'd never seen such meticulous destruction before that morning. Straddling a beam three stories above the street, two men in wool caps were shooting flame at the old building's seams, twin clouds of steam rising lazily from their blowtorches in the February chill. When I'd looked over at Dad, he was wincing, almost as if the building's skin were his own.

Shaking off the memory, I locked my bike wheel to a bent iron railing out front of a butter-and-egg wholesaler and gingerly approached Dad's warehouse. Its entrance had a speakeasy anonymity. A dented metal door, no street number, a hodgepodge of unmarked, improvised buzzers, some with wires running right up the outside of the building and into the shuttered windows. I pressed the buttons one at a time, with no results, until the only one left untried was a broken round one I hadn't wanted to touch. It hung loose by a green wire and made me think of a girl's nipple, a robot nipple maybe.

A second exposed wire was sticking out of the wall behind it, and when I touched its frayed copper tip to the loose screw inside the robot nipple, a flaming torrent of pain surged into my hand and shot up my arm. I dropped to the ground and rolled away on the pavement, desperately trying to catch my breath, a crushing weight of buzzing weariness pushing down on my chest. I don't know how long I lay there panting, but as the electrical shock faded to an intense, achy tingling in my fingers, I heard a strange squeak from above. I looked up to see one of the heavy iron shutters swinging slowly open on the third floor, and Dad's big handsome head popping out the window.

"You're late," he said, looking down at me on the ground a long moment before hauling the shutter closed again with a clang. The front door buzzed.

It was like the opening sequence of *Get Smart* in there. Just inside the metal street door was a second metal door, behind which ran a long, dingy hallway, at the end of which stood an elevator door with a rectangular window grate set into it. The elevator smelled of sweat and Chinese takeout. Wheezing and clicking, it took me upstairs in slow motion, giving me plenty of time to admire the key-scratch graffiti (YO MAMA YO MAMA YO MAMA!) on its sloppily painted gray walls.

No one was waiting for me on the third floor. But a trickle of classical music was escaping through the crack in a big metal door on my left. I followed the sound inside, then left and right through a dusty warren of hallways, until I reached its source: my father's army surplus transistor radio. It was sitting on a chewed-up worktable in the middle of a cavernous room stuffed to the ceiling with antique bric-a-brac: lion's-foot bathtubs, buckets of tarnished brass doorknobs, a moose-antler chandelier, upside-down four-poster beds, a candy-striped barber pole leaning against a crumbly brick wall.

Piled together at the front of the room was a great jumble of churchy-looking wooden panels and pews and doors and things. They appeared even more disordered than all the other antiques, as if God, perturbed by the way His house had been allowed to get as tumbledown and shabby as the rest of the city, had plucked up a cathedral and shaken loose its contents through the windows of my father's restoration studio.

I started toward the middle of the pile, where a fancy wooden bird-bath, the kind you saw at the front of churches, was lying on its side.

"Going right for the good stuff, are we?" I heard Dad's voice say. "I guess excellent taste runs in the family."

He had been watching me, and he now stepped out from behind a dark carved-wood staircase that corkscrewed ornately up to a grand but grungy pulpit. He was glittering a little, his sandy hair and one of his eyebrows speckled with gold leaf from some object he'd been gilding.

"This is actually the very stuff I thought I'd start you on," he said. "Beautiful pieces—came out of a sweet little church in Hell's Kitchen—but the dopey priests have been slapping varnish and lacquer and God knows what-all on them for about a hundred years. The archdiocese hired me to clean up the whole mess and reinstall everything."

He motioned me over to a worktable scarred with cuts and pimpled with paint.

"I suppose this isn't the kind of stripper most fathers would teach sons your age about," he told me with a half chuckle, hefting a big red-and-white can onto the table. "But I guess I'm not most fathers."

He poured some silvery goo from the can into a Greek coffee cup printed with a blue picture of what looked like a naked muscleman hurling a Frisbee.

"This is methylene chloride," Dad said. "It'll eat through just about any oil-based material. Just don't get it in your eyes or it'll blind you."

Dad mounted the spiral staircase, which was supported by cinder blocks, and appeared a moment later in the raised pulpit. He looked even bigger than usual up there.

"This poor pulpit has really suffered," he said, preaching down to a congregation of one. "You can see how dark and gooey the oak has gotten, and you see these gaudy orangey-gold highlights on the raised parts of the ornament?"

I nodded.

"That's radiator paint. Back when they invented it, everyone thought of it as gold in a can. They didn't know it would bronze over time and look phony, so they just slathered it on wherever the real gold got dulled."

Dad leaned over the top of the pulpit, loaded up his paintbrush with stripper from the cup, and gooped it onto a horizontal strip of carved ornament that looked like alternating gumballs and arrowheads. The paint on it had the cheap bronzy look he was talking about.

"What I'm going to need *you* to do is strip off the last century of goo and paint and get to the original 'parcel gilding' underneath," he said, looking down at me. "Well? Come up already. Come up, you fearful Jesuit!"

The twisting steps complained as I tiptoed up them. When I leaned over the pulpit next to Dad, the stripper fumes immediately stung my eyeballs, and I snapped my head back involuntarily.

"What're you *doing*?" Dad asked irritably. "We've got *work* to do here."

Squinting hard to protect my eyes, I leaned over the pulpit's edge again. It was all about timing. Dad showed me how to wait until the gold paint started to bubble up beneath the stripper, then to poke at it with the bristle tips, shoving the gooey gold bisque to the side. But when I gave it some elbow grease to try to get down to the layer of real gold on one of the gumballs, Dad's hand shot out and grabbed my wrist.

"*Easy* there, kiddo," he said. "*First, do no harm.*"

I looked at him.

"That's the conservator's credo." He took the brush from me and nudged the liquefied gold paint, with exquisite tenderness, to the edge of the gumball. It was hard to believe that so gentle a touch could reside within such a heavy hand. "You want to take the object back in time, to get down to the original surface," Dad told me. "But you need to make sure that in the process of trying to save it, you don't fuck it up instead by scraping off the original gold."

Dad headed back down to the studio floor, the spiral staircase groaning under his weight. With his arms crossed and his head cocked in silent appraisal, he stood down there and watched me—an eighth-grader with exactly zero restoration experience—try to save the richly carved pulpit of some New York congregation's precious nineteenth-century church.

Eyeball-stinging fumes aside, it felt like a pretty cool thing to be doing, until a drop of stripper fell from the brush onto the back of my hand. The pain was searing, a flaming drill bit boring straight into my flesh. I frantically wiped it off with my shirtsleeve.

"*What?*" Dad asked.

"This stripper stuff, it *kills*."

"*Please.* Every restorer knows it hurts like a bastard to get stripper on your skin—but it's worth it, okay? Most people go their whole lives without handling an object of beauty in any meaningful way. Most people don't even think to want to."

The stripper on my sleeve was now scalding my wrist. I rubbed at it with the other sleeve. Dad paid no attention.

"What I'm teaching you to do right now," he said, "is really the only way to learn about architectural sculpture: with your hands first, and *then* with your eyes."

I couldn't focus on what he was saying. In trying to rub the stripper off my wrist, I'd gotten some on my fingers. It felt like someone was jabbing lit matches into my cuticles.

"That's why I chose to have you work on this pulpit first," Dad went on. "It's Renaissance Revival, which means it's like a greatest hits of classical ornament: you got your Ionic capitals, your fluted pilasters, your scrollwork—and running along the top there you've got that golden oldie we've just been struggling to clean: egg and dart."

"Egg and dart?"

"Yeah, it's one of the most common decorative moldings in Western architecture. It's everywhere around the city."

"I call it gumball and arrow."

"That's great!" Dad said, his voice rising with something like excitement. "The name doesn't matter. People who study academic lingo learn *facts* about ornament, but the only way you can really come to *know* the ornament is by feeling its contours for yourself." He fixed me with those green eyes of his. "If you do that, Griffin, the whole city will open up to you. You'll find that you're suddenly seeing ornamental sculpture, really wonderful stuff you never noticed before, on buildings all over town. You'll learn to look up."

He handed me up a blue can of alcohol and a roll of cotton, told me to use them to clean off the surface when the stripper and melted paint got too gloppy.

"So I'll leave you to it," he announced. "I've got an important Stanford White grille frame I've got to finish regilding. You just keep hitting that egg and dart, and when you're done, move down to the dentil molding below it—the one that looks like teeth."

I nodded and bent to my work. When I glanced up for his approval, he was gone.

The warehouse was a busy place. Men came and went in the hallway, shouldering loads, muttering at one another with joshing aggression. Now and then the grinding shriek of a power saw echoed down the corridor from some distant room.

It was a relief to have Dad out of my face, but I sure wished I could keep the stripper fumes out of it, too, because that methylene chloride was now stinging my throat as much as my eyes.

I'd never seen a real stripper, the Times Square kind. But I was pretty sure that women's bodies coursed with danger. One Christmas Eve when our family was coming back uptown from Sky Rink, our Checker cab stopped at a red light on a side street near Broadway, a few blocks up from the colossal Gordon's Gin bottle and the giant man on the Winston billboard blowing real smoke rings out over the theater marquees and electronics shops. I was sitting on the right jump seat in front of Dad, who was reaming Mom out for getting him wobbly rental skates that made him look foolish on the ice. One side of his face kept flashing an unnatural purple, and when I looked out at the sidewalk I saw that the color was coming from a neon stripper, topless and life-size, blinking rhythmically in the window of a sex shop.

She was made entirely out of twitching electricity, which seemed to flow into her fragile outline from the pole she was straddling. Every time her body blinked, she would ride lewdly up or down that pole. I wondered, if you shattered the thin glass tube that held her, whether she would spurt out and scald you, or just leak out into nothingness.

As I snapped a pair of rubber gloves onto my hands, two men with red faces struggled past the studio door, pushing a sort of gurney weighed down with something long, thin, and awkward. It was wrapped in a filthy green bedspread.

"Stop! Stop twisting her!" one guy whisper-yelled at the other. "He said not to hurt her any more!"

"It's not *me!*" the other hissed. "It's this damn *wheel!*"

When they came hurrying back a couple minutes later, the gurney was empty. I gave the men time to get back to the elevator, then slipped down the hall in the other direction, following the cart's wheel tracks in the floor dust to where they ended at an industrial-looking sliding metal door. The door had a big padlock on it, and just behind the lock, on the dingy off-white paint, a smear of fresh blood. It was moist and thick, like finger paint.

For a second, the greasy ick of my egg-roll lunch washed up into my mouth from my insides, mixed with sour stomach acid. I swallowed it all back down and sprinted back to the studio.

I yanked off the rubber gloves and tossed them on a DECARLO FUNERAL HOME cooler, then crept to the elevator and saw the brass arrow above it pointing to 1. Right there on the landing, opposite the elevator, was a big clouded window with wire pentagons inside its glass. On a hunch, I yanked the window open and poked my head out into the dusk. Below me, parked a few feet down the cobblestoned

alley behind Dad's building, was a boxy vehicle I instantly recognized, even in the waning daylight, as a Good Humor truck. It had
the big doors in back for loading in cases of ice cream, and on its side,
faintly visible through a layer of what looked like white house paint,
hovered an enormous phantom Popsicle.

The vehicle was giving out an unnerving rumble. What could Dad
possibly need a refrigerated truck for?

One of the men from the hall, a twitchy hippie with a gray-streaked
ponytail down to the small of his back, was at the end of the alley,
peering furtively out onto the street. His head was darting around
with so much nervous energy that his swinging ponytail appeared
prehensile, as if he could use it to pull a Marlboro from his vest pocket.
When he was satisfied that the coast was clear, he sprinted back to the
side of the truck, slid open the big side window a crack, and called to
someone inside, "All right, all right, we're good!"

The rest of the maneuver was carefully orchestrated. The ponytail guy dashed inside the warehouse and came back out pushing the
gurney. As he shoved it up against the tailgate, the truck's rear doors
were thrown open from the inside, and out slid an old door on which
lay a quilt-shrouded figure about the same height as the one from the
hall. This one was roped flat to the door. With help from old Ponytail,
the guy inside the truck slid the door onto the cart, where it landed
with a heavy slam that echoed off the alley's darkened windows.

As the two men muscled the wheeled cart over the bumpy cobbled
street, the quilt concealing the bound figure's head slipped to one
side, revealing the startled eyes, tangled hair, and protruding collarbone of a woman. She was staring straight up, and our eyes met, but
before she could cry out, the ponytail guy frantically smothered her
face with the quilt again. I wondered if she would expect me to do
anything for her.

After the two men had hustled the woman into the building, I sat
there a long moment on the sill of the open window, watching my
hurried breath float out into the alley and vanish. Not a single window was illuminated in the loft building across the way. It was all up
to me.

Unable to think straight, I slammed the window shut and fled back to the studio to try to figure out what to do next. This time I hid behind an old desk so the men wouldn't see me if they glanced in as they came by the doorway. I heard the two of them rolling her past, their labored breathing and hushed curses, and after waiting a bit of time for good measure, I crept down the hall after them to that big metal door. It was slid shut again, the edges of the blood smear now thickening up to a dark, ketchupy red, and although the door wasn't padlocked this time, there was no way to slide such a heavy thing open without being heard.

I started thinking about how a real detective would get inside that room, someone like the go-it-alone smart aleck Jim Rockford from *The Rockford Files* ("Two hundred dollars a day, plus expenses"), or maybe Pete Cochran, that brooding, curly-haired member of *The Mod Squad* who Quigley thought was so cute. Rockford was my favorite, but Pete seemed to offer the more useful example. One of the Mod Squad's recent adventures demonstrated that if you wanted to crawl from one room or floor to another and do some really good spying or rescuing, then air ducts were the way to go. Just a few weeks before, that slick black dude, Linc—the one with the amazing, Jupiter-size Afro—had gotten kidnapped by some foreign bad guys and locked up in the big printing press part of a newspaper building. But before they had a chance to off him, Pete had crawled down through the air ducts from the floor above to rescue him.

I tried the doors of both rooms adjoining the one the gurney had been rolled into. But they were locked, so I made my way up a dirty, checkerboard-linoleum stairwell and slipped into the room above the one I needed to get into.

The room was down-at-heel swanky, with iron columns and those rolly wooden chairs on casters you sometimes saw in old banks. It looked like an office or a showroom. The back wall was decorated with antique gold picture frames—some empty, others surrounding old paintings of constipated-looking dukes and baronesses.

There was no sign of air ducts. But one section of the worn wooden floor did look different from the rest. Along the edge of the back wall, two holes had been drilled into the floor and a length of clothesline looped through them to form a makeshift handle.

When I kneeled and gave the handle a tug, a pair of conjoined floor-boards lifted right out to reveal a skinny rectangular slot, open to the room below, and a whoosh of musty air rose into my face, carrying a fetid smell and the low murmur of men's voices. All I could see when I peered down through the hole was a strip of the floor downstairs and, just to the side of the slot, a floor-to-ceiling rack filled with old picture frames stacked sideways like volumes in a bookcase.

The appropriate role model here, I realized, wasn't Rockford or Pete at all, but Flat Stanley. Stanley was a kid in a children's book who got brutally pancaked as he slept one night when the heavy bulletin board his parents had half-assedly hung above his bed ripped loose and squashed him. But instead of feeling resentful about his disfigurement, as any normal kid would, Stanley took his flattening as an opportunity for exploration, rolling himself up like a poster so he could get mailed to California in a tube for vacation.

Flat Stanley had nothing on me. Without thinking it through, I mailed myself right down through the narrow slot in the floor, painfully scraping my stomach and nipples on its edge. For a few seconds I hung there with my rib cage wedged in that hole, half of me upstairs and half downstairs, until I managed to swing my legs over to the frame rack and lower myself onto its top shelf.

The moment I got my bearings, crouching there just below the ceiling, I looked down and saw her. The woman from the gurney. She was flat on her back and stripped naked past the waist, her breasts breathtakingly full, the dimple of her belly button holding a tiny cup of shadow. She was made of stone, I now realized—how crazy of me to have thought she was a living woman. But in any event, she was incomplete. Below the two gentle knobs of her hips, her languorous body ended abruptly, flowing into a severe, angular bracket carved from the same beige stone. Though unquestionably beautiful, she looked freakish lying there with no legs, a magician's stage trick gone awry.

Once I'd clambered down the frame rack one more shelf, below the level of the dust-fuzzed ceiling pipes, I got a clear view of the whole room. The legless carved woman, it turned out, was a triplet. On a raised platform at the center of the room—part altar, part operating theater—lay three virtually identical half-naked half women in stone.

Each one's arms were raised above her head, palms upward, hefting an invisible burden. Each had that weird supporting bracket instead of legs.

The two men from the hall were leaning over the figure farthest from me, working on her. A dark stain ran down the middle of her face and body, and the ponytail guy was scrubbing her eyeball with a toothbrush. The beefier guy kept slapping at the lower slope of her right breast with a square of sandpaper, blowing on it to clear the stone dust, then hitting it again.

Dad came in and told them they were wasting their time.

"That's acid rain," he said of the stain, after ascending to the platform on a stepladder. "You're not gonna be able to do much with that." He stopped a moment and regarded the three figures. "They really are beauties, aren't they? Worth all the trouble."

"Absolutely," said Ponytail. The knuckles of his left hand were stone-scraped and dappled with blood. He stuck his fist in his mouth and sucked on it in thought, peering closely at the discolored sculpture. "But don't you think we should try the belt sander on this one, just a quick pass?"

Dad shook his head. "Don't worry, Zev, we'll find her a home," he said. "Some people like a little damage. Like at the pet shelter. There's always one softie who goes straight for the one-eyed cat with a bite taken out of its ear."

That's when Dad saw me. I'd thought I was hidden, crammed into the shadows of the rack between two sideways-stacked frames, but his eyes met mine and there was no getting away. He strode toward me on the platform, his face reddening.

"What in *God's* name—" he began, before losing the thread of his anger. He looked over at the room's big metal door, slid shut as before. "Wait, how'd you get in here?"

I lifted my eyes to the ceiling. He looked up, too.

"You were able to squeeze through that skinny frame slot? How's that even possible?"

"Well, I just—"

"Could you do it again?" He looked distracted, turning something over in his mind. "What I mean is, are you scared of heights? Do you get dizzy or anything when you're high up like that?"

"No, not at all. But, Dad, what *are* those things, those stone ladies?"

He took a long breath, as if deciding how much to tell me. But once he started talking, he could hardly stop.

"These, Griffin, are caryatids," he said. "They're basically stone columns, sculpted in the shape of women. Sometimes they're used to support pediments, but these were just decorative. They were holding stone urns above their heads. You like 'em?"

I nodded tentatively and climbed down from the frame rack.

"Really finely carved ones like these are comparatively rare in the city—and getting rarer. More often on New York buildings what you'll see are marvelous carved heads of goddesses or grotesques or mythological beasts."

Ponytail was nodding. "We usually just call them all gargoyles," he said.

"We do," Dad agreed, a bit annoyed at the interruption, "although a gargoyle is technically a carved creature whose mouth is a water spout."

"Where'd they come from?" I asked, making my way over to the platform.

"These three?" Dad said. "They were on the second floor of the Daedalus Life Assurance Building, on West Fifty-Third. Just off of Sixth."

"So they were knocking down the building, and they gave these things to you?"

"Not exactly."

"They weren't knocking down the building, or they didn't give them to you?"

He considered the question.

"Neither, actually," he said. "Though they did kick out all their tenants, which is how my crew and I were able to get in there last night and remove such big pieces without getting caught. And you know, owners usually don't boot their tenants unless they're preparing to demo the building."

I thought this over as I climbed the ladder to join Dad on the platform.

"So these carved ladies," I said, "you *stole* them?"

He looked at me a long moment, expressionless, until at last the corner of his mouth curled into the barest hint of a smirk.

"I *liberated* them. There's a difference. I rescue these things and I find them homes with people who actually appreciate them."

"You just go around town and take whatever you like?"

"Only the *good* ones," quipped Ponytail, chuckling.

Dad heaved a big sigh. "Guys," he said to his two workers, "I think you can knock off for the day. Just make sure one of you parks the truck back on the pier, okay?"

When they had mumbled their goodbyes and gone, Dad leaned against the curved flank of the stained woman's stomach and looked at me seriously.

"Look, son. What I'm doing is saving these things. Gargoyles are an endangered species—a whole slew of endangered species, actually. Cherubs and satyrs, gryphons and sea monsters, goddesses and kings—they're all just being wiped out. For years the city has been doing these gigantic urban renewal projects, tearing down great swaths of neighborhoods, and every time they demolish a row house or a tenement, its architectural sculptures get smashed into rubble and dumped in a landfill somewhere. So I try to get in there first and rescue them."

His middle and index fingers had found the finely wrought bones edging the stone woman's throat. They worked the hollow there, then moved up one of the two slender tendons that extended upward in a V from her collarbone. Here her stone flesh, long protected from the filthy heavens by the awning of her chin, was unstained.

"But you just said the building these came from was still standing. How do you know it was going to be torn down at all?"

"You're missing the big picture. If we wait until a building owner pulls a demolition permit, we may never get a shot at its gargoyles. The demo contractor will surround the site with fences and barbed wire, maybe even a guard. They don't want the liability of people wandering around in the rubble and hurting themselves."

"I guess," I said. There was a lot about how the city transformed itself that I didn't understand.

"Let me tell you, Griffin, it's all going fast. Between urban renewal and all that soulless, homogenized Modernist crap they keep putting up—all those housing projects, those International Style office towers, the endless blocky apartment buildings in white brick and yellow brick and now red brick—it's only a matter of time before the city's everyday sculpture is lost entirely." His fingertip had reached the subtle rise of the stone woman's neck gland, where it lingered to explore the unexpected nuance there. "Ornament is dead, son, and it's not coming back."

I was really getting light-headed and sickish from all the stripper fumes and the climbing and everything.

"Can I go home now?" I asked quietly.

"Sure, Griffin. Sure you can. But how do you think I pay for that home?" There was a weary defensiveness to my father's voice. "You think it's a breeze supporting two households in a recession? You think that whole good thing you've got, living in that brownstone, can't collapse easy enough?"

"I never said that," I protested. But the truth was, I did think of the brownstone as a forever place. It had to be. Fathers went away, or occasionally mothers. Homes were supposed to stay put. Even Lamar's apartment had survived the fire that had killed his mom.

"The first of every month, Griffin, the fifteenth with the grace period. That's when the brownstone payment is due." He nodded toward the topless stone figures. "You have these ladies to thank that the bank will get what's coming to it this month. But next month, who knows?"

I understood as little about banks as I did about women. "The bank lets you pay them in ladies?" I asked.

"Of course not," Dad said, annoyed. "But I've got to come up with the cash somehow, and nobody's buying antiques anymore, not like they used to. The collectibles market's been tanking for two years. Gargoyles, on the other hand—the living city—that's another matter. Restaurants, interior designers, collectors, lots of people around the world want a piece of New York." He seemed to be cheering himself up. "And you'd be amazed what good care they take of the stuff. Hell, they respect city artifacts more than the city does itself." His fingertips had alighted on the delicate folds of the stone woman's ear, darkly streaked by weather and slightly opened like a flower.

I started making my way down the ladder to the floor.

"I'll finish that pulpit some other time, okay?" I said. "I don't feel so hot."

"Never mind about the pulpit," Dad said, turning away at last from the carved figure. "It's the gargoyles I could really use your help with." He gave me a broad smile that showed a couple of his gold molars; he had been joking lately that if the oil crisis kept driving our heating bills up, we could always raise cash by melting down his fillings. "I'm going out again next Friday night—I've got a big buyer coming in from Houston the following week—and it would be a great help to have a nimble fellow like you along. We can just tell your mother you're having a sleepover at my place. She doesn't need to know about all this."

"I don't know," I said. "*Kung Fu* is on." This wasn't true; Thursday was *Kung Fu* night. But I knew he'd have no clue about that. He didn't even own a TV.

"Well, just think it over. If you want to help me make that next brownstone payment, just show up here next Friday around six. We'll get some spare ribs in Chinatown, maybe catch a movie, then go gargoyle hunting after midnight. Boys' night out."

"But what help could *I* be? I don't know anything about all this gargoyle stuff."

"There are things you can do, places you can get into, that I can't," Dad told me, glancing up, just for a second, at the frame slot in the ceiling. "I need you."

I could scarcely breathe. He had never said anything like that to me before.

PART TWO

THE GARGOYLE HUNTERS

6

MY MOTHER CALLED HERSELF a Manhattan orphan because every apartment house she'd lived in and every school she'd attended before age ten had vanished without a trace. Every candy store she loved, too. Every penny arcade. Every shoe shop that had dressed her growing feet in Mary Janes and canvas tennis shoes and saddle oxfords. Every Kips Bay five-and-dime, and every record store. Every soda fountain.

The way she told it, she never blamed the city for its elbow-jostling relationship with time. For one thing, no matter how often New York reinvented itself, no matter how frequently she moved house, she always took herself with her. For another, change was the city's nature. You might just as well rage at the ocean for breaking against the shore in its unending rolling rhythm, for smashing seashells into shards, then taking them back into itself as if they had never been.

When I got home from my father's studio, shuffling into a skinny brownstone that suddenly felt malnourished and fragile, my mother was at the big lion's-foot dining room table, sorting her eggshells. A dark-eyed, Gypsy-looking sort of a mom, she was an elegant sweep of shawls and scarves, jangling bracelets and two-dozen-plus-three rings.

To the untrained eye, the tools of her trade would have looked like a street person's eccentric treasures. About thirty Finast vegetable Baggies were heaped on the table in front of her, each filled with hundreds of eggshell fragments ranging in size from a sesame seed to a penny. Behind the Baggies, the table was crowded with giant Hellmann's mayonnaise bottles, the size they used in our school cafeteria's kitchen. The mayo bottles served as long-term storage for her sorted eggshell fragments. Every time our household finished a dozen eggs, she would peel away the inner membranes, toss the shells in a Baggie, smash them up inside it, and put them aside until the Baggies started to pile up. This had now happened, so the task at hand was to fill those oversize mayo bottles by matching each bag of fresh fragments with the bottle containing fragments of the same shade of white or beige or brown (and, if applicable, bearing the same subtly dappled surface). Mom and I were the only two in the family who could do it. Dad was too impatient, and Quigley couldn't tell one shade of brown from the next.

"Where've you been?" Mom asked as I plopped down in a bentwood chair beside her and pulled off my Pumas and socks to clean out the lint between my toes. "And that's revolting, by the way."

"School play tryouts," I said. Lying to our parents was easy, since neither of them ever had the faintest clue what courses we were taking, much less what extracurriculars were on offer.

"Yeah?" she asked. "Anything I've heard of?"

"*West Side Story.* I hate musicals, but the fighting could be cool."

"*West Side Story!*" Mom chirped. "Lincoln Center."

"Of course not. It's just a school play. They'll perform it in the church like always."

"No, I mean the whole neighborhood where *West Side Story* was shot was torn down to make way for Lincoln Center and Lincoln Towers. I had a Puerto Rican friend in first grade, Felicia Vasquez, who I met at a puppet show in the park. She lived in a walk-up where the Vivian Beaumont Theater is now. But my mother was afraid to go there, so I could only visit when my father was willing to take me." She held a Baggie of eggshell fragments above two mayo bottles, apparently pondering which tribe of shells the new fragments belonged to. "Then they tore down all the tenements and put up an opera house."

"Urban renewal?" I asked, liking how grown-up the new term sounded rolling off my tongue.

"I guess so. Or maybe what they sometimes call slum clearance. I don't follow the politics of it."

I began helping her sort the eggshells. I liked showing her how quickly I could identify the exact shade and pick out the right bottle for it.

"Where's Quig?" I asked.

"An audition, maybe? She was wearing some kind of cocktail dress with shoes that didn't match."

I nodded, and we sorted eggshells in silence for a bit.

It was the eggs, in all their subtle variety, that had brought my parents together in the first place. That's how they always explained it to us, anyway. This was back in the fifties. Dad had a restoration studio down near the old Washington Market, below the butter-and-egg district, and he spotted Mom at dawn while coasting home down Greenwich Street in his pickup truck, bleary-eyed after an all-night drive with a load of antique furniture from a Maine estate sale.

At the curb by Duane Park, he idled his engine, then hopped out and followed her at a distance as she went from one egg wholesaler to the next, from Fortgang to Wils to Weiss, questioning the vendors, turning the eggs over in the gathering sunlight, seeking out variations in color, shade, even texture. She herself was a variation in color and texture, an earthy figure in a lavender dress and patterned shawl moving among the pallid egg men in their white smocks and cuffed trousers.

"You take much longer to choose, lady, and those eggs are gonna be chickens," grumbled an exasperated merchant with a stub of pencil behind his ear.

She used the eggshells, crushed into fragments, to create intricate mosaic seascapes and landscapes: a single moored sailboat on a bay of shattered light; a cloud-bullying mountain peak reduced to its thousand facets. She had remarkable eyesight—20/10 like Ted Williams—and was so precise with her tweezers that you could scarcely see the gaps between the shards. One of her teachers at Pratt told her she was onto something, that he didn't always like her work but that he found it hard to stop looking at it. She had ideas about going to Italy to study art, to learn what she could do, to eat prosciutto-and-butter sandwiches on the lip of a fountain glittering with coins. But Quigley—and this is *so* Quigley—elbowed her way into the frame before my mother had been out of school six months, and when Mom next looked up she found herself in the very position she had always promised herself to avoid: pinned down in a one-bedroom Hell's Kitchen apartment with a handsome husband and a needy daughter and very little room to maneuver.

The thought that she was becoming her mother gnawed at her. Nourished daily, her self-loathing grew.

But Mom rallied. It dawned on her that the fact of Quigley, squalling and red-faced as she was, did not have to keep her—keep any of them—from making a move. She could get a part-time job during the hours Quig was in preschool. She and Dad could pool their earnings and rent a tumbledown farmhouse in the Italian countryside, maybe get another pair of young marrieds to join them. Quig could dash down the leaf-fringed corridors of a neighboring vineyard while Mom made art and had an experience or two.

Dad would have none of it, however. No way *his* wife was working. No way *he* was leaving New York after fighting so hard to make a life here, to put his Depression-era rural childhood behind him.

She let the subject drop. She knew better than to stir up his temper. She had no wish to see his face change, those blazing eyes of thunderbolt green.

That, in any event, was how Mom told me her story. She always talked to me like a peer, a confidant, spilling out intimate details of her resentments that most mothers had the good sense to save for their friends. It wasn't propaganda; she wasn't trying to turn me against Dad. It was just an unfiltered account of how she was feeling at any given moment, without any consideration of how hearing about it might make *me* feel. By turns she trashed my father and told me how exceptional he was, how much more interesting than any other man she'd ever known.

She did not leave Dad after the aborted trip to Italy—there was nowhere to go—but I'm not sure she ever forgave him.

Her art took a turn. For the next several weeks she worked late into the night painting the big wall of Quigley's nursery with a rollicking, cartoonish mural of the Trevi Fountain, water cascading and spraying, winged horses with fish tails pulling a mighty sea god's chariot amid the spume. It was a nice thing to do for Quig, who spent much of her childhood gazing up at this wondrous scene, her little bed pushed against the sparkling aquamarine pool in the precise spot, I realized years later, where Anita Ekberg and Marcello Mastroianni had stood together in *La Dolce Vita*, knee-deep in the ephemeral.

Mom returned to her eggshell mosaics. The pastoral scenes were gone, the seaside idylls. She thought of her childhood. She was an only child, the brooding, button-nosed kewpie doll her parents dressed up in ribboned dresses to complete their image of themselves as a handsome couple. Her father, who ran a small hardware store on Second Avenue, had a tremendous reverence for famous men. Every Sunday, when the weather was fine, he would dress to the nines in one of the tailored suits he got wholesale from his uncle Hiram, and he would take his wife and daughter to a different city park and tell them all the facts he had memorized about whichever great man was cast in bronze up on the pedestal there. His wife, the deputy spouse, would stroll alongside him without speaking, her arm looped possessively through his. Neither paid much attention to their daughter.

Now my mother revisited those bronze men on those high pedestals. She hadn't really planned to, she told me, but one day she found herself going around town taking snapshots of their proud, impersonal heads, the lordly expressions that as a girl had made her feel judged, scorned for a run in her tights that only they could see. She put her eggshell fragments to work, creating new portraits of these bronze personages, revealing the fault lines in their self-certainty, the hundred unacknowledged fissures, the veins of emotional absence that held them together as surely as the lead mullions in any stained-glass window. I was too young to follow fully when she explained her work to me in this way, and sometimes I got tired of hearing about it, but I did like those mosaic portraits, their spotlight on the invisible. They made me think of Rice Krispies, how that big blue box contains as much air as nourishment.

Every October, as far back as I could remember, Mom would have a big art show at the brownstone. She'd order up gallons of Gallo wine in green glass jugs, set me and Quig behind a card table as under-age barkeeps, and invite the city in. Crowds of her arty friends would come, and hangabouts from the neighborhood looking for free eats, and antiques people Dad knew. They'd get hammered, gobble up the olives and deviled eggs, grind crackers into the carpets, stay too late. Sometime after midnight, someone, usually the same lumpish Irishman, would produce a steel guitar, pluck at it with overlong fingernails, and begin singing too loudly. This would inevitably inspire several other men, usually with no musical ability, to pull copper pots off the walls and press them into service as drums, banging them arrhythmically with serving spoons and ice tongs. Everyone sung himself hoarse.

It was my job, when a mosaic portrait was sold, to affix a little red polka-dot sticker to its lower right corner. This never happened more than once or twice a show, if at all. But we were pretty low on stickers by then, anyway. Quig and I usually got bored and stuck them on our foreheads, individually as bindis, or in bunches as zits.

After I finished sorting my first bag of eggshells, Mom took the bag and a few other empties into the kitchen and threw them away. When she came back, she gave a big yawn and started in on another Baggie. Her bangles—bone and Bakelite and tortoiseshell, wood and turquoise and silver—clacked on her wrists as she worked.

"Mom," I asked quietly, as if it was no big deal. "What's that lady's face in the basement? The *half* lady's face, I mean."

She frowned, two vertical lines appearing between her eyebrows. "Oh, *that*. Nice of your father to leave that behind, huh?"

"What do you mean? Is she his? Is she related to us?"

"What are you talking about?"

"She looked like a death mask," I said. "Or what's that other thing they make by sticking straws up your nose so you can breathe while they smoosh plaster on your face?"

"A life mask?"

"Yeah, a life mask."

"No, no. She's not a real person. She's a terra-cotta ornament from a tenement façade. Terra cotta's a fired clay, and they always made those ornaments hollow so they wouldn't explode. You can't fire a solid object that big or it'll blow up in the kiln."

"What's a façade?"

"A face. The building's face."

"So she's a face from a face?"

"Yeah, I guess you could say that."

"Where'd she come from?"

"Your father brought the damn thing home when Quig was a baby. I just about throttled him on the spot."

I asked her why the woman's face had upset her so much, and recounting the story made her so mad all over again that I was taken aback. I wasn't old enough to grasp what now seems obvious to me: that you could never fully understand the situation without knowing firsthand what it was to be a sleep-deprived first-time mom left alone night and day to care for a diabolically foul-tempered infant.

Quig was about six months old, a pissy, colicky, red-faced monster known up and down the block for her fiery orange hair and her world-beating tantrums. Mom had finally given up nursing her the month before, at which point Quig seemed to discover an even higher gear of baby-rage, more or less refusing to sleep or stop shrieking ever again. Through it all, Dad did what dads were expected to do back then: nothing. At dinner parties, he liked to amuse himself by urging the other husbands to follow what he called Watts's Law of Child-Rearing: "Whatever you do, fathers, never change that *first* diaper!"

One winter day at dawn, when Quig was entering what seemed like the sixth straight hour of a crying jag, Mom simply couldn't take it anymore. She stormed upstairs, hauled Dad out of bed, and basically threw him and his demon spawn out of the house.

"I don't give a flying fuck *what* you do with her," she told him. "You can give her a shot of whiskey for all I care. Just get her the hell out of the house and don't come back before nine! I'm going to *bed*!"

Dad did as he was told, bundling Quig up and taking her out into the stirring, yawning city in her little molded-plastic stroller. The cold air and movement seemed to pacify her, and she soon nodded off. (Who said life was fair?)

Third Avenue in the upper Eighties was a kind of borderland back then, east of which things got abruptly poorer, dirtier, and more tenementy. Though I never knew it as a child, this division was a legacy of the Third Avenue El, which had once rumbled down the avenue's center, creating a right and wrong side of the tracks that persisted decades after the hulking overhead structure had been smashed apart and removed. It's not that life east of Third was all muggings and break-ins or anything, just that things got more run-down and dicey once you passed the old Puerto Rican men in their sleeveless undershirts playing dominos and arguing in Spanish out front of the little grocery on our side of Third.

But on this morning, Dad headed right across Third and down the steep hill toward Second, Quigley's stroller leading the way by force of gravity. Somewhere in this grungy district, Dad and his snoozing bundle came across a corner demolition site surrounded by blue plywood marked POST NO BILLS. A tenement had been torn down there over the past week, and at the end of the previous afternoon's destruction the workers and their yellow bulldozers had all but finished the job, leaving a hazardous moonscape of rubble where several dozen families had once made their homes.

Did Dad leave Quig alone outside on the sidewalk? Did he carry her stroller in his arms as he picked his way among the heaps of smashed brick and splintered joists? All Mom could tell me for sure was that she had been awakened from a deep sleep by the sound of Quigley screaming bloody murder, and when she ran downstairs barefoot to see what was causing all that yowling, she saw that Dad had ousted Quig from her stroller to make way for an unwieldy, burnt-red terracotta fragment of a woman's face, her hair a tangle of flowering vines.

Dad was just shutting the front door behind him, exhausted from pushing the laden stroller with one hand while balancing atop it the Elmhurst Dairy milk crate in which Quig sat wriggling and shrieking.

"Jesus Christ, Nick!" Mom screamed at him, scooping up her filthy, terrorized baby girl. "This is your daughter! Your daughter! What kind of a person does this?"

"She's *fine*," Dad protested. "She'll be fine. She didn't even cry that much until she saw the house. And just look how gorgeous this sculpture is—look at that aloof brow. She's a goddess, this one, or a *queen*. Let me tell you, even with half her forehead and one of her eyes gone, she *commanded* that demolition site with her gaze—commanded the whole damn street. And believe me, she had nothing but disdain for the cretins who pried her off that façade and hurled her down into the rubble."

That was the moment my mother first got a glimmer that her husband—her charismatic, self-absorbed, keenly observant husband—was in the thrall of something bigger, and stranger, than she would ever understand. He was in a kind of daze, staring down at his broken rescued goddess, until—abruptly—he looked up at my mother and said, with real alarm: "Good God! Do you think this is going on *all over the city*?"

The next week he showed up at the brownstone with another façade ornament, this one a massive mustard-yellow terra-cotta medallion from whose center protruded a cantankerous ox with flared nostrils and a ring on his right horn. Although Dad had left Quigley at home this time, he had again transported his scavenged treasure in her stroller, which, as he was bump-bumping its wheels up the brownstone steps, collapsed under the weight of its historical responsibility.

When my mother accused Dad point-blank of theft, he swore up and down that no, he had *rescued* that ox head from another doomed city building.

Mom stood up and walked around our dining room table to the giant mayo jars, which she began jiggling, one at a time, so that the thousands of eggshell fragments inside would settle and make room for more.

"It's just perverse to strip off a part of the cityscape and take it home with you," she said. "It doesn't belong to you—or actually it *does,* by virtue of the fact that you're a New Yorker, and it's your city, and by simply walking past that façade and looking up and appreciating it you've possessed it as fully as it can be possessed."

She stopped what she was doing.

"And so you are really just stealing from yourself," she said, peering at me closely over the mayo jars. "Why, I'd like to know, would a person do that?"

7

I WAS PERFORMING my Beak of Doom fingertip exercises in my room when I felt someone watching me and looked up to see Quigley loitering in the doorway. She looked like the orange-haired girl-monster from *Where the Wild Things Are,* the one with the pointy teeth and pigtails whose guilty smirk suggested a certain embarrassment about the outsize pleasure she took in monstering.

"Gimme your baseball," she said. "The hard one."

"It's in my closet. Get it yourself."

She did.

I was glad to get rid of her so quickly. A lot of my training equipment was out in the open—the Mott's apple juice jug, the seven-pound bag of Klean Kitty, the way-too-old-to-eat boiled ham—and I didn't want Quig to learn any of my Beak of Doom trade secrets. Dani's party was tomorrow, and though I was pretty sure I didn't have the nerve to crash it, I at least wanted to be able to peck a snippet of skin from her forearm or something if she got sassy with me in the hall at school.

I'd hefted that juice jug with my fingertips about ten minutes every day over the past week, adding another quarter inch of kitty litter each session. Now had come the moment to test my martial arts prowess.

Slowly, earnestly, with as much reverence as I could muster for the act of assaulting a boiled ham, I beaked my fingertips together and let them float menacingly above the slab of cooked pig, circling, looking for an opening—until suddenly, with the coldhearted precision that marks the true warrior, I struck, my deadly beaked fingertips darting forward, attacking the helpless cured meat and . . .

Nothing. No luck. My fingertips returned from their violent descent without even a sliver of ham to show for their efforts—not even enough to make a decent canapé.

Beak of Doom, my *ass.*

Something clattered loudly against the outside of my window frame.

I ran over and stuck out my head, scanning Eighty-Ninth Street below for the source of the disturbance. On our side of the street, I spotted Quigley bent over by the curb, dislodging my baseball from behind the wheel of a parked car. She was wearing a bunchy-necked sweater under that hideous gold lamé warm-up jacket of hers, the Adidas knockoff with the two glittery silver stripes down the arms.

"Hey!" I cried down at her. "What the hell're you doing?"

Quig, who was a lefty, ambled to the middle of the street, squared up like a chubby, freckled Jerry Koosman, and let fly a fastball straight toward my third-floor window. I ducked inside, but I needn't have, as the ball died at the last moment, plummeting harmlessly back to the sidewalk.

"What the hell?" I yelled down. "What are you *doing*?"

"Breaking your window!" Quig yelled back cheerfully.

"Why?" I was indignant. *"Why?"*

"Because," she hollered, squaring up southpaw in the middle of the street again, "if it's broken, Dad has to come fix it."

Now I understood. This was another of Quigley's delusional schemes to try to get our parents back together.

This time, Quig's aim was true. The moment my baseball left her pudgy fingers, I saw it winging straight toward me, could even make out the rotating red stitches growing larger as they approached, knew at once it was going to be a direct hit. I tried frantically to slide the window's bottom half all the way up and out of harm's way, but the damned thing wouldn't budge, and when the ball slammed into one of the panes, it showered the sill and my floor with shards of glass. I was lucky to get my face out of the way in time.

"You freak!" I yelled out the window. "You crazy freak! You stay right there!"

I sprinted downstairs to strangle her, but by the time I reached the stoop, Quig was long gone—headed, no doubt, to a pay phone to report the unfortunate damage to Dad: *I told those tenement kids not to play ball in front of the brownstone! But no one listens to a girl.*

Dad's building was the Flying Dutchman of warehouses. It never seemed to be where you left it, and you always had the sense that the only way you could ever find it was if you wandered around the deserted blocks above Chambers Street and stumbled upon it by accident. I'd stuck ten bucks in my sneaker to hide it from muggers (the three dollars of mug money in my pocket should be enough to throw them off the scent) and had taken the IRT from the Gimbels entrance on Eighty-Sixth all the way down to the City Hall stop. I'd been searching for Dad's studio on foot ever since. As long as I didn't get there too late, I figured, my mere arrival ought to be enough to thwart Quig's plan to lure Dad uptown to Mom. This was the Friday he had asked me to come gargoyle hunting with him.

Quigley was not of sound mind. Truly. Every time you turned around, she had ginned up some new stratagem to reunite our parents. One time she had badgered all our boarders into watching her perform a nonexistent role in a nonexistent Beckett play at a nonexistent interschool theater way out on Staten Island. The instant they were all out of the house, each clutching an elaborate phony map she'd made for them, she jammed her curling iron into a kitchen socket to short out all the lights in the brownstone. When Dad, summoned by Quig, showed up to the dark house to fix the electricity, he found a candlelight Swanson meatloaf TV dinner for two that Quig had prepared in the gas stove, and no one home to share it with him but Mom.

It was hard to fathom why Quig wanted our father back home so badly. Hard as he'd always been on me, he at least seemed to recognize me as his own. Quig he treated like a bewildering, scarcely acknowledged stranger dropped into his midst. Basically, I just don't think she was the sort of kid he saw himself as having. She was a lousy student, had trouble paying attention when you talked to her, seemed uninterested in little besides celebrities and clothes. She had the concentration span of a newt, and it drove him crazy to have to reexplain things he'd already told her once or twice. As far back as I could remember, he'd had a pet name for her that only he thought was cute: *Dummy*.

TriBeCa was darkening now, growing more foreign every moment. There was no question that I was lost. I kept seeing streets whose listing iron canopies looked familiar, but *all* the buildings down here had listing iron canopies. It wasn't until I stumbled onto Duane Park, the small triangular island where Dad had first tailed Mom through the egg market a lifetime ago, that I began to feel a twinge of recognition. Turning right, I found myself walking up a skinny cobbled alley, which was spanned in a gentle arc by an intimate little enclosed footbridge that connected the back of a large old brick building to a smaller one. The bigger building, Dad once told me, had begun its life as the House of Relief, one of the city's earliest emergency rooms; the smaller structure, built later, housed its laundry and horse-drawn ambulances.

Quigley's aim of getting Mom and Dad back together struck me as just about the worst idea ever, the kind of dangerous, cascading mistake you couldn't control. She just didn't get it: the trick was to keep our parents conjoined, sure, but *at a distance*—connected yet separate. The alley I found myself in was called Staple Street, a sign told me, and it seemed to me that its simple, scarcely noticed little bridge was what enabled this pair of time-tilted buildings to continue standing. That bridge looked structural to me, crucial. I imagined that the two buildings it served, the two unequal halves of the House of Relief, were a pair of living organisms that shared a heart, and this heart lay within that small, unlovely, slightly off-kilter bridge. I was that bridge. As long as I could couple my parents' two households together, both could survive. I needed to keep Dad connected and responsible for us. I needed to keep him flush with gargoyles so the brownstone payments kept coming. But I also needed, at all costs, to keep him safely away from my mother.

I was the bridge that kept my parents apart. If I could sustain that, I could save the family.

The streets were pretty quiet as I walked around to the front of the main House of Relief building on Hudson Street. Though the full-figured blond lady flouncing up the block toward me looked vaguely familiar, it wasn't until she clicked past in those knee-high Naugahyde boots that I recognized her as the woman my father had been peeping at the last time I was down here. I'd've known those knockers anywhere.

I crossed Hudson and nearly bumped right into Dad, binoculars around his neck, as he turned the corner from Worth. He seemed delighted to see me.

"Big guy!" he said, giving me an awkward clap on the shoulder. "I knew I could count on you. Let's go get some Chinese."

Dad's favorite Chinatown restaurant bore the unusual name Me and My Egg Roll. When we'd polished off their deliciously sweet spare ribs, leaving our fingers sticky and the table piled high with tooth-scoured bones, the waiter brought us two complimentary glasses of plum wine.

"Instant headache," Dad called the stuff, sliding his glass away with comically exaggerated distaste as he got up to go pee. I loved being with him when he was silly like that.

While he was in the can, I guzzled down both wines, which tasted like a mixture of duck sauce and Robitussin, then slipped the empty glasses into the greasy gray busboy tray when the waiters weren't looking. The wine made my throat warm and my head foggy, which may have been why I was so mesmerized by the movie we saw in the Village afterward, *The Taking of Pelham One Two Three*.

It was a gritty New York thriller in which Mr. Blue, a rootless out-of-towner with a false mustache, hijacks a subway train for ransom, performs a bunch of desperate acts with his three confederates, then intentionally electrocutes himself on the third rail when he's cornered by a dogged and smart-alecky transit detective played by Walter Matthau. In Mr. Blue's final moments, standing there sizzling in the train tunnel, actual smoke wafted up from inside his trench coat and wreathed his dumbstruck red face.

What I admired most about the out-of-towner was his mastery of New York's secret processes. I'd always had a feeling that the real life of the city, the things that drove the world above the streets, lay hidden. Before seeing that movie, I'd thought of these inner workings as coggy-looking engine parts or scrolled diagrams stacked in underground wine racks adapted for the purpose. Now I pictured a snaky sort of electricity vibrating all through the city's innards. Beneath every sidewalk and building, beneath Lamston's and Papaya King and the cracked concrete Children's Zoo whale whose mouth you could stand in, ran a deadly silver rail, twitching with lightning.

8

Z EV, THE FIDGETY HIPPIE from Dad's studio, was waiting for us outside the movie exit in the Good Humor truck. It was dark now, nearly midnight, the truck's phantom Popsicle only just visible by the light spilling from the old theater's double doors. Dad motioned me around to the passenger side and Zev scooched into the middle. I half expected the truck to give out a child-enticing carnival jingle as Dad drove us downtown, but the only noise it made was the sickly rumble of its old engine, the sound I'd thought was a refrigeration unit when I first heard it.

"That's our cast-iron baby right there," he said a few minutes later. Slowing by a streetlamp so I could get a good look, he pointed past me at a rust-streaked, five-story white loft building. I leaned out the window and recognized the building as the one where I'd first seen the zaftig blond lady. All the building's windows, even the lady's top-floor one, were dark.

"You see how the entire façade is made up of those really graceful two-story window bays," Dad said, "each with that nice arch at the top?"

"Yeah?"

"And you see how each of these bays is framed by those striking two-story-high columns?"

I said I did.

"Well, they call this a sperm-candle façade. That's because, to the men who put up that building a hundred years ago, those columns looked like the slender candles made from sperm-whale oil. But never mind what it's called—I just wanted you to see how stunning it is. It's basically a Venetian palazzo cast in iron."

I nodded. I didn't get how you could cast a castle, and the whole sperm thing was sort of gross, but I inspected the building more closely anyhow. It really was something, when you thought about it. An Italian palace right smack in the middle of our city. And perfectly at home here, too, somehow. A manhole moon hung above it, perfectly round and grayed-over by clouds.

Around the corner and just behind that same building, we backed into a narrow, dead-end alley blasted with graffiti and reeking of urine. Rising above us on either side were the back walls of two loft buildings. Both were of dirty yellow brick, with double-height steel doors at street level and three rows of windows above, sealed tight with rust-splotched iron shutters. The wall on the left was in especially rough shape. A paint-peeling black fire escape clung to it, descending in the usual lumbering zigzag from the fifth story to the second, where its ladder poked down through a hole cut in a sorry-looking corrugated-plastic awning someone had rigged to protect deliverymen from the rain. A long crack rode the waves of the awning's surface.

With a boost from Zev, Dad grabbed the fire escape ladder's bottom rung and hauled himself up. I followed, Dad reaching down to lift me off Zev's shoulders and away from his tobacco-sweat smell. Still unclear about what we were up to, I crouched on the fire escape beside my father and watched the operation unfold.

At the foot of the building opposite us, Zev kicked aside some flattened cardboard refrigerator boxes to reveal a plank, which he fed up to Dad through the hole in the plastic awning. The plank had to be a good fifteen feet long.

"Okay, Griffin, this is where you come in," he said. "Or rather, *that* is where you *go* in."

He pointed across the alley—over the flimsy plastic awning, over the chasm beyond it—to a window on the far wall. For the first time, I noticed that one of the two shutters on that window, alone in the entire alley, was open just a touch, no more than a foot, with a thin iron arm running from frame to shutter to hold it in place. Dad had scoped out the single chink in the building's armor.

"Once you get inside," he said, "you'll just go down the stairs to the back entrance there and let us in. Easy as pie."

At Dad's urging, I inched my way onto the plastic awning. It shuddered at this new burden, and I could feel the cracked plastic sagging under my knees as I crawled across it. When I reached the awning's edge in the middle of the alley, nothing beyond it but a fifteen-foot drop to the cobbles, Dad began sliding the plank across the awning into my hands.

"Aim it for that window opening across the way," he whispered. "Slow. *Slowww.*"

The plank got heavier and tippier the farther I poked it into the gap between the two buildings. Around the time it began to seesaw off the awning's edge, way too heavy for me to hang on to, it suddenly grew steadier and lighter in my grip. Puzzled, I peered down to see Zev holding some kind of homemade contraption, essentially a square of plywood nailed atop a long two-by-four. He was using this thing to support the plank, which he gingerly walked across the alley, with me feeding it horizontally above him. As the plank's front end approached the partially open window, Zev stopped and whisper-shouted up at me: "On *three!*" When he completed the count, we both gave a shove—me forward, him up—and I'll be damned if that plank didn't slide right onto our target window ledge.

"Go on!" Dad whispered when I looked back at him. He gave a little *shoo* motion with his hands.

What he was asking me to do—crawl a dozen feet on a skinny plank supported by a shitty plastic awning on one end and about three inches of hundred-year-old window molding on the other—was pretty preposterous. I could hear my heart blood-drumming in my ears. But when I looked back at Dad, hoping he might experience a spasm of common sense, there were those flicky hands again: *Shoo!*

So I made a game out of it. These looming walls were the ribbed flanks of two great sailing ships, rows of concealed cannon behind their shutters. And here was I—the plucky runaway street urchin, having signed on to a pirate ship to see the world—crawling across a gangplank to board a sleeping vessel at anchor. What I would do once I got in there, whether slit the captain's throat or ravish his sleeping daughter on her satin sheets, I wasn't quite sure. First I had to survive the passage.

What I did was grip that gangplank with my hands, then kind of ease myself onto it, my knees pressed against each other so I wouldn't fall off. By kneeing forward just an inch or two at a time, I found I could keep myself relatively steady. But as I reached the plank's middle, it began to sag disturbingly, and that cracked awning didn't like all this strain one bit; it kept creaking with an insistent, kvetchy urgency that scared the hell out of me.

Glancing down into the terrifying open space of the alley, I saw Zev, his cheeks ballooned with exertion, struggling to support the plank beneath me with his wooden contraption.

"*Go* already!" he grunted. "*Go!*"

No pirate boy worth his salt would plummet into the piss-briny sea this close to an enemy vessel, so I willed myself toward the window's skinny opening, scrambling the remaining few feet and angling my upper body awkwardly around the open steel shutter that jutted diagonally against the right side of the plank. This threw me off-balance, my left knee slipping right off the plank. As I began to fall, I lunged forward, got my arm inside the window up to the shoulder, worked my other arm inside, too, and hung there from the window ledge, helpless, my legs so heavy it felt like the gulf of darkness below me was pulling them down. Huffing desperately, I worked my right knee back up onto the plank, pulled myself clumsily into the dark room, and rolled onto its dusty floor, bumping my forehead as I went over.

For a long while I lay there on my back in a wedge of moonlight, sucking air into my lungs, waiting for my heartbeat to slow. But when I tried to locate my fear, I was surprised to discover that I couldn't find it. It was still there, that's for damn sure, but it had gone into hiding. And it would be a very long time before I allowed myself to

THE GARGOYLE HUNTERS   79

look straight at it again. To do so would mean questioning whether the tasks my father had in mind for me were reasonable things for a grown man to ask of a thirteen-year-old boy who wanted only to get close to him.

Dad and Zev, duffels over their shoulders, slipped inside through the alleyway door when I opened it, followed by a short, sturdy black guy I'd never seen before. He was carrying a DECARLO FUNERAL HOME & CREMATORY cooler.

"I knew you'd make it, son," Dad said. He slapped me on the shoulder a little too hard. "I could tell that *you* didn't know it, but I did. This here's Curtis. Curtis, meet Griffin."

The black guy grinned at me, revealing a mouth in need of some serious dental attention. One of his front teeth was missing, and the rest looked like they were fighting one another.

We made our way up the broad staircase, Dad's and Zev's flashlight beams gliding into each other and apart again, chopstick-fashion. Curtis followed just behind them, with me bringing up the rear. I'm not sure I understood at the time what a transformation breaking into that loft building had worked on me. There was more to it than just the terror I'd managed to stuff back inside me. The main thing was that crossing that crazy gangplank had gained me access to Dad's inner circle. Joining this company of men was like getting a promotion in my father's affection, or so I hoped. I do remember being unusually aware of my body as we climbed those stairs. The thing about not being fully grown is that, along with the anxiety over how big or tall you might eventually get, you do still have the sense of possibility. Though to this day my shoulders are not as broad as I'd like, on that night I had the sense that they were going to be, that I was finally starting to fill out.

On the top story, Dad picked a lock and led us through a door into the biggest private space I'd ever seen, a vast loft illuminated by arches of organized moonlight coming through a wall of floor-to-ceiling windows.

Curtis put down the funeral home cooler beside an unmade bed. "You sure that artist lady gone all night?"

"Yup," Dad told him. "Hasn't been here on a weekend in the six weeks I've been watching her."

"Then let's do what we come here for. Hit it and quit it." Curtis led the way up a tall metal ladder and out a square hatch in the ceiling.

The roof was an expanse of tar littered with the forgotten equipment of summer: An inside-out beach umbrella ensnared in the undergirding of a water tower. A pair of Adirondack chairs turned conspiratorially toward each other. A sodden copy of *I'm OK—You're OK*, facedown and bloated like an animal carcass.

While Curtis and Zev unpacked tools from the duffels, Dad took me to the parapet facing the street. It was chilly up here, windy.

"I want you to lean over and tell me what you see," he said. "Down on the cornice." He entwined the fingers of his two hands to form a sort of stirrup. I stepped in, and he boosted me up to the flat top of the parapet.

"I got you," Dad said into the wind. He worked the fingers of one hand around my belt in the back and held my right ankle with the other, just above my bunched sock. "Just hang over and trust me."

I rested my hands on the street edge of the parapet and Dad tipped me forward over the street, the way you might handle a gravy boat. I went with it, too, disoriented to object, pushing out from the parapet edge and looking back at the topsy-turvy building as he lowered me. My belt pulled tight across my midriff, digging in above my hip bones.

I shut my eyes tight in concentration. When I opened them, I was staring right into the upside-down face of an indignant-looking bearded man, who was protruding from the cornice. He was made of metal, with a paint-spalling nose that gave him the look of an imperious leper.

The first thing I saw after Dad hauled me back up to the roof was Curtis, staring at me aghast, his dark chapped lips open in the shape of a malformed O. I saw his eyes flick to Dad in judgment, saw him start to say something, saw him think better of it.

"Who the heck was *that* charmer?" I asked Dad, nodding toward the front of the building. "Grizzly Adams?"

"Zeus, probably. Or maybe the building's original owner. The really remarkable thing is that this is the only cornice in the whole neighborhood with heads on it—four of them, all the same fellow."

"Yeah, well, whoever that bearded guy is," I said, "he looks really ticked off."

"What do you expect? He's probably offended you never bothered to look up and notice him until now."

Curtis and Zev had laid their tools on the roof in a neat row: pry bars, a circular saw, two coiled chains attached to a sort of double-pulley, and a big upside-down wooden L that resembled a hangman apparatus.

"Looks like galvanized iron to me," Dad said of the cornice. He nodded at the circular saw. "You got the Carborundum blade on that?" Curtis nodded.

"Okay. But *please,* guys. Don't fire it up until the very last minute, and even then, only if you're *sure*"—Dad looked at Zev—"*really* sure, that you can't crank all those screws out using just the impact drivers. I'd be a lot more comfortable with this job if you didn't have to use the saw at all."

Both his men nodded.

Dad led me down the ladder back into the warmth of the buxom lady's loft. He inspected the roof filth on his palms, wiped them on the woman's pillowcase. It didn't occur to me to wonder what she'd done to deserve all this violation.

"This job's gonna be a bitch," he said, looking back up at the roof hatch. He grinned. A winning, lopsided smile. "Rubble rousers like you and me deserve something a little more fun."

9

NEW YORK PUTS YOU in your place. It's bigger than you, and more important. It's older than you, and newer, too. It's more than you: more towering, more gutter-level; more striving, more complacent; more hurried, more arrived; more refined, more depraved; more timeless, more late for dinner reservations. It has a lot of moving parts, and countless immovable ones. And it doesn't care if you have a relationship with it or not.

But the street walls, the miles of buildings rearing up on either side of you on any major avenue, could be reassuring, too. Something you could count on. Without giving it any thought, I'd learned to take these miles of masonry for granted, to feel them holding and even guiding me on my passage through the city, the way a river runner feels embraced by the certainty of canyon walls. Trundling down Second Avenue in the Good Humor truck with Dad—on the move again after a quick foray to the East Sixties to swipe an iron newel post from a townhouse railing—I felt at ease in the brick-and-brownstone-flanked corridor, block after block of solid, familiar New Yorkness scrolling past our windows.

And then it ended. Without warning, without transition, the street wall on our left, the buildings, simply vanished, replaced by a moonscape of devastation that made me do an actual double take of disbelief. A bunch of blocks east of Second Avenue in the Twenties had been obliterated. Instead of tenements and lofts and storefronts, instead of windows and stoops and lives, there was only a sprawling expanse of rubble. A neighborhood leveled.

"Jesus," I said. "What happened here?"

"Urban renewal. The city decided to pretty much bulldoze seven whole blocks of Kips Bay. Booted thousands of residents."

"Why?"

"They're putting up a slew of ugly brick towers and things, what else do they do anymore?"

We hopped a chain-link fence and walked the graveyard of the neighborhood. The crushed, shardy remains, for all their hazardous shifting underfoot, seemed oddly undifferentiated. Wreckage was wreckage, I supposed. In the crunch and stumble of our exploration, eyes fixed cautiously on my next step, I could see no evidence that the acres of jumbled rubble had ever taken the form of anything as substantial and reassuring as homes. We were treading an aftermath.

"I never get used to it, no matter how often I come to one of these sites," Dad said. "It's like a firebombed city, Dresden or something. Only this time we did it to ourselves."

"There's really nothing left, is there?" I said.

"Well, that's not quite true." He frowned at the destruction around him, his features hard-edged in the light of a droopy-necked streetlamp. "The lost are still here, Griffin. You just have to know where to look for them."

He gave a nod, strode toward a shattered slabby something slanting out of the debris. Up close, you could see it was the rounded front edge of a step made of brownstone, maybe even a stoop. I never would have spotted it on my own.

"Here you go," he said. "The gargoyles often kind of loitered around the front entrance of tenements—not unlike some of the flesh-and-blood residents, actually." He chuckled at his own small joke. "There's no real rule to it, but a lot of the time you find carved keystone portraits over the doorway or above the street-level windows. Or on brownstone or terra-cotta plaques higher up."

There was an archaeological thoroughness to the way he eyeballed the ruins, a forensic sensitivity. As I stood there blinking dumbly at the rubble, he took two unhesitating steps to his right and toe-nudged an unarticulated block of rock with his work boot. It flipped onto its back, revealing a half-smashed head of a man, hewn from a keystone the color of milk chocolate. Even with half its mouth and chin missing, the wedge-shaped face was remarkably expressive—tempestuously confident and framed by a marvelous gale of mustaches and whiskers that twisted, swirled, and tangled, transforming along the way into tendrils of ivy so finely wrought they had the grasping urgency of fingers.

"Will you look at that!" Dad cried, genuinely enchanted. "The carver must really have enjoyed making this one. I wonder how far along with it he was before he realized he was onto something spectacular?" He knelt down and ran his index finger along a storm-snarled eyebrow. It bothered me that he hadn't looked at me once the whole time he'd been talking.

Dad scanned the strewn ruins, his head held at an angle. He took a couple of steps, toed some more debris out of his way, and kicked loose a trapezoidy stone fragment with his heel. He kneeled and flipped it over with his hands.

The fragment was a jagged surviving half, or maybe third, of a rectangular brownstone slab, intricately carved. It depicted a rancorous mythological everythingbeast in full flight—a Gorgony, lion-headed sea monster with wings and fins and fangs, with scales and horns and claws, with movement and urgency and a foul mood for the ages. Oh, and flippers. It had hellacious, slap-you-six-ways-to-Sunday flippers.

Dad was transfixed. I'm pretty sure he had never in my life looked at me with as much interest.

"This one's a fever dream. What you're looking at here is an immigrant carver from the British Isles or Italy or Germany—maybe influenced by the liquid he has taken—letting his fancies go wild."

"Are you saying he was *drunk*?"

Dad chuckled. "Could be. These guys started work at six a.m., and got a beer ration from the foreman at ten. Must've needed it, too, after inhaling stone dust in the sun for four hours."

Dad had been scanning the rubble intently while he was talking,

THE GARGOYLE HUNTERS   85

and he now swept away a layer of it with his palms to reveal another carved keystone portrait, this one the head of a squirrel-cheeked lady wearing a crooked smile and a necklace of inelegant bulbous beads. Aside from her missing nose, she was in pretty good shape.

"Hey, this is a great one," Dad said. "Look how transcendently ordinary she is."

"What do you mean?"

"I mean she's a regular person. She's not Athena or Diana or the Queen of Spades."

"*So what?*" I asked, and I said it in a challenging, almost pissy voice, trying to get a rise out of him, to get him to notice me. He didn't.

"Well, the carvers clearly got tired of doing the same old idealized classical or historical figures, so they started sculpting people they knew, barkeeps and cops and dockworkers. This gal is way too funny-looking to be a goddess. She's probably the carver's sweetheart, or maybe a barmaid he's got a crush on. And he honored her, you know? He did a really loving portrait. She's got a good smile, I think: skeptical but generous."

I had to admit I could see what he meant. She reminded me of this one surly-sweet waitress who worked the luncheonette counter at the Eighty-Sixth Street Woolworth's, on your far right as you came in from Third. I liked to order cheesecake from her after I was done checking out the air rifles in the toy aisle. You could tell she hated her job—she was always rushing around, and she always had loads of coffee and mustard stains on the apron of her Amelia Bedelia getup. But she treated me, when she had time, like I was her most important customer. I'd sit on the twirly chrome stool right in front of the cheesecake I had my eye on. They kept it on a little pedestal under a clear plastic cover like the Bat Phone, and she'd lift that cover up for me with as much ceremony as Commissioner Gordon when he was calling the Caped Crusader.

"The best a global shipping magnate could do was name a boat after his woman," Dad said. "And then that ship would sail right out of the harbor, and maybe she'd see it once every few years or maybe it would sink. But a stoneworker's homage stayed put. A stoneworker could go to work in the morning and carve his sweetheart right onto New York's skyline."

I wanted to believe it mattered to him that it was *me* he was telling all this to. I wasn't so sure.

"Now what?" I asked.

The bottom of the chain-link fence had been pulled out and bent upward in one spot, making a little opening between the lot and the sidewalk that you could duck through. We put on work gloves and gathered together the salvaged gargoyles beside the fence there, a jagged little society of refugees. I couldn't believe how strong Dad was. The terra-cotta ornaments were heavy enough, but at least they were hollow. The stone carvings weighed a goddamn ton.

I followed Dad back to the Good Humor truck and helped him lift out a Daitch Shopwell cart with a wonky wheel. Then we went on a little family shopping expedition, pushing the cart along the east side of Second Avenue and hefting our battered keystones and plaques into it. We had to make several trips. On the way back to the truck the last time, Dad rooted around in the rubble some more, unearthing a toothless brownstone lion and a red terra-cotta cherub demoted to boy by the loss of his wings.

It was a pretty long drive uptown to our next destination. On Amsterdam Avenue, the Upper West Side asnooze around us, we parked alongside another sprawling rubble field, this one spanning the block from Eighty-Seventh to Eighty-Eighth Street.

At the edge of this empty lot, maybe a third of the way toward Columbus on Eighty-Eighth, a brownstone had had the bad luck to share a wall with a tenement demolished by the city's wrecking ball. The vibrations had destabilized the house, which was now slouching toward the rubble heap to its west, as if seeking to join it. The house's listing brick side wall had been braced by a cluster of wooden emergency supports: nine pale upflung arms pushing back diagonally against its will to fall.

"Lucky for us," Dad said, "they evacuated the family that lives here. They won't let them back home till the place passes inspection."

"Will it collapse?"

"Let's hope not."

Part of the troubled wall was protected by some kind of tarp or tar paper. Sensing weakness, Dad peeled back one of its lower corners and found a slanty crack and a small, street-level hole near the back of the building, where a bunch of bricks had fallen away.

He sent me through the hole with a flashlight, which I immediately trained on the inside of the wall I'd just come through. A fierce fissure, an inch wide, zigged down its plaster from the ceiling to about the height of my chest. But if you ignored that one menacing detail, it looked to be a fairly ordinary old brownstone, with a crooked spine of staircase twisting up its center and a pair of small, worn-out Wallabees left on its bottom step by some sighing mom who probably wanted them brought *upstairs, for God's sake, how many times do I have to ask you?*

Dad was waiting at the back door when I opened it, his leather-edged canvas plumber's bag in one hand.

"Do come in," I said with a low bow. "Make yourself at home."

"Don't mind if I do." He stepped in and stomped his boots on the welcome mat, a Dad-shaped aura of dust puffing from his body. "Lovely place you've got here."

We were standing in a drab, old-fashioned kitchen right out of *The Honeymooners*. Dad pulled a caged lightbulb from his bag, hooked it onto the handle of a colander hanging above the drain board, and plugged it in. It cast a low, grudging light that I hoped wouldn't catch the eye of anyone outside. He yanked the kerchunky chrome handle of the old icebox and leaned inside it.

"Hungry, Griff?"

I told him I was.

"Yeah, you looked like you were dragging a bit, back at the truck. Lemme whip you up a little something."

Dad had always been the best cook in our family. He had both the obsessive attention to detail and the gift for improvisation. He was always quoting Craig Claiborne by way of criticizing Mom's half-hearted butter deployment, and in Echo Harbor, the summer community where we'd rented a beach house when I was small, he used to doze off on the deck with a sauce-stained blue-and-green copy of *The New York Times Cookbook* on his chest.

"No pickles or bologna, I'm afraid," Dad said from inside the damaged brownstone's fridge.

It was clear why he was telling me this. Back during those Echo Harbor summers, I was small enough that I thought grilled cheese sandwiches were called *girl*-cheese sandwiches, and I frankly resented it. Instead of correcting me, Dad had invented a *boy*-cheese sandwich—strictly off-limits to Quigley or Mom—composed of several of my favorite things: Oscar Mayer bologna, Skippy extra-chunky peanut butter, sliced pickles, and pimento-stuffed olives, all held between two grilled Wonder bread slices by a glowing orange matrix of melted Kraft American cheese.

Dad now pulled a few things from the strangers' fridge and set a big pot of water on the stove. He briefly put on the flame beneath it before changing his mind and turning it off again.

"You know what?" he said. "I think we'd better get some work under our belts before we start thinking about snacks."

He handed me a kitchen chair to carry and led me up the stairs with his flashlight into the second-floor room facing Eighty-Eighth Street. It looked like some kid's bedroom, probably a little boy's. It had a bunk bed with no sheets on the top bunk, a Snuffleupagus comforter on the bottom, and a pink-plastic Big Wheel parked at its foot. A few feet away, the side wall had a long, vicious crack in its plaster, a lot like the one downstairs.

Dad found a bedside lamp and switched it on.

"There's something here we want?" I asked.

"Sure is. Intact and everything. Much more valuable than the fragments we've been scavenging. But first we've got to build a form exactly the shape of that window frame. To support the arch." He nodded toward the window on the left, whose enframement was a tall rectangle with a curve at the top.

What Dad nailed together next was something of a domestic collage. He cut up the kitchen chair with his circular saw, but he needed lumber of other sizes and shapes, too, so he kept sending me around the house to find whatever wood I could: bureau drawers, the footboard from the master bedroom, a pair of sink-cabinet doors from the hallway bathroom. The stroke of genius, the scavenged wood I could see made him most proud of me, was the base of the boy's rocking horse. I pointed out that it had almost the exact same curvature as the top of the window frame (upside-down, of course). Dad laughed with pleasure, amputated it with his circular saw, and nailed it atop the form.

"Perfect fit," he said, when we'd hoisted our mongrel creation into the window opening. "Now that's what I call an arch support."

We slid the kid's bunk bed lengthwise in front of the window to use as a scaffold. Dad climbed to the top bunk with a red Magic Marker and drew a horizontal rectangle on the plaster directly above the window. I handed up his tool bag and joined him. We sat on the top bunk side by side with our legs hanging over, chipping away at the wall with hammers and chisels. When all the plaster was removed from within the red Magic Marker rectangle, we started in on the brickwork behind it.

"What we're after, of course, is the keystone, in the center of the arch," Dad told me. "But to get to it, we've kind of gotta take the wall apart around it. Most of these brownstones were built in layers, see? Their structural walls were made of three wythes of brick."

"When you say *three widths*, you mean the bricks are back-to-back-to-back?"

"*Wythes*, not *widths*: it just means layers. And yeah, they're back-to-back-to-back, with the keystone set into the face of the building usually just two wythes deep. You and I are gonna focus right now just on the innermost wythe."

The mortar was really crumbly, freeing up the bricks pretty easily. One by one, they fell away, landing with muffled thumps on the kid's green carpet.

Dad told me to keep at it, and he headed downstairs.

It was messy work chiseling away the bricks, but not too difficult. In less than half an hour I'd chipped away the first brick layer from the Magic Marker rectangle above the window. Behind it waited another layer of bricks—except in the center, where I had exposed the back of a rough-hewn light brown wedge of rock. A thin metal strap protruded horizontally from its top, where it had been embedded for something like ninety years in the mortar layer I'd just chipped away.

"There's your keystone," Dad said when he came back. He handed up a pair of pry bars. "Now to free it up."

He joined me on the top bunk, and the two of us went to work on the remaining two layers of brick on either side of the keystone, using the pry bars to chip away the mortar and prize out the bricks. I worked without stopping, though Dad took another short break downstairs before returning to help me finish. Before too long, we had both poked through to the outside world, creating a pair of ragged windows through which you could make out the hunkered shapes of two undemolished brownstones across the street. Their own keystone gargoyles scowled back at us.

"Okay, this seems like a pretty good time to grab a bite," Dad said. "Come."

On the way downstairs, that angry crack in the first-floor side wall caught my eye again. It looked like it had gotten longer. And wider.

The water was at a rolling boil when we got to the kitchen, and Dad strained the spaghetti and poured it back into the pot. He had all his ingredients lined up, like Julia Child on her Channel 13 cooking show. With one hand, a little show-offy but great fun to watch, my father made a grand presentation of cracking an egg into a bowl and beating it with a whisk. Into the spaghetti pot went the mixed egg, followed by crumbled bacon and parmesan.

Dad folded a dishrag over his forearm and leaned forward from the waist like a waiter at a fancy restaurant.

"*Signore,*" he said, gesturing with a goofy hand flourish toward the table's single place setting. "*Per favore.*" He pulled out a chair and seated me, then filled my bowl with a steaming dish of eggy, bacony pasta. It was the best thing I'd tasted since the era of boy-cheese sandwiches.

"Mmmm," I declared, my mouth full. "What is this, anyway?"

"*Spaghetti alla Gargoilara,*" Dad said in an awful Italian accent. "Spaghetti in the way of the Gargoyle Hunters."

He leaned against the fridge, his lips curled into a grim attempt at a smile, and watched me slurp up the eggy strands. His green eyes had a lonely remoteness to them, looking right at me but also beyond me.

"Nothing like a home-cooked meal," he said.

All that remained to liberate the gargoyle was to detach it from the row of bricks above it and the row below. Dad's method caught me by surprise. He produced from his plumber's bag the very white plastic case I'd found in his toolshed, and he took out the little surgical saw that had given me the willies—the long-armed pizza-cutter-looking one with the angry-toothed wheel on the end. He flicked it on, its blade spinning so fast you couldn't see it move, and eased it into a crack between the gargoyle and its adjacent bricks. Delicately, with the precision of a jeweler, he worked it back and forth, gritty gray powder spinning into the room, until most of the mortar had been removed.

Now the keystone was all but freestanding, its bottom supported by the makeshift wooden form. Together we pushed the bunk bed right up snug against the window and then, kneeling on the top bunk, put our arms around the gargoyle and hugged it roughly into the room.

What it must have looked like had anyone been watching us from the street, I can only guess: the silhouette of a single unnamable mythological monster, maybe, with a wedge-shaped brown head, two man arms and two boy arms, gripping its own face in the middle of a ruptured wall.

When the keystone finally broke loose, it tipped backward and fell onto the bunk bed, gently cratering the mattress between us. It was oddly intimate, the three of us so close together after all that struggle, and the roguish character staring up at me from the keystone made me laugh. He was a smirking, blunt-nosed man whose cauliflower-shaped head was elaborately turbaned with bandages, as if some well-meaning friends had swaddled his poor noggin in dishrags after a barroom beat-down.

"Ha!" Dad exclaimed. "Just look at that irreverent spark in the pugilist's eye, that undimmed commitment to mischief. Is it just me or—yes! His eyes are popping, Griffin!" He cupped the stone chin in his hand, looking into the gargoyle's pupils. "That's extraordinary! The carver put lumps in his eyes to make them more expressive."

He met the carved face's gaze with his own. He did not blink. A minute passed, maybe two.

"The bridge of time is very poignant," he told me. "I think about the immigrant carvers who came over here and did this work on people's homes—itinerant nobodies, many of them, with no stable homes of their own—and I meet them across time."

Dad could see I was exhausted. He said I should sit tight while he wheeled the keystone back to the truck in the shopping cart. He would come back for me.

I was too worn-out to put the tools back in his bag. Instead, I brushed the loose mortar and brick shards from the Snuffleupagus comforter and climbed into the kid's bed. The room had really gotten quite chilly; now and then a rush of cold street air came through the hole we'd punched in the wall and made me shiver. I didn't mind. I hugged the kid's comforter tightly around me and felt very safe and at home.

When I awoke, I didn't know where I was and then I did. My head was flopped sideways. I felt a strand of slobber running from the corner of my mouth to the corduroy shoulder of the man cradling me in his arms. It was dark still, and we were moving across a rubbled lot. I could feel Dad's breath in his chest, my body rising and falling along with his labors. I must have been dead weight, big and unwieldy, gangle-armed. A burden in unexpected new ways. It was a struggle for my father to carry me, far more than when I was small. But he was doing it.

10

THE SUN COMES UP when it comes up, but the city doesn't show it to you until it's good and ready. The sky over TriBeCa next morning had that veiled brightness that told you the day had begun and that if you lived anywhere outside the five boroughs, in some backward, hillbilly place where nature still held sway, then by now you would be enjoying a quaint pyrotechnical display known, according to lore, as a sunrise.

Not here. Over on West Street, where I found myself walking uptown between the river and the elevated ghost road of the defunct West Side Highway, daybreak was more a question of feeling Manhattan gather its energies. I longed for that this morning, wanted to confront those energies head-on. I'd told Dad I had to get home, that Mom was expecting me, and he'd sent me on my way with cab fare and an onion bagel.

The waterfront was pretty ragged here, wind-burred waves breaking against the rotted pilings of vanished docks. The roadway fringed with litter.

A few blocks above Chambers Street, I found the Good Humor truck parked on a crumbling pier where we'd left it. I clambered up its bumper and hood to its roof and stood there in the wind waiting for the city to reveal itself. At the pier's end, a barge with a crane arm rocked in the water, its lines groaning now and then in concert with the incessant rope clack of its flagless pole. A green bottle blew around the pier's cracked pavement in a ringing half circle.

I turned away from the river and eyed the city, its long back porcupined with towers. The buildings in their thousands looked sullen and colorless in the unfinished morning light. But as I stood there on the truck roof, doing a shivery little jig to keep warm, the sun in an instant edged above the skyline, climbing fast and touching whole walls of windows into flame. The city came alive, had always been alive, and now my eye was drawn to individual marvels in the streetscape. Just across town the sky was pierced by a turreted, green-spired tower with the majestically oddball appearance of a drip-castle cathedral. A bit to its north, a circular colonnade atop another imposing tower was crowned with a statue of some tarnished goddess. And a few blocks downtown soared the twin behemoths of the World Trade Center, begun with great hoopla when I was in third grade and completed several years later.

It was exhilarating to think of all the gargoyles locked in the belly of the truck beneath my feet. The city was mine. I would not be sneered at, frowned upon, belittled with a smirk from on high. I would not be looked down on or put in my place. Just wait long enough and those smug stone faces would come tumbling down from their perches. Or if need be I could force them down, chisel them loose, make them my own. The city would always be full of surprises, sure, but now I was one of those surprises myself. Now I understood that you weren't required to just let New York's evolution happen around you, happen *to* you. You didn't have to hang around and wait for the city to drop your future on your head, whether that future was a gargoyle or a cornice or a lunch box.

So of course I crashed Dani's party that night. It didn't occur to me not to. The doorman of her West End Avenue apartment house was a gruff leprechaun with hairy wrists poking from his braid-edged uniform sleeves. He was standing just inside the lobby door at a card table with a clipboard on it.

"You Irish?" I asked. "A son of the Emerald Isle?"

His Irish eyes were not smiling. "Why you asking me that?"

"Only because a lot of the city's nineteenth-century stone carvers were Irishmen, and they liked to carve their buddies, and the dude carved above the doorway of that townhouse two doors down looks quite a bit like you." I jerked my thumb toward the street. "But you've probably noticed it yourself."

He stepped toward the door, which was tied open with a loop of frayed twine running from the inside knob to a brass eyelet on the wall.

"Two doors down?"

I nodded, and he took a tentative step outside to peer down the block, just long enough for me to glance at Dani's guest list on the clipboard and identify a couple of names that hadn't yet been checked off.

"You're lucky that house is even still standing," I went on. "I mean, with all the insurance fires around town, and the way the city is tearing down more than a hundred abandoned buildings every month in places like Harlem and the South Bronx, the carvings of your ancestors are really in some pretty serious jeopardy."

"My ancestors?" He looked intrigued.

"Of course. Now, I'm not saying the guy carved on that keystone is *definitely* your relative," I went on. "That would be way too weird a coincidence. But he's totally got to be a comrade of yours, a kindred spirit. I mean, the resemblance between the two of you is really striking."

"You think?"

"Oh, sure. You've both got that strong chin and that heroically miserable look of the longtime hemorrhoid sufferer."

The guy glared at me and harrumphed back inside to his card table, but when I gave him a name on Dani's list—Elliot Blum, Quigley's lab partner—he had no choice but to let me upstairs.

"I'm not one to toot my own horn," I told him, just before popping into the elevator, "but I really do know an *awful lot* about architectural sculpture."

The guy must have buzzed up, because Dani surprised me by opening her apartment door before I'd had even fifteen seconds in the hallway to plot out what I was going to say to her. She was wearing faded

OshKosh B'gosh overalls with only a black bra underneath, and I was briefly flustered by the sight of her.

"You weren't supposed to open the door," I said.

"That's why I did. The doorman said that a kid with a mouth on him was coming up."

"That didn't sound like Elliot to you, huh?"

"Hardly." Elliot was a bookish, chinless ninth-grader who seemed to spend most of his time trying not to be noticed.

"Well, aren't you gonna ask if you can take my coat? It's pretty crummy manners to leave a gate-crasher standing in the hallway like this."

She looked me over. I couldn't tell what she saw.

"Is that a present?" She pointed at the large, roundish package under my right arm.

"It *might* be." I was having a hard time not glancing at her black bra strap, so I looked down instead. She was a bit pigeon-toed, the tips of her blue-and-white bowling shoes turned in slightly toward each other. *Very* cute.

"I *like* presents," she said playfully.

I extended the package to her. It was an unwieldy thing, the size and shape of an overlarge pizza tray, wrapped in Chinese newspaper. The top story had a photo of a row of topless male Chinese study subjects holding their elbows aloft in unison so their armpits could be given a scientific sniff by a technician in a lab coat, who was going down the row with his nose extended appraisingly.

Dani giggled. "Nice wrapping paper."

She ripped open the package, and before she'd even gotten it out of the bubble wrap she was laughing.

"How did you ever know I needed one of these?" she asked, pulling my quick-release bike wheel from its wrapping.

"Buffoon's intuition, I guess."

"Well, thanks," she said. "You want some cake or something? I think there's a little left."

She turned and headed inside without waiting for me. I watched her matchstick-thin little body recede down the hall.

The apartment was one of those sprawling, prewar Upper West Side places with endless rooms and closets. I poked my head into one of the bedrooms and saw what might have been two or three couples smooching in the dark. In another room, made dim by batik fabric draped over lampshades, a circle of ninth-grade girls was gathered on the shag carpet around a turntable, listening to *Ziggy Stardust* with an "I've found God" expression on their faces. One of them was Quigley. She was wearing yellow, plastic-looking bell-bottoms and a psychedelic Danskin top with sleeves that came down almost to her wrists. She never wore short-sleeved shirts. She suffered horribly from psoriasis, a flaky-skin disorder that attacked her elbows, leaving them so raw and inflamed they looked like someone had abraded them with a cheese grater. The only way she could get enough relief to go to auditions was by slathering an icky white cream all over her elbows and wrapping the whole mess with Saran Wrap to seal in the moisture overnight. It was an awkward operation that required at least three hands, but she always performed it alone.

I'd heard her ask Mom for help over the years, the last time a few weeks earlier.

"Oh, I really would," Mom answered, her hands fluttering like birds, "but you know I'm hopeless at that sort of thing, and I promised poor Monsieur Claude I'd help him with his visa renewal." As Mom bustled away, I felt Quig's eyes shift hopefully to me, but there was no way I was doing something that gross for my sister. Sorry as I felt for her, all I was willing to offer was the invasion of her privacy. At bedtime, I spied through her door crack, her arms all pretzeled around each other, an angry pink elbow jutting, as she struggled to heal herself. One end of the Saran Wrap kept sticking infuriatingly to the other, and she kept having to throw the whole blob away, cursing and close to tears, and start all over again. When she finally succeeded in binding both afflicted elbows in plastic, Quig just sat there on the floor, exhausted and lonely, both her arms bulging in the middle with ugly, clinging kitchen wrap. She looked like leftovers.

In Dani's apartment, I wandered down a narrow back hall, searching for the room my father had asked me to find: Dani's dad's study.

On our way uptown in the ice cream truck the night before, Dad had casually mentioned that it would be a big help to him if I could poke around among Dani's father's papers and swipe anything I could find marked *Laing*.

"Her father's an architect, right?" Dad asked. I had no clue; I thought maybe he was a teacher or something.

"Yeah, that sounds like the one. He's an architecture professor at Columbia, in the grad school." My father had hoped to take me and Quigley to dinner the day after we went gargoyle hunting, once he was done fixing my broken bedroom window. But Quig told him she was going to Dani Gardner's party. Intrigued by Dani's last name, Dad looked her up in the class list and discovered that her father, Aaron Gardner, had the same name as an architect whose work he was interested in. If he turned out to be the same man, it would really help Dad's business a bunch to know more about his designs and business partners.

Doing my sneaky best, I slipped quickly into the first of a pair of side-by-side maid's rooms, which turned out to be Dani's bedroom. It was dark, and I nearly broke my neck stepping on something that tried to slide out from under my foot. When I switched the light on, I saw that the offending object was a small silver pizza tray with two loops of black Velcro attached to its center. After mulling it a few seconds, I figured out it must be a homemade shield of Dani's own invention.

Dani was a Dungeons & Dragons nerd. D&D was a new fantasy game that one of her big brothers, Luke, was always playing on the weekends with friends like Max Schloss, older brother of Lamar (a.k.a. Fathead). They usually let Dani play, and once Max even brought Lamar along when they needed an extra player. Lamar was always trying to tell me about the game, how much I'd like it, but its rules involved way too much phantasmagorical mumbo jumbo for my taste.

From what I could gather, D&D centered on a bunch of adventures in which each kid took on the role of either a human or a fantastical creature like an elf or a dwarf. The players were all supposed to be on the same team, tackling monsters and ethical dilemmas together. But the game was so sketchily conceived, with so many holes in its proce- dures, that it always degenerated into a big shouting match, a roomful of pimpled, self-righteous lawyers hollering at one another about Hit Points and the Axis of Morality.

Dani loved the fantasy element of the game, all that role-playing stuff about pretending you were a muscle-bound medieval warrior. But listening to boys argue irritated the hell out of her, so she had introduced her own, more streamlined method of conflict resolu- tion: hand-to-hand combat. Following her example, all the boys made swords by wrapping a length of broomstick with foam rubber and duct tape, and whenever two players had a disagreement over the rules, they would face off in the living room, walloping the crap out of each other for thirty seconds, at which point the less bruised com- batant was declared the winner.

Dani was good: small but quick. She had three older brothers, so she took special pleasure in besting boys, and she took the swordplay so seriously that she even signed up for after-school fencing, to work on her moves. I, too, had signed up for fencing, to watch her work on her moves.

I stepped back into the hall to resume my search. A peek inside the other maid's room next door revealed that it was indeed Dani's dad's study. But it wasn't safe to sneak in there yet, I realized. Coming from the kitchen, just a few steps away, I could hear the gravelly murmur of a stultifyingly dull man boring someone to tears with his conversa- tion: ". . . a manifest abdication of city government's fiscal responsi- bility . . . short-term debt obligations of $3.4 billion . . . unsustainable reliance on the municipal bond market . . ."

I poked my head around the corner and saw a small man in a tweed jacket leaning against a butcher-block countertop with a glass of red wine in his fist. His back was to me. Opposite him, more or less pinned against the stove by the guy's torrent of blather, was Kathleen Shaw, a pretty ninth-grader who wore her painter's pants too high. Her mouth seemed paralyzed in the shape of a phony half smile and her eyes had a look of pained stupefaction, as though she would rather slit her own throat with a rusty penknife than listen to even one more tedious word. It was obvious she would make a break for freedom at the first opportunity, so I was definitely going to need help keeping Dani's father occupied while I snooped around in his study.

I couldn't find my buddy Rafferty anywhere—maybe he'd been one of the lucky kids smooching in that dark room—but Kyle was in the living room, perched on a leather chair next to a kid with a bowl haircut whom I'd never seen before. Kyle waved me over. He looked as serious as I'd ever seen him.

"Griffin, come have a seat. Me and Greeley here were just talking religion."

I said hi and sat down.

"Greeley goes to St. David's. Headed for church college when he graduates—seminary, he said they call it."

The kid nodded self-importantly. He had milky eyes and a bland, kindly face.

"Kyle clearly hasn't had much religious instruction," he told me. "But he has an open heart, and that's all one can really ask."

Kyle leaned in close to Greeley. "Now, I admit I've never been much of a religious guy," he told his new friend, "but what you've been telling me is *totally* fascinating. Because if I understand you properly, God is *everywhere*."

"That's right."

"Everywhere?"

"Everywhere."

"So God is all over the world at this very moment," Kyle said. "He's in this room, He's at the top of the Eiffel Tower, He's down on the Bowery—"

"Yes, that's all true," Greeley interrupted. "But it's not just the physical world we're talking about, of course. It's the spiritual world. God isn't just all around us, He's within us."

"*Within* us." Kyle's eyes lit up.

"Within us."

"So God really *is* everywhere."

Greeley smiled. "Yes, that's what I've been saying."

"He's in you."

"Yes."

"He's in Griffin here."

"Of course."

"He's in me."

"Sure he is."

"He's in my soul, and in my mind, and in my heart."

"Now you've got it."

"He's in*fus*ing me, filling every part of me."

"Yes, he's *everywhere*."

Kyle leapt to his feet. He couldn't suppress his glee.

"So God is in my *butt*!" he crowed.

"I'm sorry?" Greeley looked up, astonished.

"God . . . is in my *BUTT*!" Kyle cackled. "You just said he's everywhere! So God is in my butt!"

There was no holding him back now. Every other conversation stopped and all eyes turned to Kyle as he cavorted joyously around the room doing an exuberant, sashaying booty dance, his chin down near the carpet, his buoyant rear end hoisted high in the air: "God is in my *butt*! God is in my *butt*!"

By the time Kyle finally stopped to catch his breath, Greeley had melted away into the party, utterly mortified. I caught Kyle by the sleeve.

"That's quite an epiphany you just had there," I said. "Talk about finding God."

"Yeah," Kyle said, his face flushed. "Turns out you just have to know where to look!"

I told him I had a little something going with Dani, and I desperately needed him to run interference with her dad while I made my move in one of the maid's rooms. We both knew I'd never really made a move on anyone—not one that worked, anyway. But boys have to have aspirations, and for Kyle to point out my miserable track record would have been to cast doubt on the very viability of our eternal shared goal of getting in a girl's pants.

"You gonna get her to tickle your Twinkie?" Kyle asked.

I hesitated.

"Yank your Yodel? Surely you're gonna get her to yank your Yodel."

"Kyle . . ."

"Dandle your Devil Dog! You should totally—"

"Dandle?" I asked.

"Dandle, yeah. It's *dandle,* isn't it?"

"I think you mean *diddle. Dandle* is something you do to babies. On your knee."

"It's not *dandle?*" His brow furrowed. "You *sure* it's not *dandle?*"

"Jesus, Kyle, will you shut up already? Are you gonna help me out or what?"

In the end, he was everything a friend could ask for in a wingman, chatting up Dani's father in the kitchen while I slipped into the old guy's study just down the hall.

Mr. Gardner's desk lamp, one of those pretentious old-timey brass ones with the green glass shade, was already on when I snuck in there. It was a very skinny room. One of the two long walls was lined with cork and covered floor to ceiling with photos and blueprints of buildings, all overlapping and shoving one another out of the way. The bookcase on the long wall opposite was stuffed with volumes bearing titles like *Historic Preservation: Curatorial Stewardship of the Built Environment.* On the shelves in front of the books, jutting into the room at all angles, were dusty balsa wood models of buildings. The effect of being in this overcrowded space was like that of walking down a narrow city street with all the façades leaning aggressively inward from both sides.

I ignored this shiver of claustrophobia and went to work. Most of the blueprints on the wall had client names in the lower right corner, but none said *Laing.* Some of the models had names or addresses written on their bases, but again I didn't see what I was looking for—though I did find a hip-flask-shaped bottle of Smirnoff vodka tucked inside an apartment house marked 840 Fifth Avenue. (A fifth on Fifth: Was this a private joke of Gardner's, or just a way to remember where he'd left his hooch?) I took a swig from the bottle, but the stuff was so nauseating that I instantly spat it all over the bookcase, showering several townhouses with a boozy monsoon.

The house phone buzzed in the hall outside the study, making me jump. Mr. Gardner answered it and told the doorman, in his lugubrious monotone, that it was okay to send someone-or-other up.

"That's just *so* interesting what you were telling me," Kyle was saying now, just outside the study door. "I didn't know that something as hard as stone could be so, you know, vulnerable."

"Oh, yes, sandstone is notoriously fragile, especially in this climate, and brownstone is just a species of sandstone." As I rifled through the papers on Mr. Gardner's desk, his soporific murmur oozed right into the room: "Sedimentary rock is formed in layers, you see, in planes parallel to the earth. But when the city's townhouses were constructed, their brownstone façades were typically installed with the sedimentary plane parallel to the plane of the building."

"Wow, that's just *sooo* intriguing."

The drawers of Gardner's desk were mostly filled with junk: nasal spray, ticket stubs, another vodka bottle, binders full of plumbing specifications.

"That's why brownstone façades spall so terribly," Mr. Gardner blathered on. "They're weak along those planes, and gravity simply flakes off the strata."

As quietly as I could, I eased open the top drawer of the green metal file cabinet behind the study door and began going through it. Mr. Gardner was uncomfortably close; I could see a tweedy swatch of him through the crack between the door's hinges.

About halfway through the second file drawer, I found it: a folder marked *Laing, Edgar.* Inside it was a sealed manila envelope and a few receipts. I stuck the whole folder in my knapsack and slid the drawer closed gingerly.

"That's really just absolutely *fascinating*," Kyle was saying now. "You know, I learned something else fascinating tonight, Mr. Gardner. Did you know that God is everywhere?"

I froze. But instead of answering him, Mr. Gardner suddenly barked out: "Whoa whoa whoa! Hold on a minute there, Piggy. Do you really need to have *seconds* on birthday cake, when you're only having *one* birthday? Here, let me toss that out for you."

The study's doorknob gave a little jiggle. I grabbed my knapsack and fled into the bathroom between the two maid's rooms, quietly pulling the door closed behind me. When I tried to shove open the bathroom's far door, I found it was locked, but from my side. I slid the little bolt open and pushed my way into the other maid's room, where I bumped right into Dani. She gave a little gasp of fright and then hit me in the chest with her open palm when she realized it was me.

"You jerk!" she cried, fighting tears. "What are you doing in my room?"

I closed the bathroom door behind me and glanced around. Her pizza-tray shield was still on the floor, along with a jumble of album covers and sneakers and a worn copy of *The Fellowship of the Ring.* I reached out and took Dani by her slight shoulders. They were warm and smooth in my palms.

"Hey," I said gently.

She shook me off. "Where have you been? I've been wandering *all over the place* with your stupid cake, *looking* for you!"

"You shouldn't let him make you feel bad," I said. "It's idiotic what he said. It's just cake."

"But I didn't even *want* the cake, I *hate* cake, it's *your* cake!" She was shaking.

"I was only saying—"

"Get out of here, will you? Get out of my party!" Her eyes were rimmed with red. "I don't want you here, don't you get it, dumb-ass? You weren't even *invited.*"

I was confused, but did as I was told, edging out of the room as best I could without crushing any albums underfoot. My stomach felt awful.

I found Kyle alone in the kitchen, gorging himself on the disputed dessert. Instead of cutting himself a slice like a civilized person, he had impaled the entire remaining half a cake on the tines of a bone-handled carving fork, which he was rotating methodically so that not a single square inch of frosted surface area could escape his wide-open maw. His eyes were alight with amusement.

"What?" he spluttered with balloon-cheeked mock innocence when he saw me, a small avalanche of cake crumbs spilling from his mouth

and down his shirt. "Why are you looking at me like that?" His face was smeared with a disturbing clown smile of brown frosting, and he was very, very pleased with himself. He stifled a giggle.

"We've gotta go," I told him. "We're not welcome here anymore."

"*We?*"

We got our jackets, and Kyle followed me out the kitchen door, across the hall, and into the back stairwell. It was grimy and dimly lit, each floor with a clouded window and a wide gray door behind which elevator cables ticked and sang.

On the far side of the landing, I stopped and regarded the fire hose, all neatly coiled in its hanging rack and culminating in a brass nozzle.

"What?" Kyle asked.

"You ever wonder how they get water pressure all the way up here? It's a miracle of mechanics, really. Fighting gravity all the way."

"No, Griffin. I never wondered that." He continued down the stairs. "Come on."

"But the thing is, how do you really know it'll work unless you test it?"

"I'm sure they do test it. Just like the elevator. Let's go."

I put my hands on the red wheel.

"*Griffin?*" There was urgency in Kyle's voice, distrust maybe.

"But how do you know?" I asked. "How do you know how safe you really are until you test it?"

I leaned into the red wheel and gave it a twist. It resisted a moment, then began to turn. There was a jerking rumble from somewhere far below, then a delay during which nothing much seemed to happen. And then, as Kyle's eyes grew big as Super Balls, there came a distant jolt—I could feel the vibrations in my hands—followed by a surging *shhhhhhhhh* sound from somewhere downstairs, rapidly growing louder. We stared at each other a long moment, expectant and half-disbelieving, as the sound rushed closer—until the base of the coiled hose lurched spasmodically and began to thicken with water.

Kyle let out a cackle. "You *jackass!*" he cried. "You total jackass!" And then we were running, giggling and sprinting down the stairs, feeding off each other's laughter.

The wheel on the next landing turned more easily. This time there was much less delay before the coiled hose began filling itself.

"Griffin! That's enough!" Kyle could barely get the words out, he was laughing so hard. *"Seriously!"* We ran. Ran and giggled.

By the following floor I had my technique down, slap-gripping the wheel with my left hand, turning it just enough to open the valve while keeping my overall momentum moving down the stairs. It was crucial that we reach the lobby ahead of the deluge.

And the deluge was coming now. At first the flow was just a leisurely plashing from above, descending step by step. But as the waters from the uppermost hose reached the waters from the hose on the landing below, their force and volume multiplied, rushing down to join the next hose's output, and the next, the stream becoming a river becoming a flash flood.

"Dude," Kyle chortled, *"Poseidon Adventure!* I'm Ernest Borgnine!"

"No way! *I'm* Borgnine! *You're* Gene Hackman."

"I don't want to be Hackman!"

"You're Hackman," I insisted. "The priest who's questioning his faith—wondering if maybe God is in his butt!"

"All right, all right," Kyle said. "But if I'm Hackman, you have to be Shelley Winters."

"Is that the annoying fat lady who swims up a storm and then keels over?"

"That's the one."

"Bastard!"

We discovered we could move faster if we alternated floors. While Kyle spent a few moments turning a hose wheel enough revolutions to really open the floodgates, I sprinted right past him and spun open the next one. I liked the rumbling vibration in my fist, the feeling of power as my palm flew off the wheel.

Things were getting pretty wet. Somewhere above us, the water had risen high enough to spill through the metal uprights into the stairwell's open center, waterfalling the full eleven stories from Dani's floor to the lobby level. By the time we got down to the bottom, the center of the first-floor landing was filling with water, the pool widening as the stairwell Niagara poured into it. Kyle high-stepped it around the edge of the pool, and I tried to follow, but halfway across, my stomach hurt so much from laughing that I had to stop and collect myself.

"Hurry, Shelley, *hurry!*" Kyle cried. "You can make it, old girl! Remember those swim lessons from your youth!"

Together we stumbled, giggling, through a heavy door, slamming it shut behind us. We found ourselves in an ornate side hall of the lobby, with gilded moldings and chandeliers whose bulbs were shaped like flames. We stood on the Persian carpet, still snorting with laughter, and stared expectantly at the door through which we had just come, wondering when the water would begin flowing from the crack at its bottom.

"What are you boys looking at?" the doorman's grumpy voice demanded from behind us. "What's going on here?"

We turned to face him.

"I'm thinking maybe someone left the tub running or something," Kyle said. "Because things are getting a tad moist back there. You should really do something about that."

We speed-walked past the doorman and out to the sidewalk, and though I never actually saw him open the stairwell door, I told Kyle as we hurried down Ninety-Third Street that I liked to imagine the guy being carried straight out to West End Avenue in a raging flood, arms cartoonishly akimbo.

We were almost at Riverside, where the bums slept behind the bushes that surrounded the Joan of Arc statue, when a booming voice caught up with us: "Hey! *You two!*"

We turned around to see a cop loping down the street toward us, holding his flashlight like a cudgel. At the corner behind him was a police cruiser. A second cop was standing beside it listening to the doorman, who was pointing at us and gesticulating furiously.

"Yeah, *you!* Come back here!" the nearer cop yelled at us. "I wanna talk to you!"

He stopped, maybe fifty yards away, and waited for us to obey.

Kyle and I looked at each other, flabbergasted.

"What the hell?" I said under my breath. "How'd they get here so fast?" It didn't make any sense; it was as if they'd just beamed down from the *Enterprise*.

"I don't think they came 'cause of us," Kyle said. "Some Collegiate boys were throwing soggies out Dani's window before you even got there."

"So we're innocent."

Kyle looked at me, slack-jawed and petrified.

"We're totally innocent," I said, and I started walking, unhurried, back toward the cop. Kyle came along. "That's why we're so relaxed," I told him. "*You're* relaxed, right?"

"Yeah, I guess so," he said, sounding anything but. Then, after a pause: "*Why* am I relaxed?"

"Because we didn't do anything. We simply left the party after those terrible Collegiate guys, and now we're just walking on back to talk to the nice policeman."

"Right," Kyle said, still walking alongside me. "And we're just chatting together in the unworried sort of way that innocent people talk."

We had nearly reached the cop by now. He looked bigger up close. He had two thick, angry eyebrows joined by a furry isthmus. He gave us the once-over.

"No bullshit now. What have you two been up to in the last five minutes?"

I looked him in the eye and told him how we had just left Dani's party. I was respectful but not too jittery or suck-uppy. I told him how we'd heard a weird hissing from a few floors above us in the back stairwell, like a burst steam pipe maybe, and how it freaked us out, and how we'd hightailed it out of there as quickly as we could.

"What was it, officer?" I asked. "Is everyone okay? I hope no one got scalded with steam or anything."

He looked at me a long moment, and just when his posture started to soften, something seemed to occur to him and he got all puffed up and suspicious again.

"But the doorman ID'd you!" he said. "He says he saw the two of you standing in the lobby staring at the door to the back stairway, like you knew water was about to flood out. You're gonna have to explain that."

Kyle looked at me. His expression was completely blank, but I knew him well enough to recognize that blankness as terror. I looked at the cop. He was staring down at me, waiting.

"Well, it wasn't the door, actually," I said.

"What wasn't?"

"The thing we were staring at, it wasn't the door."

"What was it, then?"

"It was the molding *above* the door, along the ceiling."

The cop cocked his ear. "What about it?"

"Well, its gilding isn't real gold, for one thing," I said. "It's a poor restoration job done with gold radiator paint. Back when they invented it, restorers thought of it as 'gold in a can.' They didn't know the paint would bronze over time and start to look crummy."

The cop was eyeing me closely. "And that's why you were staring at it?"

"Well, not that *exactly*," I said. "What I was mostly doing was pointing out to Kyle here what a cool example of egg and dart that molding is."

"Egg and what?"

"Egg and dart. It's one of the most common decorative moldings in Western architecture. And the really special thing about that lobby's ornament, and why I wanted to show it to Kyle in the first place, is that just below the egg and dart there's also a really nice Dentyne molding."

Kyle was nodding.

"They call it that because it looks like teeth," I explained quickly. "It's a classic design. There's Dentyne moldings all over New York, not just inside buildings but outside, too: carved in stone on windows, porticos—you name it."

The cop stared at me a long time without talking. I kept quiet, too, deferring to his authority. Finally, with a grudging nod, he said, "All right, you two, get out of here."

We did, and this time we didn't say a word to each other until we'd turned the corner on Riverside.

Kyle's face was ghostly pale. I gave his shoulder a playful little shove and said, "Oh, don't be such a sourpuss. If you ask me, that really might've been my finest—"

"Griffin?" Kyle interrupted, stopping to make sure I was looking him in the eye. His voice was shaking, and he looked like he might throw up.

"Yeah?"

"Fuck you."

11

M Y WINDOW WAS GOOD AS NEW when I got back to my room. The fresh pane my father had put in was better than the old one, too, because aside from a few smudgy Dad fingerprints along the edges, it let you see things clearly; the original one had had that wavy antique glass that made you a bit seasick to look through.

I got out one of the cigar boxes I'd cadged from the Te Amo head shop on Lex and gingerly began filling it with the shards of glass Dad had left all over my floor. I think I would've almost enjoyed the challenge of not cutting myself had Quigley not been tap-dancing above my head like a crazy person. Her room was right above mine, and although I'd gotten pretty used to her practicing her tap routine up there for the school talent show, this was an entirely new level of mania. This was a staccato, skull-jabbing racket that sounded like Woody Woodpecker with a gizzard full of amphetamines. Or a small army of hypercaffeinated, cane-wielding blind men conducting a Morse code competition.

I had to bang on Quig's door a good long time before the mad tapping stopped and she opened up.

"What the hell is going on up here?" I asked her. "Are you okay?"

Quigley was wild-eyed, her freckled cheeks flushed. Her orange hair was slick with sweat along her forehead.

"They kissed!" she said breathlessly. "At least I think they did—my breath kept fogging up the window!"

"What are you *talking* about?"

"Mom and Dad, they kissed! I got them to kiss and I was trapped outside totally barefoot and it was freezing cold but everything was going really great—better than great!—until it wasn't. There are just too many people around here, Griffin, too many—it's impossible!— I can't do it any better than this, I can't, I did my best, I really did!"

I got her to sit on her bed and tell it to me slowly. Quig, it turned out, had left Dani's party early to see how her latest matchmaking scheme was working out at home.

My father had let himself in as usual without calling ahead, but my mother didn't let it bother her this time; she even went up to my room to thank him as he was smoothing down the last of the window glazing with his index finger. Quig was spying on them from the hall the whole time. Dad slid down my storm window to protect the regular window from any future wayward baseballs, and when my parents headed upstairs to close the fourth-floor storm window, too, Quig slipped up toward the fifth floor to avoid them. This turned out to be a tactical error, because when Mom asked Dad to take a look at a strange bulge up on the fifth-floor wall, Quigley found herself trapped. As our parents climbed the steps, she had to slip out the fifth-floor door to the roof to avoid being caught.

The fifth floor of the brownstone wasn't technically part of the brownstone at all. Our house, in its original form, was only four stories tall, but a little after I was born, Dad had built Mom an art studio atop it. Invisible from the street, this new fifth floor was basically a little suburban cottage plopped down on the tar roof amid the chimney pots and vents and pipes. Its own roof was pitched, and it had white clapboard siding and window boxes and a glass-louvered front door that opened onto a tar-paper lawn. In better times, Mom had painted trompe l'oeil green shutters on its façade and Dad had planted old spackle buckets with tomatoes. This fifth-floor cottage was where my parents sometimes used to sneak off to smooch in private, back when my father was still living with us.

Before Dad moved out, he moved upstairs. He emptied his closet and his dresser and brought everything up to the cottage, where for several months he slept on the floor on an old mattress, with a hot plate and a rotund electric coffee percolator for company.

I really had no clue at the time where things were headed. To me, Dad's new upstairs digs were more special than worrisome; he just seemed to be taking a sort of extended camping trip I could drop in on whenever I liked. I could see that he was in a foul mood most of the time and that it cheered him up when I visited him in the mornings, and that made me feel important. I'd put on my powder-blue robe with the white piping—the one I'd worn to the emergency room the time Quig smashed my head into the metal trundle bed—and I'd play the part of his happy little manservant, aglow with my usefulness as I brought him milk for his coffee.

I especially liked putting together the percolator, whose peculiar assortment of archaic-looking parts—the perforated disc! the gray metal tube! the sproingy spring!—reminded me of one of those ingenious inventions in the Leonardo exhibit Dad once took me to. Leonardo wrote everything into his notebooks mirror-image with his left hand, immediately encoding his answers to the very problems his inventions were meant to be solving. The percolator was its own problem, an intricate puzzle that, when properly assembled, reshaped Dad's whisker-grim face into a smile and made the coffee burble up into the little glass knob on top.

Quig peered through the glass door as Mom showed Dad the place on the far wall where some of the cottage's Sheetrock was swollen and stained. He didn't look impressed, and seemed to tease her a little about being alarmed by something so trivial as a roof leak. She gave him a playful little shove and he shoved her back, gently, his hand on her collarbone. They were laughing a little, discovering an unexpected intimacy in their months of shared conflict. Not far away on that same wall, Mom's latest piece was under construction on a slanted architect's table. It was a new subject for her: a huge mosaic portrait of a brownstone that was probably ours, the curlicue cursive words *Ceçi n'est pas un oeuf* spelled out in eggshell fragments and hidden like a Hirschfeld *Nina* in the looping decorative ironwork of our front-stoop railings.

Mom went to the mosaic to pick at a loose piece with a long maroon fingernail, and Dad joined her to have a look and said something to her and she considered his words and replied and in a moment they were doing something I guess they hadn't done in a very long time, which was listen to each other. Dad moved in to inspect the work more closely and Mom leaned in, too, dropping from Quig's view behind his body, and then it seemed their mouths must have met, because Dad's head and back were curving urgently forward, with all of Mom's form swallowed up in his, all but her wine-red fingernails clutching the back of his neck.

Quig's toes were growing numb out on the cold roof, but she was euphoric. She kept looking away and back, away and back, unsure of the proper protocol for a girl spy under the circumstances. And then Dad's head whipped around: there was Mr. Price, rumpled and embarrassed at the head of the stairs, a ratty wicker basket of damp laundry in his arms. Realizing his blunder, he began to blurt apologies and backtrack, but Dad was already surging across the room at him.

"Jesus *Christ*! Ever hear of knocking?"

Mr. Price's neck and face flushed deep red all the way up to his ears as he muttered muddled explanations about how he sometimes dried his laundry up there by clipping it to the lines Mom had strung up for her woodcut prints. Mom hurried over to insist that Mr. Price was telling the truth, that it was an honest mistake—and just like that, the fleeting tenderness between our parents vanished as quickly as it had come.

12

EVERYTHING ABOUT THE CITY FOLLOWED hidden rules, if only you could uncover them. The subways had cryptic subterranean signals and unpublished schedules and phantom stations that rushed past you in the darkness according to some overarching logic of momentum. The water system had aqueducts and gatehouses and six thousand miles of concealed mains through which a million gallons of water sluiced each day, all following an arcane plan I imagined to be the handiwork of mustachioed engineers in belted trench coats. Even the weather could be understood, if you possessed the secret knowledge that allowed you, with an authoritative swoop of your Magic Marker, to sketch a scowling storm cloud over the Battery or Hell Gate, the way weatherman-cartoonist Tex Antoine did on *Eyewitness News*.

My father's anger, like all the bewildering infrastructure governing my world, must follow some unseen pattern as well, I felt sure, its eruptions issuing from obscure yet knowable fault lines beneath the asphalt. But unlike the secrets of the transit and water systems, some of which I'd puzzled out over the years by squinting at the yellowed maps and documents that had flowed through our house en route to eventual resale, the rules behind my father's mood swings had always defied discovery. Only by dumb luck, in fact, did I finally stumble on a system for decoding and, at least for a while, containing his temper.

The solution was hiding in plain sight. The day after my father's blowup with my mother and Mr. Price, I crept up the stone spiral staircase that led from our school's cinder-block basement classrooms to the church upstairs, from which the school rented space.

The Church of the Heavenly Rest was an impressively gloomy structure, a vast vaulted world of soaring stone arches and bloodred stained glass and humorless whiskered personages carved in the wall behind the altar. Since our school had no auditorium of its own, we performed all our plays and musicals up there. By sneaking up to the church after school on this afternoon, I hoped to catch a glimpse of Dani rehearsing her swordplay performance for the talent show. But I'd picked the wrong day. This was the afternoon they were setting up the stage, and before I had a chance to slip away, Mr. Krakauer, the drama teacher, spotted me.

"Watts!" he called. "Stop skulking around in the shadows and give us a hand here!"

During a little self-granted break after an hour of hauling sets, I found my eyes drawn to the group of three-digit numbers posted on the broad stone surface behind the pulpit. I'd surely seen them dozens of times over the years, but never before had it occurred to me to wonder why those numbers were there, or what their specific sequence might signify.

Prominently displayed on a massive wall of stone blocks, the numbers seemed to speak of permanence. But they were ephemeral, too, each digit printed on an eggshell-yellow card of its own and slid into a small track like the ones you sometimes saw at coffee shops announcing the special of the day.

The numerals put me in mind of the carved naked ladies on the altar down at Dad's studio, the upper arms of which, I now recalled with a kind of tingling recognition, were also marked with three-digit numbers, in yellow chalk. I grabbed a stubby little pencil and a Join Our Parish card from the wooden shelf beneath the pew and scribbled down all five three-digit numbers from the wall. I felt certain I was on the cusp of understanding something here, something crucial.

While Mr. Krakauer was squinting at his stage diagram, I slipped to the darkened edge of the church and then out to the street.

The explosion of sunlight on Fifth Avenue was blinding after all that time in the lugubrious belly of the church. But I was too excited to mind the way it hurt my eyes. I blinked until the numbers I'd written on the card became unblurred: 592 was the first one.

592. It looked familiar.

Before I even had time to contemplate why, my feet were carrying me uptown, past the ornately textured brick-and-limestone mansion of the Cooper Hewitt Museum.

Two blocks up from school, I saw them: a pair of lushly maned lion heads, carved from rich red stone and roaring down, full-throated, from atop two columns flanking the door of a townhouse. I'd never noticed them before. The expression on the lions' faces was so epically peevish, and the details of their open mouths so finely wrought, that you could practically smell the caribou on their breath and diagnose which pointy teeth in their jaws might be afflicted with a touch of gingivitis.

I looked up at the two yellow street signs jutting, perpendicular to each other, from the lamppost on the corner: E 92 ST and 5 AV.

92 & 5: 925.

Or flip the signs around: 5 AV and E 92 ST.

5 & 92: 592! Just like on the church wall. I'd done it! *I'd cracked the code.*

It took me more than a week, because the five three-digit church numbers referred to blocks all over town, but I scoped out all the relevant intersections, and at all but one there was a building façade with a gargoyle or some other architectural ornament that looked precious enough for Dad to want to own and sell. Here at last was the hidden system that ordered and nourished my father's obsession with possessing the city. Here, if I knew how to use it, was a blueprint for keeping his nettling dissatisfaction at bay.

The next time I went to watch Dani rehearse her swordplay act— and I have to say, she looked way better in her cutoff jeans and red bandanna headband than the ordinary pretty ballet girls in their pink

Danskins—the numerals above the pulpit had changed. This time, though, I was properly equipped. I carefully recorded them in a moleskine notebook I'd gotten at Blacker & Kooby: 237, 348, 590, 256.

I didn't tell anyone about those church numbers. Not Kyle, not Quig, not Mom. I wasn't sure what to do with the information, whether I should reveal to Dad that I knew how he decided which gargoyles to target, or if learning that his secret was out would cause him to turn his rage on me. It was important to play it right.

The matter was further complicated by the disturbing certified letter from Chase Manhattan Bank I signed for and tore open one of the many afternoons Mom wasn't around to answer the doorbell. It was a NOTICE OF ARREARS informing my father that he was several months behind on the brownstone mortgage. I'd never seen or heard the word *arrears* before. It sounded like being mooned by a financial institution.

With Dad short of cash, I needed to take matters into my own hands. By the time it got dark, I had swiped Quigley's old violin case and filled it with the few things I thought I might need for my mission. Mom didn't come home all evening—she never seemed to be around much anymore—but Quig was still bustling about in the dining room and kitchen. She couldn't stand the chaos of the house, how the boarders never cleaned up after themselves. In an effort to restore some of the order that had eroded along with our parents' marriage, she always crept downstairs after the boarders had retired and emptied the ashtrays, pushed in the chairs, did the dishes. She couldn't bear to start a new day with things in such disarray.

At 11:17, when Quig finally went upstairs to listen to her show tunes, I snuck out to the street. I'd had hours to choose my first target from the list of numbers in my moleskine notebook: 590.

Ninetieth and Fifth was easily the closest of the city intersections indicated by that week's three-digit church numerals, and happened to be the location of the Church of the Heavenly Rest itself. I hoofed it over there with my tools rattling around in the violin case. There

were doormen in long coats behind the glass doors of the two apartment houses facing each other across Ninetieth Street on the west
side of Madison, and a broken checkerboard of lit and unlit windows
above each lobby. But as I headed toward Fifth, everything residential
slipped away behind me and the only light came from the jaundiced
glow of the tall silver streetlamps curving their necks to peer down at
my slinking progress. On Fifth Avenue and Ninetieth, only two of the
four corner streetlamps were even functioning properly. A third, on
the southeast corner where the hulking stone church loomed, flick-
ered a jittery light down onto me. Nothing much worked in the city
these days.

So where was the architectural sculpture I was supposed to take?
The most obvious choice to yield up its treasures was the church itself,
whose heavy stone entrance was richly framed with carved crowns
and shepherd's crooks and all sorts of other God paraphernalia. But it
seemed unlikely that the number 590 had been hanging on the wall
inside as a prescription for pilfering the carvings on the church itself,
so I ventured across the street to take a look at the iron-and-granite
fence that ran around the courtyard of the Cooper Hewitt Museum.
The fence did have a blocky sort of column at its corner, but the big
urn-like stone ornament at its top had to be a good eighteen feet above
the street, and way too huge to remove.

This was frustrating. The wind was beginning to find its way up
my pant legs and between the folds of my scarf to my throat. I started
working up to feeling good and sorry for myself, noting how each of
my breaths wafting toward Central Park was clear evidence of how
horribly cold I was, when I realized I was looking right at what I'd
come for.

Across the asphalt moat of Fifth Avenue stood the two stone pillars
of the Engineers' Gate, one on each side of the park entrance. I closed
my eyes tight and made a quick deal with myself not to contemplate
what a stupid idea it was to get any closer to the park, which everyone
knew teemed with muggers and rapists and every other sort of crimi-
nal you could imagine. When I opened my eyes again, I was pleas-
antly surprised to find that no one had lurched from the shadows and

jumped me. I crossed Fifth Avenue on the red and stood at the base of the uptown gate pillar. Some vandal had knocked out the light of the streetlamp above it with a rock, but you could still see quite clearly that an elaborate—and, frankly, quite freaky—coat of arms had been carved into the pillar's front panel. It looked like a psychedelic Peter Max poster wrought in stone, or the sort of fever dream a court sculptor might come up with if someone had planted a tab of acid in his morning crumpet. At the carving's center was the head of a pompous-looking cougar or lion wearing a wackadoodle pharaonic headdress and surrounded by a junk closet's worth of regal bric-a-brac: garlands and wreaths and so forth. What it all meant I hadn't the slightest clue. This was how grown-up power encoded itself.

I looked around to make sure I wasn't being watched. Here on the park side of Fifth, the empty street beside the curb was decorated, at regular intervals, with piles of moonlit glass shards, where some previous night's marauder had gone along and smashed the passenger window of each car to get at its radio.

I rested the violin case on the curved stone bench at the base of the gate pillar and took out a hammer and chisel. The pillar was made of stacked stone blocks, like a built-in ladder, with large grooves in between, so climbing up to the really good details of the carved panel was pretty easy.

The moment I got up there, I zeroed in on a little stone eaglet about the size of a grown man's hand. He was really the only part of the carving that stuck out enough for me to get at; even his wings were pretty flat against the panel. But it was no problem to get the chisel edge behind the bird's rounded shoulder. I gripped the pillar with my knees, made sure the angle of the chisel was right, and began hammering the round red top of its handle.

The noise the eaglet and I made was rhythmic, and seemed to get swallowed up in the textured darkness of Central Park. After I'd chipped away behind half of the little eagle's body, I shifted the chisel to the bird's other shoulder and went at it from the opposite side. When I could feel that he was only held on by a sliver of remaining stone along his spine, I let the hammer drop to the sidewalk, cupped the creature gently in my left hand, and worked the edge of the chisel behind his back again. A violent jerk of my right wrist was all it took. The eagle popped loose into my palm, leaving his wings behind.

High above Fifth Avenue, I opened and closed my fingers around the bird's little breastbone and beak, admiring his solid fragility.

13

MOM WAS STILL OUT when I got home. I had no idea where. Though she was supposed to be the one who *hadn't* left, it somehow felt as if I saw even less of her than of Dad.

She had always needed time away from us, time to herself. "I'm off duty," she would announce, sighing with theatrical exhaustion, and she'd disappear for a morning, an afternoon. Quig and I would trade rueful one-liners about how she was never really much *on* duty, so how could you tell the difference?

But you could. When I was little, maybe four or five, she had taken a class in wood-block printing. Each week she brought her new knowledge home to me like a birthday present in colored tissue paper. She let me handle the Japanese carving tools, the gleaming new-moon blade my favorite. She showed me how to approach the wood at an angle, how to pressure the narrow handle with my thumb. Together we gouged out a sliver of sky, a skeptical eyebrow, a zebra's haunch. I liked the feeling of her cool-ringed hand over mine, the comforting bite of its ornament.

"Mommy," I told her one day, the words popping out of my mouth without forethought, "I love you more than the leading cough drop."

I helped her make a few woodcuts for my room: A rendering of my three-wheeler, which she called *The Princeling's Tricycle*. A portrait of my green-breasted parakeet, Pistachio, before her grumpy black cat, Mencken, got him. I loved the sweetly toxic smell of the oil paint, its

sticky resistance as you spread it over the carved boards with the rubber roller. I appreciated that my mother was an original. My friends'
moms smelled like purply hand soaps; mine stunk of turpentine. That
was quite all right by me.

I certainly didn't do arts-and-crafts with her anymore—no thirteen-
year-old boy wants to hang out with his mom *too* much—but I had
never stopped visiting her studio. She liked to hear my take on her
work, called me her best critic. I even let her drag me to an art exhibit
in the neighborhood now and then. For years we'd observed a pretty
straightforward quid pro quo: if I let her show me some wacky paintings at the Whitney or the Guggenheim, she'd take me for hot dogs at
Papaya King when we were done. Quig, who hated museums, sometimes met us afterward for ice cream sodas at Agora, that antiquey
place on Third with the stained-glass windows and the long ice cream
spoons.

But all of this camaraderie had slipped away since our parents'
breakup. Mom had become preoccupied, evanescent, hard to see in
certain light. She no longer announced her departures; she just went.
She always came back, and that was something, but you could tell her
heart wasn't in it.

I wasn't sure the situation was reversible. Her days off from us were
really just a progression of what she'd done for ages. It was no secret
that she'd always wanted to travel, to live abroad. She'd abandoned
that ambition after Quig showed up, but that didn't mean she was
staying put. If New York was to be her world, then her ports of call
would be people. She went straight at them whenever she could, and
once she had identified a man or woman or couple who interested
her, they tended to remain on her itinerary indefinitely. She dropped
in on them unannounced at home, at work. Stopped by to bring them
a straw-cloaked bottle of Chianti or an unusual oyster plate she'd
spotted at an antiques shop. One evening her destination might be
the rangy tai chi instructor who rented the servants' quarters atop
the Duke mansion on Fifth Avenue. Another it was the Czech oboist
shacked up in a SoHo loft with a puppeteer who had once operated
the Cookie Monster's arms.

Her impulsive gregariousness had always put her at odds with my father. Dad hated parties, feared the unfamiliar, was forever accusing her of collecting acquaintances. "Why do you need new people all the time?" he would complain. "What's wrong with the ones you already have?"

But it wasn't so much others she was collecting; it was herself. She sailed out into the city to discover parts unknown within herself. Parts that could only be revealed, or created, with the help of others. "It's so surprising sometimes to see how you are with them," she told me, "who you turn out to be."

She liked to decorate herself: patterned shawls, translucent silk headscarves, jostling bracelets of bone or onyx or mother-of-pearl. More lush than luxurious. At her hips she wore a clothesline belt, knotted below her navel in looping, Escher-like infinity. Its frayed ends she had cauterized with a borrowed Gauloise cigarette.

Mom had a way about her, a bemused openness, that strangers responded to: bus drivers, doormen, maître d's. Once, when she and I paused on a sidewalk to watch two pigeons tussling over a bialy, a white-haired man in a straw boater, thinking we looked lost, left his Buick running with the door open in the middle of Third Avenue to come offer us directions.

I hated when her room was dark, her many-pillowed bed empty. There had been a time, before Mencken died, when she always left her bedside light on, so he could warm his fur beneath it, and her radio playing QXR, so he wouldn't grow lonely in her absence. Now all was charcoal silence.

I stood in the doorway of her room. There was a cabinet under her cushionless window seat that had always been my secret hiding place, ever since I was little. My body was growing too ungainly for its confines, but I still liked to retreat in there to visit all the knickknacks that had accumulated over the years: a stack of Mad magazines, supermarket machine toys, a worn copy of Watership Down, a joy buzzer. It was cold in the cabinet, but private. I curled up in the dark in there, my head on one of her faded taffeta throw pillows, and told myself I was too old to miss my mother.

14

MY FATHER WAS IN NO MOOD for company when I turned
up at his studio a couple days later. I heard him barking at one
of his workers as I came down the fourth-floor hall, and he left me
standing in the doorway a good long while before he finally looked up
from the crate he and Zev were packing and said, "Not the best time,
big guy. What's up?"

The room was a mess. There were wooden crates everywhere, and
packing materials all over the floor. Zev was hammering a strip of
wood inside one of the crates.

"Send that one ahead to the Laing place, too," Dad told him. "It can
go out with the others."

"You *sure*? Don't you even wanna give Crowley a taste? He's been
after me all month about these."

"No, Laing gets 'em all. They'll be a great fit, trust me."

Leaning against a workbench not far from Dad's boot stood an eye-
poppingly colorful terra-cotta medallion almost as tall as me. King
Neptune glared out from its center, wearing a golden crown and gripping a burnt-orange trident. His stormy green hair and beard surged
from his head with roiling fury, a swollen sea overspilling the medallion's edges.

"Where'd *he* come from?" I asked.

"Coney Island," Dad answered. "City knocked down the Washington Baths—well, their Annex, actually—on the boardwalk last

year, where old Neptune had been gazing out at the ocean for God knows how long. A guy Curtis knows, works the Tunnel of Laffs out there, pulled it out of the rubble with some friends. We made him an offer."

I leaned in to inspect Neptune, his glazed face crazed with cracks.

"You have someone who'll buy it off you?" I asked. "More than you paid?"

"Of *course* more than I paid," Dad said irritably. "Look, I gotta get back to shipping all this stuff. What do you want?"

I took from my inside pocket a small object wrapped in chamois and put it in his palm.

"*What?* What is this?"

He began unwrapping it impatiently, but when the little eagle poked its beak from the fabric, Dad suddenly became very gentle, pulling back the edges of the cloth with extreme tenderness, as if helping a baby chick hatch out of its egg.

"Oh! Now isn't this a sweet one?" he said, running his finger over its feather-etched breastbone. He looked up. "Thank you, son. Thank you."

The gift seemed to cheer him right up. He held it at arm's length and grinned at it.

"Now let me guess where you got it," he said. "I can practically see it in my mind's eye: it came from a kind of tableau or pediment." He closed his eyes tight, then sprung them open: "Was it the National Arts Club, on Gramercy Park South—the old Tilden house? No, no, this one is granite, not sandstone . . ."

He thought awhile more and then poked the air with his index finger. "Got it! Engineers' Gate. Central Park, across from the Carnegie Mansion." He gave a laugh. That's why it was so familiar to him. He'd passed it practically every morning for years on his way to jog around the reservoir.

"You're right about the gate, Dad, but it's across from the Cooper Hewitt, not the place you said."

"I said the Carnegie Mansion. Same thing. The Cooper Hewitt *is* the Carnegie Mansion. Andrew Carnegie lived there with his family."

"A family lived in a museum?"

"No, they turned the family's home into a museum after the family was gone."

That rubbed me the wrong way. Anybody rich enough to build himself a palace on Fifth Avenue ought to be able to hang on to his home and not have fat midwestern tourists with Instamatics rambling around the bedrooms gawking at all the stuff.

"Did he have a son?" I asked.

"I don't remember. But never mind that." He gripped the little carved bird and poked its tail at me for emphasis, the way black-and-white movie fathers did with their pipes. "You did a good job here, son. There's certainly a little market for fragments like this, especially if they've got the provenance this one has."

So we made a game of it, the two of us: part scavenger hunt, part quiz show. I'd bring the artifacts in from all over town, and Dad would guess where I'd gotten them. It was remarkable how well he knew the city, or at least the ornamental creatures that populated it. Quite a few times he nailed the exact façade. Even when he didn't, he could almost always tell me the building type and neighborhood.

His favorite carvings were those that made his own past present.

"I'm guessing this is a gryphon talon from a sandstone plaque on one of those brownstone tenements in Little Italy," he'd say. "Right around Mott Street. I noticed those the first time I took your mother to the San Gennaro festival. The generator for the Ferris wheel was making the street vibrate, and I told her that all that seismic shaking was because they'd built the street over the San Gennaro Fault."

As pleased as my father was with the gargoyle fragments I brought him, I was a bit disappointed with his reaction when I gave him the Laing folder I'd worked so hard to steal from Dani's father. "Oh yeah, thanks," he said, setting it down on top of a DECARLO FUNERAL HOME & CREMATORY cooler. "Forgot I asked you about that."

.   .   .

Over the next couple of months, I kept Dad's spirits up by bringing him scraps of streetscape I'd hunted down, delivering them to his downtown studio with the predatory neediness of a cat laying a parade of dead mice at his master's doorstep. Every Monday a new batch of numbers would appear on the church wall, guiding me to particular street corners. There wasn't always a façade ornament at every intersection, and even when there was, a lot of the time the carving or casting was too high for me to reach or too flat to chisel off. But in every batch of numbers lay the coordinates of at least one treasure.

Since most of the pieces were far too big to remove in their entirety, I had to satisfy myself with fragments. As a result, the jumble of riches I brought Dad was a bit of a witches' brew. There was no eye of newt, but I did manage to snag the ear of a mare from an old stable on Sixty-Third and Third (633), the snout of a bulldog from a tenement on Fifty-Sixth and Ninth (569), the nipple of a demigoddess from a bank on Fifty-First and Sixth (516), and the horn of a Viking from a brownstone on Forty-Seventh and Eighth (478). All of these Dad assembled into a cluttered ensemble of partialness he displayed in a waist-high glass case.

When he was feeling voluble, he gazed back across the bridge of time and told me what he saw: The harried architect conjuring tenement after tenement to house the grubby multitudes disembarking at the piers and jostling uptown on the clattering new Els. The bellowing construction foreman, seeing again that the architect hadn't bothered to sketch any ornament on the blueprint, pointing curbside to a blank block of stone destined to crown a window arch ("Hey you! Carve me a Moses or a Mary or something!"). The sore-thumbed carver, free to invent in a way rarely permitted in Europe, incising his imagination into our city. Trotting from job to job with chisel and apron, transforming our streets into fantastically quirky public art galleries.

15

SOMETIME BETWEEN VALENTINE'S DAY and St. Paddy's Day, Mom took in another stray. This one was different, though. He was his own center of gravity; he wasn't looking for my mother, or our home, to provide one. He had interests, friends, a closet full of finely tailored suits and elegant neckties. He cut his own angles through the city, striding, even when dressed informally, like a man wearing a cape with a top hat and cane. This courtliness he wore not as a barrier but as an overture. He had an easy smile, one incisor turned slightly inward as if it were a tad shy.

His name was Shelby Forsythe, he'd grown up near New Orleans, and Mom, needing the money, had emptied out her top-floor studio for him to live in. He was the first boarder Quig had ever been able to stand. He showed her card tricks, wiggled his ears for her. He stood against a door, slyly rapping on it with his hidden left hand while knocking on the thigh of his trousers with his right to "prove" he had a wooden leg. Quig pretended to fall for it, punched him playfully in his gabardine shoulder, taught him how to tie a knot in a cherry stem with his tongue.

Mom had met Shelby at Hurley's, the Time-Life hangout a block down Sixth Avenue from Radio City. He was a failed actor—that's how he introduced himself—who wrote promotional copy for *Fortune* and other Time-Life magazines. He liked to sit, his long legs crossed, in the upholstered chair Mom kept near her bed, laughing and sipping vodka gimlets, discussing Tennessee Williams and Noël Coward late into the night. Though normally a Bushmills gal, Mom always had what he was having.

Shelby took Mom and Quig and me to dinner once, at one of those expensive hole-in-the-wall bistros near Madison Avenue, where everything on the menu was too disgustingly obscure and French for me to eat. Quig ordered the snails and gulped them down with effort, her eyes popping uncomfortably with each sophisticated swallow. Another time, he invited us to a performance of *The Front Page* at the Amateur Thespians Society, a black-tie-and-Champagne-bubbles theatrical group whose all-male membership—moonlighting bankers and lawyers and the like—had been putting on shows at their Murray Hill clubhouse since 1884. Shelby had just a small role, as a jaded, smart-alecky reporter haranguing the sheriff to move a scheduled hanging up a couple of hours so it could make the morning paper. But he cut a dashing figure up there on the stage in his checked vest and shirtsleeves, barking into the tube-like mouthpiece of the old-fashioned phone.

After that, Quig was always in Shelby's room of the brownstone, having scared up whatever excuse she could to gain entry. He let her. He had an enormous collection of antique *Playbills* he kept in a thrift-store set of Mark Cross luggage. She loved to leaf through them, smell the musty theatricality of their old pages. She asked him questions about the Barrymores, which he answered patiently and fondly. He poured out steaming Darjeeling tea for the two of them and played obscure show tunes for her on his turntable, his door always slightly ajar.

There was a night, a quiet one, the sound of the streets muffled, when I came home from Kyle's to find the house darkened. I don't know why I didn't turn on the lights, or what made me keep climbing the stairs after I'd reached my own floor. I don't know what I was expecting to find. On the landing outside Shelby's room, unlit like all the others, a sharp sliver of light slanted from his door crack. I crept closer and peered through the narrow opening, squinting into the shock of light. They were kneeling on the floor, the two of them, face-to-face. My sister's hands were clasped behind her head, her eyes cast down. His hands were raised, doing something to her. He was touching her, the tips of his long fingers rubbing white cream on the raw pink knobs of her extended elbows. I could hear her breathing.

He lowered his hands, struggled with something in front of his body I couldn't see. He gave a little grunt of effort, then delicately raised his right hand and held it in the space between him and Quig, something wide and sheer dangling from his fist. Saran Wrap. He murmured something to her. She nodded, smiling shyly, and unfolded one of her arms for him. He touched it with his free hand, turned the inflamed knob of her elbow to face him. Tenderly, without a word, he draped the clear plastic over her wound and wrapped it like a gift.

16

I LEARNED TO BE FLEXIBLE with my scavenging. Like the time one of my church numbers (595) took me to the intersection at the southeast corner of Central Park after midnight. With all the liveried doormen around, I had no shot at chiseling any stonework off the Plaza or the Sherry-Netherland, and the GM Building had no ornament worth taking, unless you counted the décor of the Auto Pub in its sunken plaza, where we used to have family dinners in booths shaped like race cars.

So instead, I boarded the RR, the angriest subway in the world, and headed downtown to the next target on my list, Twenty-Seventh Street and Fourth Avenue (274). Though I didn't know that area at all, I had teased the RR strand out of the underground map's spaghetti tangle of train lines.

When the doors jostled open at Twenty-Eighth Street, however, I was greeted on the platform by a jabbering silver-haired lady wearing a soiled drum-majorette's hat, who looked to be either squatting like a baseball catcher or taking a dump. I opted not to find out which.

The next station, Twenty-Third Street, was empty, thank God—just a gum-splotched platform whose tiled walls were the usual riot of graffiti. I climbed a grimy stairwell and emerged opposite a flat dark park edged with the shadows of skyscrapers. Across the street on my right, below the park, was the great prow of the Flatiron Building, looking like it might sail right up the avenue and crush me if I didn't get moving.

Though it was surely a stupid thing to do, I crossed over and walked uptown through the deserted park so I could get a good look at the buildings around it. The view seemed worth the risk. On the park's eastern fringe, an Italian-looking clock tower needled its way into the night sky. Across the next side street, two office buildings were conjoined high above the pavement by a pedestrian bridge far grander than the little one down on Staple Street. And a couple blocks north stood perhaps the most extraordinary building of the bunch: a lavishly ornamented, multi-tiered wedding cake of a tower, surging skyward and topped by a golden pyramid.

I ventured over to this vertical extravagance and did a slow lap around it, discovering that the building took up the entire city block. NEW YORK LIFE INSURANCE COMPANY read a bronze plaque beside its Madison Avenue entrance. Had the street coordinates been the ones I was searching for, the building would have been the perfect candidate for my architectural salvage, as the curving bands above its street-level archways were magnificently carved with all manner of animals, plants, and fairy-tale characters.

But the skyscraper occupied the block from Twenty-Sixth to Twenty-Seventh Streets between Madison and Park Avenue South. It was not in the right spot, and in fact *nothing* was in the right spot. I double-checked the church number in my notebook—274—and walked all the hell over the place trying to find where Twenty-Seventh Street crossed Fourth Avenue. But it never did. I found Fifth Avenue, and I found Third Avenue several blocks to the east, but there was no such thing as Fourth.

It was maddeningly disorienting. I leaned against a mailbox on Park Avenue South, trying, I guess, to steady myself on the city grid.

"You oughta say *hi*," a scratchy voice said from behind me.

"What?" I whirled around to see a dark lump in a vestibule a couple doors down.

"That's three times you pass by me now. You oughta say *hi*."

I was a little alarmed. "Oh, um, sorry. I didn't see you."

"No," the voice said with amusement, "I guess maybe you wouldn't this time a night, but I been seein' *you*."

The lump arose from its darkened nook and revealed itself to be a very tall, stooped black man in a droopy brown overcoat. He had a ragged gray-flecked beard and was sucking on a lime wedge.

"I been watchin' you tramp back and forth all around here. Look like you lookin' for somethin' you don't know what it is."

He came closer, but not too close. He only made me a little nervous; something about the loose-limbed way he carried himself gave me the idea he was okay.

"I know what I'm looking for, all right," I said. "*Fourth Avenue*. I mean, who in his right mind designs a city that jumps right from Third Avenue to Fifth Avenue? Where did the geniuses hide *Fourth*, anyway?"

"But you *on* it," the man said.

I squinted at him, more confused than ever, until I saw that he was pointing, across the avenue and toward the sky. I followed his finger. High up, at least twenty stories above the street, the brick side wall of an old office tower was painted, in faded white block letters, with the words FOURTH AVENUE BLDG.

"What the hell?" I said. "Then why do all the street signs say Park Avenue South?"

The man shrugged and gave his lime a suck. "Things change," he said.

I was grateful to him and all, but even after I said goodbye and thanks, I couldn't get rid of the guy. He followed me up the block to the big arched entrance of the New York Life building and watched me scope out the multitude of carvings on its white stone façade. One especially caught my eye. The band that curved along the edge of the archway was incised with leaves and berries and doodads, culminating, maybe ten feet above the sidewalk, with the grinning head of a man. Big-nosed and snaggletoothed, this bulbous cranium hung like an irreverent teardrop off the bottom of the band of ornament.

I could sense the humor of the anonymous artist who had carved it, and I wanted it, wanted Dad to have it.

A few feet below and to the right of the head, an old-fashioned rectangular bronze sign jutted from the wall: INTERBOROUGH SUBWAY. This massive hunk of bronze looked to be an ideal platform for my salvage work. But there was no way I could have reached it without my new friend. Maybe it was because I gave him my RC Cola and half my bologna sandwich, or maybe he just had nothing better to do, but as soon as he saw what I was up to he went and wheeled over the shopping cart from his vestibule. He let me stand on it, then let me climb up his shoulder to the subway sign.

"Just one boost and I'm outta here," he said. "And you oughta get gone, too—get right home to your parents, you know what's good for you."

"I will, I will. Soon as I'm done."

He handed me up the crowbar and hammer from my violin case and then took off. The irregular, abrasive sound of his cart grew fainter until I stopped hearing it anymore.

The crowbar was just long enough for me to reach the carved head. But the most I could hope to remove was its big crooked nose; the rest of the carving was too firmly embedded in the wall. I pressed my right shoulder against the building, angled the sharp edge of the crowbar against the side of the nose, and went to work.

My technique had improved over the past couple months. After probably no more than five or six minutes of hammering the end of the crowbar, the nose popped off its face and fell to the pavement.

"Shit!" I cried, when I saw a little corner of the nose chip off and skitter away as it hit. But when I lowered myself to the sidewalk I found that the damage to the nose was pretty minor. And as proboscises went, this one really had a lot of character. Up close, you could see how much effort the carver had put into delineating the tiny veins, not to mention the bemused flanges of the nostrils. It was my favorite city fragment yet. I pocketed it, quickly gathered up my tools in Quig's violin case, and headed up the darkened side street toward the subway.

I was feeling pretty pleased with myself. I imagined Dani giving me one of her challenging smirks and asking, "Is that a nose in your pocket, or are you just glad to see me?"

The jittery black guy who leapt out of the doorway in front of me caught me completely by surprise. He was breathing heavily, his nostrils flaring, and he held a souvenir wooden Yankees bat cocked menacingly above his right shoulder. The chips in the bat's blue paint suggested that it had seen prior service.

"Gimme your money!" he said. "Quick. *Quick!*"

I was petrified. I pulled all my cash—a wad of three or four dollar bills—from my pocket and extended it to him. He grabbed the bills in his left fist and snorted at their meager denomination.

"Don't fuck with me!" he said. "What else you got in your pockets? I want it *all!*"

I yanked my left pocket inside-out to show it was empty. From my right I withdrew the freshly harvested nose and held it out to him, my palm shaking.

He stared at it incredulously, his eyes bugging out. "I *said* don't *fuck* with me!"

"I'm not! It's a sculpture! You can sell it! It's history!"

He looked at me hard. "You a wack dude, you know that? What the fuck do I want with a fuckin' *nose*?" He shook his head furiously and turned to go, then, almost as an afterthought, wheeled around and smashed me across the bridge of my nose with the bat.

I went down, blood pouring from my face. Overcome with nausea, I felt sure my nose was destroyed, shattered bone and smeary pulp smashed down into my skull. The pain was so staggering as I lay on the pavement that I didn't even feel the guy yank off my Pumas and take the twenty-dollar bill I'd hidden under my left insole.

"You poor bastard," Dad said when I turned up at his studio. "That's a pretty good knock you got there."

He carried me to an old soft chair with stuffing sprouting from its arms and had me lean my head back with a bag of frozen peas on my nose. He stroked the hair from my forehead. The throbbing had retreated from my nose and settled behind my eyes. I must have seemed pretty down in the dumps, because Dad tried to make me feel better by telling me about the time he'd gotten knocked down and kicked in the face by a bartender who caught him stealing a neon Ruppert Beer sign in college.

"I was three sheets to the wind, and I'd forgotten to unplug the sign," he told me. "I stuffed the thing under my sweater, and as I got up to go with my roommate, the bartender saw my sweater blinking: RUPPERT! . . . RUPPERT! . . . RUPPERT! Not my finest moment."

Dad now clasped his hands behind his back and regarded the piece of New York I'd brought him, which sat atop an otherwise empty worktable.

"Anyway, Griffin, you did good tonight. This, my boy, is a nose to be reckoned with. A schnozzola of stature."

I looked up from my haze. "Yeah? So where'd I get it?"

Dad peered down at me, impressed. "Ah, even struck down on the field of battle the young jackanapes thinks he can stump the band, does he?" He plucked up the nose and held it up to the lightbulb above the table. "I'm afraid this is an easy one, son: the New York Life building, on Madison Square. Not much challenge there. It's one of the most celebrated skyscrapers in the city. Designed by Cass Gilbert, one of the big boys of New York architecture, and put up right before the Depression."

"You're *good*, Dad."

"Yes, I am. And as I think about it, as bad a bonk as that bandit gave you, you're in pretty good company being assaulted on that spot. Maybe it's a pedigree to be proud of."

"Huh?"

"Well, there's a bit of a history of violence there, you might say. The old Madison Square Garden—probably Stanford White's greatest New York building, mind you—was built on that site around 1890, and old Stanny liked it so much that he actually kept a studio in its tower. The building had a famous roof garden the smart set would go to, and White was taking in a musical up there one night when a deranged Pittsburgh millionaire, the jealous husband of a girl White had bedded back when she was a teenager, strolled up and shot him dead. Just like that."

"Whoa."

"Yeah, it was about the most famous scandal of its day. And then, if being killed on his own roof weren't indignity enough, the green-eyeshade gang at New York Life came along a few years later and ripped down the whole damn Garden to make way for their new Cass Gilbert tower. We're talking about maybe the signature building of New York's most revered architect—smashed into rubble for the landfill." He sighed. "New York Life indeed."

The bag of peas was thawing and getting squashy. I sat up to remove it.

"Boy, you look rotten," Dad said. "But you know, maybe there's some good to be salvaged from all this. Maybe there was something serendipitous in your bringing me an artifact off that particular building."

"What do you mean?" Had he guessed that I knew about the church numbers?

"Well, I've had it in mind for a while to liberate a major sculpture from the crown of an even more remarkable Cass Gilbert tower. It's probably an opportune time, 'cause they're restoring the original Gothic terra cotta, and it seems a pretty good bet that in order to finish their work, the restoration contractors are going to have to do us the kindness of building some scaffolding up there in the clouds. A Stairway to Heaven, if you will."

He paced around a bit, tapping his lips with an index finger in thought.

"Dad, I'm not sure if I really—"

"Nonsense. It's about time we raised our sights. No more scraps of things! We're better than that. From now on, we take only entire ornamental sculptures, and only the most spectacular ones from the most spectacular buildings."

He went to the big wall of windows and shoved open the iron shutters on one of them.

"There!" he said, pointing exultantly downtown.

I struggled up from my chair and stood beside him. It was probably four in the morning. Other than a few stray lighted windows, Lower Manhattan was dead. Beyond the loft building across the street, all I could make out was different qualities of darkness layered atop one another.

"I don't see anything," I said.

"Oh, you will. You will. And you'll see it in a way few New Yorkers ever have."

17

THE PITY AND ADMIRATION I was counting on were nowhere to be found when I got home to the brownstone the following afternoon. All the way uptown on the subway I had crafted a touching and heroic tale to explain my swollen-potato nose and the throbbing mask of mottled purple around my eyes. The story involved my fighting off a couple of teenage thugs who'd been abusing either a limping old Polish lady or an adorable stray dog (I hadn't settled on which). But I never got to tell either version. There was a major ruckus going on upstairs in Mom's room.

"*Protecting* me?" Quig shouted. Her voice sounded freckled and raw. "Oh, come off it! You fill the house with one creepy soup-kitchen reject after another, and then suddenly you've got this big problem with the *one* guy I can talk to?"

"It's not the talking I've got a problem with," Mom said.

"What's *that* supposed to mean? You don't know *anything* about us!"

"You're barely fifteen years old. It's inappropriate."

"Oh, that's a good one," Quig snorted, "coming from *you!*"

She stormed out of the room and clomped up the stairs a few steps before turning to shout down one last thing: "We *both* know why you did this!"

When silence had settled over the house—and boy, was there a silence—I quietly climbed the stairs past Quig's bedroom to take a peek at the top-floor studio Shelby was renting. Everything was gone: his luggage full of *Playbills*, his fancy suits, him. It was jarring how quickly the room's emptiness took me back to that worst of all days. The only things left on the floor were that same old mattress and sad little hot plate Dad had left behind when *he* had moved out.

Shelby never returned to our house, but that didn't mean Quig accepted his exile. Before coming to us, he had lived with a friend in a tenement apartment above Drake's Drum, an English pub on Second Avenue near Eighty-Fifth that had a wooden ship and dusty signal flags in the window. Apparently Shelby had moved back there, or at least Quig hoped he had. My friend Rafferty lived a couple of blocks farther downtown, and practically every day on his way home from school he saw Quig haunting that pub building, either right outside it or directly across the avenue. She was pacing back and forth, looking up at the apartment windows upstairs, hoping to catch a glimpse of the only grown-up who had ever paid any attention to her.

18

T HE MEN IN KYLE'S FAMILY were a peculiar bunch, every one of them a scientist. Kyle's grandfather was a British field surgeon in World War II who was credited—true story—with inventing the holes in Band-Aids. Kyle's father was a wry Park Avenue gynecologist considered one of the world's foremost experts on the G-spot—which meant that if he didn't quite invent the holes in women, he certainly conducted major research on them. We all wanted *his* job when we grew up.

On Friday afternoons when his folks weren't around, Kyle's house was easily everybody's favorite place to hang out. For one thing, he lived in a fourth-floor apartment right across Madison Avenue from the Jackson Hole hamburger place, which meant that we could get the world's tastiest bacon cheeseburgers delivered, without exception, in somewhere between six and a half and seven and a half minutes.

The second reason we liked Kyle's house was that Dr. Sherman, his dad, possessed probably the finest collection of smutty Victorian literature in the United States. The stuff was everywhere—leather-bound volumes as well as Grove Press paperback reissues—scattered all over the house with the dirty bits studiously underlined by Kyle's father. None of us really had any clue what a G-spot was, other than the obvious understanding that it was as perfectly round, clearly labeled, and easily illuminated as an elevator button.

Kyle always said that his dad's special genius was in proving the existence of the G-spot through not just scientific evidence but also literary. Women's bodies were women's bodies, Dr. Sherman maintained, no matter what century they happened to live in or however little most men understood about them. What this meant was that if the G-spot's existence was a physiological fact, then accounts of the Old Faithful gushers it generated must surely appear in dirty books throughout the ages.

To prove his point to the medical community, Dr. Sherman had gathered in his Madison Avenue home all the antiquarian smut he could get his hands on. Wherever you turned in that apartment, you were practically guaranteed to stumble over a dog-eared pornographic Victorian novel.

Dr. Sherman's helpful underlining made it much easier to find the dirty parts in his books than in my mom's collection of Anaïs Nin stories, which required you to wade through pages of snoozy description about Parisian artists before you got to the good stuff.

Another advantage to Kyle's place was that his folks weren't around much. They hadn't officially separated the way mine had, but things were pretty obviously headed in that direction. Kyle's father was openly dating a hot thirtyish photographer, and his mom was never at home when I was over there, giving me the distinct impression that she, too, was sleeping around; all Kyle would tell me was that she was in the NYU library studying for her Ph.D. in English literature. The single time I made a crack about his mom "boning up" for her "oral exams," Kyle shot me a look that warned me I would never say anything like that again if I wanted to remain friends.

One Friday night when Kyle's parents were out and a bunch of us were sleeping over, his dad came home early with his hot photographer while we were all lying around in front of *Star Trek* in our sleeping bags, reading his vintage porn novels. I was the last to notice Dr. Sherman standing in the doorway, so I didn't hide my book fast enough.

He couldn't conceal his amusement. He asked to see the novel, and I showed him the cover illustration. It depicted a whip-brandishing lady in petticoats and ankle boots riding a similarly dressed lady, who was down on all fours.

"Ah, *The Bawd of Fontainebleau*. One of my personal favorites," he said in his posh English accent. "You like it?"

I nodded. "Way better than *Beowulf*, anyway."

"Oh God, yes," he agreed. "I can't abide that Grendel."

Greta, his hot photographer, was just behind him in the hall.

"Why don't you show them your slide show, Nigel?" she asked. "You certainly couldn't ask for a more enthusiastic audience."

Dr. Sherman loved the idea. "You know, that's an awfully good notion! Would you boys care to see my G-spot lecture? I'm presenting it next month at Mount Sinai, but a dry run could actually prove quite useful."

Our rush to his bedroom, where he told us the show would be presented, was nothing short of a hormone-fueled stampede. While Dr. Sherman fussed around with the slide carousel, we stole randy glances at Greta, who had perched herself on one side of the bed.

She caught me staring at her and smiled at her power. "Anything I can help you with, Young Raccoon?"

I felt my cheeks go red. My twin black eyes had faded a lot since that Yankees fan had busted my nose, but the matching dark rings around my eyeballs still made me look like a cartoon burglar. It was Dani, actually, who had initiated the whole raccoon line of ridicule, weeks earlier. Even before the nose incident, she had had me squarely in her sights. Twice she had cornered me in school and told me some detail about the flood damage in her apartment building—how the repairs had cost her dad two thousand dollars, how they hadn't yet caught the boys who did it. And both times she had then fixed her hazel-flecked blue eyes on me and said, "I'm willing to go easy on you if you come clean. Is there anything you want to tell me?" In response, on both occasions, I had given her a look of bewildered innocence. I guess this didn't satisfy her, because when I showed up at school for the first time with a pair of black eyes flanking my misshapen nose, she lost no time in dubbing me Rocky, as in Rocky Raccoon, and making sure that everyone, including Kyle and Rafferty and even Lamar, began humming the Beatles tune of that name whenever I walked by.

Dr. Sherman told us he was going to need a few minutes to set up the projector properly.

"Cool," Kyle said. "That'll give us time to visit the snack bar."

While Kyle jiggled the Jiffy Pop over an open flame in the kitchen, the talk ricocheted from the girls' basketball team to Valerie to Quigley.

"Dude," Rafferty told me, "I saw her coming *out* of that door next to Drake's Drum yesterday! Did you know your sister's actually going up to that old guy's apartment now?"

Of course I knew, I told Rafferty, though it was the first I'd heard of it. Playing it cool was the only way to avoid a barrage of lewd comments.

I cut the subject short by going to Kyle's room to dig out the remains of his Halloween candy, and by the time Dr. Sherman lowered the lights to begin the most eagerly anticipated entertainment experience of our lives, we were fully provisioned with movie snacks. Rafferty, his mouth stuffed with Charleston Chew, made a crack about how much he was looking forward to the "coming attractions."

I don't know what exactly we were expecting, but Dr. Sherman's presentation was downright tedious, a ponderous parade of clinical anatomical lithographs and scientific jargon, all presented in a stuffy prewar apartment whose radiator kept blasting out waves of soporific heat. As the good doctor laboriously surveyed the scientific literature, beginning with Reinier de Graaf's tiresome 1672 observation of diffuse glands around the female urethra, I kept sneaking peeks across the darkened room to see if I was the only one undersexed enough to be having trouble staying awake. I sure wasn't. As Dr. Sherman rambled on, every boy in the room waged a valiant, droopy-eyed struggle against sleep, lest he miss some "good part" of this yawn-inducing lecture that must surely be right around the corner. Even Kyle was nodding off, and by the time we got to 1895, and a comprehensive account of that era's evolving perception of the clinical ramifications of Skene's glands, Rafferty was out cold, his curly blond head lolling.

As my comrades dropped like flies, I determined to resist at all costs the lulling combination of the room's darkness and Dr. Sherman's scholarly drone. For a boy so committed to staying awake as I, it surely couldn't hurt if I rested my eyes for just the briefest moment while our lecturer recounted his discovery that female urethras typically returned positive results for prostatic acid phosphatase, manifestly demonstrating their homology with the male prostate and . . .

AAAAAAAAH!!! A bolt of eye-scalding lightning jolted me awake, terrified, from the deepest, most coma-like sleep of my life. Someone had switched on the lights. Blinking wildly, I surveyed the bright room and saw everyone else sitting abruptly upright and wiping the sleep out of their eyes.

"So then, lads," Dr. Sherman asked with a grin. "Any questions?"

For a moment nobody stirred. Then Rafferty, struggling to stifle a yawn, raised his hand and asked groggily, "Yeah. Um, where *is* it?"

19

NOW AND THEN KYLE MANAGED to get some girls to come over for one of our Friday afternoon burger fests. Since his house was less than two blocks from school, we could sometimes scoop up whichever girls happened to be hanging around with nothing to do after classes got out. Dani came along only once. Besides the slight awkwardness of being a ninth-grade girl hanging out with eighth-grade boys, she didn't really fit in with the other girls who were willing to come over; she lived on the West Side, she didn't own any alligator shirts, and she said she didn't like how obnoxious we were to the delivery guy. She seemed particularly unimpressed with my role as Ceremonial Greeter. Wearing white Rawlings batting gloves and the tails that Quig had bought for her tap performance, it was my job to open the front door with a flourish and take receipt of the bacon cheeseburgers, sometimes enveloping the flummoxed delivery boy in a vigorous, jiggly bear hug.

But one day the burgers didn't come. It was a bit embarrassing, because we'd managed to get Laurie Daniels and Rachel Gottlieb, two of the cutest eighth-grade girls, to come over for the first time, and they were looking forward to it.

But six minutes rolled around, then eight, then ten, and still no burgers. Finally the phone rang and it was the delivery guy. He told Kyle that Jackson Hole had a new policy regarding Kyle's building, which he conveyed to Kyle with an unmistakable note of pleasure: he was no longer permitted to come up to people's apartments, but he could bring our order to the basement service entrance if we liked.

So down I went in the elevator wearing Quig's tails and my matching black Chuck Taylors with the white rubber toes. When the elevator door slid open in the basement, I was more than a little astonished to see Dani standing there, wearing the broadest smile I'd ever seen on her face. She blew a strand of copper hair from her eyes and drew from her backpack, with ninja-like precision, her duct-taped foam sword.

"Special delivery, funny guy!" Dani cried, and began gleefully walloping me about the head and shoulders. "You didn't think you could just flood my building and get away with it, did you?"

"Actually," I said, laughing in between blows, "that's exactly what I thought." I wrapped my arms around my head in self-defense. Though the hits didn't hurt much, it was impossible to escape them. "But hey, it's not exactly chivalrous to beat the crap out of an unarmed man, is it?"

"Who's unarmed?" Dani pulled a fencing foil from a loop on her backpack and handed it to me. "A trained fencer like you should have no problem fending off a girl with all those nifty moves you've learned from Mr. Cavar this semester, right?"

I had no moves, had cut every fencing class since the first one, and Dani had to know that. Though I raised my foil in feeble defense, it took her no more than three or four deft maneuvers of her own sword to knock my weapon right out of my hand. It clattered to the elevator's linoleum floor and she advanced on me, raining blows on my head.

"My nose!" I bleated. "Watch out for my nose!" But she was too skilled to come anywhere near it, beating me into submission instead by battering my ears and the top of my head.

She was really enjoying herself. "You know, I do have to admit: the whole flood thing was actually pretty amusing," she told me. "You should've seen how pissed off my dad was. I thought he was gonna pop a vein in his forehead."

"Yeah, well, it couldn't happen to a nicer guy."

She gave me a smack on the head for that one, but she was giggling, and so was I. This ambush was turning into a pretty good time, and I was cowering in the corner now, playing along by begging for mercy. When Dani stepped all the way into the elevator—to finish me off, I guess—the door began to close behind her. She immediately threw her backpack in the path of the door to keep it open, turning away from me just long enough for me to grab her sword and give it a yank. She fell on top of me, but quickly recovered by pressing my shoulders against the elevator wall and kissing me, hard. I kissed her back, laughing and clumsy, and now we were sprawling on the floor, pretending to fight, but kissing mostly, feisty little nips at one another's mouth. We pulled our bodies into each other.

Dani was wearing a gray T-shirt, the one with the Led Zeppelin album cover of the old grinning hermit hunched over beneath the weight of a giant load of sticks. Her breasts were right there inside that T-shirt, pressing up against my chest, small and warm. I could hardly believe it. If I could just work up the nerve to get my palm on even one of them, this whole ambush by Dani would make a terrific story to tell Kyle and Rafferty, rather than a humiliating one about getting my ass kicked in an elevator by a girl.

Dani's T-shirt had pulled up a little, exposing a magnificent swatch of flat white stomach. I put my fingers together in the shape of a trowel and slid my hand under the fold of fabric and up toward the promised land. But before I even got past her first bony rib, she shifted her weight expertly and pinned my arm underneath her, then countered my move with one of her own: she grabbed my hip, really gripped it, then slid her hand over my Levi's toward my crotch. Whoa. *Way* too close to my Johnson. I was terrified. Definitely not ready for that. *I* was supposed to be the one putting the moves on *her.* I leapt up, pushing her off me and into the wall, harder than I meant to.

"What the hell, dude?" she asked, rising to her knees.

But I'd had enough. This wasn't fun. The Jackson Hole order was sitting on the floor just outside the elevator, a brown paper bag filled to the top with foil-wrapped burgers. I guess she'd bought them off the delivery guy and put him up to calling us. I grabbed the burger bag and headed out the service entrance and up the ramp to the street. Dani was right on my heels, demanding to know what was up with me.

"*Nothing,*" I grumped. "I'm just hungry, okay?"

I had never been more relieved to see Kyle than when I found him standing in his kitchen, grinning down like the Cheshire cat at Laurie and Rachel. Both girls were sitting in ladder-back chairs at the kitchen table wearing strained smiles, Laurie with her knees together, Rachel with her arms knotted in front of her chest. Rafferty, his mouth open in pleasure, was sitting on the stove.

"Hey, Griffin," Kyle called to me. "Just the guy I wanted to see. Oh, hey, Dani, what's up? Listen, you guys, for some reason the girls are having trouble believing that my dad keeps a tray of vagina cadavers in our kitchen freezer." He nodded at Laurie and Rachel. "Griffin will tell you."

"Of *course* there are vagina cadavers in the freezer," I said, happy to have an excuse to leave Dani in the kitchen doorway and go lean against the counter beside Kyle and his cheerfully aggressive grin. The kitchen was split into two groups now, the three of us boys on one side, smiling complacently across at the three girls.

"That's just what I was telling them," Kyle said.

I nodded. "I mean, how else could your dad have done all the important research necessary to complete his *seminal* work on the G-spot."

The girls looked at me skeptically.

"Oh, yeah," I went on, feeling my bravado mounting. "Doc Sherman totally has a whole *slew* of vagina cadavers in there. And whenever he gets bored, he takes them out of the freezer and runs electric current through them, just to see which ones like him the best."

"A man has to have a hobby," Rafferty said.

"*Exactly,*" Kyle added. "So I was telling Rachel and Laurie how they're right in the freezer door there."

"Bullshit," Dani said flatly.

This surprised us all.

"Well, if you don't believe it," replied Kyle, "then just open the freezer and take a gander."

"Why don't *you*?" Dani countered.

"Because we've already seen 'em," Kyle said.

"All the time," Rafferty agreed. "We're on, like, practically a first-name basis with them."

Kyle bore down: "So if you really don't believe us, Dani, why not just open the freezer and look?"

Laurie and Rachel were still smiling, but you could see they were pretty horrified.

Dani gave a little eye-roll and then, with a complex half smile I couldn't quite read, put her hand on the freezer handle. She stared at her fingers a long moment and took a deep breath. But as long as she stood there, she just couldn't quite bring herself to open that freezer door.

Finally, she let her hand drop and turned back to us, laughing reluctantly. She looked from me to Kyle to Rafferty and said, shaking her head, "Did anyone ever tell you guys you're pigs?"

The three of us boys looked at one another awhile in silence, considering the question, before Kyle brightened a bit and asked Dani, "*Charming* pigs?"

20

THE OLD CITY WAS ATTACKING the new city. Fighting back in the only way it could. Under assault for decades, yielding block by block to boxy modern towers with no surface ornament to speak of, no imprint of the individual, the old city now discovered that being genuinely over the hill gave it a potent new weapon unavailable to it in middle age.

The first salvos of the resistance went unnoticed. A rust-ravaged Italianate iron bracket, murder on its mind, loosened itself from the lavish façade of the B. Altman dry goods store's erstwhile home on Sixth Avenue and Nineteenth Street; it plummeted forty-four feet but landed harmlessly among some trash bags at the curb. A few days later, a cracked terra-cotta rosette hurled itself from the sixteenth story of an elegant prewar Riverside Drive apartment house and dented a mailbox near the corner.

This was the story of the city's decay my father told me over spare ribs, again and again, in the weeks after I'd gotten my nose smashed. I couldn't remember him ever reading me fairy tales when I was little, so I was not unhappy to let him play catch-up now. Each time he told it he added new details of location and architectural style, until the story itself became so encrusted with ornament that there was barely room for more.

Before long, such violent potshots from above could no longer be ignored. In architecturally lush sections of town, at unpredictable intervals, hunks of exuberantly crafted nineteenth- and early twentieth-century ornament hurtled streetward from the skies. In Morningside Heights, one-third of a *pressed-zinc Beaux Arts cornice dropped off the former Home for Indigent Gentlewomen and ripped straight through the fabric roof of a Barnard sophomore's Triumph convertible. In Murray Hill, another wayward strip of cornice—this one copper, Florentine-influenced, and cantilevered majestically eight feet out from the façade—plunged eight stories from the top of the Gorham Silver Company's former showroom on Fifth Avenue, killing a passing librarian.*

Landlords all over town were roused from their slumber. Consulting their innermost hearts, most of them immediately concluded that any flicker of responsibility they might feel toward the crumbling Victorian and Beaux Arts architecture under their care was trumped by their distaste for expensive repairs. Phone calls were made. Supers and their odd-job cousins were dispatched. From the warehouses of TriBeCa to the row houses of the South Bronx, from the commercial palaces of Ladies' Mile to the grand apartment buildings of the Upper West Side, hundreds and hundreds of vibrantly embellished façades were stripped of cornices, corbels, pediments—any projecting ornament, really, that might harbor ambitions of shaking loose and bludgeoning a pedestrian.

The story, of course, was true. My father made sure I understood that. And though a few enlightened owners did turn their minds to restoration rather than amputation, not many did so with anything like the sensitivity he felt the old buildings deserved.

This was the gong he had been banging for weeks, every time I visited him downtown. He had a lot of time to get riled up about all this stuff, too, because we weren't rescuing architectural sculptures anymore. Why not, I wasn't quite sure. There was a sense in his studio of things about to happen, of needs pent up for too long. But it was hard to know if the change we were waiting for lay outside in the city or inside Dad.

Even DeCarlo was wondering what was going on. "Thanks but no thanks, Deke," I heard Dad saying into the phone. "I'm just not doing any harvesting right now. Though I know I still owe you a cooler."

I didn't ask Dad about this big pause in operations. My broken nose and raccoon face were almost healed—*finally*—and I wasn't in any hurry to give the city another crack at hurting me.

The best part was that we now spent our time together doing normal father-and-son things. We built a model of the *Andrea Doria*. We went to Little Italy and devoured a couple of zeppole so rapaciously that the sugar powdered our eyebrows white. We went to the movies. Dad was nuts about the silent-film comedians, especially Buster Keaton and Harold Lloyd; he wanted to share them with me. We'd take the subway up to Midtown and laugh our asses off inside the Carnegie Hall Cinema, a wonderfully crummy theater that was tucked like a shabbily dressed stowaway into the humid basement of the legendary concert hall. You went in through a seedy side entrance on Seventh Avenue near Fifty-Sixth.

Then one Friday night I showed up at Dad's studio to find him and Zev on their toes, hollering into each other's face.

"I swear to God I'll kill you if we miss our shot at those tourelles, Zev!"

"I get it, all right? But we can't rush this. We need—"

Zev stopped short when he saw me in the doorway.

"Maybe *you* can talk some sense into Ahab here," he told me, throwing up his hands. "He certainly doesn't listen to any of *us* anymore."

Zev grabbed a fistful of paperwork and headed for the door, turning back just long enough to add, red-faced: "Look, Nick, I know you've got the guard in your pocket and everything. But this isn't just any old building—that's all I'm saying. We need to be more careful than usual."

I stepped aside so he could get by. When he was safely gone, I asked Dad what all the hullabaloo was about.

Dad chewed on his lower lip awhile in thought. "Here, I'll show you."

We climbed the two stories to the uppermost floor of the warehouse. At the top of the darkened stairwell, a ladder was bolted to one wall. Dad went up it, shoved a cover off the square roof hatch, and climbed into the night. I followed, rising through the square hole from darkness into darkness: black tar roof, moonless overcast sky, Dad a breathing shadow I could sense more than see.

"Look," his voice said. "Turn around."

I did, blinking dumbly at what I saw. Amid all this downtown darkness, illuminated from below by a necklace of blazing floodlights, a soaring slender cathedral pierced the sky, its creamy surface rich with ornament and shimmering with mist. It was several blocks away, but against the great building's brightness I could make out tiny workmen on hanging scaffolds, wielding what must have been high-pressure hoses. The mist they made seemed alive. It billowed as the wind caught it, gathering up the light and moving in wet waves across the tower's magnificently textured façade.

"What is that thing?" I asked. "A skyscraper church?"

"No," Dad said, chuckling. "Or sort of, I guess. It's an office tower; it only looks like a church to you because Gilbert—your old friend from the New York Life building—designed it in a flamboyant Gothic style. He was hired to create the world's tallest building, which it very much was when it went up in 1913."

"How tall is it?"

"Sixty stories; it dwarfed absolutely everything when they put it up. But its design didn't come easy to Gilbert. When he was planning the tower, he found himself struggling with the problem of how to *clothe it in beauty,*' as he put it—how to give the great city the great building it deserved. Architects gave a shit about things like that back then."

Gilbert, Dad explained, settled on Gothic because he was going for that surging verticality that cathedrals manage so well. "In fact, a local bishop even nicknamed the building the Cathedral of Commerce during his speech at the Woolworth's dedication dinner."

"A bishop ate at Woolworth's?" It seemed ridiculous. I imagined the miter of a pink-faced holy man tilting over the Woolworth's lunch counter on Eighty-Sixth Street as he carefully sipped the top half inch or so from his coffee cup without spilling it.

"No, no," Dad said, laughing. "That skyscraper is called the Woolworth Building. It was commissioned by Frank Woolworth."

"As in *Woolworth's* Woolworth?"

"That's the guy, king of the five-and-dime. It was a huge deal at the time. Huge. All the papers had the Woolworth Building on the front page, and the president, Woodrow Wilson, opened the skyscraper by pressing a button in the White House that lit up the Woolworth with eighty thousand lightbulbs in one go. Not too shabby."

I asked Dad if this was the same tower he'd told me about the night I got my nose broken.

"Yeah, it is," he said. "For my money, it's the most spectacular terra cotta in the city."

I looked again at the delicately fringed skyscraper, ablaze with floodlights against the black backdrop of Lower Manhattan, and recognized it for the first time as the same tower I had admired, from farther away and under far less dramatic lighting, while standing atop the Good Humor truck on the pier.

"But what are they doing to the building now?" I asked. "I mean, besides cleaning it. What's with all the scaffolding?"

"They're restoring it, or at least that's what they claim. But Zev has been getting the inside scoop from this young architect he knows over at D.D.&M.—they're the firm running the job—who says they've been cutting all kinds of corners. See, they did this huge survey of the building's surface, and they concluded that *twenty-six thousand* pieces of its terra cotta were so shot they couldn't even be saved."

"So isn't it good that they're fixing everything up?"

"It would be if they were *doing it properly*," Dad said. He spat out these last three words with a sudden hostility I didn't understand, until I noticed that Zev had climbed through the hatch and joined us on the roof. Dad's anger was directed at him.

"But instead of casting terra-cotta replicas of Gilbert's ornaments," Dad said fiercely, "the Neanderthals have been replacing those thousands of marvelous originals with—you're not even gonna believe me when I tell you this, Griffin—precast concrete. *Concrete!*"

"Why would they do that?"

"Well, I'm sure I don't know," he said, giving his voice a sardonic edge. "Why don't you ask Zev here? Old Zev thinks it's a perfectly *swell* idea to turn a masterpiece of skyscraper design into a five-and-dime knockoff of itself by cladding it in concrete."

Zev exhaled a weary breath. "What do you expect them to do? The terra-cotta industry's basically dead. The world has moved on, Nick. No one makes this stuff anymore."

"Bullshit. What about Gladding, McBean in California?"

"No way. You know damn well the modern forms they're using don't allow undercutting the way the old sand molds did. And even if they *could* pull off this job, it'd be way too expensive."

"That's just what I'm saying! Woolworth's is too cheap to do the right thing."

"They're *not* cheap," Zev said. "They're doing the best they can with a building that's basically rejecting its own flesh. It'd be a whole lot cheaper for them just to strip the entire tower of ornament and be done with it. But instead, Healey told me, they're shelling out twenty mil for the restoration. Now, I know that doesn't guarantee you're gonna like all their choices when you see them up close, but if you could just hold off till Monday to go look—"

"Oh, good God, Zev! Tell me you didn't follow us all the way up here just to keep badgering me into waiting on those goddamn tourelles!"

"Yeah, I did," Zev said. "I was able to get Herm on the phone just now; if we can hold off a couple days, he says he can get loose from that bank demo in Philly by Sunday. And Curtis'll be back from Rochester by then, too. Just give me two days to pull a crew together. *Two days*. Those tourelles aren't going anywhere between now and then."

I was tired of listening to them argue.

"What *are* tourelles, anyway?" I asked. They sounded like hip-swaying, sequin-gowned fifties backup singers: *Ladies and gentlemen, please give a warm welcome to our very special musical guests . . . Frank Woolworth and the Tourelles!*

Dad gestured at the gleaming tower of the Woolworth Building, which surged skyward from its broad, ornate base. The tower was crowned by a pyramidal roof with a delicate unlit lantern at its pinnacle. The jewels of this crown, Dad said, were the four little towers, or tourelles, at its corners, each one about five stories high and intricately adorned with vivid terra-cotta decorations in a rising rhythm of textures and colors. I couldn't make out any of this detail, though, because you could only see three tourelles from the studio roof, and all of them were obscured. Two of the three were ringed with scaffolding. The third one was concealed, too, its bottom part behind more scaffolding, and much of its top under a shroud of black netting.

"You *have* to see them, son. Every inch of these things is encrusted with terra-cotta ornament, glazed in absolutely gorgeous blues and golds. It was all modeled by an Italian sculptor, who finished off each of those tourelles with the most marvelous gargoyles you'll ever see: peculiar, old-soul creatures of such vitality you'd swear they were alive. I used to sit on the roof of my old studio near Washington Market with binoculars and watch the clouds move across those tourelles—and I'd watch those gargoyles watching me. Made the hair stand up on the back of my neck."

I stood alongside Dad and squinted at the scaffold-caged towers.

"Drives me crazy I can't see what the contractor's doing under there," he told me. He was bouncing on his toes. "I *have* to get up there."

It looked like there was still a pretty clear way to avoid getting involved in all this. Sunday, when Zev would have his crew together, was a school night; I'd be safe in bed uptown.

"Sure, Dad," I said. "But really, if you've waited this long already, what's the rush?"

There was a long, uncomfortable silence, during which I could've sworn I felt the rising heat from Dad's face fill the space between us.

"*Well,* Zev?" he barked at last. "Tell him! Tell him what Healey told you today."

Zev sighed. He pulled up a plastic milk crate for me to sit on, and sat down himself on the parapet. Dad remained standing.

The ornament on the Woolworth Building, Zev explained to me, got more elaborate the higher up you went. The tourelles, then, were about the biggest pain in the ass on the entire restoration job, precisely because they were so intricate. Parts of them were also in horrendous condition. One of the four tourelles had originally been an open-topped, coal-burning chimney, which had spewed filth on the building's crown for decades, damaging the terra cotta. So at the outset of the restoration project, the architects at D.D.&M. simply wrapped all four tourelles in black-mesh safety netting and left them alone. For two years, while they cleaned the rest of the tower from the thirtieth to the sixtieth floors, and then replaced thousands of its simpler terra-cotta blocks with precast concrete, they agonized over what to do with those tourelles.

Now, as I could see with my own eyes, they had moved on to cleaning the base of the building, the lower twenty-nine stories. But they had also finally begun tackling those tourelles way up top.

"The head honchos at D.D.&M. finally settled on an affordable restoration plan," Zev said. "That's why they started scaffolding the tourelles all of a sudden last week. But even my guy doesn't know what exactly they're doing up there. They're keeping it all very hush-hush."

"Which I don't like *at all*," Dad grumbled.

"But we don't even know if it's a problem, Nick! I mean, if they're doing a faithful restoration, you may just want to leave all that terra cotta right where it is, let the next generation enjoy it. But if they're prepping it for even a limited demo, believe me, the pickings are gonna be so rich that you'll be thanking me for hiring you a full crew to carry out all that material."

In the end, Dad grudgingly acknowledged the wisdom of sitting tight for a couple of days. He sent Zev home and whipped me up an American-cheese omelet on his hot plate. It was illegal to live in any of the lofts or warehouses down here, so Dad had to make do with equipment that could be justified to fire inspectors as work-related; in the case of the hot plate, he told them he used it to heat rabbit-skin glue for his antique-frame restoration. As for bedding, he slept on a horsehair mattress on one of his half-dozen vintage four-poster beds. It was his only mattress, so whenever I slept over I shared that bed with him, covering my ears with pillows against the elephant-seal roar of his snoring.

On this night, though, he never came to bed. And I can't say I was entirely surprised when he woke me around two and told me to get my clothes on.

"C'mon, kiddo," he said, a lumpy army duffel slung over his shoulder. "We're gonna get a bit of fresh air."

21

BY THE TIME WE REACHED the far side of Broadway at Warren Street, sky and skyscraper had swapped lighting. The Woolworth's floodlights were extinguished now, the building a looming shaft of shadow above the tree-edged wedge of City Hall Park. But a bright scythe of moon hung above it, silhouetting the tower's pointed peak and tourelles.

The sidewalk, dry on every other block, became an obstacle course of puddles as we approached the building. On the park side of Broadway, across from its entrance, stood a construction trailer and a skinny plywood sentry box shaped like an upright coffin. I peeked through its scuffed Plexiglas window to make sure there was no Rent-a-Cop in there—there wasn't—but Dad barely gave it a glance. Instead, he led me across the street, straight under the tall carved arch of the skyscraper's entrance, and through the front door, which he seemed to know would be unlocked.

No matter how old I get, I'll never forget walking into that building that night, how radically different it felt from the circumstances under which I left it just a couple of hours later. I've been back to that block a lot over the years. There's a terrific little hole-in-the-wall restaurant called Sole di Capri nearby on Church Street, where Quig and I meet, when she's in town, to devour pasta made by an Ecuadoran man who cooks like an Italian grandmother. The number 2 subway I take from Brooklyn lets me out right at the foot of the Woolworth, but only once in the past forty years have I been able to bring myself to set foot in the building again.

Still, my recollection of that night is as sharp as if it were just last week. The building looked as much like a cathedral on the inside as outside. The lobby was shaped like a great cross, its stained-glass ceiling bordered by dimly lit bulbs, its walls made of churchily carved marble and fringed with bronze filigree.

Dad strolled up to a pair of elevators. He tapped the button and waited, whistling absentmindedly, as if this were his place of business and today just another day at the office.

"Oh," he said. "C'mere. You should see this."

He pulled from his duffel what looked to be a homemade miner's headlamp, a powerful light attached to a stripey Björn Borg headband. Holding it in his palm, he directed its brightness toward a small stone bracket supporting a ceiling beam. Into the bracket was carved the hunched caricature of a bespectacled oldster with a mustache and a handful of coins.

"That's Frank Woolworth," Dad said with a chuckle. "Counting his nickels." He swung the lamp to another funny-looking figure, carved on the bracket directly opposite. "And over here is Cass Gilbert himself."

Gilbert was clutching a model of the Woolworth Building. His mustache was droopier than his employer's, his round glasses a bit more owlish. Both men were depicted with bulging superhero biceps.

The elevator arrived with a chime, and we stepped into a sumptuous, oaky compartment whose name, according to a curlicue inscription, was Otis.

Dad grinned. "This is an express, and you've gotta think about what this felt like back in 1913—a straight shot, seven hundred feet a minute, right up to the fifty-third floor. This, my boy, was one hell of a ride."

After rising less than a minute, during which time my ears popped, the elevator chimed open and deposited us in an empty hallway. Quickly, almost hastily, the elevator closed its doors behind us and hurried away, taking its light with it and leaving me, here in the darkness beside Dad at the top of the city, with a sudden burden of loneliness that caught me by surprise. I didn't know why I was here. The grandeur of the hallway's decorations, its little Gothic doodads and fastidious attention to beauty, struck me as desperately pointless.

Up here in the tower, the skyscraper was skinnier than in the lobby, the corridors shorter. Dad followed a trail of filthy boot prints down a construction-paper pathway to the end of the hall, past a clouded-glass door marked FULMER & ASSOCIATES, then left to two side-by-side windows in the middle of the building's western wall. The right window of the pair was not even latched; it slid open easily. We bowed our heads and stepped through the window, out into a gutter just a foot and a half wide and bounded by a little parapet that didn't even come up to my knee. The air chilled my cheeks.

I took a sudden step back in self-protection, my shoulder blades against the window frame. I couldn't tell what I was seeing. The sky downtown was striped in a thoroughly disorienting way: two huge black vertical columns with a lighter one in between. Not until I looked up and saw the blinking red airplane-warning lights atop the two outer columns did I realize I was looking at the Twin Towers of the World Trade Center, a vertical band of night in between. They were the highest buildings in the world, just as the Woolworth had once been. I wondered how anything that tall could possibly stand by itself, wondered if they planned to fortify the pair by conjoining them with a bridge like the one over on Staple Street.

Dad was shaking his head ruefully in the darkness.

"What is it?" I asked.

"Oh, nothing really." A defeated breath escaped him. "It just kind of hit me all at once, what a crazy amount of destruction the gargoyles up here have seen."

I scanned the West Side, where he was pointing. I didn't see any destruction. What I saw was *con*struction. The Twin Towers, as every kid in town knew, had been officially dedicated with a big old ceremony just last year. And here they were now, robust and looming, only a couple of blocks downtown. At the foot of the southern tower, another, much smaller building was on the rise. I could just make out the latticework shadows of its steel skeleton and the ungainly crane beside it.

I asked what destruction he was talking about.

"Well, this wasn't a *cornfield,* you know. Anytime anything goes up in New York, especially anything big, you can be sure something went down to make way for it. That entire area, the neighborhood around Washington Market all the way up to Hubert Street, was cleared to make space for the World Trade towers and a community college and a bunch of other ugly stuff. More than sixty acres."

"Huh," I said, trying to sound thoughtful. I had no clue how big an acre was.

"You know how I told you I used to sit on my studio roof on Murray Street with my binoculars," Dad said, "how I used to watch the gargoyles up here?"

I nodded.

"Yeah, well, even then, I think I always knew they'd outlast me. I watched them watching me, craning their necks to get a really good look—and then one day I was gone, evicted along with the rest of the neighborhood, and the gargoyles watched that, too. Watched me get forced out of that remarkable building."

"Your old studio? What was so special about it?"

Dad laughed mirthlessly. "Everything."

"Like what?"

"Well, for starters, it was pretty much the only place in New York I've ever felt at home—and actually, if you want to know the truth, you yourself were conceived there." He looked at me with sudden interest. "Why don't I show it to you sometime?"

"You mean where it used to be."

"No, I don't mean that. Don't tell me what I mean."

I hesitated. "I thought you said they cleared the whole neighborhood. They didn't tear your studio down?"

"Yeah, they did. Every scrap of it."

"So how can you show it to me?"

He looked at me thoughtfully, as if considering just how far into his life he really wanted to admit me.

"Never mind," he said quietly.

Over the years I've wondered if there was something I should have said at that moment, something that might have settled him down enough to prevent what happened next. My father so often talked like he wasn't waiting for a response, wasn't interested in one, but now I'm not so sure if that's what was really going on. Kids, even sensitive ones, have a way of focusing mostly on themselves. Maybe there was something useful I could have given him then, had I been thinking less of my own unease and more about what sort of outraged loneliness would drive a man up here to the wind-battered roof of the old city in the middle of the night.

Dad pushed away the memory of his eviction and headed right, along the narrow gutter. All business now. Tentatively, I followed. The low parapet keeping us from tumbling off the building was fringed with terra-cotta frippery, pointy protuberances I grabbed onto every time I thought I might fall; it felt like clambering around atop a colossal wedding cake. Up ahead, at the tower's northwest corner, stood a tourelle, completely encircled by pipe-frame scaffolding. Close up like this, the tourelle looked a lot like a big white asparagus spear: a narrow upright shaft with a pointy top. As we approached it, our gutter narrowed treacherously until it was no more than one sneaker wide. Normally, there would have been a two-foot gap between the building and the tourelle. But fortunately for us, this gap was bridged by the scaffolding, which rose, like the tourelle itself, from a landing a few stories below.

Dad was already climbing up when I reached the tourelle; I stayed put and watched him swing up to the first level of scaffold planking above me.

"No!" he cried out. "They didn't *dare*!" There was real anguish in his voice, mixed with indignation. "What could they be *thinking*?"

Then he was swinging down beside me—"C'mon! C'mon!"—and charging back along the gutter in the direction we'd just come from. He seemed oblivious to the precipitous drop just to our right.

"This can't *be*!" he was yelling when I reached the second tourelle. The dark knot of his body moved about in the crosshatch of scaffolding above me. "This just can't be! How could anyone in the restoration business possibly be this destructive?"

I craned my neck. "What is it? What did they do?"

A weak, strangled sound emerged from his throat.

He tried again: "They stripped the whole . . . *the whole goddamn thing*! Both tourelles. Even the gargoyles!"

Before I could work up the nerve to climb up and see what a missing gargoyle looked like, Dad was already jumping down beside me.

"Maybe we're not too late," he murmured as he raced along the south-side gutter to the third tourelle, the more downtown of the two that overlooked Broadway. "Maybe they're not done yet." He was running much too fast, too carelessly. He lost his footing, started to go down—but steadied himself at the last moment on a decorative bric-a-brac protrusion. Unfazed by this stumble, he kept moving.

This time he must have expected the bad news that awaited him. No cries of anguish came to me from the tourelle above, no cursing. Using the skinny ladder built into the scaffolding, I climbed up and joined Dad on the first level of scaffold planking.

He was on his haunches, peering at the violently scarred surface of the tourelle.

"But why?" he was muttering. "See, they haven't actually taken all the terra cotta off—not all the way to the brick underlayer, anyway, like you'd think they would. They've just hacked off all the ornament that projected more than an inch or two." He pressed his palm against an open wound in the tourelle's eggshell-white skin. "What are they up to? *What are you up to, you cynical shitheads?*"

He climbed down quickly and hurried along the gutter to the fourth and last tourelle, the open-topped one that had once been a chimney. I followed, slowly and carefully, stopping halfway to look at the black ribbon of river and the Brooklyn Bridge, whose harp-strung spans sparkled with white lights.

Another groan, almost more animal than human, came to me from up ahead.

"What is it?" I asked, scrambling along the gutter to reach Dad, who was standing on a makeshift bridge—a few planks laid across steel beams—that connected the building to the tourelle.

There was no scaffolding on the inside portion of this tourelle, making its asparagus-spear shape easier to discern, and when I got up close, I recognized right away that something very strange was going on with the skin of its shaft. Unlike the rough, scarred surface of the tourelle we'd just come from, the surface of this one looked smooth and modern and brand-spanking-new, almost fake. Dad shone the beam of his headlamp across its surface. It was metal—flat metal— with very simplified lines, all painted in tacky golds and browns, like a Disneyland or Vegas version of the real thing.

"What a disgusting thing to do!" Dad cried.

I reached out my hand. The surface of the tourelle was cold to the touch, its textureless expanse unbroken except by the slight bump of screwheads at regular intervals.

"I don't understand," I said.

"That's because it's *incomprehensible!*" Dad roared. "These vandals couldn't even be bothered to replicate the terra-cotta ornament up here in *concrete*. No, even concrete knockoffs would be showing too much respect for New Yorkers' architectural patrimony. So what are they doing? The philistines have decided to just strip off hundreds of square feet of our skyline's most exquisite terra cotta and replace it with fucking *aluminum siding!*"

It was hideous, no question. "But it can't really be aluminum siding, *can* it?"

"That's *exactly* what it is! It's a mock-up, don't you see? They mocked up the inside surface of this tourelle to show their bosses at Woolworth, just this section the workers could reach from this plank bridge here without any scaffolding. So then they marched the Woolworth suits up here and got them to sign off on this approach for *all* the tourelles, told them how they'd save a fortune on maintenance for the next thirty years—all that sort of horseshit. And as soon as they had that okay, they began throwing up scaffolding around all four tourelles and hacking off all the projecting ornament. See, the siding gets installed right on top of the terra cotta, so they have to tear off any protruding elements that'll get in the way."

At the top of the tourelle's aluminum-clad shaft, right where it met its asparagus-tip top section, two matching beige aluminum *things* jutted out horizontally from the wall, several feet apart. They looked like giant toothpicks.

"What are those supposed to be?"

Dad gave another groan. "That's where the *gargoyles* used to live! I guess instead of just doing away with that projecting visual element altogether, the architects at D.D.&M. wanted to suggest the gargoyles' long-necked forms from a distance, so when you look up here from the street you won't get the feeling that something's missing." He spat, barely avoiding his own boot. "But you *will*. I guarantee you will. Architecture is intuitive. People will look up and sense, without knowing quite why, that something is wrong. At least for a while. Then, after a few years, it'll all come to seem normal. This city has no memory, and after a time the skyline will sort of close up its wound until nobody even remembers anymore how much has been lost."

Dad put on the headlamp and stood on his tiptoes, peering first around one side of the tourelle and then the other. But without any scaffolding here, there was no way for him to get far enough out.

"Can't see a damn thing," he muttered. "Do me a favor. Go climb the scaffolding on that other tourelle there, the first one we looked at. Lean out as far as you can, and tell me if you see . . ." But I guess I didn't look like I was in any hurry to do any climbing. I rubbed my nose, which still had a souvenir bump on it from its encounter with the souvenir bat. "Oh, Christ," Dad said. "Never mind. I'll do it myself."

It amazed me how comfortable he seemed, swinging his body around on those scaffolds. From my safe spot at the base of the northeast tourelle, I watched him make his way up the northwest one, the blue pipe-frame shuddering as he hung off the outside to get a better view. I must have been feeling his every movement as if it were my own, because when he let loose a sudden caw of exultation, I was so startled that I grabbed hold of the edge of the aluminum siding to steady myself.

"There's *still one left!*" he told me breathlessly when he rejoined me, gripping me by the shoulders and trying to shake me into sharing his excitement. "There's *one gargoyle* they haven't butchered yet! One! Out on the farthest corner, above Broadway!"

The top twenty-five feet or so of the tourelle—ten feet of shaft topped by about fifteen feet of conical tip—rose above the fifty-third floor here. But only the shaft could be easily accessed with ladders. This meant that the uppermost fifteen feet—the conical open grillwork of the chimney top—was left untouched by the demo workers, as were the ornate terra-cotta "pinnacles" that poked upward from the top of the shaft every few feet around its perimeter. But below those pinnacles, the workers had been merciless in stripping off as much of that tourelle's projecting ornament as they could reach, up to and including the gargoyles.

The catch, of course, was that they couldn't get to the outside of the building without scaffolding, so they had only been able to cut off seven of that tourelle's eight gargoyles; the eighth and final gargoyle remained out of reach, perched on the tourelle's most distant corner, where it leered across City Hall Park at the twin-domed, copper-corniced Park Row Building.

But that was all going to change, and soon. Over the past week, the demo contractors had been brutally efficient in erecting scaffolding around the other three tourelles, building upward from the forty-ninth-story setback and then quickly stripping off all of those tourelles' projecting terra cotta, including their gargoyles. This northeast tourelle was the last to receive its scaffolding.

"At quitting time today, they'd reached the fifty-first or fifty-second story," Dad said. He went to the low wall and pointed down. "Right *there.*"

"Okay, so as long as you and Zev and everybody get up here Sunday night—"

"No, Sunday's too late. In another half day, they'll have the scaffolding up to the top and they'll be stripping the rest of the tourelle." He was bouncing in place on his toes again, trying to burn off some of his nervous energy. But his eyes never strayed from mine. "We have to get that gargoyle *now. Tonight.*"

My throat felt like it was stuffed with a balled-up tube sock. I wanted to back Dad down with the power of my reasoning, the flash flood of my language, the way I sometimes could with kids at school. But just standing beside Dad, the force of him, so often rendered me inarticulate. His imminent disapproval was a weight I could never quite stop trying to push off me.

In the end, all I could manage was a small, quiet question: "But how do you know *they* won't save the gargoyle? The workers, I mean."

Dad made a clucking noise with his tongue. "How do I *know*?" He seemed amused by the question. "Because, son, demolition contractors are not subtle men. Demolish things is what they *do*." He was on his knees by his duffel now, pulling out a nicked-up power saw of a size and shape I'd never seen before; it had a curved trigger and a very long blade with fierce teeth.

"You know," he told me, "the first terra-cotta casting I ever saved was a woman's face some demo goons had half destroyed by hurling it down from a tenement in Yorkville; it's the one I caught you monkeying with in my basement studio in the brownstone. And the second piece I rescued was an ox head I got off one of the most exquisite terra-cotta civic buildings ever put up in the city: the Produce Exchange, down by Bowling Green. They were repairing some of the open mortar joints or something, and the Exchange was all conveniently scaffolded, so I just moseyed on up there with some tools after dark one Saturday and pried that ox head right off. Brought it home on the subway in your sister's stroller."

He blew some air through the space between his front teeth, a whistling sigh. "The fifth floor of that building was festooned with these absolutely stunning terra-cotta animal heads, and a couple years after I was up there, they tore the whole thing down and destroyed every last one of them. I never forgave myself for not rescuing more of them."

The first thing Dad did when he was done talking was pull a coiled yellow extension cord from the duffel. He went back along the Broadway side of the building, pushed open an ornately gabled window, and found an electrical outlet inside somewhere. He returned a minute later, playing the cord out behind him, then plugged the saw into it.

"This is a Sawzall," he told me, firing it up. He had to raise his voice

to be heard over its phlegmy growl. "Got a nice reciprocal blade on it."
I'd never seen a tool like that. It was ferociously loud, with a serrated
saw blade that went *zhigga-zhigga-zhigga* in and out. Dad motioned
me to stand back, then went to town on the aluminum siding, the
Sawzall making horrible shrieking noises as it chewed through
the sheet metal.

"Footholds," he said simply when he was done, gesturing at the
series of irregular, jagged-edged holes he'd cut all the way up the aluminum flank of the tourelle. "Only the best for my boy."

I must have said, *"Me?"* because Dad immediately snapped, "Of
course, *you*. I weigh a hundred ninety-five pounds. You think you can
belay *me?*"

Up above us, vertical terra-cotta pinnacles ringed the top of the
tourelle's shaft like the pointy parts that stick up around the periphery
of a crown. Dad took a length of rope from his bag and, wearing work
gloves, climbed far enough up the tourelle's side to reach up and feed
the rope's end around one of these pinnacles. He climbed down and
tied the rope to the back of my belt, giving me a bit of a wedgie as he
tugged the knot to test it.

"Pretty good, I think," he said, handing me the gloves. "Up you
go." Again with that shooing motion of his hands. He'd gotten himself so worked up that I didn't dare protest. I knew how scary he could
get when he thought you were standing in the way of something he
wanted.

Up I went. While Dad looped the rope around his back and bent
his knees in a ready-for-anything stance, I began picking my way up
the tourelle, using the holes he'd cut in the aluminum as hand- and
footholds. Dad kept the line taut between me and the pinnacle.

What surprised me most when I pulled myself up to stand in the
wind on the tourelle's rim was that I was even more afraid of falling *into* that tourelle than off it. Unlike its three purely ornamental
siblings, which were closed on top, this tourelle was open to allow
coal smoke to escape. So I was essentially standing on the rim of an
enormous defunct smokestack, with an open grillwork cone rising
above me.

I'd always had a terror of falling into holes, and that's what the inside of that tourelle was: a seven-hundred-foot-deep hole. If I was clumsy enough to tumble in, my spindly body would plunge straight down to the basement furnace, arms wheeling.

"I don't like all the abrasion that pinnacle is giving our rope," Dad called up to me. "You're going to need more mobility than that. Hang on a second and let me see what equipment I can find down where they're working on the twenty-seventh floor."

"Wait!" I cried into the wind, but he was already gone, disappeared around the corner below, where he either couldn't hear me or pretended he couldn't. He had left me again. I felt my testicles tighten up close to my crotch in fear, as if they wanted desperately to retreat clear up into my stomach. It was a sickening feeling. You never feel more alone than when someone was with you just a second ago.

I made a point of not looking around while he was gone, instead crouching on the rim and hugging the pinnacle, which was sooty gray and cracked. I tried to imagine what Dad might be up to from moment to moment—breaking into a storeroom downstairs somewhere, poking around in a tool chest with his powerful hands, hurrying back to see me. Surely if I concentrated hard enough on him, he would in turn think of me, and that would be almost like being together.

When Dad came back, he was carrying a big oval object that rattled as he walked. He told me to untie the rope from my belt and feed the end down to him, still keeping the rope looped around the pinnacle. When I fished the rope back up, my catch was a big wooden pulley with a green box cutter duct-taped to its side.

"That's a pulley from one of the hanging scaffolds they're using to clean the façade," Dad said. "Got some other handy stuff, too, but I'll send that up to you later."

For now, I was to untie the pulley, drop the rope back down to him, and climb around the rim of the tourelle to the gargoyle. "When you've got a nice angle on it, just clip the pulley to the grillage above you and wait for me."

I did as I was told. No longer tied to anything, no longer protected in any way, I gingerly made my way around the crumbly rim of the tourelle with the pulley under my right arm, stopping periodically to catch my breath and try to get my heartbeat to slow down. The wind was picking up, blowing across the open ring of the tourelle with a resonant, melancholy hum—a deeper, more haunting version of the sound made by a breath across the top of a Coke bottle. For a moment, I again imagined falling in, and started to feel sickish. To distract myself and keep warm, I tucked my chin into my chest, blowing hot air into the front of my down jacket.

The outside of the tourelle's shaft below me was still covered in black netting, with some weird exceptions. Every few feet, the top of the netting had been shredded. Peering down in those places, I saw a kind of terra-cotta stump, which I guessed was all that remained of the gargoyle that had once made its home there. It was easy to see what had gotten Dad so hopping mad. It did something to your stomach to see a violent absence up close like that.

After passing two or three of these stumps, edging far around the tourelle toward the dark gulf above Broadway, I looked down to see this time not an absence but a presence: a sharply defined, long-necked figure jutting from the wall with prickly alacrity. The creature's body strained against the taut black netting that covered it, and if I hadn't known what it was, I would have thought it was alive. You could feel the energy coming off it, and the more I peered down at it, the more details of its exotic body I could make out: curled claws gripping the façade; muscular, distrustful haunches ready to spring; a spread of feathers that might have been wings; an arched back and tense, alert neck. All watchfulness and cold coiled power.

And then, something amusing, or so it seemed to me; something that cried out for closer inspection. But first to free up my hands. The old wooden pulley had a kind of clip at the top; I stood up tall and attached it to a steel crosspiece on the grillwork above me, then untaped the green box cutter from its side.

Crouching down again and releasing the blade with a thumb flick, I began to slash at the black netting that shrouded the gargoyle. It was satisfying to watch the mesh fall away, and when I'd laid bare the gargoyle's form I saw that I'd been right to be amused, for the surging terra-cotta creature was wearing what appeared to be an improvised leash. Looped around his neck and running in a taut diagonal up to a bolt in the wall above him was a weathered, small-linked chain.

"Oh, good going!" I heard Dad's voice call to me from somewhere down below. "You figured out why I sent up the box cutter. So we're ahead of the game already."

I peered down toward his voice just in time to be momentarily blinded by a work light Dad was setting up for me atop the pipe-frame scaffold, a good fifteen feet beneath the gargoyle. He had evidently taken the interior stairs down to the forty-ninth-floor landing—what architects call a setback—where both the tourelle and its scaffolding originated, and had then climbed up the incomplete scaffolding to a spot right beneath me and the gargoyle.

"Yeah," I called down. "I got him all freed up from the netting, I think. But what's with this leash? 'Please curb your gargoyle'?"

Dad looked where I was pointing and laughed out loud when he saw the little chain. "Well, that's a novel approach, but not so surprising, really. No one had ever used terra-cotta cladding for such a huge building, so the stuff started to fail pretty much the moment they installed it in 1913. They've been putting half-assed protections like that all over the building for decades."

Dad told me to look alive, and he tossed up a rope with a metal clip tied to the end. On the third try I caught it. Following his instructions, I looped the rope through the pulley on the grillwork above me. Then I fed the rope back down to Dad. A minute later he sent up a sort of harness clipped onto the end of it. The harness was fastened through the handle of a circular saw, which trailed a thick orange extension cord.

"Put that Skilsaw to the side and get that harness on," he called up. "It's what the guys operating the hoses have been using downstairs."

The harness was little more than a thick leather belt sewn into a heavy, canvas-padded waist strap maybe eight inches wide. By the time I was all cinched in, my hips were uncomfortably constricted by that strap, which had a D-shaped ring at the back into which the rope was clipped. The rope, in turn, ran up around the pulley and down to Dad. I wasn't sure whether I felt like a mountain climber or a marionette.

I knew how to work the circular saw. In Echo Harbor, Dad and I had used it to make a birdhouse for Mom. We'd wanted to attract songbirds, but we made the holes too big and a family of astonishingly bitchy squirrels had routed its feathered tenants and moved in instead.

"That gargoyle probably has a bronze rod running through its center," Dad said from below. "The front end is likely fastened with a washer and nut inside his mouth, and the back end extends beyond the gargoyle and ties into the structural steel of the tourelle."

But first things first: we had to get through the terra cotta before going to work on that rod. My first step, then, was to cut around the gargoyle's neck as close to the tourelle as I could manage; I didn't need to worry about hitting the rod inside the gargoyle, Dad assured me, because the circular saw's blade was too short to come into contact with it. "Just try to get us as much of his neck as possible, kiddo, and when you're done with that cut I'll tell you how we sever him from the building."

One of the books Kyle and I were always quoting back and forth to each other was *Catch-22*, and I kept thinking about a gross description in there of a guy who'd fallen from a building and gone splat on the sidewalk, where his pulpy body lay motionless like "an alpaca sack full of strawberry ice cream, pink toes awry." We'd always thought of it as a pretty funny passage, but now the idea of that pavement-tenderized dead guy made my stomach feel empty and bloated at the same time.

Still, I had a plan how not to become that leaky corpse down by the curb. Basically, I just straddled the rim of the tourelle to the right of and just above the gargoyle, gripped that wall tightly between my knees, and leaned over to hold the saw's teeth above the terra-cotta creature. I steadied myself and squeezed the trigger, lowering the whirring round blade onto the gargoyle's neck. Despite the hissing whine the blade made on contact, it cut into the terra cotta without much resistance, and I eased it carefully around the curve of the sculpture as far as I could reach. Oddly, though I was leaning out into a fifty-three-story drop, I felt almost relieved to be getting away from the yawning mouth of the tourelle.

After switching off the circular saw long enough to squiggle my butt back a bit on the tourelle's rim, I twisted my torso, reached lower at a more treacherous angle, and managed to continue the cut around the bottom of the gargoyle's neck—his throat, I guess you'd call it. I had to squint to protect my eyes from the powder the saw's blade spun up toward me, but other than that it wasn't too hard. And by the faint but ever-present pressure around my waist, I could tell that Dad was adjusting to my movements with great subtlety, playing out and pulling in rope as needed. We made a good team.

"Now what?" I called down when the saw's whining blade had spun back into silence. The gargoyle's neck was mostly severed, a thin line of clay powder on either side of the dark cut. But it was still very much attached to the building.

Dad had me unstrap myself and send the circular saw back down to him in the harness. It was easy to see how excited he was, manic almost. He talked very fast and moved around on that swaying scaffold down there probably more than he needed to. Before too long, he sent the harness back up with the Sawzall strapped inside it.

When my loins were all uncomfortably girded again, I permitted myself a glance at my surroundings. The sky was a touch lighter, the city a tad less protective of its secrets. The bulky smudges of darkness downtown were beginning to resolve themselves into something like buildings.

"Now, this tool is jerkier than the circular saw," Dad called up from the scaffold planking. "So, to get better leverage, you're going to want to lock the blade in the 'on' position by hitting the little button above the trigger with your thumb. Then you're just going to ease the blade into that cut you've already made. When you're ready, just put a little extra pressure on that top handle with your left hand and guide the blade slowly down onto the rod. When you've cut all the way through, that chain leash should keep the gargoyle from falling very far."

By the time I was comfortable with my angle and balance, my head was tipped down so far that I could feel the blood thumping in my temples.

"Don't worry; lean over as far as you need to," Dad said. "I've got you." And he did, too; I could feel the rope's reassuring tug on the back of my harness, could see him below me, playing out more rope as I stretched down to get my left palm in good position on top of the Sawzall.

I eased the blade into the slot on the gargoyle's neck the way he'd told me, squeezed the trigger, and thumbed the blade lock. Right away, I could tell something was wrong. I'd forgotten you're supposed to turn on a saw *before* making contact with the thing you're cutting, and as soon as that crazy *zhigga-zhigga* blade started trying to jerk up and down, I realized it was fighting me, and fighting the gargoyle, too. The blade was jammed in that slot, and it didn't like it. To try to loosen it, I leaned farther off the building and shoved down with my left hand, driving hard from my elbow. At first the saw didn't dislodge, just struggled further, its motor growling, all that pugnacious herky-jerky energy transferring not to the blade but up through my hands and arms, causing me to shift my weight abruptly to keep from falling. Maybe that sudden movement bent the blade or jogged something loose, or both, but for one quick moment the Sawzall seemed to move as it should, its blade sliding down into the slot, sawing rhythmically up and down—until I felt it jolt against the rod, felt it catch and stutter and then kick back toward me with startling violence, the butt of the saw handle smashing me in the shoulder and knocking me off-balance.

I was falling then, tumbling sideways right off the building, dropping the Sawzall to throw my arms around the gargoyle's long neck, a lunge of desperation that seemed, remarkably, to stop my fall, until I felt that wonderful abrupt tug at my waist and realized that it was not the gargoyle but Dad who was supporting me, holding strong at the other end of the rope that connected me to him.

In that moment, practically strangling the gargoyle with my arms in my confusion of desperation and gratitude, I saw the Sawzall dropping toward the scaffold beneath me, its jagged teeth sawing the air. It didn't hit Dad. It landed on the planking a couple of feet from him, but with its blade still pumping fiercely back and forth, it skittered wildly across the wood toward his ankles, forcing him to leap out of its path.

There was no way he could have held on to that rope. I felt it go limp at my waist, felt the burden of my own weight grow suddenly enormous on the gargoyle. I gripped him tighter in my desperation, heaving my skinny chest farther up onto his skinny neck, which, to my amazement, remained attached to the building. Then, slowly, almost serenely, the skyline creature began dipping his head toward the street. There was a contemplativeness to his movement, a deliberation—until his neck snapped cleanly at the cut I'd made, the little chain leash yanked right out of the wall, and I was plummeting through the open air toward the street, hugging this useless, dragon-eared hunk of terra cotta to my chest.

Time flattened out then. I didn't see Dad as I plunged face-first past the top of the scaffolding, but I did see the cross-pipe he'd tied the rope to, and I saw that rope in its last instant of slackness, uncoiling from its pile on the planking and flying frantically upward toward the pulley. Then the rope stiffened suddenly and gave a fierce yank on my harness, arresting my fall for only the merest moment before tearing the cross-pipe right off the scaffold and releasing me again to plunge toward the pavement.

I was in free fall now, the smeary yellow lights of Broadway's streetlamps rushing up at me, the cold air so strong in my face and throat that I couldn't breathe or even blink. This time when the rope jerked violently on my harness, I was completely stunned. The sudden force of the harness belt against my stomach was so wrenching that it knocked the wind out of me, and now the gargoyle and I were swinging on the end of that rope straight toward the broad cliff face of the Woolworth's flank. I gripped the gargoyle tight and shut my eyes tighter, opening them cringingly just as we smashed into the ornamental edging of an elaborate terra-cotta canopy, the gargoyle taking the brunt of the impact and sending fragments of shattered crockets and pinnacles flying in all directions like Gothic bowling pins. Away we swung from the wall again, spinning counterclockwise to gaze out involuntarily over Lower Manhattan—the high-rise hodgepodge of the financial district, the spangled-harp spans of the Brooklyn Bridge, the dirty-gold goddess topping the columned tower across City Hall Park—then swinging back into the canopy's upper edge, my right shoulder sharing the impact with the gargoyle this time.

We collapsed, the two of us, onto the flat top of the terra-cotta canopy, where I lay gratefully with my eyes closed for a very long time, breathing, just breathing, exulting in the sensation of being completely at rest. My crotch felt oddly hot, then cold, and I realized I had pissed myself.

When I dared open my eyes again, I was startled to find myself face-to-face with the gargoyle, which I'd forgotten I still held in my arms. He was staring at me with penetrating, deep-set eyes. He had the facial features of a Labrador retriever, or a gryphon or dragon, or maybe a lion; he was all these things and yet not quite any of them. But I liked him. He was giving me a sneaky, conspiratorial grin, which I appreciated.

He also had something around his neck. Fighting the overwhelming exhaustion that pressed on my eyes, I lifted my head to peer more closely at this odd, comforting creature and saw that he was still wearing his little chain leash. That made me laugh.

"Good dog," I said, laying my head down again beside him and shutting my eyes against the world.

22

O N A HUNCH, ZEV CAME in to work the next morning, a Saturday. He just figured he'd be needed, he told me, either to bail my dad out of jail or to pack up some rare Gothic terra cotta for immediate shipping: "You don't work twelve years for a man like your father without figuring out that he tends to do what he wants to do, especially when he's in one of those revved-up phases of his."

We were sharing some day-old macaroni salad at a card table in the office, the big fourth-floor room with the framed oil portraits and that Flat Stanley slot in the floor. My father was on the phone, leaning way back in the swively oak chair with his big boots on the desk. He was grinning broadly.

"Well, the thing is, Don, it's going to cost you," he was saying. "It's the last one. The very last one. And *I've* got it."

Dad listened awhile, dabbing Neosporin on the vicious pink stripe of raw flesh that the flying rope had burned into his left palm as I was falling last night. When he was done ministering to his left hand, he began, with a wince, to apply the ointment to the matching wound in his right.

"Sure, sure, of course," he said. "You can come see it anytime you're in town. I'm just saying, I'm not gonna be able to give you a number right away, that's all. I've got to live with the piece awhile first. Pricing the priceless is a tricky business."

There was only one place in TriBeCa that sold even rudimentary groceries—Morgan's, a butcher shop on Hudson—because the few artists and eccentrics who lived down here were doing so illegally. But Morgan's didn't have an ice machine, so Dad had sent Zev to the Towers Cafeteria on West Broadway to beg some ice from Artie and Joan, the couple who ran the place. Wrapped in a stained dish towel, the frozen cubes helped numb the pain in my shoulder quite a bit.

Zev was trying every way he could think of—short of coming right out and saying it—to convey to me how horrified he was that my father had sent me out into the night to fall off a skyscraper. The whole time I'd been telling him the story, he kept shooting sardonic, disgusted looks at Dad. Zev wanted me out of the gargoyle-hunting business once and for all.

"Don't you have friends you could be hanging out with instead of us boring old people?" he asked. "Isn't there a chick you might like to take to the movies?"

But trusting your parents is an occupational hazard of being a child, and which of these men was I going to put my faith in, anyway? My passionate father with his invigorating sense of mission or this lanky, gray-ponytailed hippie with his fretful pinprick eyes?

Finally, frustrated, Zev dropped all pretense of tact. "Look, Griff, what I'm trying to tell you is that your dad's getting into some pretty heavy shit you don't know about that it'd be a real good idea for you to steer clear of."

I wanted to punch him in the nose. Why was he trying to separate me from Dad now that I'd finally gotten him back? Surely my father wouldn't have put my life at risk without a really good reason.

The melting ice was beginning to soak my shirt. I left the wet dish towel on the card table and went over to take a look at my gargoyle, which was lying aslant on the oak desk. I wanted to get another look at his sneaky grin, feel again that strange energy coming off his body.

But all the vitality had drained out of him. Just like that. Here on a desk with a bent bronze rod sticking from its neck, that terra-cotta gargoyle was just an object. A thing. Without its high-rise perch, without the Woolworth—without the *city*—it had lost its magic.

I reached down to touch its dull beige surface, but Dad, glancing up from his conversation, flicked me away with his fingertips. I was stung. I went and sat back down at the card table.

"I could've told you that would happen," Zev said, his mouth half-full of macaroni salad. "He's already forgotten that you're the one who actually climbed out there and sawed the damn thing off."

He gave a long look over at Dad, who was now cradling the gargoyle's head in his hands and staring at it with hungry wonder. After several moments in that posture, the phone pinched awkwardly between his chin and shoulder, he abruptly laid the head down again and sat upright in his chair.

"Well, I'm sorry you think I'm being difficult," he said into the phone. "I did mean it when I said you'd get first crack at it. But the fact is, Don, it's *mine*. And if I say I've got to live with it awhile, that means I've got to live with it awhile. *Okay?*"

Zev was still watching him. Chewing his macaroni salad in thought. He leaned in close to me without taking his eyes from Dad, who was now glaring at the gargoyle, his fingers resting on the ragged edge of its neck.

"It's a funny thing about collecting," Zev told me. "It starts out as love. But it becomes something much more grasping and corrosive."

23

MOM WANTED TO HAVE a word with me. In her room. *Now,* if I wasn't too terribly busy.

This was the conversation I'd been dreading. Back when they were still living together, my mother had made it clear she would leave my father on the spot if he stole even one more piece of New York. So what did that portend for my future in the brownstone if she'd learned of my serial larceny?

I was pretty sure she suspected. I'd seen her inspecting the stone powder on my jacket sleeves, and once she'd even found a chisel in the pocket of my down jacket. But I could tell she didn't want to believe I was preying on the streetscape. She'd seemed downright relieved when I assured her that I'd gotten my broken nose and bruised shoulder during fistfights over a girl.

This time, however, she had clearly discovered something that alarmed her.

"Griffin," she said, as I sat on the end of her bed facing her. "I'm going to ask you a question, and I want you to give me an honest answer. You understand?"

I nodded.

"Griffin, I found—" Flustered, she stopped short, then tried again: "Griffin, I'm not mad—I mean, why would I be; I guess it's all perfectly natural for a boy your age, and God knows I'm no prude. But I guess, well, I just really need to know the truth about this one thing:

Why in heaven's name do you have *a slab of boiled ham* hidden under your bed?"

Now it was my turn to be at a loss for words.

"It must've been under there for *ages*," she went on, her eyebrows furrowing in worry and disgust. "It stunk to high heaven. And when I think what you must have been doing—"

I could see it wasn't a good idea to let her keep talking.

"Well," I started, "it's not the easiest thing in the world to talk about, but have you ever heard of, um, the Beak of Doom?"

"The beak of what?" She looked vaguely appalled.

"The Beak of Doom. I mean, not too many people can even do it, but there's this legend that, well, and I guess they probably didn't even use ham in Malaysia—but I just thought if I practiced really hard I could kind of learn to beak my fingers together and . . ." I let the sentence drain away. The slab of ham under my bed wasn't something that could be explained in a way an adult could understand.

But my mother had heard all she needed. Her eyes grew soft. "It's okay," she told me, leaning forward to give me a reassuring little pat on the shoulder. "You don't need to explain. I've read *Portnoy's Complaint*."

I didn't know what this meant, but it was clearly time to change the subject. I asked her if she was going to go see Quigley in the talent show at seven.

"Oh, goodness, is that tonight? I guess I really should, but I'd be afraid I'd run into your father."

I told her there was no chance of that. "He said the same thing when I asked him, that he couldn't go because he didn't want to risk seeing *you*. I think you really oughta go."

"Are *you* going?"

"God no," I said, and I started backing out of the room. "But I'm not her mother."

"Well, I'll think about it. Oh, and if you're going downstairs, would you make me a cuppa? There should be some Medaglia d'Oro instant right by the stove."

.   .   .

Against all logic, Quigley had saved three seats in the front row, each marked WATTS FAMILY. I sat in the middle one and tried to spread myself onto the two empties like a really fat guy making himself right at home. The wait for Quig to come on was brutal. I had to sit through a god-awful recorder duet and a wobbly, keening rendition of "Greensleeves" played on a saw with a violin bow.

But Quigley made quite an entrance. The church went pitch-black, except for the red EXIT rectangles every fourth arch or so, and this darkness lasted much too long. Then, just as everyone was beginning to rustle around uncomfortably in their seats, an enormous spotlight shone onto the stage and a deep, syrupy man's voice intoned over the loudspeakers: "Ladies and gentlemen, we are privileged tonight to present to you, live on our stage: the one . . . the only . . . *Watts Sisters!*"

Out strutted just one girl, a proud one: Quigley. She wore a sparkly gold top hat, black tails, and a Danskin top with a tuxedo shirt and bow tie printed on it. She carried a silver-tipped black cane, which she swung around with an air of self-assured razzle-dazzle. As she stepped into the circle of light at center stage, she was grinning so broadly you could see quite a bit of her pink gums above her upper teeth. A slightly too red and too round circle of rouge decorated each of her freckled cheeks.

With a pull of a concealed string, someone unfurled a homemade red-on-gold satin banner bearing the words THE WATTS SISTERS in swoopy, showbizzy letters. In the pews all around me, necks were craned and murmurs were exchanged, until at last the crowd came to realize that this was it—this one girl up there was the only Watts Sister they were going to get—and a ripple of what I took to be admiring laughter made its way through the church.

When Quigley opened her mouth, out came an astonishingly throaty, husky voice, so unexpected issuing from this proud, freckled imp that it seemed as if she must have swallowed a gruff fifty-six-year-old carpet salesman from Canarsie: "Let me . . . enter*taiiin* you," she growled melodically. "Let me . . . make you *smiiile* . . ." It was a song from the musical *Gypsy,* which she'd been playing endlessly at home on her portable beige plastic record player.

She was having the time of her life up there, grinning so widely it practically made my own jaw hurt to watch. The crowd loved her— her gumption even more than her singing voice—and she was loving them right back, until her eyes, scanning the audience to take stock of her fan base, spotted me sitting in the front row, flanked by matching empty seats. I saw her eyes dart around the church—searching the aisles for late arrivals, I suppose. When she didn't find what she was looking for, her face flushed burgundy and she glowered down at me, as if it were obvious that our parents must have been there until just a second ago, and only some unforgivably obnoxious act on my part could be responsible for their absence.

I was mortified. As soon as she looked away again, I got the hell out of there. I knew she had a second number at the end of the evening's program, a tap solo in the middle of a full-cast finale, and I figured it might not be too late to make things right. While I jogged home, down Ninetieth Street, right on Madison, then left on Eighty-Ninth two blocks past Dalton and Service Hardware, I tried and failed to make sense of Quig's whole strange decision to call herself the Watts Sisters. It was just the two of us kids in our home, Quig and me.

As I crossed Lex, I saw the boarders down the block, hightailing it out of the brownstone en masse, in the way of animals fleeing a forest fire. When they reached the sidewalk they quickly dispersed, Mathis trotting my way, the other two making for Third Avenue: Mr. Price in full scurry, Monsieur Claude somehow managing to look languorous and bored, even while moving at speed.

By the time Mathis saw me, it was too late for him to change course. He practically bumped right into me.

"What's wrong?" I asked. "Where's everyone going?"

"Who knows, who knows," he said, woggling his head uneasily. "I just felt a bit of private time might be in order. Why're you out of breath?"

I told him about Quig's performance, and the empty seats. I asked if he'd go fill one of them; it was only a few blocks away.

"Tough to say, tough to say," he muttered, moving his fingers quickly in front of his face as if he were trying to count something very fast. "How do I know there really *is* a show? You Watts kids are a slick pair. Quigley sent me on the Staten Island Ferry last October to a Beckett play that didn't exist. And you told me you barely knew the rules of backgammon, and now I owe you two hundred thirty-seven dollars and seventy-five cents."

That gave me an idea. I told Mathis he wouldn't have to pay me his backgammon debt if he just went to see Quigley's tap-dancing number. His eyes lit up behind his Gandhi glasses.

"I'll do it!" he said. "I'm a man of honor, you know. I always had every intention of winning that money back from you."

Mom and Dad were too busy yelling at each other to hear me unlock the front door. They were in the dim middle room at the base of the stairs, where everyone's mail was always sorted on a small wicker table. I wondered if my Sea-Monkeys had arrived; I had ordered them from the back of an *Archie* comic almost six weeks ago.

"You're losing the brownstone, aren't you?" Mom was saying in a prosecutorial tone. "You're losing the brownstone on purpose!"

"Ex*cuse* me? Get your head out of your ass, Ivy. *I'm* the one who owns this place. If the bank takes it, I'm the one who loses, not you."

I stayed in the front room, standing just out of sight on the Persian carpet's threadbare edge.

"I *live* here, Nick. The kids live here. This is our home!"

"Don't be an imbecile! You can't lose anything when you don't own anything."

I wasn't quite sure what to expect. The drawing in the Sea-Monkeys ad showed a cheery, web-toed pink king with his tail covering his privates and his arm around his queen and their two scaly, smiling offspring. There were jolly bubbles all around and a castle in the background. The queen had a bow in her antennae and was heavily made up, with plump red fish lips and flirty eyelashes.

"WORLD-FAMOUS Sea-Monkeys are so full of surprises you can't stop watching them," the ad had promised. "They swim, play, scoot, race and do comical tricks and stunts." It was unclear how that fun-loving aquatic royal family could actually be shipped through the mail, but it was understood that when they arrived I needed only to pop them in a glass and add water to make them come to life. I had Scotch-taped six quarters, two dimes, and a nickel to a piece of cardboard for the privilege, mailing it all off with an order form to something called Sea-Monkey Aquarium at 200 Fifth Avenue.

"How the hell am I supposed to pay a bill I never saw, anyway?" Dad was saying.

"It wasn't one bill, Nick. This says Third Notice. *Third* Notice of Arrears."

I stepped into the room. Both my parents looked at me, their mouths half-open in mid-assertion.

"Did my Sea-Monkeys come yet?"

Both Mom and Dad crinkled their eyebrows at me, taken aback, maybe, by the childishness of my question. But neither answered. Instead, they turned back and resumed their important grown-up business of yelling at each other, as if none of this had anything to do with me. For a brief moment I thought how nice it would be to Scotch-tape them both to a giant piece of cardboard, or maybe a blue plywood sheet from a demolition site wall, and ship the pair of them off to 200 Fifth Avenue. I wondered how many stamps it would take, and if there was a kid at the Sea-Monkey Aquarium who would sign for them, as I had signed for Dad's Notice of Arrears.

"What the hell are you doing opening my mail, anyway?" Dad asked Mom. "Who's signing for certified letters that belong to *me*?"

"I only signed for this *one*, Nick. But that's beside the point. That's not what we're talking about here!" What we were talking about was how he was squeezing her, how his lawyer had rigged it so his payments to her were alimony rather than child support, so that she had to pay taxes on it all. What we were talking about was how irresponsible he was being with our home.

"*Irresponsible?*" His eyes grew wide with indignation. *Who had been on-the-ball enough to refinance the brownstone with a fixed rate way back before interest rates went through the roof? Who had gotten them into that affordable health insurance plan? Who had made one well-researched financial arrangement after another that she was either too lazy or too stupid to even try to understand?* "And then you repay me for all that by rifling through my goddamn mail?"

He moved to the table and grabbed a fistful of our boarders' letters in his left hand. With his right, he began shredding them, ripping corners and edges off envelopes and letting them fall through the air like ticker tape.

"You think it's fine to just rip open other people's letters?" he raged. "Invade their privacy? I wonder how you and all your men will like being treated with the same—"

"Stop! Stop! That's not yours!" She was grabbing at his hand, jumping and scrabbling and scratching at his wrist with her maroon nails as he held the mail above her reach. "How dare you, Nick! How *dare* you!"

I stepped forward then, went right at the middle of them, and grabbed each one by the wrist. I was taller than her, smaller than him, but mostly I was just in the middle, the most pivotal and horrible place to be, and I used my position there to shove them apart, get my reluctant body between them. I couldn't look at them, either of them, didn't want to see the ugliness in their faces. But I sure felt them. Mom's wrist was tiny and veined, with little bones running lengthwise under my fingertips. Dad's was meatier, with coarse hairs that tickled my palm grotesquely. But my parents were exactly alike in one way. The flesh of both their wrists quivered with a hostile buzzing energy, a pent-up current of rage itching for release. And standing between them, gripping their wrists, I completed the circuit. I became—or maybe had been for years—the crucial connection through which that destructive current could pass. The jolt was immediate. I felt that itching torrent of hatred, or corroded love, or whatever name you give to such a thing, surge from both my parents and meet inside me. I felt it vibrating through my fingertips—like the time I touched the robot girl's damaged nipple at Dad's studio door, only much, much worse—coursing up through the soft skin of my inner forearms and through my armpits to my heart and throat. It made me short of breath, and it made my face hot from the inside out, and it made me—well, it made me *furious*.

"What in *FUCK'S NAME* is *wrong* with you people?" I heard myself shouting. "What are you even *doing* here?"

My parents stared at me, utterly startled. As if they'd only just noticed I was in the room. I had never cursed in front of Dad before, had never dared. I had never even raised my voice around him.

Later, with my separated parents separated again, I retreated alone to the winter darkness of the backyard. There, resting my butt against the huge gnarled filth tree for support, I bent over at the waist and gulped for air, unable to breathe.

The light had come on in Mom's room upstairs, turning the curtained rectangle of her window into a kind of shadow box just above where the swollen tree branch approached her sill. She began to undress, her distorted bosomy shape moving about behind the jagged Roman ruins.

24

OUR PARENTS' FRONT-ROW ABSENCE from Quigley's performance, the public loneliness of that evening, worked a change in my sister. Starting the very next morning, she no longer dressed to capture attention. She no longer even tried. Gone was the rainbow-leather newsboy cap, the gold lamé jacket, the yellow bell-bottoms with the wide, built-in belt and oversize buckle. Gone was the Liza Minnelli mole over her left cheekbone—and all makeup for that matter. Now Quig mostly wore plaid flannel shirts, a khaki army jacket from Weiss & Mahoney, ordinary Wrangler jeans with no embroidery. Even her freckle-stained lips were exposed to general view, unconcealed by tangerine lipstick. She never again went on an audition.

At first she shut the world out, locking herself in her girl cave pretty much the moment she came home in the afternoon. But after a couple of weeks she stopped coming home after school at all. Instead, she would appear hours later—eight, nine, even ten o'clock—weary but with a strange, knowing calm about her.

"None of your *business*," she'd say when Mom insisted on knowing where she went, who she was with. "Like you actually *care* what I do."

Then, just when we were getting used to Quig's mid-evening arrivals, she took her disappearances to the next level. All at once, she started coming home around midnight. On weekends she slept till noon.

I'd like to say I was worried about her, and maybe I was a little, but the main reason I finally followed Quigley after school one Friday is that my curiosity was eating me alive. Quig headed east on Eighty-Sixth Street as I expected, but instead of continuing past Lex and Loew's and on to Shelby's place above Drake's Drum, she surprised me by ducking into the IRT under Gimbels. I hid myself in the crowd at the far end of the subway car and tailed her when she got off at Thirty-Third.

Turns out she was headed to Shelby after all. On the south side of Thirty-Sixth near Third, Quig knocked at the red door of the Amateur Thespians Society clubhouse and slipped inside when it opened. The moment the door shut behind her, sealing her in there with *him,* an unexpected wave of disgust washed through my innards. Though I'd known in the abstract that Quig was probably messing around with Shelby, it wasn't until I actually saw my frizzy-haired fifteen-year-old sister sneaking around town to meet a grown man with graying hair and thick fingers that the creepiness of the whole thing hit me.

I wasn't about to tell on Quig to Mom, who might well call the police or Dad, but I could see that this situation was way too skeezy to be allowed to continue. I decided to catch them together and confront them.

The Thespians' performances were formal, invitation-only affairs. You couldn't just buy a ticket and go, and on weekends adult audience members had to wear tuxes and gowns, though boys could get away with only a sports jacket and necktie. Since I couldn't borrow these items from Shelby, as I had when we'd come to see him the last time, I went home and swiped a gray jacket and fat polyester tie from Mr. Price's closet. The jacket was too big and swathed me in a spicy funk of old sweat, but it made me presentable enough. When the play let out a little before eleven, the well-dressed audience of couples and families spilling onto the sidewalk through the arched double doors, I mixed in among them. The play, I saw from the program in a lady's hand, was *The Cherry Orchard.*

After a time, the dressing rooms were opened upstairs and those with friends in the cast went back inside and marched up the carpeted steps to visit them, as Mom and Quig and I all had after seeing Shelby in *The Front Page*. The clubhouse had a ramshackle elegance. In the second-floor lounge, ladies in fancy dresses reclined on worn velvet banquettes while men popped corks and filled up little plastic Champagne glasses. The walls above the wood paneling were covered with framed programs and cast photos from almost a century of performances. The curved shades on a couple of the ornate wall sconces were crooked and bulb-blistered.

I followed some merrymakers out of the lounge and into the warren of dressing rooms behind it. Little explosions of laughter burst from some of the rooms as I passed. At the back, near a wall of costumes hanging from a horizontal pipe, I found Shelby's dressing room. I didn't really have any kind of a speech planned or anything. I was kind of just hoping that my catching them in the act would help both him and Quigley see the whole affair through my eyes, maybe show them how pervy the whole thing was.

I threw open the door. Inside, two heads turned to look at me in astonishment. One belonged to Shelby. He was lounging in a chair pulled back from a mirrored dressing table, wearing a silk Oriental robe and those leather half slippers that dads wore on shows like *Father Knows Best*. His made-up face looked overripe and plasticky. Leaning against the table facing him was a younger man with a stiff mustache and wavy brown hair that tumbled down past his shoulders. The top three buttons of his wide-lapeled green shirt were open.

"Where is she?" I demanded, surprising myself with my vehemence.

Shelby looked at his companion, then back at me. It took him only a moment to recover.

"Jerome, this is young Griffin, child of Ivy, my erstwhile landlady. Griffin, Jerome."

I refused even to look at the other guy. "I mean it," I said. "What have you done with Quigley?"

Shelby stood up. He was quite a bit taller than me. "The question you should be asking," he said, "is what has she done with herself?"

He put his hand on my shoulder and guided me, firmly but not roughly, out the door and a couple of steps down the hall.

"Why don't you go downstairs: *here*"—he gestured to an open door with an uncarpeted, industrial-looking stairway behind it. "You have not been extended an invitation, and I think it would be best for all concerned if you took the back way out."

I felt foolish. A pipsqueaky little "Okay" was all I could manage.

At the bottom of the steps, the landing opened up into a broad backstage area with black fabric draped all around. It was dead quiet. Everyone was upstairs. I spotted a program on the floor with a footprint on it. I picked it up and scanned the cast list. I knew the club sometimes brought in women from outside to play female roles, but Quig's name was not there, and she had to be too young, anyway.

I wondered if I'd missed her in the audience. I went to where a black curtain met the side wall and peered out at the auditorium. It was dim and empty, filled with the lonesome quiet of recently departed crowds. The double doors to the street were now closed. A smattering of abandoned programs littered the floor.

I was heading down the side aisle to go home when something onstage caught my eye. It was Quigley, her back to me. She was standing alone, holding a clipboard, in a room of dilapidated grandeur. There were no curtains on the room's richly carved windows, no pictures on its walls. The few remaining pieces of elegant furniture were piled up in a corner as if for sale.

Quig was wearing black jeans and a plaid shirt, her frizzy orange hair back in a ponytail. A rolled script poked from her back pocket. I stood in the shadows and watched as she lifted an overturned chair from the top of the furniture pile and set it down at center stage, meticulously adjusting it until its two front legs aligned with strips of glow tape on the floor. As she went back to the pile to fetch a small table and a chair, I looked again at the program in my hand, squinting at the letters in the dark. Still I didn't find what I was looking for, until I flipped to the crew list on the back cover and four words leapt out at me: QUIGLEY WATTS *(STAGE MANAGER)*.

By the time I looked up again, the chairs were assembled at angles around the little table as if in conversation. Quig brought over a standing lamp from the pile, positioned it on its mark, stepped back to admire her work. She wasn't satisfied, though, not yet. She nudged a chair just a smidgen, shifted the table's angle a tad. Getting it all ready for tomorrow's performance, everything in its place, everything just so.

25

I T'S TEMPTING TO TRY TO FORCE the past to behave in the retelling, to make it lie down flat for once. But some memories, usually
those involving my casual destructiveness, stand up like a cowlick.

If it wasn't the coldest morning of the year, it sure felt like it. While
everyone milled about in front of school, shoving their hands in their
armpits and laughing about what geniuses the teachers were for
choosing such a miserable day for the field trip, Kyle and I took advantage of the big crowd to stage our most high-profile slobber race of
the year.

To the right of the school entrance, which was built into the side of
the church on Ninetieth Street, a low wall of limestone blocks separated the sidewalk from an enclosure full of stinking garbage bags.
Kyle and I climbed into that trash pit and stood on the pile of bags
with our chins atop the wall, facing the street. At a signal from Rafferty, we each began slobbering down the outside of the wall as copi-
ously as we could. The trick, we'd learned during past races, was not
simply to produce more spit than one's rival, but to create at the outset a nice, cohesive phlegm blob, then to generate a steady stream of
slobber for that blob to ride down the wall to victory. If you had the
proper technique, it was like sending a barrel down a waterfall. First
slobber blob to the bottom won.

The contest was nip and tuck right from the get-go, with both of us
launching genuinely handsome blobs down the wall. A crowd of kids,

mostly eighth-grade boys, gathered to watch, chanting with a fervor usually reserved for fistfights:

"Slob-ber *race!*"

"Slob-ber *race!*"

"Slob-ber *race!*"

I had a good rhythm going, but just when I felt my salivary glands really kick into gear, my phlegm blob began freezing to the wall, barely halfway down to the sidewalk. Kyle's blob, I quickly noted, had also stopped descending, but it was a couple of inches ahead of mine. And whatever I did, I couldn't get mine to make up that distance. With my slobber trail frozen like a glacier, all my slobber reinforcements froze solid, too.

Naturally, I argued that the game should be called on account of weather. But Kyle maintained that the match was official because both slobber trails had descended across five stone blocks, just as a Major League Baseball game became official after the fifth inning. The crowd sided with him, and Rafferty leapt to the top of the wall.

"The *winnnah!*" he shouted, hoisting Kyle's arm aloft to roisterous applause.

I spotted Dani at the edge of the crowd, looking grudgingly amused. She was wearing a big fuzzy hat like Brezhnev wore in the newspaper. It looked a lot better on her.

The last of the yellow school buses pulled up with a moan, and a surge of excitement went through the crowd. Two teachers with clipboards tried to muster the kids into the right groups. A couple weeks earlier, everyone in the eighth through tenth grades had filled out a form listing their preferred field trip destination among the five offered. Kyle chose the observation deck of the Empire State Building, from which he hoped to murder a pedestrian with a tossed penny. Rafferty was going to the aquarium to check out the sharks. Both those trips sounded pretty okay, but I'd chosen instead to go with Mr. Darrow, the art teacher, on the theory that he was Dani's favorite and she would choose whichever trip he was leading.

Turned out I was right, and I celebrated my ingenuity by completely ignoring her as I got on the bus. Tipping my head away casually in the manner of a wily waiter avoiding eye contact, I breezed right past her and strode toward the way back, where I discovered too late that the only seat left was next to a notorious tenth-grade dickhead named Zaccaro. Immediately living up to his reputation, Zaccaro started right in on me, informing me in a braying voice how he liked the cut of my jib ("I *do,* I just *do!*") and telling me loudly, to the delight of all his dickhead friends, that "henceforth, young fellow, your name shall be *Otto!*" Then someone made a stupid crack about "Otto-eroticism," and how well the term applied to a wanker like me, and the whole chorus of dickheads took up the theme, all the way down the FDR Drive until they lost interest somewhere around the U.N.

When our ferry pulled away from the dock at Battery Park, most of the kids hurried around to the far side of the ovoid deck for an early look at our destination, the Statue of Liberty. But I didn't see what the rush was. Instead, as the boat growled its way out into New York Harbor in a gray mist, I stayed on the unpopular side of the deck with a smattering of chilly tourists. Aside from a gawky German and his plump dumpling of a wife, I was the only one at the railing as Ellis Island's onion-turreted main building slid past. A half-sunken ghost ferry lay tilted in the slip, its rusted funnel poking forlornly from the choppy water.

When our own ferry swung around Liberty Island and headed for the dock a bit later, I looked over to see a fuzzy hat beside me; it was attached to Dani.

She nodded at Lady Liberty, who loomed above us on her pedestal, growing more gigantic by the moment.

"Kinda freakish, no?" she said. "This giant green chick guarding Manhattan?"

I had to laugh. "Completely! You ever see *Godzilla*?"

"I *know*! I keep expecting Megalon to stomp out from behind the Verrazano and do battle with her."

We settled into a comfortable silence, watching side by side in the biting cold while our ferry, groaning and backing into its own fumes, parallel-parked at the dock. As we walked up the cracked path and prepared to climb under the enormous green lady's skirts, Dani was still at my arm.

The park ranger inside Liberty's base wore the same sort of goofy round-brimmed hat as his Yellowstone counterpart on *Yogi Bear*. Standing on the first of the 315 steps that led up to Liberty's brain, he gave us an earnest orientation lecture: no running, no pushing, no throwing stuff or hanging banners from the crown, no climbing to the torch.

"Wanna climb to the torch?" Dani whispered in my ear.

I nodded. She took hold of my upper arm through my puffy down jacket and led me to the side so we could let the other kids go ahead. With her fuzzy Brezhnev hat a little off-kilter atop her unbrushed coppery hair, and her cheeks still flushed from the cold, she had a roguish lopsidedness about her I quite liked.

The pedestal stairway was spacious enough, but the moment we climbed from the pedestal into the shadowy confinement of Liberty's insides, I began to lose my bearings. As long as you kept going up the claustrophobically narrow spiral staircase, there was no way to actually get lost, but the staircase ceiling was so oppressively low, and so much colossal infrastructure pressed in on you from all sides, that it was impossible to know quite where you were or what you were looking at. As far as I could tell, twin staircases—intimately entwined but usually invisible to each other—corkscrewed up the statue's center, surrounded by an elaborate steel skeleton that looked something like an oil derrick.

"You all right?" Dani asked me. She was twisted partway round to look down at me.

"Sure, maybe just a little dizzy from all this walking in circles."

"C'mon up. There's a bench thingy here."

Hanging off the side of the staircase was a kind of broad bucket with a metal bench inside it. I sat down next to Dani, or more accurately, next to her fuzzy hat, which rested between us. I pretended to scratch it under its chin.

"Does this thing have its shots?" I asked.

"Shhh. You hear that?"

High-spirited chatter wound its way up the stairs to us from some-where below. It turned out we weren't the last kids to come up after all. Dani motioned me to stay put and stepped back into the spiral stairway, her right arm raised as if to defend us from marauders. Then, deflated, she let her arm fall.

"What total buffoons!" she said. "They built this staircase back-wards."

"How can a spiral be backwards?"

"Because it *can*. This one spirals counterclockwise, which favors the attacker. Whereas every medieval castle designer without his head up his butt knew you had to make the stairway spiral *clockwise*, so it was the *defenders* who got to swing their swords forehand."

As the chatter drew closer, Dani made a sword blade of her right hand and raised it to her left shoulder in readiness. "See," she whis-pered, "if these were Huns or Vandals coming up the stairs, rather than giggly little knuckleheads, they would be running up toward me right now with their swords raised forehanded, while I would be forced to defend the tower entirely with my backhand. And with that kind of disadvantage, I couldn't realistically expect to have success killing my attackers like . . . *THIS*!!" Here she brought the blade of her right hand slashing down, lightning-quick, to the throat of poor Julia Watkins, a painfully shy classmate of mine who was just coming round the bend from below.

Julia let out a bloodcurdling shriek, which she quickly swallowed when she saw that her assailant was only Dani.

"What are you *doing*?!" Julia cried. "That's not even *funny*!"

"Sorry," Dani said with a shrug. "I thought you were a Visigoth."

We gave the knuckleheads some lead time to climb up ahead of us in their Frye boots.

"You really have a way with people," I told Dani. "I can see why you're so popular with all the other girls."

"*Me*? You're not exactly a born charmer, Cadaver Boy."

I stood up and hugged myself a little for warmth. It was way too chilly to be sitting around this long.

"I know," Dani said, leading the way upstairs again. *"Brrrr!"*

The shape of Lady Liberty's insides changed constantly as we climbed, darkened recesses and half-seen folds always just beyond identification. A shadowy little canyon off to our right seemed ripe for exploration, but Dani kept on climbing. Finally, when we reached what turned out to be Liberty's forehead, the spiral staircase ended and things widened out enough to let us stand upright on a strut that ran around the perimeter of her skull. Here, too, Dani paused for no more than a moment before heading up a short final staircase to a metal platform speckled with flattened chewing gum.

Another park ranger was up there, this one a boyish woman with close-cropped brown hair. She was finishing up some explanation about plaster casts while four or five kids, including Julia Watkins, blinked into the Arctic wind that poured in through the arched windows of Liberty's crown.

"Cold as a witch's *tit*," I whispered to Dani, hoping to make myself a little more comfortable by making her a little more uncomfortable.

"Colder," she countered, unfazed. "Colder than a brass monkey's *balls*."

The interior of Lady Liberty's scalp—the rounded ceiling—was a clutter of graffiti, hundreds of men's names and nicknames scrawled lengthwise down the narrow rivulets of her hair. Apparently Tito72 had made the pilgrimage to his nation's enduring monument to freedom, as had a fellow patriot called the Puss Man.

Dani and I elbowed our way up to the windows and peered out. Brooklyn lay low and uninviting across the slate-gray water, heaps of sullen clouds above it. Whatever dark weather those clouds held was heading our way.

The ranger told us all that it was just about time to head back to the bottom with her. While she was busy identifying one last geographical feature that Julia had spotted out the window, Dani and I started down ahead of the others. As soon as we reached the bottom of Liberty's forehead, we bypassed the "down" staircase and slipped down the "up" staircase a few twists to hide.

Huddled mid-spiral in our down jackets, we listened in silence until we could no longer hear the descending clang of boots on metal steps. But as we rose to make our assault on the torch, a low, thunderous rumble reverberated through the statue, right up through my hands on the railings and my feet on the stair treads.

My old fears about lightning flashed through me. How high above the harbor were we, anyway? Plenty high enough to be at risk, that's for sure. And to make matters worse, Lady Liberty, oblivious to the danger, was thrusting her torch heavenward, fairly begging to be zapped. Her whole posture was so irrational for a fifteen-story-tall metal woman that it wouldn't have surprised me to learn that she was actually standing on her tippy toes, trying her damnedest to brush the tip of that torch against a storm cloud and draw down its voltage, the way the pole on the back of a bumper car sucked its power from the electrified grid above it.

Was Lady Liberty grounded? It was a funny word, *grounded*. Dad had taught me that it was an electrician's term, the method by which wayward voltage could be tamed and guided safely down to the earth, rather than coursing all through the house turning ordinary objects deadly. *Grounded* was also the punishment Mom gave Quigley the time Quig stole a half-smoked joint from the coat pocket of one of Mom's musician friends. But *grounded* had yet another meaning. Some of the boys at school used it to describe any girl who seemed to have her shit together. They meant it as a compliment, as in *not crazy*. But I didn't hear it that way; whenever someone said a girl seemed really *grounded*, what I heard was *dull*.

"Let's go, Pokey." Dani was motioning me up the stairs, her too-tall hat under her arm, her coppery hair alive with static electricity. No one would ever think to call *Dani* grounded. She was too unpredictable. Too herself.

A little ways up, one of the pockets of darkness out beyond the steel skeleton seemed to curve upward into a vertical tunnel.

"That's got to be her shoulder joint, and her upraised arm," Dani said, clambering out onto the steel framework. "C'mon."

But when we reached a paint-chipping steel platform with a bolted ladder leading up from it, we found a padlocked mesh gate blocking the tube of Liberty's arm.

"Crap," Dani muttered, climbing back down. "No torch for us. Want to explore a bit?"

We returned to the staircase. A couple more twists up, Dani stopped at the dim canyon that had caught my eye earlier.

"Her face!" she said. "Look, you see the negative of her nose in the dark, way back there? And those roundish indentations have to be her eyeballs!"

"Ha! I do see it. Very cool."

We were standing inside her neck. Dani and I helped each other up the penny-pink copper wall of Liberty's throat and nested in the giant woman's chin, snapping our down jackets together for shelter. Mine was a cheap mustard-colored one from Herman's that clashed with the red of hers, a superior item she'd probably gotten at Paragon. Kneeling face-to-face, we must have looked like a pair of heads poking out the top of a puffy, two-tone igloo. I could feel the heat of her body filling the space between us, mingling with my own to form a dome of warmth within this freezing copper silo of a statue.

"It's like winter camping," I said, just to say something. "Only with cold knees. And I mean *really* cold knees."

Dani regarded me with a smirk.

"*Pussy*," she said, and she pressed a hard kiss on my lips, backing me against the cold wall of Liberty's cheek with her little breasts shoved up against my chest. Her mouth tasted sweet, and not fake sweet like Franken Berry cereal; more like bananas.

But what was she doing with her lips? It was exciting but confusing—terrifying, actually. Her mouth kept forming into a tight little wet circle, an open passage, as if she had an urge to whistle, or blow a secret down my throat. Why? Why did she keep doing that? No matter how many times I pulled away and tried to restart things with a normal kiss, there it was against my lips again: that open, expectant wet circle of her mouth. And when I opened my eyes, hers were fixed on me—so *close*—with a terrible look of irritation.

"*What?*" I asked.

"What do you mean, *What?*"

"What are you doing?"

"What am *I* doing? What are *you* doing? Or what *aren't* you doing, is more like it!" She pulled away from me. "Don't you even know how to *French*?"

Before I could answer, an obnoxious, high-pitched cackle startled both of us. We turned to see Zaccaro standing on the staircase in his bomber jacket with two of his dickhead pals.

"Ohmyfuckin'god!" Zaccaro brayed, pressing his palms to the sides of his wool Jets hat in a show of disbelief. "Little Otto snagged himself an older woman and he doesn't even know how to French-kiss!"

The other dickheads joined in the laughter.

Dani looked from them to me, embarrassed, and hastily unsnapped her jacket from mine. For a moment, as she pulled it around her body and snapped it all the way up to her neck, I thought she was going to say something kind to me. But at the last instant, her eyes ticked over to Zaccaro and she said, "I guess that's what I get for going after an *eighth*-grader. Do you *seriously* not know how to French?"

I felt my face redden. How could she? I thought we were on the same side.

Zaccaro and company *loved* all this. They were still guffawing about my incompetence as they continued up the stairs. When they were safely gone—we could hear them cackling and roughhousing up in the crown—I turned to Dani. I was livid. I couldn't believe she had betrayed me like that just to save face with a douchebag like Zaccaro. I wanted to hurt her for that. I wanted to punish her.

"I *do* actually know how to French," I said. "But I'm a little rusty. Why don't you show me. Remind me how, and I'll do it with you."

She was flustered. "*You're* the guy, not me. I can't keep being the one who has to initiate *every*thing."

"No, I know. Just show me how to French-kiss and I'll do it to you." I pointed to a pair of depressions in the wall just below the statue's nose: her two giant lips. "Liberty is French, isn't she? Just French *her*, and then I'll do it to *you*."

The weirdness of this suggestion appealed to her. "You'd like that, wouldn't you? A little multinational girl-on-girl action?"

"*Ooh-la-la*," I said.

So she did it. She crawled over to Liberty's enormous inverted lips, opened her mouth, and gingerly touched her little wet tongue to the freezing copper wall.

You could see in her eyes that she knew at once she'd made a horrible mistake. Once her tongue tip fused to the metal, there was no getting it loose. Just as I'd planned. She made some terrified noises with her throat. She began to cry. And then she did the only thing she could: she pincered the tip of her tongue between her two index fingers and tore it free, leaving behind a little flap of flesh.

After she was gone, running down the staircase with blood pooling in her mouth, I felt violently ill. It wasn't until hours later, when my urge to throw up still hadn't subsided, that I realized it wasn't Dani's wounded mouth that was making me sick. It was me. I couldn't stand to be around me anymore.

PART THREE

WE TOOK MANHATTAN

26

THE END OF THE SCHOOL YEAR was tough going. I found myself alone a lot, scuffing my Pumas down the long halls or peering busily into my backpack when friends went by, as though there were something crucial hiding in there somewhere, if I only knew where to look.

It was unclear how much the story of my misadventure with Dani had gotten around the building. Maybe not at all; maybe it was as humiliating for her as for me. No one mentioned it, anyway. No one teased me, or challenged me about it, or even shot me a look of wary disgust. But something had changed. A distance had opened up between me and my schoolmates, Kyle included. Whether everyone was pushing away from me or I from them, I couldn't quite tell.

As for Dani herself, she seemed to come through our encounter surprisingly undamaged. She was back in school after only two days, and she seemed okay, aside from a slight lisp that lasted a week or so. She, too, never talked to me about the field trip, choosing instead to express herself more directly. Once, when I was hurrying to sixth-period Latin, she tripped me down the stairs with her skinny ankle and I chipped a front tooth on the slate floor under the water fountain.

From that point on, she mostly ignored me. Whenever she passed in the halls I tried to convey a sense of brooding sensitivity by staring into the middle distance, hoping she might perceive—telepathically, I suppose—how shitty I felt about what I'd done to her.

It occurred to me that this effort might be more successful if I developed powerful jaw muscles of the sort possessed by Steve McQueen and the male models in the copies of GQ that Quigley hid under her bed. So for three straight days I bought a fifty-piece box of Bazooka gum at the Sweet Suite after school and camped out alone in the back of the shop chewing it all in one sitting. This made my mouth muscles sore as hell, but as often as I checked myself out in the shop's full-wall mirror, I could detect no improved manliness to my jawline.

I needn't have gone to all that trouble. The last week of May, Dani stopped coming to school altogether. I was fairly sure it had nothing to do with her tongue, because more than two months had passed since the field trip. But I couldn't get any good information, either. None of the ninth-grade girls I asked seemed to know squat about her whereabouts or, to be honest, to care all that much.

"I heard she was sick or something, I don't know," Quig told me. "What are you, her truant officer all of a sudden?"

The last thing I had expected, after school let out for the summer, was to miss our boarders. But as the weather warmed and they hung around less and less, I became more aware of the empty well of darkness at our brownstone's center. Hollow and cool, with the sagging staircase twisting around it floor by floor, this unlit core of our home was suffused with a melancholy languor. Mom wasn't around all that much, and even when she was, she was rarely available. Her door was closed.

A closed door could mean any number of things, all of which translated to: *You're on your own, kid.* Two of the more common scenarios were that she was napping or that she had a boyfriend in there. Of course, she never used the word *boyfriend,* possibly because the personnel changed too often to justify the term. "He's a *friend,*" she would say, in the same way she would never acknowledge being drunk when Quig called her on it, no matter how sloppy-fond Mom and one of her *friends* got around the Bushmills bottle at night. "No, we're not *drunk,* honey," our mother would say, stretching catlike on the black sofa with a great show of sensuous dignity. "We've *been drinking.*"

Likewise, Mom would never quite own up to napping during the day. If she happened to sack out with her door open and you startled her awake at two o'clock on a Tuesday afternoon, for example, she would cage a yawn behind her ringed fingers and languidly assure you that she had not been *napping;* she had merely been *lying down.* All of this, we were given to understand, was part of her *creative process.*

Thus, anytime her bedroom door was closed, as it so often was that June, there was no sure way to tell whether Mom was receiving children that day—that is, whether she was simply *lying down* and would enjoy a visit from a son bearing a cuppa, or if, on the other hand, she had *been drinking,* was with a *friend,* had *been drinking* with a *friend,* or was even *lying down* with a *friend* with whom she had *been drinking.*

Working through all these domestic permutations was just exhausting. Quig avoided the whole thing by spending most of her time at the Thespians' clubhouse, where she was now learning about set design and lighting; I headed outside and tried to get Dad to do summer stuff with me. Although he'd never mentioned my outburst that time when I separated him from Mom, he hadn't been back to the brownstone since, and I had the sense he'd been trying to go easier on me.

We both liked to hang around the boat pond near Seventy-Fifth Street, beside the Alice in Wonderland sculpture, whose bronze toadstools I sometimes still clambered up. There was something reassuring in the realization that my own grappling hands and scuffling feet had contributed, at ages three and five and eight and so on, to a timeless vitality of wear that continually polished Alice's nose and the White Rabbit's pocket watch at the points of the climbers' greatest exertion. Surely my mother's struggling ascents, too, had once lent their burnishing friction to these very same spots.

My newest enthusiasm was the radio-controlled sailboats that tacked around the pond with urgent, tilting grace. If I stood too close to the alligator-shirt kids working their expensive remote controls, my envy became almost too much to bear. But one of the doughy middle-aged regulars, a gentle redbeard in a Model Yacht Club T-shirt with yellowed armpits, confided to me that a boat cost only half as much if you bought a kit and put it together yourself. I thought the idea of building something would appeal to Dad, and it did; when I showed him a boxed Lightning inside the boathouse, he pulled out two twenties and bought it for me on the spot.

"This'll be good," he said. "You help me with my project, and I'll help you with yours."

I was so excited about my model sailboat that it didn't occur to me to wonder where we were going until we reached the speckled, hexagonal-stone pavement of Fifth Avenue.

"So what's your project, anyway?" I asked. "Will it take long?"

"Well, it might," Dad said, putting his palm up to stop a car as we crossed Fifth on the red. "We're going to steal a building."

Quig and I had been discussing lately whether Dad might be starting to lose it. This latest ambition of his seemed to lend weight to that idea.

"Dad . . . ," I began carefully, but he cut me off with another raised palm.

"It won't be anything like the Woolworth, I promise. No climbing! And I've got a whole crew lined up to do all the lifting this time."

Down in TriBeCa, I tried to get some details as we walked in twilight from Dad's warehouse after swapping my model boat for Dad's army duffel. My curiosity only irritated him.

"No, not *part* of a building, son. What we're going to steal is a *building*—the whole damn thing, cornice to curb. Just stop asking so many questions and you'll see. *Okay?*"

He was leading me toward the Hudson. Past once-grand commercial palaces of weathered marble. Past proud old factories with broad brick arches and drooping iron canopies. Past a squiggle-roofed, Dutch-looking oddity, its brick façade ablaze with puffy-lettered orange graffiti. Though I obviously understood that stealing a building was impossible, I tried to guess which grittily picturesque old structure Dad might fantasize about taking home with him, in some world where the laws of physics didn't apply.

Ahead of us, the city seemed to fall away abruptly. As the day's remaining brightness faded, Dad led us into the barren band of blocks on the island's western fringe. Three high-rise monstrosities of puke-brown bricks were rising just uptown, behind which, Dad said, an equally hideous community college would one day be built. But for now, we were walking a grid of rubbled lots, each surrounded by a chain-link fence.

"This is what I was telling you about up on the Woolworth," Dad said.

Dad stopped at a vacant lot where weeds had grown up around some piles of metal junk. He leaned against the chain-link fence with his back and offered me a Life Saver, the wintergreen kind that sparked in your teeth if you bit down on them in the dark. I took one and sucked on it. I liked the way you could force your tongue tip through the ring as the candy dissolved.

"Are the others meeting us?" I asked. "What are we waiting for?" I was starting to feel uneasy.

"I just want to be sure we're alone."

We were. There were ONE WAY signs on the corners, but no cars to obey or ignore them. No one walked the smashed sidewalks. Back in the direction from which we'd come, on the far side of what might have been Greenwich Street, a weak beam of light flashed briefly across the inside of a third-floor loft window.

Squatters, Dad explained. Artists with flashlights who didn't want to be seen by city building inspectors. "Of course, at this hour all the inspectors are home on Staten Island with their families, eating pasta fazool," he said. "But the threat of eviction makes you paranoid, believe me."

Dad walked around the corner of the lot whose fence we'd been leaning on. The lot was a funky shape, like a candy corn. Near its skinny end, just across a wide street from the piers, he stopped at a padlocked gate and pulled a pair of long-handled clippers from his duffel.

"Wait, we're going in *here*?" I asked. "Why?"

Dad applied the clippers to the curved chrome part of the lock and cut it cleanly with a powerful jerk of his hands. He slipped the lock off the gate and pocketed it.

"Welcome," he said grandly. "Feel free to look around."

There was nothing to see, other than some windblown trash flattened against the fence and the piles of metal debris at the wide end of the lot. He wandered over and laid hands on two broken pieces of a long, skinny rectangular box, muttering to himself: "That must be how these go, yeah. They must've—*shit!*" He yanked his hand back and shook it in the air. "That edge is sharper than it looks."

He turned my way. "It's a really good thing you came along. Much better to do this methodically. You see those big piles over there?"

I nodded warily. Not five minutes in this crappy vacant lot and he was already giving my precarious trust a poke.

"Well, what I need you to do is just drop down in the spaces between them for me, starting with the two on the left." He patted his belly. "I'm afraid I'm getting a bit too broad in the beam for that sort of thing."

He pressed an unlit penlight into my palm.

The piles of mostly flattish metal were grouped by shape and size, no pile more than four feet high. Turned out it was actually no problem to slip into the narrow space between the first two piles and crouch down on the dirt as he instructed. I liked it in there, I was surprised to find. The dark was darker, the quiet quieter. It was comfortingly private, like the cabinet beneath Mom's window.

"You got your bearings?" Dad's voice asked from above. "Now look at the undersides of any panels whose edges might be sticking out where you can see them. Start with the left pile."

I clicked on the penlight. The ground in here was weedless and dusty.

"See any numbers? We only need one from each pile, or maybe two to be sure."

The panels closest to the ground were too low for me to look beneath. Starting about a foot off the ground, though, I began seeing stenciled yellow numbers on some panels, three digits each, in yellow paint as bright as the graffiti we'd passed earlier.

"Three ninety," I called up. "Three forty-one. Three-oh-six."

"Do they *all* begin with three?"

I confirmed that they did, and we repeated the process on the second pile—long, grooved half cylinders of some kind, each stenciled with a letter and a number: c4, c8, c5. When I popped my head back out the top, Dad was scribbling into a composition notebook. I tilted the penlight beam toward his face. Even wincing away from the light, he looked more hopeful than I'd seen him in a long time.

"Dad," I asked, emboldened. "What is all this junk, anyway?"

"Junk?" he cried, with mock indignation. "Did the young fellow say *junk*? That's no way to talk about a man's home."

I was at a loss. "What do you mean?"

Dad laughed, enjoying my confusion.

"I told you I'd show you my Washington Market studio sometime, didn't I? Well, you're standing in it. Your mom and I made you inside this thing."

27

When I awoke in his four-poster bed the next morning, Dad was nowhere to be seen. The pillow beside me, where his big head had been snoring raucously most of the night, was now occupied by a dog-eared antique booklet the size of a comic book. It was missing its cover.

You could tell by the greasy thumbprints on its pages, and the occasional stains from someone's nineteenth-century lunch, that this wasn't the sort of jealously guarded manuscript that had spent its life locked up in a library. This thing was meant to be *used*.

The booklet was drawings mostly, intricately executed, black on white. The first one had a rollicking quaintness that reminded me of an old-timey Ringling Bros. poster. It depicted a cheerfully industrious "manufactory"—"*ARCHITECTURAL IRON WORKS: D. D. Badger and Others, Proprietors*"—with puffs of smoke issuing from its eight perky stacks and a beneficent wind holding aloft the pennant that crowned its cupola. The rest of the booklet was more abstract. Interspersed with illustrations of entire fancy building façades was a grab bag of minutely rendered architectural odds and ends: *Plate XLIII: Window Lintel Architraves & Sill; Plate XXXII: Cornices, Arches & Arches Ornamental.*

I heard the heavy whine of the opening door before I saw Dad coming through it. He was in high spirits, cradling a brown paper bag mottled with grease stains.

"Oh, I see you've met Mr. Badger," he said when he saw the booklet in my hands. "I thought that might interest you."

"It does, sort of. But what is it?"

"Well, it's a rather remarkable thing. It's an original catalog from one of the foundries that produced components for cast-iron buildings in the mid to late eighteen-hundreds. Badger's office was right down here on Duane Street. His factory was over on Thirteenth and Avenue B, right by where that Con Ed plant is now."

"Is that what all those metal pieces were yesterday?"

"Yep. The whole system was basically pioneered by a New Yorker called James Bogardus. Clever fellow." Bogardus, Dad said, would start by having a foundry pour molten iron into sand molds to individually cast the component parts of a building. Then all those pieces would get delivered to a building site, where they'd be bolted together on the spot like a giant Erector set to make either a freestanding iron building or, more often, a handsome classical façade that could just be attached to a regular old brick-and-wood building.

"Like a mask?"

"Yeah, but a *beautiful* mask, and convenient. In fact, iron-front buildings became so popular that a bunch of different foundries, like Badger here, started designing their own iron modules. A lot of the history's been lost, though, so that of all the surviving cast-iron buildings in New York, there's only one, over on Leonard Street, that we know for sure was actually designed by Bogardus. And since none of his construction drawings of whole buildings survive, no one even knows exactly how his system fit all these interlocking components together."

I flipped through the Badger booklet. Page upon page of *Capitals*, *Corbels*, and *Pilasters*, each identified in florid calligraphy.

"So how is this a catalog? Could you actually buy a building out of this thing?"

"Sure could. Or you could design your own and they'd cast it for you. It was kind of an architect's dream, because it let them design remarkably intricate façades that could be put up quickly and then painted to look like stone. It was practically like ordering from a Chinese menu: 'Gimme a Number Twelve—the Second Empire mansard roof—with a side order of Palladian windows and a couple servings of broken pediments.'"

"'And make it snappy!'"

"That's right. I know you're joking, but it really was quick. Took only two months to put up my Washington Market studio back in 1849. Which only made it easier for the barbarians who run this city to tear it down."

I asked when they'd done that.

"Three years ago—*you* remember. I took you over to watch. You liked the way the blowtorches spat sparks when they were cutting the bolts."

That morning of destruction came back to me. The burly men straddling a beam three stories up. The way they peeled off the building's skin and winched it down with a chain, one panel at a time. The raw hurt on Dad's face.

"Breakfast dumplings!" he said now, trying to wrench us back to the present. He extended a fried lump to me on the tip of a chopstick. I plucked it off. Steam escaped from the round puncture wound.

I bit the dumpling in half. It was delicious, a compact little explosion of grease and salt. But Dad must not have looked at my face until my pleasure had turned to revulsion.

"Oh God, son. Don't do it!" he said, laughing. "Don't you know the first rule of eating Chinese food is never to look inside a dumpling?"

It was a little after nine when we clattered up to the fenced lot in a big brown delivery truck Zev had brought by the warehouse. Dad turned up the radio as loud as it could go and hopped out, leaving the door open so the cheesy love song on his oldies station could be heard by anyone who might happen by. He wanted it to appear as if we belonged here.

Wearing a blue hard hat, Dad opened the padlock with a key attached by a chain to his belt loop, and waved Zev through the gate. We trundled in over the uneven dirt, then backed up to the cast-off iron panels.

"What does he want that stuff for, anyway?" I asked Zev.

"Scrap iron. Any chop shop up on Hunts Point'll pay a hundred bucks a ton, easy."

When Dad rolled up the truck's overhead rear door, Curtis stood up and hopped out, followed by an older, slightly stooped black guy who had been sitting on a DECARLO FUNERAL HOME cooler. His skin had a bluish tint and a dusty look to it even before he started working. No one introduced us, but everyone called him Furman.

Dad made me stay out of sight in the back of the truck all morning with the composition book. My job was to count each iron panel the crew loaded into the truck and record its stenciled number in the notebook.

"The foundries kept pretty good production records of each panel's specs," Dad explained, "so the numbers you got me last night allowed me to look up how much each component weighed. This way, as long as you keep careful track of how many of each type we take, the scrap yard won't be able to rip us off on weight. Everyone knows their scales are rigged."

The truck got pretty full after only a couple of hours. Some of the pieces, like the skinny, ridged columns with the bolt holes on their edges, took only two guys to lift. The larger panels took three or even four. My favorite pieces had at their center a beetle-browed lady with writhing, twisty hair. Dad said she was Medusa. To me she just looked like an unhappy woman who didn't like to get out of bed in the morning.

It must have been about 105 degrees in the back of the truck. The hotter it got, the more I found myself stealing glances at that DECARLO cooler, recalling with repulsion the putrefying meat smell from the cooler in our backyard and dreading finding out what was inside this one.

A little after twelve, I got my answer. My father—followed closely by Zev, Curtis, and Furman—climbed into the truck and slid the cooler to its center.

"And now, boys, the moment you've all been waiting for," my father said, lifting the top with great fanfare. "Let's just see what our kind benefactor Tony has sent us today."

Curtis and Zev peered inside eagerly, but I couldn't bring myself to do it.

"Not bad at all," my father announced, poking around inside the cooler. "Turkey, ham, Swiss—oh, and those stuffed olives you like, Curtis. A pretty good haul."

I looked into the cooler, and sure enough it was full of rolled cold cuts and other hors d'oeuvres on plastic trays covered with Saran Wrap. These, my father explained, were the leftovers from the previous day's memorial reception at DeCarlo's "body shop."

"Is that what's *always* in those coolers you have around?" I asked, as relieved as I was surprised.

"What else?" Dad said. "No one ever eats at those services—too busy grieving—so Tony always ends up swimming in leftovers. Won't even take any money from me for them."

The guys took turns filling their plates with cold cuts and cheese cubes, and we all sat down amid the scavenged scrap iron to eat. Around the time Curtis started grumbling about needing a Yoo-hoo to wash it all down, Dad declared our work done for the day. He was in a terrific mood as he locked the gate behind us.

"We'll take Man*hattan*," he sang, his head bobbing, "the Bronx and *Staten* Island, too . . ."

Zev rolled his eyes at the bad pun. "Christ almighty, Nick. Not in front of the child."

Dad hopped back into the cab, and we rumbled across town and up the FDR Drive toward the Bronx, with me up front between Dad and Zev, and Furman and Curtis in the back with the scrap iron. I tried not to show my disappointment when Dad had Zev drop me off on Eighty-Ninth and Third, rather than letting me continue with them across the Third Avenue Bridge to watch the thunderous machines shred metal in the Bronx.

On the cracked steps of the tenement near the corner, three old Puerto Rican men with saggy socks were drinking cans of Schlitz and yelling in Spanish at a staticky transistor radio playing the Mets game. A little up the block, a Puerto Rican boy played handball against himself with a Spaldeen.

It wasn't until I was almost home, passing the apartment house with the ripped green awning, that I realized just how little I wanted to be inside the dark, airless brownstone.

28

O VER THE NEXT COUPLE OF WEEKS I stayed over at my
father's as much as I could. I found that if I got up early enough,
he'd help me put my model Lightning together for a bit before it was
time to go load up the scrap iron. I could never have managed the
boat's motor without his help. He'd grown up in Rhode Island in the
thirties repairing tractor engines with his brothers, so this kind of
work came naturally to him.

Carting away the cast-iron fragments became a routine. In the
morning, before it got too hot, we'd pull into the lot in the brown
truck and get to work. Zev and Curtis would bicker a little about
which way to tilt the panels as they came off the piles. Furman would
wait for them to work it out and then silently lend his muscle to the
effort, never smiling or complaining. I stayed out of sight in the truck
and recorded the stenciled numbers in the composition book.

Sometimes I wondered how I would look to Dani if she ever saw
me here, whether I would come off as a rough-and-ready laborer performing man's work or if I might just seem like a secretary taking
dictation.

After locking the gate behind us, we always headed across Chambers and then uptown. I never got used to the sting of being dropped
off on Eighty-Ninth Street instead of completing the trip up to the
scrap yard in the Bronx.

One afternoon after watching the brown truck speed up Third

without me, I walked up the block and kept right on going past the brownstone. My hand didn't pull out my key ring, so my eyes didn't search for the new key marked with maroon nail polish that Mom had given me after changing the lock on our front door. Perhaps out of habit, my feet took me past Finast and the Paulding Pharmacy on Lex, over to school on Ninetieth Street, and through the Engineers' Gate to the dusty black bridle path ringing the reservoir. On the West Side, I emerged at Ninety-Sixth Street and kept on going, past Fowad, an emporium of shitty used clothes sold for profit, and past the Salvation Army, an emporium of shitty used clothes sold for charity. By the time I took a moment to think about where I might be going, I looked up to find myself standing in front of Dani's building on West End.

I stood there awhile, rocking on my heels. The door was open, a giant circular fan standing just inside the lobby, disturbing the air with a whirring noise worthy of a jet turbine. Steely Dan was playing on the doorman's radio: *Any major dude with half a heart surely will tell you, my friend: Any minor world that breaks apart falls together again . . .*

I squinted into the sun and counted up to the eleventh floor, where the windows were framed by Greeky terra-cotta ornament the bland beige of Alpha-Bits cereal. Which windows were her apartment? Might she be looking down at me this very moment? What if she had moved away, or was too unwell to even sit up?

I took a couple steps toward the building before seizing up with fear. What if that ornery Irish doorman I'd deluged with hose water was on duty today?

Yeah, and what if he wasn't? It wasn't too common, after all, for a guy who worked weekend nights to suddenly be working weekday afternoons.

Maybe, but you could never be too careful.

I headed down toward the Eighty-Sixth Street crosstown without even poking my head inside the lobby.

Wuss.

29

FURMAN AND I HAD AN ARRANGEMENT. Dad refused to buy me junky desserts, and Furman only liked the outside of his Ring Dings. So Furman would give me his snack cakes' spongy innards (half-life twelve thousand years, give or take) in exchange for my share of any olives and cornichons that came out of the DECARLO lunch cooler. I watched his weathered face as he carefully gnawed the flaky frosting off each Ring Ding, first around the circumference and then the top and bottom. The flesh beneath his eyes was bunched and gray-blue, like the skin of an old elephant. His broad nose whistled when he breathed.

Zev and Curtis usually spent lunch giving each other shit about something trivial, like which one of them looked more like a Smurf in his blue hard hat, or whether women preferred Lee jeans or Levi's.

"In *your* sitch-a-ation it don't matter *any*how," Curtis told Zev, "'cause you ain't got no butt to stick in them jeans you *do* buy." Curtis shook his head sympathetically. "Ain't a woman alive trust a man with no butt!"

Sometimes we even ate breakfast at the lot, plopping down for a morning picnic on what remained of the scrap iron. I especially liked sitting on the pile of flat spandrel panels, facing the derelict piers with my legs dangling down. Across West Street, behind the serenely decaying corpse of the elevated highway they'd shut down last year (after a dump truck plunged through the roadway to the street below), an *R* had gone missing from the front of Pier 21: MARINE & AVIATION, it said; ERIE LACKAWANNA AILROAD.

I tried joining Dad in the cab of the truck a couple of times, but it was obvious it annoyed him. He didn't fraternize with us enlisted men during meals. He ate alone up front with his *New York Times*, staying aloof from his crew the way Captain Scott did in his expedition's Antarctic hut the winter before his doomed assault on the South Pole. It pissed me off, but I worried that if I complained he'd just send me home.

I wasn't the best note-taker. Zev, who usually kicked me in the rear about it a bit, was working back at the warehouse today, so instead of taking inventory I was sitting in the back of the truck trying to draw a halfway-decent Tribble. Dad, Furman, and Curtis were loading a double-sunburst panel into the truck when we were all startled by someone shouting outside: "Hey! *Hey!* What're you doing with that?"

Dad didn't miss a beat. "Stay *inside!*" he hissed to his men. He gave an urgent nod in my direction: "Keep him *out of sight!*"

Outwardly calm then—acting almost bored—Dad stepped from the tailgate and ambled out of view toward the front of the truck.

"*What's* that, bud?" I heard him say.

"You with the Commission?" the stranger asked suspiciously. "They didn't tell me anyone—"

The truck's cab door slammed. The ignition fired up and the truck lurched out of the lot, knocking me off my feet and churning up dust behind us.

"*Heyyy!*" the stranger's voice yelled again. "*Stop!*"

I tried to get a good look out the back at the guy, but a big brown Curtis hand gripped my skull and shoved it back down like a clown head in a jack-in-the-box. The truck swerved right, then right again, sending all three of us tumbling. The engine gave a growl, the truck picked up speed beneath us, and we hurtled uptown, the scrap iron shifting and jittering all around us.

"Dude was writin' somethin'!" old Furman, rising to his knees, told Curtis. "Mighta seen our plates, maybe."

"*Mighta?*" asked Curtis. "Or *did?*"

Neither man said any more. Curtis was practically sitting on me now, but in the spaces between his limbs I saw Furman struggle to his feet and toward the back.

The overhead door clattered down and we were bumping along in darkness.

The truck shuddered to a halt. We had driven half an hour, maybe more. Curtis told me to hush, his callused hand oddly gentle against my chest. There was shouting outside—urgent, rankled—and someone out there rolled up the rear door, the sudden sunlight jabbing my eyes. A ferret-faced teenager in a dirty T-shirt poked his head inside, then vanished again.

Curtis and Furman immediately began unloading the scrap, tossing it, clanging, into a pile beside the truck.

We were in a vast, oil-stained yard with a trailer on one end and a mountain range of mangled metal on the other. A brick wall ran around it. Dad wasn't in the cab of our brown truck. I found him inside the trailer, talking intensely to an unshaven fat guy who was eating a meatball hero at a metal desk. Farther back, a wiry old man in a filthy black-and-orange New York Giants baseball cap sat on a salvaged car seat, an ass divot in the upholstery beside him.

Dad's eyes caught me in the doorway, expressing no interest before flicking back to the meatball hero guy. I wandered off to explore.

The scrap yard was outrageously cool, a land of ordered mayhem lorded over by two giant yellow claws. The entire topography of ruin, if you looked closely, seemed an elaborate sorting system, an outsize version of Mom's mayo jars full of eggshells. There was no overlap among the mountains of smashed metal. Each had a different texture, and some had distinctive colors. The tallest one seemed to be a lot of sheet metal and auto bodies and silver kitchen ducts; a hill off to the side was darker and might have been iron; nearest me was a tortured alp of copper—twisted pipes and cables glinting in the sun.

The sound of sustained destruction was deafening, a layered clattering and groaning and *beep-beep*ing. Now and then one of the machines would pause and give out a breathy sigh, then swivel over to renew the assault.

The truck in front of ours was a battered green pickup whose rusted wheel wells looked like astonished eyebrows. With help from the ferrety teenager, a slope-shouldered Puerto Rican guy in plastic sandals struggled to slide a refrigerator off the tailgate and onto a hand truck. His two little boys, too small to give a hand, shrieked with pleasure as their dad galumphed it onto the scrap yard's big scale. The fridge had colored alphabet magnets on its door, and part of what looked like a child's painting. While the dad and the scrap worker were haggling, one of the boys bolted from the safety of his father's side and tried to grab the painting off the fridge. His dad chased him down and yanked him back, giving his ass a big smack and chewing him out in Spanish. The kid howled.

The ground at the yard's edge sloped upward. I climbed it until I reached the back wall, which turned out to be an embankment on some kind of narrow river or canal. The sluggish water was slicked with oily rainbows. Three barges hugged the shore below, one empty, the others partly filled with scrap metal. One of the gargantuan yellow claws swiveled into position above a barge and dropped a clattering load of debris. Back near the scale, the second claw descended on the Puerto Rican family's fridge, which slipped from its grasp ten feet in the air and smashed to the ground. The claw swooped down again to get a better grip, its pointy tips easily puncturing the fridge's flanks and crushing it. The claw rotated abruptly and hurled the fridge onto one of the mountains, sending a minor avalanche of shredded metal skittering down its side.

Not far from the trailer, the ferrety teenager and two other workers had propped up several of our cast-iron panels against the brick wall and were going at them pretty aggressively with power saws, cutting each one into halves or thirds. Dad stood nearby, sometimes instructing them to cut up a piece further. He seemed anxious to make the panels unrecognizable.

Something was worrying me. If private investigator Jim Rockford were on our trail, it wouldn't take more than an hour for his bald buddy at the force, Sergeant Becker, to run our truck's plate number and then leave its owner's name and address on the newfangled answering machine in Rockford's mobile home. And once Rockford found the truck, it was only a matter of time before he found *us.* Wouldn't any real-life detective be able to track us down just as easily?

"We're toast!" I bleated at Dad when I joined him by the growing pile of destroyed iron panels. I pointed at our brown truck, which someone had pulled forward, near where we were now standing. "Our fingerprints must be *all over* that thing!"

Dad managed a joyless smile. "I've taken care of that. You might want to stand back."

I followed his gaze just in time to see the claw close itself up into a huge tight fist, then slam directly down onto the truck—*POOM!*— ripping through its steel roof as easily as if it were canvas. In my terror, I leapt back needlessly and gave a girlish squeak I hoped no one could hear over the clamor. The claw rose again, lifting the truck off the ground a couple of feet as it shook itself free, then hammered down through the windshield, shattering the glass and caving in the truck's hood and engine.

As the claw continued its thunderous beat-down, Dad stuffed a wad of bills into Furman's hand.

"Tell your cousin," he said, "I'm sorry about his truck."

30

BEFORE I EVEN KNEELED DOWN to lift the *Times* off our stoop the next morning, the headline leapt right out at me:

150-TON CAST-IRON LANDMARK FACADE
PANELS STOLEN HERE

A horrible, pukey dread swept up from my stomach to my throat as I read:

Working in daylight under the startled eyes of a construction contractor, three thieves made off yesterday with a truckful of panels of a 150-ton city landmark—a 125-year-old cast-iron facade of a four-story structure described as an architectural treasure.

The audacious theft of the cast-iron panels from the Bogardus Building was spotted at 11 A.M. by Gerard Varlotta, the contractor, at a lot at Chambers and Washington Streets in lower Manhattan.

Mr. Varlotta told the police that he saw three men wearing blue construction helmets putting the panels into a brown truck at the site. He said he ran toward the three men, who, when they saw him, jumped into the truck and roared away. He said he was able to jot down the license number of the truck before it got away.

Last night the police disclosed that they had one of the three men in custody and were questioning him and that a search of a junkyard in

*the Bronx was under way. Capt. Paul G. Mannino, commanding officer
of the First Precinct, said that the theft of the facade panels had taken
place over several weeks, and he said he doubted whether all would be
recovered.*

"This stuff looks just like junk," he said.

The market value of the cast iron was said to be about $100 a ton.

I couldn't read any more. I was pretty sure I was going to throw up
on my moccasins.

"Give that here!" Mathis said brightly as I shuffled into the dining
room with the paper. "See!" he cried at Mr. Price, poking the headline
with his index finger. "Here it is! A *landmark* they stole!"

He read the top of the story aloud, shaking his head in delighted
astonishment. I listened without hearing.

"There!" Mathis said suddenly. "This is the part I was telling you
about! It was all anybody at the A.P. could talk about yesterday."

I tried to make myself invisible as he continued reading:

*The theft became public when Mrs. Beverly Moss Spatt, chairman of
the city's Landmarks Preservation Commission, dashed into the press
room at City Hall yesterday and shouted, "Someone has stolen one of my
buildings."*

*She added: "It was an architectural treasure—the finest example of a
cast-iron building in the city."*

*The original building was designed by James Bogardus and built at
97 Murray Street in 1849. It was regarded as one of the finest examples
of cast-iron structure in the world. A section of the facade of the architectural treasure is in the Smithsonian Institution in Washington.*

*The four-story facade, which could be disassembled, moved and reas-
sembled at another location, was made a landmark in 1970. A year later,
when the building was torn down to make way for the Washington
Market Urban Renewal project, the facade was disassembled at a cost of
$80,000 and stored in the lot.*

*Mrs. Spatt said that the federal government had given the city $450,000
in 1971 to reconstruct the facade as part of a new community college.*

"I've worried so about this building," Mrs. Spatt said. "I've pleaded with the Housing and Development Administration to store it in a safe place. Now it's gone and I'm heartbroken."

"Bloody unbelievable," said Mr. Price, chuckling with horrified superiority. "You Americans've got little enough history as it is; you'd think you'd mind where you left what heritage you *have* got."

"Oh, let's not get so high-and-mighty here, Price," Mathis said to him. "You're telling me you don't have bottom-feeders back in London?"

There was more to the story. Mr. Price stood up to read the paper over Mathis's shoulder. Both were silent as their eyes darted back and forth across the columns of newsprint.

I was pretty sure I would spontaneously combust if I had to keep standing there pretending not to be too interested in the stolen landmark. So I hid out in the crapper at the base of the stairs until it sounded like everyone had gone. Then I raced to the dining room table to read the rest of the article:

The Bogardus Building was the first with a complete cast-iron facade constructed in the city, and it became a prototype for all subsequent cast-iron facades. It was said to have foreshadowed the eventual development of the skeleton-steel construction of the skyscraper.

The arrested man was identified as Furman Boyd, 46 years old, of 121 East 120th Street, Manhattan, who was booked on a charge of grand larceny.

(Fuck.)

The police said they expected to take two other men into custody.

(FUCK!!)

According to the police, the cast-iron pieces were found in a junkyard at 850 Edgewater Road, the Bronx, based on information supplied by Mr. Boyd. All were broken pieces, they said.

The police added they would look in the junkyard later today in an
effort to find further parts of the structure. The police said the junkyard
operator had had no idea of the historical value of the iron pieces.

Dad, it must be said, was not too thrilled to see me show up at his
studio that morning.

"What are you doing here, son?" He shot Zev a nasty look for letting me in. "You should be staying as far away from me as you can
right now."

Dad looked awful. He was wearing the same dirty flannel shirt and
jeans from yesterday. His eyes were shot through with red.

"Zev!" he barked. "Take Griffin to lunch! I'm trying to *think* here."

Zev got up as if to lead me out, but I ignored him.

"The paper said that was a *really* important building we stole, Dad."

"Hell yeah, it was important. Why do you think I was so upset
when they booted me out of it so they could tear it down?"

"But they were going to put it back together! They spent a buttload
of money saving the building so—"

"*Saving* it?" Dad asked bitterly. "Sure they were saving it—just the
way Teddy Roosevelt 'saved' all those exotic animals by shooting
them and putting them on display at his natural history museum. The
city's a living thing, son. You don't save it by dismantling it."

"But the paper said they had like *half a million dollars* set aside to
rebuild it."

Dad shook his head. "Son, I'm sure some of those people over at
Landmarks mean well, but their plan was a farce."

"It really was," Zev agreed.

It must have been clear from my face that I had no idea what they
were talking about.

"Look, the city has this powerful new landmarks law," Dad
explained, "which they could easily have used to keep the Bogardus
standing forever, right where it was built. *Instead,* they tore down
hundreds of historic buildings around Washington Market, including
the Bogardus, to make way for the Twin Towers and the community
college and those repulsive Independence Plaza high-rises. They piled
the Bogardus fragments in an unguarded lot—*you* saw them!—and

basically dumped the whole preservation problem in the laps of the poor architects designing the college."

"Seriously," Zev said. "It's about the screwiest arranged marriage you ever heard of."

"What is?" I asked.

"Landmarks has been forcing the college to incorporate the Bogardus into their super-duper-modern new campus," Zev said.

"The best they've come up with is this ridiculous plan to reassemble the two cast-iron curtain walls of the Bogardus as a freestanding screen in one of the courtyards," Dad said. "The kids could throw their Frisbees back and forth through its windows."

I looked at his red face, weighing whether it was safe to say what I was thinking.

"Isn't a courtyard kind of better than the scrap yard?" I asked.

"*No!*" Dad exclaimed. "It damn well *isn't.*" A wide blue vein was standing out in the middle of his forehead. "The Bogardus is meant to be a *building*—a living structure you can get *inside,* make a home or a business out of! What they had in mind for it would be as phony as the bogus plywood town in *Blazing Saddles.*"

Man, did I love *Blazing Saddles.* It had come out back in February, and since it was rated PG, Kyle and I had gotten this nice bald guy on line at the Beekman to pretend to be our dad and take us in.

Dad went to his little bachelor's fridge and took a swig from a milk carton.

"It's basically pretty simple, son. The city didn't respect the Bogardus, so I"—he shot me a pointed look—"*we* put the building out of its misery. And even though we got caught before we were able to scrap the whole thing, we still managed to make some pretty good money off this selfless act of mercy."

I was not comforted. "They arrested Furman!" I said, my voice going all girly-high again. "Will *you* be arrested? Will *I?*"

"I doubt it. I paid those guys enough to keep quiet, and they'll probably get off with only a few days at Rikers, anyway. For guys like them, that's practically just a cost of doing business."

"But how can it be for only a *few days?* The paper said it was *grand larceny!*"

Dad raised his palms toward me. "That's ludicrous. All the iron we took over the past couple weeks was already trashed beyond recognition by the time the cops started snooping around the scrap yard yesterday. So they can't pin those earlier thefts on anyone—no evidence. And grand larceny means you stole something worth a *grand,* which they didn't, not in that single day's haul." He looked at me impatiently. "The Bogardus may have been priceless as architecture, but architecture has no street value. Scrap iron does: ninety-seven dollars a ton. So in the eyes of the law, those guys didn't steal a treasure; they stole a pile of scrap. There's no way Furman gets locked up for too long."

Maybe not, but it just seemed like whenever a group of men or boys got together to do something, one of them, usually the most vulnerable, got totally hosed. A memory came to me of Lamar, the time an after-school mob of us, chanting "Fathead! Fathead!," stuffed him in a forty-gallon garbage can and lifted it up on a classroom table so he couldn't tip the can over to escape without risking falling on his head.

In *Blazing Saddles,* there was this huge thickheaded lummox named Mongo, who worked for the bad guy played by Harvey Korman and whom Kyle and I always told Lamar he reminded us of. The way Mongo finally met his end was that his enemies put a stick of dynamite inside a box of candy and delivered it to him at a campfire: "*Candy*gram for Mongo! *Candy*gram for Mongo!"

Mongo never saw the explosion coming.

I wondered what went through Furman's mind up in Harlem when he opened his door to the police and his decision to trust Dad blew up in his face.

31

Z EV'S PLACE ON THOMPSON STREET was pretty much a
dump. A *very* tiny tenement apartment directly above a tailor
shop with a flickery green neon sewing needle and spool in its window. As we hunched over Zev's little table, sopping up our Dinty
Moore with slices of white bread, the sound of the sewing machine
downstairs jittered up through the floorboards in irregular bursts.

"You like living here?" I asked, looking around.

Zev shrugged. "It's home. I don't spend a whole lot of energy thinking about what I don't have."

What he did have was pretty unusual. His floor was mostly covered with small, haphazardly overlapping Oriental rugs, including
one really beautiful red one that looked like a dog had taken a bite out
of it. Not an inch of space in the room was wasted, yet nothing in it
seemed useful. There were piles of antique tins—cigarette tins, and
tooth-powder tins, and tins painted to look like wicker baskets. There
were unframed oil paintings of sheep and old women and a peacock
who was missing a leg. There was a window shelf of brightly colored
glass seltzer bottles, no two alike. There was a red wax Empire State
Building whose spire had drooped in the heat.

"How old are you now, anyway?" Zev asked me. "Fourteen?"

"*Thir*teen."

The number hung there in all its maddening ambiguity, neither
very much nor very little.

"You like it, being thirteen?"

I looked at him. "What do *you* think?"

"Yeah, I guess that's a pretty dumb question." He smiled. "It's a pretty rotten age, way I remember it: nothing to do, and no one to do it to."

A silence grew.

"You have to admit," I said finally, "it *was* pretty fucked up of him to just go and trash that one-of-a-kind landmark like that. It *was*."

The tailor's sewing machine vibrated through the soles of my Pumas in tommy-gun bursts: a Thompson on Thompson.

Zev sighed. "Look," he said, "your dad is not an easy man. But he loved that building, and they tore it down. People respond in unexpected ways when things they love get damaged. And yeah, his way sure isn't the only way." He watched his own fingers drumming the metal tabletop. "Can I show you something?"

I followed him to a three-foot-tall Hostess CupCakes display cabinet under his narrow loft bed. On its white grillwork shelves stood a number of unusual, very old objects. The only thing they seemed to have in common was that every one of them had something wrong with it.

"I call these Poignant Repairs," he said. "They're antique objects, some of them completely unremarkable to begin with, that broke at some point in the past but whose owners were so fond of them that they went to extraordinary lengths to fix them. In doing that, they transformed the object, by their ingenuity and affection, into something completely new and singular."

Zev squatted down so his face was only a few inches from his ragtag collection.

"Kids do this all the time," he went on. "A favorite stuffed animal loses an eye, right, so in its place they have their mom sew on a button from last year's winter coat. Or a toy car's tire goes missing, so they replace it with one of those little round rubber bands from their big brother's braces. But most adults forget how to care that much. They get impatient. All they see are the flaws, in the object and in their own craft. So into the wastebasket it goes."

Zev picked up a pitcher whose glaze looked like brown lava cascading down its sides.

"Take a look," he said. "This is a Bennington earthenware pitcher made probably around 1910. At some point its handle broke off. But instead of just tossing the pitcher out, someone took remarkable care to fashion this handsome replacement handle for it out of tin, which they attached with nuts and bolts through two holes they had very artfully drilled in the pottery."

The handle totally didn't match the pitcher, but that made the whole thing look cooler somehow. Less ordinary. You could even see the hammer marks on the tin, where the guy had beaten the handle into a graceful curve. Zev put the pitcher in my hands. I closed my fingers around the handle, which curled perfectly into my palm the way a cat nestles in snug behind your knees when you're sleeping on your side.

"And check it out," Zev said, taking the pitcher from me and turning it sideways. "The guy who did this repair, a Mr. Frühman, was so proud of his handiwork that he even crafted a brass plate for his name on the inside of the handle."

Zev returned the pitcher to its shelf, alongside a glass goblet with a prosthetic marble foot and the carved white king from a chess set whose crown's lost cross had been replaced with a typesetter's tiny *X* turned slantwise.

"So isn't this all just a particular kind of restoration?"

"No way. Restoration is basically a fancy word for trying to hit rewind, struggling to take an object back to an earlier version of itself. This is actually kinda the opposite. It's an act of idiosyncratic *creation* that carries within it a pretty violent implied *destruction*—the destruction of any possibility of returning the object to its former state."

"Of *unbreaking* it, you mean?"

Zev laughed. "Yeah, of unbreaking it." He gnawed an already gnawed thumbnail. "Because unbreaking something, as you put it, even if it was possible, is a pretty unimaginative thing to do. It may be a craft, but it sure ain't art."

He picked up a two-toothed tortoiseshell comb carved with swirling, dragony-floral designs.

"My pal Marilynn Gelfman gave me this one. You can see that at one time it snapped at its two weakest places—probably, Marilynn figures, while fastening one of those Spanish lace shawls to a woman's coiled mass of dark hair. But you see those beautiful little silver reinforcements that are holding the comb together now?"

I peered closely and saw the absolutely *tiny* silver scraps he was talking about, each smaller than my pinky nail. They were engraved with impossibly fine floral designs, and fastened to the two halves of the tortoiseshell comb by the most infinitesimal nails I'd ever seen. I can't say I'd ever really given a crap about a woman's comb before, but this one *was* pretty amazing.

"The damage was the opportunity, you see," Zev said. "Without damage, there's no discovery." He was marveling at the thing as if he were laying eyes on it for the first time. "It was a pretty nice comb to begin with, you know, like a lot of pretty nice combs." He returned it to the shelf. "But now it's the only one like it in the world. Now it's perfectly *itself*."

I mulled this over, unsure why it made me feel both lonesome and energized.

32

A BOY OF ONLY FAIR-TO-MIDDLING COURAGE does what he has to do. I waited till Dani's cranky Irish doorman slipped around the corner for a smoke, then snuck through her lobby. All the way up the gray staircase, the bottom foot or two of its walls were snowdrifted with white swoops of spackle. Patched up, sure, but *very* West Side to still need painting after all these months.

I'm not certain what my plan was, but I know it didn't include getting busted by one of Dani's obnoxious college-age brothers the very *second* I popped my head into the eleventh-floor hall. He had poofy black David Cassidy hair parted in the middle, and he was just coming out their front door when he spotted me. He looked me over skeptically while I tried to explain myself.

"Y'know what?" he said, before I'd gotten very far. "Save it. I suddenly realize it's *way* too much work to pretend I'm interested." He shouted over his shoulder: "Yo, *Dani*! You got a little admirer skulking around out here. Squeaky voice like his balls haven't dropped yet." He thought a minute, then yelled into the apartment, "*See?* I *told* you you had friends!"

A TV spasmed with canned laughter from somewhere inside. After a few moments, Dani appeared at the door in a Bruce Lee T-shirt and blue pajama bottoms, looking thin and winter-pale. A little "Oh!" of surprise escaped her when she saw me.

Her brother studied her. "Looks like *someone* wasn't expected," he said, peering at her in a way that somehow seemed both mocking and protective. "Shall I show your gentleman caller the gate?"

"No, no," Dani said. "This is Griffin. From school. It's fine."

Brother was not satisfied. "What's in the *Big Brown Bag*, Griffin from School?"

I was, in fact, carrying a big brown bag, which was helpfully printed with the words *Big Brown Bag*.

"None of your *bees*wax, *Brian*," Dani said, leading me inside by the elbow. "Don't answer him," she ordered me.

What do you bring someone who's sick? Food, right? Homemade chicken soup or a tray of lasagne or something. Much better than one of those hokey Get Well cards from Lamston's—because what if Quig was totally full of it and Dani wasn't sick at all? Food would work either way.

"So what *is* in the Big Brown Bag?" Dani asked me. We were sitting on the saggy blue velvet sofa in her living room, not far from several enormous homegrown avocado trees. Their leaves were big green paddles.

I lifted a large Tupperware tub from the bag and placed it on the Lucite-cube table. "Hungry?"

She didn't say anything.

"This is a little breakfast delicacy I whipped up at home," I told her. "Just for you, as a kind of peace offering. Me and Kyle invented it at the beginning of the year. It's evolved over time, but today, I'm really pretty sure, I per*fect*ed it!" I peeled off the top—"*Et, voilà, mademoiselle!*"—and tipped the tub toward Dani.

She peered in reluctantly, then jerked her head back in horror. "*Gross!* What *is* that? It looks like somebody already ate it!"

That cracked me up. "I know, I know," I said. "But it's as tasty as it is ugly, I *swear*. All we need to do is heat it up."

"It's *green*! What the hell are you trying to feed me here?"

"Well, it's a scrambly little breakfast masterpiece I like to call the *Eggsorcist*. Repugnant, yes, but so dia*bo*lically delicious that after just one bite it's sure to possess your body and soul"—Dani's face was a total blank—"and maybe even lift you up in the air and spin you around above your bed while a gnarly old priest shrieks at it to release you." (I'd never actually seen *The Exorcist,* but everyone knew about Linda Blair getting twirled around all freakily by Satan, and I thought pretending to have seen an R movie might make me seem less middle-schoolish.)

Dani didn't say anything, so I kept blabbering: "Its ingredients are pretty simple: six jumbo eggs, six ladlefuls of Seabrook Farms creamed spinach, a six-ounce can of StarKist tuna, six tablespoons of lard, six Steak-umm strips, six dollops of Hellmann's mayo, and six tablespoons of bacon grease—you know, that congealed goop from the coffee can you keep on the stove. All of which—and I think this is safely within the Recommended Daily Allowance—adds up to roughly six hundred sixty-six thousand calories a serving."

For the longest time, Dani just stared at me, her face betraying nothing. Then a Dani-esque smile began to play across her lips.

"What?" I asked.

Her smirk grew broader. "You are an extremely considerate bozo, you know that?"

"But it's the *Eggsorcist*!" I protested helplessly. "Surely you are not shunning the Eggsorcist?! Have a bite! You'll love it."

Dani was laughing openly now.

"What?" I pleaded. "What is it?"

She put her hand gently on my forearm. Still grinning, she looked into my eyes and said, "You *do* know that I was hospitalized for my anorexia last month, right?"

I'd never even heard of anorexia. Everyone knew that chubby girls like Quig ate too *much,* and *that* was a problem, but I'd always thought the skinny girls were doing just fine.

"So it means you can't eat?" I asked, after she'd spent a few minutes trying to teach me about the world of eating disorders.

"I *can.* I just don't. Not enough, anyway."

I nodded as if there were something sensible going on in my head.

"And you know what?" Dani went on. "It's weird. *Deciding* not to eat kind of felt really *good* sometimes, in a way. Like I was in control of myself for once. Like I'm choosing—*was* choosing—stuff entirely for me."

She took me to the fridge in the kitchen and showed me a bunch of special milk shake cans she was supposed to drink three times a day now; they were all stacked up in the back, chocolate mostly, with a couple of pink ones that must have been either strawberry or cherry. They looked sort of gross and industrial, but she said they'd "fattened her up" to 106 pounds from the 94 she'd weighed when her mom checked her into the ICU the second-to-last week of school. Though I had no clue what a girl was supposed to weigh, neither number sounded like a whole hell of a lot. Last I'd checked, my own weight was 133 with my tighty-whities on.

"Did you know you're the only one who came to see me?" Dani asked. "Except Valerie—she came the first weekend I got back from Roosevelt, and acted really weird, like I was *contagious* or something, and then she never came back. Other than her, it's like no one at school even noticed I was gone."

Dani padded over to the kitchen table and carefully lifted herself onto its enameled metal top. She let her skinny pajama'd legs dangle.

"I mean, my brothers have been *okay,* in a Neanderthal kind of way, and Mom fusses over me in this totally annoying, *How could any daughter of* mine *do such a thing to herself* way—at least when she's not at one of her hairy-armpit conventions with her lefty friends up at Barnard." She gnawed on her lip. "But otherwise, you know, I kind of got to feeling that if I stopped eating completely, I'd just"—she looked away from me, down at her swinging feet—"I'd just disappear."

I went over and sat beside her on the kitchen table. Her thigh was surprisingly warm where it touched mine.

"You wouldn't . . . ," I started. "I mean, you didn't. I mean . . . *I* noticed."

Neither of us said anything for a long time. When I finally turned to look at her, I was startled to discover that she was studying my face.

She smiled a small smile. "You're pretty hard to figure, you know that? I mean, for such a nice guy, why do you do such *jerky* things?"

I looked down at my sneakers, my palms on the worn-smooth knees of my Levi's cords. "Maybe I'm a jerky guy who does *nice* things?"

Nothing happened for a bit. Then I felt her small hand come to rest on top of mine. I'd never looked closely at her fingers before. They were elegant and bony: *elegaunt.* Maybe she was two things at the same time, too.

Dani's breath warmed my ear. "I'm glad you came," she said.

33

WHILE MONSIEUR CLAUDE was in the kitchen lighting one of his stinky unfiltered Gauloises on the stove, I snagged the *Times* from his place at the table and fled upstairs with it to the one spot I knew I couldn't be found: inside the cabinet under the window seat in Mom's bedroom. I'd been spending a lot of time in there the past few days, scouring the paper for any scraps of information about the police investigation into the stolen Bogardus.

This morning Mom came back before I was even halfway through the first section, but I was prepared for that: when I saw that she was settling in on her bed, I carefully pulled the cabinet door closed from the inside with a rubber band looped round its knob, and I switched on the nifty headlamp I'd rigged by gaffer-taping Dad's penlight to the bill of my Mets helmet. It was reassuringly familiar there in my old hiding place; the exposed brick wall under the window gave the space a cavy coolness I'd always loved.

The first bit of unsettling follow-up news had been buried in an article just two days after we were spotted loading the Bogardus into the truck. I still had the clipping here inside the cabinet. The story was headlined RIVERSIDE BRIDGE STRIPPED OF BRONZE, PART OF A WAVE OF THEFTS. Apparently someone had swiped seven sections of an ornamental bronze railing from the Riverside Drive bridge at Ninety-Sixth Street. The article said it was a big deal because the bridge had been the work of Carrère and Hastings, the same architects who had designed the world-famous Lion Library on Forty-Second Street.

There was a photo, too. It showed a guy and his daughter—or maybe his long-haired son—leaning on a railing whose elaborate, curving decoration looked vaguely like a row of bronze violins. Attached to it was the city's pathetic wood replacement for a stolen section: a bunch of two-by-fours banged together in the most primitive way you could imagine.

The article listed a bunch of other cool-sounding architectural treasures that had been stolen from around town, including two lavishly adorned lampposts from the Firemen's Memorial on Riverside and 100th Street and an entire bronze statue of a big-time nineteenth-century architect named Richard Morris Hunt, which someone had swiped right off its plinth in Central Park.

Most of the stolen bronze is not recovered, but in one instance a bronze urn torn from its base at the Grand Army Plaza monument in Brooklyn was traced and recovered at a belt-buckle factory in the same borough. Its thieves were later apprehended.

This was the first time it occurred to me that Dad wasn't alone in preying on the city. The whole damned place was cannibalizing itself. But the part of the article that made me queasy came right at the end:

In a related development, the police arrested two men and were seeking a third yesterday in the theft of cast-iron panels of a dismantled landmark, the Bogardus Building. The two were apprehended after the police traced a truck that had been seen leaving a storage area at West and Chambers Streets with several of the panels.

Arrested were Furman Boyd, 46 years old, of 121 East 120th Street, and Curtis Knowles, 28, of 155 East 104th Street, both laborers.

Every time I reread those last two paragraphs, I recalled the feeling of Curtis's big callusy palm on my forehead, shoving me down into the truck to protect me from being seen. Why should that hand get cuffed behind Curtis's back at his roachy Harlem apartment while I got my own bedroom in a five-story brownstone? Was Dad right that only "laborers" got arrested for this sort of thing, or did he think the police were onto *him* now, too, the "third man"? Is that why he'd been so jumpy when I confronted him down at his studio?

Today's paper was loaded with the usual sorts of cheerful news: more than five hundred American unions were on strike, mostly over low pay; Nixon's cohorts were complaining that the head of Congress's impeachment panel was biased; one of the Watergate "plumbers" was unveiling a new legal defense; Bobby Fischer had renounced his world chess title over a rules dispute (no one knew if the chess federation would accept his resignation or negotiate); both the Mets and the Yankees were in last place; the Equal Rights Amendment was on the rocks; and Harry Browne, best-selling author of gloom-and-doom books about "dollar devaluation and runaway inflation," was in town—he'd told a crowd at Carnegie Hall that a depression was just around the corner and that he was preparing for it by loading a three-year supply of canned goods and Chianti into an emergency retreat in the frozen north, four hundred miles above West Vancouver.

There was nothing else in today's paper about the Bogardus or any other architectural thefts. I wanted to get out and stretch my legs, but when I popped the door open a sliver to peek out, Mom was hunched over a woodcut on her bed with her legs crossed, her yellow peasant dress hiked partway up her thighs. She was wearing maroon underwear, which I really didn't want to see, and she was using one of her little U-shaped blades to gouge out long strips of wood that curled, as they came loose from the board, in a way that reminded me of the grotesque World's Longest Fingernails belonging to that wrinkly Indian guy in *The Guinness Book of World Records*.

She clearly wasn't going anywhere soon. There was a cuppa on the travel-scuffed Louis Vuitton steamer trunk she used as a bedside table. Every so often she yawned and took a sip.

There are worse things than being trapped into taking a summer nap, though. I pulled the door tight again and shifted around in my little cave. There were more than enough odds and ends of my childhood in there for me to make myself comfortable. *The Return of the King* was a couple inches thick and made a perfectly passable pillow once I took off my pajama bottoms and bunched them on top of the book to make it softer. And a few old issues of *Ranger Rick* spread out on the floor made it a bit less cold against my naked legs.

The only way I could fit lying down was by curling into the fetal position, but I liked that. It was comforting drifting off to sleep in there like when I was little. Now, as then, I could faintly hear the twittery classical music from Mom's radio, which was tuned to QXR as usual. Except for a thin rectangle of light seeping in around the cabinet door, I was cocooned in darkness.

The terrifying bass-note *THUMP* that startled me awake sometime later felt like nothing less than all that darkness collapsing onto my head. The impact was right on top of me, shaking the too-small walls of my sleep. At first I thought I was back in our Echo Harbor cottage, where daybreak seagulls dive-bombed our roof with clams to smash them open. But as I shook off my disorientation, I quickly identified the sound as a big shoe stomping onto the cushionless top of the window seat above me. Someone had broken in by climbing the tree branch I'd failed to cut.

I heard a kind of gasp of surprise from Mom—less a scream than a startled intake of breath. My heart drumming, I pushed the cabinet door open a crack and blinked into the light to see a big man kneeling on the bed in front of Mom, leaning desperately into her. He had her by the shoulders, and seemed to be trying to wrench her body toward him so her mouth would meet his.

"Stop it! *Stop it!*" she cried, squirming and slap-grappling at his hands on her body until he gave out a horrible throaty groan and abruptly pulled away from her, staring in startled agony at her woodcut tool, whose little U-shaped blade was lodged half an inch deep in his upper arm.

"You *bitch!*" he roared, pulling the blade out with his fist and throwing it aside. Enraged, he pushed her down and kneeled on top of her, pinning her arms with his hands, her dress hiked up to her waist and her naked legs splayed on either side of him. Again, he leaned in and tried to kiss her, but she shook her head violently from side to side, battering his face with her chin.

"Get *off* me!" she yelled. "Get *off*! What the hell do you think you're doing?"

"*Me?*" the man snarled. "Where do *you* get off locking me out of my own home!"

"It's *not*—" Mom began, but he thrust his mouth against hers, and maybe his teeth cut her lip, because her words dissolved into a hard little bleat of pain. For just a moment more Mom struggled, and then she stopped moving and so did he, the two of them locked together on the bed in motionless misery.

I don't know if I pushed the cabinet door so hard on purpose, but it swung all the way open on its hinges until its porcelain knob banged against the outside.

Both bodies on the bed jolted in response as if electrocuted, and both my parents' heads turned abruptly to look my way, their eyes wide with oddly similar looks of panic. Dad was crying, red-faced and helpless even in his position of supposed dominance. Mom was indignant and out of breath.

She blinked away her indignation then, blinked away my father. I saw her look over at me kneeling in the little doorway of the cabinet in my underwear—really look at me, as if seeing me for the first time in a very long while.

"Oh, Griffin," she said in a voice you could barely hear. "I am so sorry."

PART FOUR

SALVAGE

34

Hᴇ ɴᴇᴠᴇʀ ᴄᴀᴍᴇ ʙᴀᴄᴋ that summer. We never heard from him at all.

My mother's drowsy aloofness had vanished. She seemed more alert, more *there,* than I could remember seeing her, like when you sharpened our RCA Victor's fuzzy picture by crumpling knobs of tin-foil onto its rabbit ears. She was also newly, overbearingly attentive to me.

At first, I liked it. Eating a hot dog in the spray of that nifty man-made waterfall in Paley Park wasn't bad, and neither was drinking an egg cream at Agora. But she kept asking me if I wanted to talk about stuff.

I didn't. At least not the kind of stuff she had any clue about. The thing that was worrying me most, if she really wanted to know, was the condition of George Thomas Seaver's left hip. It was hard to over-state how bad the Mets had sucked all season. Just last fall we'd come within one World Series win of knocking off the scary-swaggery Reg-gie Jackson–Catfish Hunter Oakland A's. (Was there a more dumb-ass team name in *all* of sports than the *Athletics*? Was there a relief pitcher *any*where who looked more like a mustache-twiddling silent-film villain than Rollie Fingers?) But this season our team was just fall-ing to pieces. Willie Mays had retired, Buddy Harrelson was reduced to pinch-running duties by a broken hand, and the pitching perfor-mances of Seaver—by far my favorite player—had gone from lights-out to ordinary. Today was the exact halfway point in the season, Game 81 of 162, and we were in last place, a putrid ten games under .500. Seaver, after winning nineteen games and the Cy Young the year before, actually had a *losing* record of 5–6. It all came down to the health of his hip.

My mother was pushing to take me to Tru-Tred for new penny loafers that afternoon, but there was no way I was missing Seaver's start. Even watching the game on Channel 9 was a fallback plan. For weeks, I'd been drinking quarts of Dairylea milk like a madman, cutting the waxy rectangular coupons out of the back of each carton in hopes of collecting the twenty you needed to earn a ticket to Shea. I'd only gotten to sixteen, though, so Channel 9 it was going to have to be.

Lindsey Nelson, wearing one of his customary hideous plaid jackets in the Shea booth, had just gotten through telling Bob Murphy how urgently the struggling Mets needed "Tom Terrific to be terrific again" when the phone rang. It was Dani.

"You busy?" she asked me. "I could use your help with something."

I thought I heard Quig or Mom pick up downstairs and palm the receiver, so I played it even cooler than I probably would have otherwise. I told Dani all about Seaver, and the game, and how I couldn't possibly miss it.

"So watch it here," she said. "I've got it on anyway, and Seaver usually goes eight or nine, so you've got plenty of time to get over here and still catch most of his start."

"You're a *Mets fan*?" I asked.

"What kind of a question is that? I thought you *liked* me. You think I'd root for the *Stankees*?" The disgusted way she said it, it was as if I'd implied she was a die-hard fan of the raw sewage flushed into the Hudson from the houseboats at the Seventy-Ninth Street Boat Basin, where Kyle and I sometimes went turdwatching.

I didn't know what was safe to bring Dani anymore, so I didn't bring her anything. I just sniffed the pits of my orange "Ya Gotta Believe"

T-shirt to make sure I smelled okay, and gave my tongue a few pep-perminty Binaca blasts every few minutes on my way over on the Eighty-Sixth Street crosstown.

Seaver had already come out to the mound for the fourth inning when I joined Dani on her parents' bed to watch. We were the only ones in the apartment. Our guys were up five–zip over the Giants, but for some reason I still couldn't get comfortable.

"Would you stop jiggling your foot already?" Dani said. "You're making me nervous."

"Sorry."

"I tell you what. Why don't you go get us a bottle of something or other from my dad's booze cabinet. It's in the hall outside my room, that low thing with the painted-over glass door."

There were about a million liquor bottles in the cabinet, but every one I pulled out was so nearly empty you wondered why they hadn't just thrown it away. Finally I found two half-full ones whose funny foreign names sounded like Monty Python characters. I brought them to Dani on her folks' bed.

"Noilly Prat?" she asked, crinkling her nose. "You think we're gonna drink straight vermouth?"

I shrugged. I'd never heard of vermouth.

"And Fernet-Branca?" She held out the second bottle. "You know what this stuff is?"

I searched my memory. *Fernet Branca* did kind of ring a bell.

"Wait," I said, "isn't that the guy who gave up that home run to what's-his-name—Bobby Thomson? *You* know: 'The Giants win the pennant! The Giants win the pennant!'"

She stared at me. "Are you serious?"

I was. The name *Fernet Branca* sounded so familiar. I thought maybe it was a liquor named after a ballplayer, like a grown-up version of the Baby Ruth bar.

Dani had begun to giggle.

"That's *Ralph* Branca," she said. "Not *Fernet*-Branca." She put her hand on my cheek and looked at me in this really wonderful, affec-tionate way. "Ralph Branca is a toothy Brooklyn Dodgers pitcher who gave up the most heartbreaking home run in, like, his team's entire history. *Fernet*-Branca is a disgusting Italian after-dinner liqueur. My dad brought it back from Rome. Said one of the professors there told him it could cure any head cold in twenty-four hours."

She twisted the top off and motioned for me to take a swig.

"What if someone comes home?"

"Not gonna happen. Brian's my only brother who's even around this summer, and he's at his stoner girlfriend's in Amagansett."

"What about your folks?"

"They're house-hunting in Philadelphia—or just outside it, I guess." She gestured with the bottle again. Its contents smelled vile.

"You're *moving*?"

"Who knows? Dad got an offer from UPenn. I guess he's considering it. He loves New York and all—he's nuts about it, actually—but he says the city's dying."

"So he's *moving*? Are you kidding me? What a *wuss*."

"Why're you getting so mad?"

"Who said I'm mad? I just think your dad's a wuss, that's all. So what if the city *is* dying? He's just gonna up and leave?"

"He's got a job offer. What's he supposed to do? Go down with the ship?"

I grabbed the bottle and slugged back a throatful of Fernet-Branca. It was viscous and fiery, with a hideous bitter kicker of an aftertaste. I had to clench my teeth to keep from throwing up. Dani took a swig, too, wincing as it went down.

"It *is* pretty gross," she said, wiping her mouth on her wrist. "But believe me, you get used to it."

I took another swig, then another. It was a little less repellent each time. I was starting to feel more . . . I don't know, at *home,* maybe. I felt like I was right where I was supposed to be. I settled back into Dani's parents' poofy pillows, and Dani joined me there, her bare shoulder just touching mine.

Seaver froze the Giants' hitter, a lefty, with a curveball at the knees for strike three. I pumped my fist. Two outs.

"Maybe there *is* hope," I said. "My man looks good."

"No, he's laboring."

"What're you talking about? He just struck the guy out looking."

"He's not finishing his pitches." She pointed at the screen. "Here, watch."

Seaver wound up and threw a riding fastball high and inside. The hitter danced out of its path.

"There!" Dani said. "See that?"

"See what? Just a little chin music, that's all."

"You're not looking."

"I am too looking."

"No, you're not. Not if you don't see how off he is today. The first rule of looking, Griffin, is to *look*."

Seaver wandered around the mound, rubbing the ball between his hands, scowling at its seams. It would've been awful to be that ball and have him looking at you that way.

"I'm telling you," Dani said, "he's not finishing his pitches. Seaver gets his power from those big thick legs of his, driving toward the plate. But look at his right pant leg—there's barely any dirt on it."

"So?"

"So when Seaver's right, he rotates his hips and follows through so completely that the front of his right pant leg always drags in the dirt. It's usually filthy by the fifth inning, right on the knee, where no other pitcher's uniform ever gets dirty."

"I never noticed that."

"Yeah, but today his knee's not coming anywhere near the dirt because he's not coming all the way toward Grote."

Seaver was back on the pitching rubber. He shook off a sign from Grote, then threw a breaking ball, which the batter bounced to Milner at first for the third out. During the commercials, one for Rheingold and another one I don't remember, Dani and I took a couple more swigs of the booze, which we had taken to calling "Mr. Branca," out of respect. I was feeling pretty excellent—until, that is, the broadcast came back on and Bob Murphy told us something that pretty much sank the Mets' season then and there: Seaver had taken himself out of the game with a sharp pain in his left hip.

Dani and I groaned in unison.

"*Ohhh,* that's a *te*rrible blow to the New York Metropolitans," Bob said in that folksy, not-from-here way he said everything. Yogi Berra, our manager, was already trudging out to talk to the home plate umpire about the pitching change.

"It's *over,* Yogi!" I yelled at the TV. "The whole damn season."

Dani went and turned the volume all the way down. But even without sound, I couldn't bear to watch anymore.

"What was it you needed help with, anyway?" I asked.

"Huh?"

"Help. You said you needed my help. That's why you called me, remember?"

"Oh, yeah yeah yeah, sure I do. Wait here a sec."

She came back a couple minutes later with a plastic serving tray containing a bunch of unusual items: a Popsicle still in its wrapper, some paper napkins, a bottle of rubbing alcohol, a great big sewing needle, a few nipply-looking white-tipped matches, and a little square of wood that seemed to be a blank Scrabble tile. She pushed her mom's hand mirror aside and set the tray down on the bedside table, on top of a small pile of *Ms.* magazines.

"What's all this for?"

"Well," she said playfully, "there are some things a girl can't do herself." She lay down flat on her back with her slender arms raised on the pillows above her, her burnished-copper hair spilling onto the white bedspread. "I've decided I'd look pretty fabulous with a single gold hoop earring. Kind of piratey, you know?"

"I guess."

"So you're gonna pierce my ear for me."

A prickle ran up my spine. I told her I didn't think I wanted to do that.

"Sure you do. I'll talk you through it."

Dani held the unopened Popsicle to her left ear to numb it, squirming a bit at the cold. I sat on the edge of the bed. At her instruction, I struck a match and poked the needle tip into its flame, then put the needle aside for a second. I rubbed alcohol on her earlobe with the corner of a napkin, and she squirmed again.

"That *tickles*!"

"This was *your* brilliant idea," I said. "Shove over."

She did, and I kneeled on the bed beside her with the needle in my right hand, carefully pressing the wooden Scrabble tile against the back of her earlobe with my left. This was *such* a terrible idea. There was no way this was going to end well.

"Stop giggling!" I said. "Your ear is jiggling all around."

"Then *clearly*, Doctor," Dani replied, "you need a better angle," and she pulled me on top of her.

"Careful!" I cried—it was all I could do to hang on to the needle without stabbing her in the face with it—"I could really hurt you."

I was now straddling her at the waist, her hip bones digging into the insides of my thighs. I felt the first tinglings of a stiffy pressing against her flat stomach. I wondered which would be more embarrassing, if I popped wood right then or if I didn't. It was very confusing.

"Well?" she said. She took the Scrabble tile from my hand and held it tight against the back of her own earlobe. "What're you waiting for?"

It was a big sharp needle. The thought of jabbing it into her flesh was pretty horrifying. She told me I needed to get it all the way through in one push, "otherwise it's gonna hurt like a motherfucker."

I took the Scrabble tile from her fingers, and she turned her head to offer me her ear. Her neck looked extraordinarily fragile, the branching veins slender and blue beneath her thin skin. The Visible Woman.

I wanted to touch her. I put the needle down on the tray and reached out my hand until my middle and index fingers found the delicate bones edging her throat. There was a little hollow there, a private place as perfect and smooth as a sake cup. I pressed my fingertips into her flesh in that spot, just lightly, just enough to feel less outside of her, then moved them up one of the two slender tendons that extended upward in a V from her collarbone.

My fingers stopped at the rise of her neck gland. It was so exposed, that little bump, such a measure of trust that she would offer it to me. I surprised myself by leaning forward and touching it with my lips. It felt lumpy and odd, but terrifically real, too, so different from the cloying perfection of a marble goddess or a grinny cigarette-ad model (*Newport, Alive with pleasure!*).

I got a little embarrassed then, and got back to business. I held the Scrabble tile firmly against the back of her earlobe, which was surprisingly rubbery but also kind of beautiful. I picked up the needle and held it above her neck. For all her bravado, I could see her eyes getting all slitty in anticipation of pain, her cheek flushing marbly red. It bothered me that she was scared. I didn't want to be someone who scared her.

I brought the point of the needle toward her earlobe, gritted my teeth, and took a deep breath. But my hand did nothing. I couldn't bring myself to jab her with it.

"What's the matter?" She opened her blue eyes wide and looked up at me. "You afraid of needles?"

"No," I said. "I'm really not."

"Then what is it?"

I looked down at her body under my body. Fierce and fragile in her T-shirt and cutoff jeans.

"*My* ear," I said.

"What?"

"*My* ear. I think you should pierce *my* ear."

The idea caught her by surprise, but she liked it. A lot. She propped herself up on her elbows and gave me a sneaky smile. "Why do you want your ear pierced?"

I shrugged and rolled off her. I *didn't* want my ear pierced, actually. But with the memory still fresh in my mind of my father pinning my mother down, the thought of making Dani bleed sickened me. And I figured the only way she was ever really going to trust me after I'd tricked her into tearing her tongue was if I gave her a chance to hurt me back and trusted her not to.

Dani pounced. Before I had a chance to change my mind, she'd pushed my shoulders down into the bed and climbed on top of me.

"Here." She grabbed her mom's hand mirror from the bedside table and held it above my face, which looked flushed and not unanxious. "Which ear?"

I pointed at my left one, and she gave me the Popsicle to press against it.

"No *way* am I wearing any piratey gold hoop, though," I said. "Just so you know."

She took the Popsicle. "Of course not. We'll get you a cool little stud or something." She dabbed alcohol on my ear, tossed the clumped wet napkin on the floor. She looked down at me with a little grin. *"Ready?"*

I nodded, and a maniacal electric bee descended from nowhere and—*"Yaaggh!"* I hollered—rammed its pitiless stinger through my poor earlobe. Dani gave a happy cackle and pulled the needle out.

"There," she said. "Now, that wasn't so bad, was it?"

I nodded. Remarkably, the psychotic bee had vanished in seconds, leaving only a minor pulsing discomfort in the bottom of my ear.

I started to mutter something I hoped might sound clever, but Dani shut me up with a kiss, our tongues swimming together like dolphins wrestling. Her mouth, the flavor of Fernet-Branca and Cheerios, was a private hungry place she welcomed me into, and until that moment I didn't know you could feel so magnificently lost and at home at the same time. I dove into that feeling, warm and woozy and not worried about anything for a change, and as we rolled onto our sides she took my hand and guided it under her T-shirt, up her flat stomach and over the cage of her ribs, to the soft warm Dani-ness that rose and fell and rose over her fifteen-year-old heart.

I awoke sometime later from a deep Fernet-Branca snooze to find Dani curled up beside me, pushing something pointy and cold through the new hole in my ear.

"Just a sec," she said. She placed a flat something against the other side of my lobe and pressed it firmly. It felt pinchy but not painful. "There. Go take a look." She smiled at me. "I found something way better than a stud. I think you'll like it."

In her parents' bathroom mirror, I saw affixed to my ear a small tarnished disc that looked exactly like a subway token, only much smaller. It was like a Shrinky Dink after you put it in the oven to reduce it to a miniature of itself.

"Is this a real token? From before they made them big?"

She laughed. "Yep. My dad hoarded a bunch before they raised the fare 'cause he's cheap and thought they were bluffing about changing the token. When he got stuck with them, he had this one made into a tie pin. But I thought it'd look better on you."

I looked at the new me in the mirror, the sophisticated, nearly ninth-grade me who had Frenched a girl and felt that girl's left boob and then Frenched her again. I had to admit, the antique mini subway token did look pretty cool. I closed my eyes and touched it, to see if I could differentiate the angular cutout letters with my index finger: *N . . . Y . . . C.*

"Holy shit!" I hollered. "Holy shit! Oh *no!*"

"What? What is it?"

"It's the *gay* ear! You pierced my *gay* ear! The right one's the gay one, *right?*"

She turned my shoulders so I was facing her and studied me a moment. Then she exploded in laughter. "I'm so sorry!" She covered her mouth with her hand, but the laughs kept rippling out between her fingers. "I didn't *real*ize, I really didn't! That's the one you *told* me to pierce!"

"*Yeah,* but *I* was looking in the mirror. The left was the right. You should've corrected me!"

She was still laughing. "But I was *facing* you! Your right was *my* left, too!"

"You made me gay!"

Another little giggle escaped her. "I *swear* I didn't do it on purpose. But it doesn't matter, anyway. I mean, nobody believes all that stuff about left and right, do they?"

"I guess not."

I was leaning on the sink, my palms flat on its porcelain. I could feel Dani's warmth pressing against my back. She put her arms around me from behind, looping them across my chest like a scarf.

But then, in the mirror, I saw her shake her head. Something was bothering her, something serious.

"What is it?"

"Nothing," she said, hesitating. "It's just that . . ."

"*What?* Tell me."

She looked at me very earnestly for what seemed a long time, her face growing more and more distressed. She didn't blink. Then, shaking her head in wonder, a fond, gamine smile creeping across her lips, she said: "I can't believe my boyfriend's a *homo!*"

Best. Day. Ever.

35

FALL FELL. Still no sign of my father, which was forcing some pretty big changes in our house. With the spigot of alimony checks turned off, paying for private school was an impossibility. This had caused me enormous anxiety through most of the summer—it's tough enough to have your dad vanish without also being separated from your friends—until my mother finally went and had a big meeting with Dr. Townsend, our principal. The upshot was that the school agreed to come up with the financial aid to let me stay; though I was sometimes disruptive and a real headache for my teachers, he told her, I was still one of their stronger English students. But he wouldn't offer the same support for Quigley, who hated school and often cut class to smoke clove cigarettes or pot on the bridle path by the reservoir. She was sent to Julia Richman, a horribly overcrowded public school on Sixty-Seventh and Second, which she clearly considered my fault, though in the end I don't think she disliked her new school any more than her old one. She just wasn't much of a school person.

Dani moved to the Philadelphia suburbs over Christmas vacation. Her father had taken the UPenn job. He was going to teach grad students all about the built environment and the fraying urban fabric and how New York was dying. I was pretty upset about Dani's leaving, but we smooched a bunch in her still-unpainted back hallway, and she assured me that we were still going out; her father was keeping a small, rent-controlled apartment in Morningside Heights, and she'd be back to see me on vacations. Whenever I missed her over the coming months, I took the homemade foam sword she'd left me as a souvenir, and I made myself feel better by biffing Quigley with it for no reason.

Dani did come back for a few days in March, brimming with horror stories about the soul-deadening sameness of the suburbs. For the brief time she was in town, she wanted to explore it with me as much as possible. We snuck into the south gatehouse of the Central Park Reservoir, the one where the torture scene in *Marathon Man* would later be filmed, and fooled around in there while the joggers did their laps around the path outside.

Kyle told me I was a pussy for getting hung up on one girlfriend who didn't even live in the city anymore. He, meanwhile, was always disappearing into closets with girls at parties so he could tell us all later how far he'd gotten with them. I chatted up a few girls that ninth-grade year, too, but none of them were really Dani-like enough to tempt me. So much of the time you could see they were saying what they thought you wanted them to say, which I hated. Kyle didn't care much what they said, as long as he could get his hand down their pants. Part of me was jealous of his success, but I was also put off. He seemed to exult in casting off his girlfriends, and one time he even tape-recorded himself dumping a Town School girl who wore too much eyeliner.

We drifted apart during the year, and I found myself hanging out with Rafferty more. We both liked to make awful puns and write silly stories, and we were competitive with each other about it. Most of our best work was contained in *The Punishment Book,* a giant volume kept by my favorite teacher, Ms. France, the head of the upper school. She was more interested in language than in discipline, so in lieu of detention she offered miscreants the opportunity to write a shaggy-dog story in that big book. As a result, Rafferty and I were always contriving ways to get into trouble so we would be allowed to pen another entry. I wrote mine in pencil, returning often to erase and rewrite, erase and rewrite. For me, nothing was ever finished.

The city continued its deterioration just fine without my father.

There was no money to fix or clean anything. Sometimes the subway cars were so defaced with graffiti you couldn't even see out the window. Cables had snapped on the Brooklyn Bridge, and the West Side Highway was still a ghost road two years after its collapse had forced its shutdown. David Schapiro, a friend of Rafferty's who lived in Chelsea, went roller-skating on it all the time, until he sprained his ankle jumping over a pothole. His skates were sneaker-skates, and while he was limping home, three kids from the projects jumped him and yanked them right off his feet.

New York had become world-famous as a hellhole of street crime, arson, and general mayhem. And just in case we were tempted to stop seeing ourselves that way, Hollywood was good enough to keep reminding us. The year my parents broke up, Martin Scorsese, himself a New Yorker, had given us *Mean Streets*. Then came *Death Wish* and that subway-hijacking epic Dad took me to, *The Taking of Pelham One Two Three*. This next cycle of the calendar would bring us *Dog Day Afternoon,* with *Taxi Driver* close on its heels, followed by *The Warriors*.

The TV was full of decay and desperation, too. Mayor Abe Beame, who seemed about as feckless as the mayor in *Pelham One Two Three,* got in front of the microphones and pretty much begged everyone to lend the city money by buying some kind of "notes." But no one wanted to take the risk.

By spring, the city was flat broke. Literally couldn't pay its bills. Who knew such a thing could happen? Beame warned of coming "horror cuts" to the city budget. He scheduled waves of layoffs: cops, garbagemen, hospital workers. Tens of thousands of protesters crowded into the skinny streets of the financial district to rail against some bank the city owed a buttload of money—apparently they were mad that the bankers had gone and said out loud what everybody already knew: that the city was at serious risk of going under.

One day Mathis brought home from the A.P. newsroom a scare-mongering pamphlet that the city unions (police, firefighters, and others) were threatening to distribute to tourists if Beame went through with firing all those cops and firemen. WELCOME TO FEAR CITY, the cover said above a drawing of a skull. A SURVIVAL GUIDE FOR VISITORS TO THE CITY OF NEW YORK.

Inside the little booklet, tourists were advised that the "incidence of crime and violence in New York City is shockingly high, and getting worse every day. During the four-month period ended Apr. 30, 1975, robberies were up 21%, aggravated assault was up 15%, larceny was up 22%, and burglary 19%." If the mayor now laid off public safety officers, the pamphlet warned, "the best advice we can give you is this: Stay away from New York City if you possibly can."

The guidelines offered to visitors who ignored this friendly advice were a bit over-the-top, but it was hard not to be unnerved by them anyway—after all, these were *the cops themselves* who were writing all this scary stuff: "Stay off the streets after 6 p.m.," the pamphlet cautioned, helpfully adding this warning: *"Do not walk:* If you must leave your hotel, summon a taxi by telephone." As for public transportation, "Subway crime is so high that the city recently had to close off the rear of each train in the evening so that the passengers could huddle together and be better protected. Accordingly, you should never ride the subway for any reason whatsoever."

Beame went ahead with his cuts anyway, and the unions got ornery. When the mayor's "crisis budget" took force in early summer, the garbagemen went out on strike, leaving tens of thousands of tons of stinky trash bags on curbs all over town. Just in time to bake during summer's ninety-degree afternoons.

In the early months of this gathering crisis, I made a habit of going down to look at my father's warehouse about once a week. It was always completely sealed, worn iron shutters and all. No sign of life. No answer when I buzzed the robot-girl's nipple. For a good while I also phoned his studio regularly. No one ever picked up, and eventually I started getting that cheery phone-lady's voice saying that the number I had dialed was no longer in service. ("Please check the number and dial again.")

I tried to forget about him, as Mom was clearly trying to. And for a while I thought I'd succeeded. But she had more distractions than I did, now that she was working six days a week at a friend's gallery down in SoHo. She had bills to pay, bills and more bills. Not me. So

264 THE GARGOYLE HUNTERS

in early July, with nothing to do now that school was out again, I decided to pay one last visit to Dad's warehouse to see if maybe he'd come back for the summer.

I picked the wrong day. Even before I got out of the subway station at City Hall, I could hear that something aboveground was very, very wrong. Ladies were clicking hurriedly down the steps in their high heels to get away. A low murmur of inarticulate fury cascaded down the stairs.

Out on the streets, hundreds of beefy men, most of them white guys who hadn't shaved, were milling about outside City Hall with a seething rage that seemed to be casting about for a target. Some held beer bottles, others handwritten signs.

BURN CITY BURN, one of the signs read. BEAME IS A DESERTER, A RAT, read another. HE LEFT THE CITY DEFENSELESS.

There were police all around, but they didn't seem to be doing anything to stop the chaos. One of them, way up on a horse with his nightstick and gun bulging out at his hips, actually looked like he was *begging* the angry men to calm down.

"What's going on?" I asked a nervous-looking man in a business suit.

"Laid-off cops," he told me.

All at once, the crowd found a direction. Swept up by its momentum, I was carried along against my will to the Brooklyn Bridge, where some of the angry men had blocked traffic with police barricades. Others were going around with keys, letting the air out of the stalled cars' tires. The traffic had backed up as far toward Brooklyn as you could see, and a cacophony of car horns broke out. Drivers shouted at the unemployed cops, who shouted back. A few of them surrounded a car and pounded on its windows.

"Turn it over!" someone yelled. "Turn it over!"

The driver inside, a small dark-skinned man with a pert mustache, looked petrified.

Three or four more men surrounded the car and began to rock it side to side. Several uniformed cops, including a silver-haired boss guy in a white collared shirt, trotted over to intervene. He had a hand on his billy club.

I didn't stick around to learn what was going to happen. Making myself as small as I could, I ducked under the sea of shoulders, darting into every opening I could find, forcing my way off the bridge. Down Park Row, around the bottom of the park, and west across Broadway.

The crowd thinned as I passed the Woolworth Building, then all but vanished by the time I reached West Broadway. I doubled back past a warehouse block that smelled of smoked cheese and made my way up to Dad's block. I needn't have bothered. The buzzers weren't even there anymore. Someone had yanked the robot-girl's nipple right off, leaving two exposed wires and nobody home. Alone on this block of working warehouses, each one's streetfront heaped high with uncollected trash bags and reeking food crates, the curb outside Dad's place was pristine.

36

DANI ONLY CAME TO THE CITY for one July afternoon that summer, and during even those few hours she seemed to be doing her best to avoid me. She was leaving for sleepaway camp the next morning, and the only way I got to see her at all was by agreeing to meet her at the Scandinavian Ski Shop on Fifty-Seventh Street, where I tagged along like a barely tolerated puppy while she bought last-minute camping supplies. I'd been hoping to talk to her about my missing father—the subject was pretty much avoided in our home, and I had trouble talking about real things with my guy friends—but she just seemed too far away for me to even bring it up. Instead, I tried to rekindle her old interest in exploring Manhattan with me, all the places Dad had told me about that I was pretty sure we could sneak into if we tried: the abandoned penthouse ballroom of the Pierre, now used as a giant attic to store old hotel furniture; the train tunnels under Riverside Park, gaudily graffitied by spray-can-wielding Invisible Men; the vaulted subterranean chamber just south of the reservoir, where you could walk the Loch Ness Monster–y iron back of a huge water main before it plunged into the earth and headed down Fifth Avenue.

But Dani was done exploring, done even trying to enjoy New York.

"I hate it here," she told me. "All being in the city does is make me miss it."

"Miss *you*," I wished she'd said.

. . .

When I got home, feeling bruised and bewildered, Mom was busy in the dining room with her lawyer. I didn't much like the look of him. He was a little guy, with a sparse failure of a ginger mustache and a briefcase scarred with cat scratches. He looked worried all the time. Every few weeks that summer and fall he came and snapped open the briefcase, took out a fat accordion-sided file, and talked to my mother in low, milquetoasty murmurs.

Mom didn't like to give me much detail about money matters, but it was understood we were losing the brownstone. All her lawyer and his sad little almost-mustache could do was delay. Make a mortgage payment here and there, hold off the bank a little longer, persuade a loan officer or a judge to give us more time. Delay.

My mother's SoHo job seemed to have stabilized things a bit. It turned out she was pretty good at explaining to rich people why a photorealist painting of a ketchup bottle or a horse trailer was just the thing they needed to make their classic-eight apartments on Fifth or Park stand out. And I overheard enough grumbling from Monsieur Claude and Mathis to know that she had managed to get them to come up with most of their back rent. But none of this was enough to stop the flow of those certified letters from Chase Manhattan. It was all about delay. A week, a month, another month. Buy Mom time to meet with the folks at the housing department again, fill out the paperwork, climb the waiting lists. Delay.

For all this uncertainty in our home, though, the city's finances were, if anything, in even rougher shape than ours. Wherever you went that fall, all any of the grown-ups talked about was *default*. It meant the city was going bankrupt. One day soon, someone was going to present a gigantic bill we couldn't pay and the city would go belly-up.

It was late October, the day President Ford was supposed to give his big speech. The one announcing whether he was going to bail us out. Everything depended on it, and Mathis was going crazy waiting for the answer. He was terrified the picture on our RCA Victor would pull its usual trick and become a shimmying wall of static just as Ford started speaking.

I couldn't stand all the anticipation. I wandered out to the back-yard, where I heard the urgent hubbub of a bunch of other TVs tuned to the same speech. When I rejoined Mathis, Ford was standing at a podium on TV, all big-lipped and bald and irritated.

"The message is clear," the president was saying, looking out at us with barely concealed contempt. "Responsibility for New York City's financial problems is being left on the front doorstep of the federal government—*unwanted and abandoned by its real parents.*"

I went out into the hall. It was chilly. To save money, my mother had been cheating the thermostat down to sixty lately, sometimes fifty-eight. I padded downstairs to her floor in my socks and poked my head in her door. She didn't notice me. She was lying on her bed in dungarees and a bunchy sweater, reading what looked like an Agatha Christie. I could see a black bowler on the cover, two swoops of a black mustache. Mom wasn't interested in President Ford. She wasn't interested in Dad, either. Not anymore. She didn't care if he came back or not: she wasn't letting him into her life again, and that was that.

For a time that had been good enough for me, too. Until it wasn't. You can choose your husband, which I suppose means you can unchoose him. But you can't choose your dad. Whether you like it or not, whether you like *him* or not, you are fused together. Like that time when I was four and dozing on his shoulder at daybreak as he carried me through the majestic ruins of New York's old Penn Station, the felled granite columns strewn like giant pick-up sticks across the marshy junkyard of New Jersey's Meadowlands. I was part of him, my small body lifting and subsiding with his every breath.

37

THE CRUMBLING BRICK TENEMENT at 155 East 104th was even more of a shithole than I would've guessed. Darkened with filth from a century of neglect and the elevated train down the street on Park. A deformed cherub's-head keystone hung above the entrance, its weather-worn face repaired grotesquely by some forgotten handyman with a bucket of plaster and a trowel.

Two old black guys chatting on the cracked steps next door abruptly stopped talking when they saw me coming. I tried not to look directly into their distrustful eyes. This was the first time I'd ever been above Ninety-Sixth Street on foot, and even the air felt different here: chillier, more charged.

The vestibule smelled like piss, but the mailboxes told me which apartment I wanted, through the front door with the busted lock and up three flights of creaky linoleum steps. I'd heard about drug dealers working out of Harlem tenements like these, and I'd certainly seen plenty of yellow-tape crime footage of these kinds of dim rabbit-warren hallways on the news. I hoped maybe I could stay safe if I just kept moving and acted like I knew where I was going.

Curtis answered his door himself, lots of little brown heads taking turns poking out from behind the thick trunk of his body. He looked at me impassively. Not unfriendly, just tired.

"Well, look who we got here! Can't say as I was waitin' on a visit from the son a the Cast-Iron King." He chuckled drily, his prunish lips pulling back for an instant to reveal the tumult of teeth behind them. "How'd you know I got out, anyhow?"

"The paper. Same place I got your address. Said they let *you* out, but Furman had another four months to go."

Curtis nodded. Hand on hip.

"Look," I told him, "I'm totally sorry about what happened to you guys." To avoid meeting his eyes, I stared at the triangle of light in the space between his bent arm and torso. "It wasn't fair."

Curtis shifted his weight in the doorway. "Well, gettin' arrested sure don't make it easier to find work, I'll tell you that. But at least I got sprung early 'cause a what I done for 'em. Did your paper tell you how I helped the city get some a them panels back from the junkman before they was all tore up?"

"Yeah. It said the D.A. asked the judge to go easy on you and stuff, that thanks to you they still had a third of them left."

Curtis waved his hand dismissively. "Yeah, only I don't know why they gone to all that trouble gettin' them panels back and pilin' 'em all up with the ones we didn't get a chance to take if they was only goin' to go store it all in another dumb place anyhow."

"How do you know it's in a dumb place? I thought where they moved it was this big secret."

Curtis scoffed. "Everybody know. All the scrap dudes, anyhow. City got it hid away in Hell Kitchen over by Tenth Avenue, in some old building the Urban Renewal folks got there. Only thing is, anytime anything happen with the Urban Renewal folks, every scrap yard in town know about it in like five minutes. 'Cause if you think about it, them urban renewals is what give 'em they best business, you know? It's like a—a whaddayacallit, a pipeline."

A little girl with tight black pigtails appeared at Curtis's side, hugging his leg. He rested a fond palm on her head and she squirmed away.

"But I'm thinkin' you ain't here just 'cause you missed my good looks," Curtis said to me. "There's somethin' you want."

I felt myself redden. "Yeah," I said.

"So what is it?"

I ground an imaginary bug into the ground with my sneaker. "Well, my dad's gone. Maybe you heard that?"

Curtis nodded. "Sorry 'bout that. I never gave him up, you know."

"I know that. At least I figured. But I've been thinking about something you said one time, one morning at the lot on West Street."

"Yeah?"

"Yeah. You didn't think I could hear you, 'cause I was in the truck, but you were complaining to Furman about how Dad said he left your pay envelope at his country house."

"Uh-huh. I sure remember *that*."

"Yeah, well, we don't *have* a country house. So I figured he was just lying to get out of paying you. But now I'm not so sure. Did he ever say where this country house *was*?"

Curtis shook his head. "Never told us. Just used to say that was where he been anytime he been gone awhile. I got the idea maybe there was a—hope you don't mind my sayin'—a woman, maybe."

This surprised me, though I don't know why. "And he never said anything else about where it was? Just that it was his country place?"

"Well, that's just it. A couple times he told us he was goin' to his country place, but then later, like the same day, I hear him tell Zev he was goin' to his Men-*hatin'* place."

"His *Manhattan* place?"

"I guess. Only he said it funny, with a kinda accent: 'Men-*hatin'*.'"

This only confused me further. "Was there any, like, *pattern* to when he went there? Could they be two different places?"

Curtis gave a long sigh. "Lookit. I never understood much about white people and all they houses anyhow." He shook his head. "The crazy ways them houses make 'em act, too, when they either gettin' 'em, or losin' 'em, or gettin' ready to get 'em or lose 'em."

The girl was back, tugging at his pant leg. He let her pull him inside a step.

"Mebbe it *was* all a lie," he said with a shrug. "*I* don't know." And now a little boy in a Buster Brown T-shirt was shoving the door closed. "But you take care a yourself, you hear, Griffin? Nobody else goin' to."

38

"FOR CHRISSAKES, takes you people long enough to answer the phone, dontcha think?" The voice on the other end of the line was gravelly, unfamiliar. A less slurry version of the old guy hawking Fudgie the Whale cakes in those Carvel ads. "Is Nick Watts around?"

"He stepped out for a moment," I said.

"We're talking about irritatingly handsome antiques-nut Nick Watts, with all the old frames and shit, right? *That* Nick Watts?"

"Yeah, he's my dad."

"Well, tell him *Larry* said he better get his ass down here quick. *Wash*ing-machine-sculpture Larry, from *Annie*'s building. Tell him they're putting all his shit out on the street."

I found Mathis sitting opposite Monsieur Claude at the dining room table, hunched over a map in the *Times* with all kinds of bands and arrows on it. Mathis allowed as how he was "a bit light of pocket" this week and couldn't possibly give me cab fare, notwithstanding the $67.25 in new backgammon debts he'd racked up with me since summer.

"I regret the circumstances," he said, turning back to his paper. "But there it is."

I tried to reengage him. "What's that map?"

Mathis looked up, his round glasses glinting. "Oh, it's the weather.

This here is the projected path of that tropical storm that just hammered Jamaica. You hear of it?"

I shook my head.

"Emma, they're calling her. They're not sure if she'll build into a hurricane before coming ashore." He stroked his chin collection. "Why do you suppose they always name storms after women, anyways? Someone oughta get Gloria Steinem on the case."

"Is it coming *here*?"

"Unlikely. It's tracking the East Coast right there, see, then it's supposed to swing in and make landfall somewhere between Hatteras and Atlantic City. We'll probly just get some bad rainstorms."

He went back to reading the article that accompanied the map.

"You sure you can't lend me five bucks? *Please?*"

Mathis shrugged. "Afraid not. Your mother just cleaned me out for rent. Even made me pay her back for that camera my nephew stole when he was staying here."

I looked over at Monsieur Claude, whose bored face was wreathed in Gauloise smoke. He had one leg crossed loosely over the other, a yellow espadrille with a hole in the big toe dangling from his left foot.

"How about you?" I asked him. "I swear I'll pay you back."

Monsieur Claude sniffed absently. "I had a lover from Hatteras once, a Fulbright scholar," he said. "She taught English to Arabs in Lille, at an execrable little *école*." He exhaled a weary plume of smoke. "A soft girl, and grateful for my company. She cried when I left."

Another brouhaha was in full swing when I emerged from the City Hall subway station. The crowd was even bigger than the mob of laid-off cops from last time, but the atmosphere felt less dangerous. The protesters were more defiant than enraged, and they looked less like hooligans and more like regular people.

The villain, as far as I could tell, was Jerry Ford. No longer the harmless stumblebum of Chevy Chase's *Saturday Night Live* imitations, the president had been transformed into New Yorkers' Public Enemy No. 1. Everywhere you looked, people were jabbing the air with giant blow-ups of the recent *Daily News* front page: "FORD TO CITY: DROP DEAD. Vows He'll Veto Any Bail-Out."

I'd had more than enough of crowds. I skirted this one by hurrying west on Chambers.

The foul-mouthed sculptor guy on the phone had been right: someone *was* putting all Dad's shit out on the street. As I came jogging up the block, two thick-necked men were grunting a rolltop desk through the front door and out to the curb.

"What's going on here?" I asked.

"Eviction," the one with the bulgier cheeks said. "Nonpayment of rent, I'm guessing. There's a lot of that going around."

"Who sent you guys?"

"Mr. DeCarlo, who else?"

"*Tony* DeCarlo?" I asked. "What's he got to do with it?"

"Everything. He owns the building. Now, if you don't mind getting out of the way, kid, we've got a lot more junk to bring down."

"Some decent stuff here mixed in with the crapola, too, though," the other thick-neck added, already heading back in for the next load. "Help yourself. It's all gonna get soaked to hell when that storm gets up here, anyway."

It was surreal seeing the inside outside. As odd a place to live as it may have been, that warehouse was Dad's home. And now here was his four-poster bed, the one I shared with him whenever I slept over, slanting off the sidewalk onto the asphalt-patched cobbles; someone had already made off with one of its carved-pineapple finials. Right next to it, tucked close like a bedside table, was his little cube-shaped bachelor's fridge with the fake-wood door. Nearby, a claw-foot bathtub leaned against a lamppost, filled with a jumble of household items and antiques: Dad's disemboweled percolator, a framed black-and-white photo of Ebbets Field, and an old-fashioned scale painted with the words TOLEDO HONEST WEIGHT.

The banished contents of Dad's warehouse extended all the way down the block to West Broadway. Piles of antique picture frames. Coffee tables lying in the gutter all legs-up and rigor mortis-y.

I cast my gaze down the street, the long line of jetsam washed up on its curb. I didn't want any of this stuff, not really. But wasn't I responsible for it? I mean, wouldn't Dad be furious if he came back and found I'd just abandoned it all here on . . .

But what a bozo you're being, I realized. *What a rockhead. He isn't com-*ing *back.*

Isn't. Coming. Back.

Someone had dumped a big pile of Dad's vintage postcards in a porcelain chamber pot by the curb. Every one of them depicted a scene of lost Manhattan, a few from this very area. One picture—shot, it said on the back, from the former A. T. Stewart dry goods store on Chambers Street looking downtown—showed City Hall Park and lower Broadway in 1905. No Woolworth Building yet, but the lower end of the park was occupied by an ornate post office with a zillion rounded mansard roofs billowing forth like sails with their bellies full of wind. The next postcard, bearing a 1909 postmark no doubt stamped in that very post office, showed the exact same view, with the prominent addition of a slopey-topped skyscraper in the background, a slender beauty labeled "Singer Building, highest in the world." I'd never seen it or heard of it. It was as gone as Dad.

On a third card, postmarked 1913—again from the same vantage point, looking down Broadway from Chambers—the Gothic, dripcastle tower of the Woolworth Building had risen to its full, world-topping height, lording it over the Singer Building and everything else. Just below the Woolworth's pinnacle, my eye was drawn to a small, energetic architectural element jutting over Broadway from the northeastern tourelle: *my gargoyle!* In the intervening years, before I severed him from his home, that vivid watchful skybeast must have witnessed both that big post office and the Singer Building being smashed to rubble. And now, just a handful of blocks downtown from where I stood, the mighty World Trade Center loomed over the Woolworth, nearly twice its height, having transformed the Cathedral of Commerce, in the eyes of most, into a quaint afterthought in the city skyline.

I flipped through some more antique cards: grand vanished hotels, mansions, and clubs—the Manhattan Club, the Union League Club, the Progress Club—each with dates and locations printed on the back. Some of the cards were organized in stacks held together with rubber bands. I stuffed a brick of them in my shirt pocket and another brick in each of my back pockets. They were awfully uncomfortable. If I wandered over to the piers and happened to fall into the Hudson, the weight of the lost city would pull me under for good, as surely as the cement shoes of any mob victim.

In the bottom of the chamber pot, uncovered when I removed the cards, was an age-browned clipping from an 1856 issue of *Harper's New Monthly Magazine*. "New York is notoriously the largest and least-loved of any of our great cities," the story said. "Why should it be loved as a city? It is never the same city for a dozen years altogether. A man born in New York forty years ago finds nothing, absolutely nothing, of the New York he knew. If he chances to stumble upon a few old houses not yet leveled, he is fortunate. But the landmarks, the objects which marked the city to him, as a city, are gone."

A bit of action was stirring down the block. An old man and woman, both dressed head to toe in purple and wearing oversize fly-eye glasses, were filling an industrial laundry cart with oddments. Grinning and chattering to each other, they moved antically from pile to pile in their floppy purple hats, occasionally holding up an artifact for the other's approval. I wandered over to check out the objects in their cart, whose randomness, I found, unaccountably enraged me.

That wasn't the only thing bothering me, either. I had an idea that the pointy bulge in the woman's purply tie-dyed shoulder bag might just be the mast of my radio-controlled Lightning sailboat. I couldn't imagine actually wanting to play with that boat anymore—I was too old for that now. But after piecing the vessel together with my own hands, right down to the filament-thin hawsers and the tiny cleats, I didn't like the idea of its living in someone else's home. I imagined the boat cloistered lonely in the darkness of that bag's insides.

"Um, excuse me, miss?" I said, half pointing with a crooked index finger at the purple lady's purple bag. "But if that's a sailboat in your bag and you, um, got it from one of these piles of stuff? Well, then I think it's possible it might actually be mine."

For a moment there came no answer, and I was about to repeat myself when the purple lady suddenly wheeled on me, bared her big beige teeth like a rabid squirrel, and shrieked in my face with the primal ferocity of a woman whose baby is being yanked from her arms: "What? WHAAT?! You *think* . . . you *OWN* . . . the *STREEET*?"

39

IT WASN'T JUST MY FATHER who was missing that fall; it was Dani, too. She never seemed to be home when I phoned and never called back with an answer to all my messages asking if she was coming to visit over Thanksgiving vacation. When I finally did reach her, it was obvious from the startled, peevish way she said, "Oh, hi, Griffin," that taking my call had been an accident.

She was not sympathetic when I tried to tell her about my father's eviction and the lousy luck I was having searching for him. She listened awhile in silence before interrupting me: "You know I know it's bullshit, right?"

"What's bullshit?" I was thoroughly taken aback.

"All this garbage about you not knowing where your dad is. You steal shit for him, you're his little right-hand man and everything, and you honestly expect me to believe you have no clue where he's living?"

It took a whole lot of probing and arguing before she finally told me what this was all about: the Laing folder.

"A few weeks ago Mom got so tired of me asking why we couldn't move back to the city that she finally told me the real reason Dad had to leave Columbia—that he was such a drunk, he'd lost the whole freakin' folder for, like, his most important project. But then when she said it was the weekend of my birthday party last year that it disappeared, I totally realized it was *you* who took it. I mean, I *saw* you blunder into my room from his study with your backpack. And the more I heard about how screwed up that Laing project ended up getting, the more obvious it became to me you must've stolen the folder for that weird business of your dad's." Her disgusted sigh blew through the receiver. "I can't believe a word that comes out of your mouth, Griffin, and I don't want you calling me anymore. *Okay?*"

I was so stung by her anger, so shamed by both my guilt and my ignorance, that I could barely speak. The few words I could get out did nothing to convince her that I didn't even know who Laing was, much less what was in his folder.

"I thought you were on my side," she said. "I mean, here I am, stuck in this fucking awful *Stepford Wives* suburb where nothing ever happens, and now it turns out that it's all because of *you*."

40

Z EV DIDN'T ANSWER HIS BUZZER. The old tailor downstairs, his shriveled head as intricate as the carved knob of a walking stick, looked up from a pinned hem long enough to tell me that he did know Zev but hadn't seen him in some time.

How odd that I'd worked with a guy all those months without ever learning his last name. I couldn't get his phone number without it, so I'd just have to keep coming back until he was home.

Or maybe not. Turning the corner on King Street to get back to the subway, I had a stroke of luck: there at the curb midblock, parked on an angle, stood the Good Humor truck. In the slanting November light, the brushstrokes of house paint over the phantom Popsicle looked more textured than before, the anatomy of the concealment more visible.

I peered inside the passenger-side window. Nothing much in there. Take-out wrappers and a bottle of fabric softener on the seat, sand and dead leaves on the floor mats. Wait—*fabric softener?*

The windows of the Laundromat down the block were too fogged for me to make out anything but hazy forms moving around inside. One of them turned out to be Zev, putting a badly folded pair of jeans on a pile of other badly folded jeans.

He gave me a surprised grin when he saw me come in. "Perfect timing, Griff. Can you give me a hand with one of these?" He nudged one of his two laundry sacks with a boot toe. "Truck's parked a few doors down."

The back of the ice cream truck was filled with tools and spackle buckets and two more bulging laundry bags.

"What's with all this laundry?" I asked.

"Been away awhile." He was looking at me funny. "You mind helping me schlep this stuff upstairs to my place?"

He got behind the wheel and leaned across to unlock the passenger door. "Here, let me get this junk out of your way." He swept his arm across the seat beside him like the clearing mechanism on a bowling lane, knocking to the floor a crumpled white paper bag and a sheet of creased wax paper with a crust of something in it.

The truck smelled of cigarette sweat and tartar sauce.

"My dad got evicted from the warehouse," I told Zev as he began the short drive back to his apartment. "Or at least his stuff did."

Zev nodded. "Well, it was only a matter of time, I guess. DeCarlo is certainly not known for his patience when someone owes him money."

I didn't like the sound of that.

"Do you think he'd *hurt* Dad over that back rent?"

Zev thought it over. "Maybe, maybe not," he said. "They do go way back. Besides, he'd have to find your father first. And *that*, as you probably know by now, is no mean feat."

I turned in my seat and looked at him sharply. "Do *you* know where my dad is?"

"Yeah," Zev answered after a pause. "Sure I do. I've been helping him out. *Was* helping him out." He turned a corner, more aggressively than necessary. "Never again, that's for sure. *No one* talks to me that way. *No one.* Especially after all the crazy things I've done for him."

"Where is he? Is he at his Manhattan place now?"

"The warehouse? You just said he was evicted."

I paused. "No, I mean his Men-*hatin'* place."

Zev looked at me, startled. "You *know* about that?"

"Sure," I bluffed. "But where is it exactly?"

"I can't tell you that, sorry. I gave him my word." He tightened his fists around the steering wheel. "But it's just as well, Griffin, believe me. You've already lost him. We all have. It's really better that you stay away."

Something was poking me in the butt. I fished around on the seat under me and found the culprit, an object so unexpectedly familiar, even across such a distance of years, that seeing it actually made me flinch with recognition. It was a blue plastic swordfish, flat and see-through. The kind of thing they pierce through sandwiches to keep them from falling apart. On its side was a stylized letter *S* whose bottom curve ended in a little fishhook barb. My butt had snapped the poor swordfish in half at the base of his pointy nose. I pocketed both pieces anyway.

"Here we are," Zev said, trying to sound upbeat as he pulled up in front of his walk-up.

"Yup," I said. I got out and headed up the street toward the subway again.

"Wait," he called after me. "Aren't you gonna help me with my laundry?"

I turned a moment to answer. "No time," I said. "There's someplace I just realized I need to be."

41

I N *From the Mixed-Up Files of Mrs. Basil E. Frankweiler,* a popular children's book Quig hated because it involved running away from home, two suburban kids get to New York City by finding a commuter train ticket with one unpunched adult fare left on it. My method for funding my trip in the opposite direction—*out of* town—was admittedly less clever: I swiped the cash from Monsieur Claude's billfold. I figured he owed me—if not for wolfing down so many breakfasts that by rights should've gone down the gullet of a certain growing boy, then as a penalty for repeatedly afflicting my eyeballs with the ghastly sight of his saggy sweatpants and pallid Gallic posterior.

Port Authority. Don't make me describe its foulness in any detail. Just imagine a bus terminal tucked deep down in one of the more rancid and overstuffed corners of Smaug the dragon's colon, several hours after he's taken top honors in a hobbit-eating contest.

The bus seats were threadbare and uncomfortable. I used my blue duffel as a pillow, and tried not to think how much easier this trip would be if Dani were traveling with me, if my father hadn't driven her out of my life with that whole Laing business.

From my spot near the bathroom in the back, you could hear the septic fluids sloshing around mintily as the driver made the wide turn into the Lincoln Tunnel. After the initial assault of ugliness when we emerged into New Jersey—the electrical plants and the gas stations and the choking tangle of infrastructure—the highway unspooled through an increasingly green and uncomplicated landscape, the sort of comparatively verdant remoteness that passes for nature to a native New Yorker.

My bus window was either childproof or broken. After a struggle, I managed to slide it open a few inches, enough to feel the air growing chillier and thickening with salt. Did they still have softshell-crab sandwiches this time of year?

After the bus dropped me off across from the Echo Harbor General Store, which was closed for the day, I headed over to visit Mrs. Krauss, the old lady who adopted all the cats abandoned by the summer people every Labor Day. Maybe I longed for something solidly familiar amid the disorienting wash of memory, or maybe I thought she might have seen Dad.

I was immediately sorry I'd come. There were no cats. There was no old-lady tricycle. The cottage had been torn down and replaced by a bigger and swankier bungalow that shouldered its way out to the property line. A station wagon sided with fake wood panels was parked at the curb. A preppy dog, one of those golden Irish setter retrievers that annoying happy families always have, sat at prick-eared high alert on the porch, the way all house pets do when heavy weather is coming.

It was weird how well my body knew its way around, even though I didn't remember many street names. The round cedar picnic tables were right where I remembered them on the deck of the Sandcastle, our family's favorite seafood place, which stood as always at the end of one of the many narrow canals Echo Harbor was known for. My stomach gave me a little rumble of reminder that I was supposed to be providing it with a softshell-crab sandwich, but the Sandcastle was all boarded up. Someone had printed a note in block letters with a Sharpie on the plywood nailed over the door:

TO "OUR CUSTOMERS,"
HOPE TO SEE YOU AGAIN SOON AFTER EMMA BLOWS THROUGH.
—"NORMA AND ED"

God, it made me crazy when people used quotation marks for no good reason.

HEY, "NORMA"! I thought. WHY DON'T YOU AND "ED" DO US ALL "A FAVOR" AND LEARN HOW TO WRITE "AN ENGLISH SENTENCE"? AND WHILE YOU'RE AT IT, HOW ABOUT STICKING AROUND TO SERVE A HUNGRY KID A "CRAB SANDWICH" OR TWO?

At the Sandcastle, you had to order something on bread if you wanted one of those blue plastic swordfish that Quig and I always used for our epic swordfights. She usually ordered a BLT. I got the softshell-crab sandwich, whose fried claws I enjoyed dangling in her face.

The bungalows in Echo Harbor were mostly of two kinds: charmless, one-story rectangles that looked like boxcars with windows, and pitched-roof cottages resembling human-scale birdhouses. Mrs. Krauss's place had been the boxcar kind, while ours was a birdhouse, complete with a little round window just beneath the peak. Most were arrayed along the canals, which had been created at the same time the original developer filled in the area's marshland with landfill he could build on. In summer, many of those houses had boats tied up out back.

Alive with families and recreation in my memory, Echo Harbor was bleak and windswept this time of year, particularly with a tropical storm hurrying up the coast for a visit. The windows of most of the houses I passed were X'd with masking tape. Some were sealed with plywood.

Even with daylight slipping from the sky, it was easy finding our old bungalow. It was one of the exposed ones right on the beach, looking out at the Great Bay and its distant island and the ill-tempered ocean beyond. The house looked pretty much the same as I'd remembered it, that basic birdhouse shape with the deck, except that its seaglass-blue paint on the ocean side was peeling off in long, thin strips. As with all the houses directly facing the sea, its windows were boarded up.

I suppose it was unrealistic to expect to find Dad sitting in a director's chair in the living room waiting for me. Or a potful of *Spaghetti alla Gargoilara* warming on the stove. When I peered through the glass-louvered side door, it was clear enough from the sheets over the furniture inside that no one was home.

No house key hung on the nail where it used to live, so I found a length of metal flashing among the debris under the house and used it to pry out one of the glass louvers on the side door, as I'd once seen Dad do when he lost his key. From there, all I needed to do was tear a hole in the screen and reach my hand through to unlock the door.

Nothing and everything had changed. The musty beach-house smell was *exactly* the same. I went around and yanked the sheets off the furniture with a series of *presto!* wrist flicks, revealing each time a tired wicker chair or a cheesy, nautical-themed table edged with rope. The floor had been painted an unforgivable bright yellow since our time, but in the chair-scraped ring surrounding the dining table you could still make out traces of the eggplant-purple floor Mom always loved, as well as intervening layers of green and blue. What lives, what losses, had played out in this room during the green and blue eras? Had the people who lived those lives ever regarded the chair scrapes and wondered about the eggplant-purple days our family had spent here before them?

My stomach felt scooped out with hunger. The fridge, of course, was empty, its door propped open with a Kadima paddle to keep mold from growing in there during the winter. The mice had already gotten to the Quaker oatmeal I found in a cabinet. But there was plenty of canned stuff. I cranked open some Chef Boyardee and forked it into my mouth right out of the can.

The family room was artificially dark with its big windows sealed up for the winter. I found a cat's claw in the tool closet under the stairs and used it to pry off the plywood nailed to the outside of the window frames.

All the beds had been stripped down to their mattress pads. I went from room to room, gathering whatever folded sheets and blankets I could find. These I unfolded and piled up on my old cot at the top of the house, right under that small round window beneath the roof peak that at bedtime had always made me feel like a little bird tucked away in safety.

Without removing my down jacket, I crawled under the mound of bedclothes and hugged them around me for warmth. They had the same old mildew smell as ever, mildly unpleasant yet comforting in its familiarity. If I craned my neck just a bit I could see out the little round window, where night was falling over the Great Bay like a scratchy charcoal blanket, obscuring the distant tuft of Fish Island. Every so often the clanging of an unseen buoy called out from the water, lonesome and arrhythmic.

I must have dozed off, because when I awoke the world had gone black. I thought I heard the rumble of distant thunder. It had that noncommittal quality that far-off thunder sometimes does, as of the skies clearing their throat, trying to decide whether they meant business. I hoped they didn't. The last time I'd weathered a lightning storm in this cottage had been terrifying.

They say lightning is white, but I remember it as blue. I bolted awake with cannon exploding in the roof beams and a flood of sky in my bedroom, bluing every shadow. When the room went black again and the air stilled, the memory that left me shaking was the spooky way the corduroy fish on my mobile, reds and purples in daylight, had all been bleached that same dead color.

That was the summer of my craze about lightning rods. For weeks I'd been peppering Mom and Dad with questions: Did our cottage have a lightning rod? Did it have enough lightning rods? Were these lightning rods the right lightning-rod height? How did lightning know to hit the rod and not our house?

I was under the sheets now, cocooned in cotton, listening and trembling. Out of the silence came a thin, sizzling sound, as of tracing paper ripping cleanly, until that awful blue light flared under the edges of the bedsheet, burning my eyes. The next instant, another explosion shook my mattress.

There was no point yelling for anyone, because the top of the house was empty except for me. It was our last weekend at Echo Harbor, and Marion, the mother's helper who'd shared my room all summer, had already gone back to Bard. Mom had taken Quig home to New York, too, for a friend's birthday party. It was just me and Dad left. I'd never been alone with him overnight, and I'd been nervous about it.

I crept out of bed and down the stairs, feeling my way along the scratchy burlap walls. I could hear the wind shoving the darkness around outside. But I didn't run. This was the most dangerous game of flashlight tag I'd ever played. I didn't want the lightning to notice me. If it guessed that I was out of bed and alone, if its next blue bolt caught me tiptoeing down the hallway, I'd be a goner.

When I got to my parents' bedroom door, I reached for the knob but felt only a draft wafting into my pajama sleeve: the door—the whole door!—was gone. I ran into the room and felt around the taut sheet for Dad, cautiously at first, then more frantically as I felt only hardness and button dents and the fine wire grid of the electric mattress pad beneath the sheet. He was gone—the door was gone and the bedcover was gone and Dad was gone.

Seized with panic, I went tearing around the house searching for him, in the bathrooms, in the kitchen, until at last I got up the nerve to look in the most exposed place of all—the family room, whose wall of windows faced directly onto the Great Bay. What I saw out there was horrible. The storm was crashing in the sky right in front of me, tree limbs thwacking against our windows, dark clouds sizzling blue every few seconds like the Insect-o-cutor the butcher hung behind his pork slabs.

I saw him before he saw me. One bare foot resting lazily on the coffee table, my father was sitting on the sofa without fear, a soft statue watching the storm.

"Oh, Griff," he said when he noticed me. "You're up. Come have a look." I ran around the L of the sofa and burrowed my head into his armpit. He held me in there with a flannel forearm.

"This is really something, isn't it," he said, his hand cupping my rib cage. "It's been like a light show at the planetarium out there."

That caught me off guard. I liked light shows.

"What do you mean?" I asked his chest.

"I mean it's beautiful. You couldn't paint it this beautiful. And the thing of it is, the sky does all the work—all we have to do to be part of everything is just sit here and watch."

We sat together like that for a long while, lightning flashing off his chin. As far as I could tell, he was making no effort to calm me down. He just stared out the window with that look people get when they gaze into a fire and lose themselves.

I started to get sleepy. Even with jags of electricity zigging into the bay outside our window, I could feel my terror draining away. I tried to get it back.

"I think our lightning rod must be busted," I said, "'cause the lightning hit the roof right above my bed!"

Dad shook his head. "I don't think so. Though it is pretty nearby—for a while it was striking the water out by Fish Island, and now it's moved closer, near where Mr. Christie keeps his crab traps."

"Won't that hurt the fish?"

"Nope. And come to think of it, I bet the electric eels are having a pretty grand time of it."

"Even the little ones?"

"Them especially—they can get their batteries all recharged tonight, see, and tomorrow morning, when the sharks come out of hiding and try to catch themselves some nice eel breakfast, they won't believe how speedy the baby eels have gotten."

I laughed a little. I was pretty sure he was making all this up, but I liked knowing that he was in control of the truth.

A frayed thread of lightning flashed over the bay. Trees writhed against our windows. We sat together and watched, the two of us, staring when it was dark and blinking when it got bright. And though I can't say I thought the lightning was beautiful exactly, it did seem less like it was coming for me.

The next rumble shook me awake, and I hadn't the faintest inkling where I was until I lifted my head. I threw that big pile of blankets off me and sat up in the chill to look out the round window at the bay. Morning had broken.

It was startling how white all the whites were out there: the foaming tips of the waves, the single seagull riding the wind currents. Blinking through my grogginess, though, I realized that the whites hadn't changed at all. The rest of the world had. Both sky and bay were a brooding ash-gray that lent the whites a charged immediacy.

Lightning crackled in the distance, descending through the sky with jerky, Etch A Sketch movements. Mostly it vanished into the serrated water far out in the bay.

I was leaving Echo Harbor without discovering what I'd come for. I suppose it shouldn't have made my insides feel so hollow. Just because Zev happened to have had a take-out sandwich from the Sandcastle didn't have to mean that this town was where he'd been working for Dad all these months. It had only been a hunch of mine, after all, based on nothing more than a cheapo plastic swordfish that used to mean something to me.

42

T HE GENERAL STORE WAS NOT ONLY OPEN this morning;
it was downright hopping. A crowd of ten or fifteen people were
clustered under the sagging overhang outside, some with bags and
pet carriers. One guy had a TV in a folding shopping cart. None of the
faces was the one I was hoping to see.

The lanky old man behind the counter inside had gotten a fair bit
wrinklier since I'd last seen him. He had a chapped red face and a neck
like a turkey vulture's.

"Bus ticket, young man?" he asked.

I nodded. "Yeah, to New York."

He took my last twenty dollars and gave me change with my ticket.
I asked about departure times.

"Just the one at eight forty—that's in, ah, nineteen minutes," he
said, holding his watch at arm's length so he could see it clearly. "Don't
you miss it, either. They're shutting all their routes down at noon up
and down the Northeast, on account of Emma."

"Is she coming here for sure? Do they know yet?"

"Well, they make like they kinda know. Weatherman says she
might could hit us right in the teeth, but then he hedges his bets saying the thing's gonna make landfall somewheres in a seventy-mile
swath from Cape May to Long Beach. But it doesn't much matter if it
hits us direct or not, you ask me. The real trouble *I* see is the moon."

"The moon?"

"Yeah, storm's supposed to come ashore at high tide tomorrow. It does that and I can tell you, the flooding around here won't be any joke."

A middle-aged couple in yellow slickers came in to buy tickets. I headed over to the cookie aisle and picked up a box of Nilla wafers for my trip.

There was a seating area in the back with two little round tables and a serve-yourself coffee corner. On hooks above the big percolator hung a couple dozen ceramic cups belonging to the store's regulars. Each cup was painted with an identical striped bass but personalized by a first name brushed on with gold nail polish. I looked them over carefully. None had the name I was looking for.

The wall above the tables was decorated with framed old newspaper clippings and fishing rods and old-timey black-and-white photographs of the area.

AW, SHUCKS! ran the headline of one story, about a local kitchen worker who'd won two hundred dollars in a clam-shucking contest at Long Beach.

"OLD STINKBOX" GUTTED BY FIRE, announced another, above a grainy picture of a four-story factory with flames roaring from its roof. HARBOR RESIDENTS REJOICE.

The yellow-slicker couple went outside to wait for the bus.

"That Fish Island factory," I said to the old turkey-necked guy. "The Stinkbox. Was it burned down by lightning?"

The guy gave me a slightly patronizing smile. "Oh, I sure don't think so, son. Arson, you'd have to think."

"They don't know?"

"Well, sometimes you can know a thing without knowing it, know what I mean? Wasn't a man in town—exceptin' the factory manager, I guess—who wasn't glad to see the Stinkbox burn down."

I asked him why, and he laughed. "Well, how do you think it got its name? Worst thing you ever smelt in your life. When the wind come up in summer, the stink blew right in over the bay and the whole damn village here stunk of dead fish." He crinkled his nose. "It'd get in your clothes, your hair. I can practically still smell it now, twenty-five, twenty-seven years later."

"So you think someone from town here just got fed up and set it on fire?"

The old man chuckled. "You'd have to think it's a good possibility. Though lightning did use to hit the factory's water tower now and then. So who's to say for sure?"

"I just saw lightning hit it this morning."

He cocked his head. "Oh, I don't think so. That water tower collapsed back in the fire. Anyways, it's hard to see anything clear out there from so far away."

He was right about that. The island was distant enough that from our deck it didn't look like much more than a green blur on the horizon.

"So that was the end of the fish factory?" I asked. "The owners just, like, walked away?"

He peered at me closely. "You want they should've rebuilt it?"

"Why not? I mean, how do you just abandon a whole factory? Did the guys who worked there all lose their jobs?"

"I suppose they did. They weren't from around here, though. Mostly fellas from the south. They'd come up for the season by the boatload and live in bunk houses out on the island. Never even came to the mainland here to shop. But there was little sense rebuilding anyhow, son. The whole men-*hatin'* industry was over the hill by then. Everyone knew it was only a matter a time till they fished 'em out."

I goggled at him. "*What* did you just say? The *what* industry?"

"Men-*hatin'*. That was a men-*hatin'* factory."

I couldn't have been more confused. "You mean Man*hattan*?"

"'Course not," he said, raising his voice a little. "Men-*hatin'*! M-E-N-H-A-D-E-N: menhaden!"

"What's menhaden?"

"You don't know? They're a nasty little fish too oily and bony to eat. Bunkers, some folks call 'em. They used to grind 'em up and make fertilizer and animal feed out of the scrap. Lamp oil, too, all up and down the East Coast. Stinkbox's real name was the Great Bay Menhaden Fertilizer and Oil Works." He looked at me like I was an idiot child. "You really never heard of menhaden?"

I shook my head.

"Where you from, anyway?"

I sighed. "Manhattan."

"Man*hattan*?" He stifled a laugh.

"Yeah, Manhattan."

"You're from *Manhattan* and you never heard of *menhaden*?"

I nodded.

"In that case, son," he said, pointing a spindly finger at me, "I got just one question for you."

"What's that?"

"Who's on first?"

43

I T TOOK ME PRACTICALLY ALL DAY to get up the nerve to swipe a boat. I kept making excuses for myself. First I had to go home to our bungalow to carbo-load on Beefaroni for my expedition. Then I decided it wouldn't feel right to leave without tidying up first, so I carefully folded all the blankets I'd used and dumped my dirty food cans in the neighbors' trash bin. A couple of times I had to duck behind the wicker love seat when an Ocean County Sheriff's car came by broadcasting a recorded loop of staticky urgings that "all persons" should voluntarily evacuate coastal areas. This was all the encouragement I needed to put off embarking on a sea voyage in favor of organizing the game cabinet and alphabetizing the food cans. It's amazing how many hours you can fritter away doing busywork like that.

After a while, the sheriff's car stopped making its rounds. In an upstairs closet, I found a black wool cap and a man-size Irish fisherman's sweater that smelled of tobacco and rain. I put them on and tugged my down jacket over the sweater's lumpy bulk. Back on the first floor, I wrapped two thick blankets in a thirty-gallon Hefty trash bag, stuffed them into my duffel with the Nilla wafers, and headed down to the beach, where a burly Jersey-looking guy and his son were working offshore to tie up their moored motorboat with four lines. The guy was up to his waist in the agitated gray-green water; the boy was in the boat's cockpit, feeding him rope. He looked cold and unhappy.

I wandered the village in my down jacket and jeans, up and down the canals, peeking through cottage windows. Nobody home. With only a couple of exceptions, the place was a ghost town.

There was no shortage of boats to choose from. Most of the bigger ones were probably in a shipyard somewhere for the winter, but in every second or third canal I scoped out, someone hadn't yet gotten around to hauling his boat out for the winter. Most of these neglected vessels were banged-up skiffs whose owners probably didn't worry too much about losing them to the weather.

In the canal behind Howells Road I spotted a docked fishing cruiser with looping chrome rails and a pair of two-hundred-horsepower engines. I steered clear of it. As a little kid I'd always watched Dad's every move as he fired up the *putt-putt*ers he rented to take me fishing, and a bunch of times he even let me steer. These serious machines, though, I had no clue how to operate.

The boat I settled on was a dinky Boston Whaler with a thirty-horsepower engine, tied up in the slip behind a birdhouse bungalow on Surf Walk.

I'd forgotten that woggly feeling you get in your knees and hips the moment you step into a small boat, the way your arms rise and your fingers splay in reflexive, stick-'em-up surrender. I bent low to collect myself. In my mind, someone was always watching me to see if I looked cool or dorky. So even though I kind of half kneeled on the fiberglass seats while untying the lines, I tried to do it without looking afraid. I even tipped up my chin confidently as I pushed off the dock, easing the boat out of its slip.

Neither of the life preservers fit me. The grown-up one was too big and the kid one too small. I tried not to dwell on it, instead tilting the little motor into the water the way Dad had taught me. I clicked the gear lever into the middle, guessing that must be neutral, and gave the rip cord a few good yanks.

The motor gurgled to life. I sat in the right stern the way Dad always had and gripped the vibrating handle to steer. Another click of the gear and my little boat lurched forward down the opaque green runway of the canal.

The wind seemed to pick up and begin shoving my boat around the moment the canal's artificial order gave way to the wide-open churn of the Great Bay. Instead of puttering ahead in a straight line, my little whaler labored forth in an irregular corkscrew motion, the motor's vibrations in my steering hand punctuated by the *galUMPH-galUMPH* of the boat's snub nose banging off the waves. Rain spattered down in fat drops, chilly on my cheeks and hands. The sky thickened with moisture, blurring the speck of Fish Island on the horizon.

Umoored. Untethered. At sea. This was the first time I really understood what those words meant. For a long while, the charcoal smudge of shoreline behind me grew more remote without Fish Island appearing to get any closer. I couldn't imagine feeling more alone—God, I wished Dani were there with me. But slowly, gradually, the hulking, malformed ruins of the menhaden factory emerged out of the haze, as imposing and forlorn as a sacked island fortress.

My boat rumbled closer across the waves and troughs until I began to make out distinct structures up ahead. On the near shore, the felled water tower lay on its side like a great stricken daddy longlegs, its scorched limbs twisted up beneath it. I steered left around the curve of the island, coming broadside of the two main factory buildings. Decrepit and huge, they were about the same rectangular shape and size. One was weather-battered but intact, with ripply metal skin. The other was its dead twin. Its flesh long since burned away to expose its steel beams, it now lay half-collapsed on the beach like the rust-red carcass of some gargantuan beast.

Darkness was falling. The wind was rising. My jacket was wet, and my teeth were chattering.

I was anxious to land. But pulling up anywhere near these two factory buildings was out of the question. Aside from a small section of charred planking, all that remained of the dock was its upright wooden pilings, which juddered in the water like teeth loose in their gums. Even if I managed to tie up to one of them, there was no getting ashore from here. The concrete landing that had once connected the dock to the factory was too high to reach from such a small boat. Worse, the edge of the landing was fringed with the corroded remains of what must once have been steel reinforcement but which had deteriorated into a row of jagged rusty stalagmites jutting upward from the water.

Keeping a good distance away to avoid any unseen wreckage under the surface, I motored past the intact main building, from whose rooftop cupola a strange gridwork structure, almost like a small railway, arced down to the concrete landing. Around the next curve of the island, tucked back from shore among a wilderness of puffy-topped beach weeds, I spotted another, smaller building, under assault by green vines. A bit farther along, I cut the engine and glided into a marshy shallows.

My feet were pretty well soaked already from the rain and sea slosh. I took off my shoes and jeans and hopped, shivering, into the shallow water and muck among the marsh grasses. *Christ*, it was cold, stingingly cold, instantly tightening the muscles of my left calf into a painful charley horse. I hauled the boat up onto the flat as best I could, sending a crowd of fiddler crabs scurrying, and looped the yellow rope and its anchor round the trunk of a scraggly tree. Boy, was I relieved to be off that goddamn water. I tugged my jeans and sneakers back on, leaving my balled wet socks in the muck among the mussels.

I could've used a machete. The overgrowth on this crazy island was like the Amazon or something. As soon as I got up the beach I was confronted by a wall of those bamboo-like beach weeds, easily six feet tall and knit together by a chaos of vines. The wind racing through the stalks made a tremendous, layered shushing sound.

Though the building wasn't far away, getting to it was slow going. I found a fallen limb, snapped off its branches, and used it to hack an uncertain path through the forest.

The concrete landing on the beach side of the building had collapsed. The doorway was above my head. I fought my way through the weeds and rubble and heaved a length of driftwood up to the doorway as a ramp. Grabbing the thicket of intruding plants for support, I clambered up the slant of wood and into a long, mostly empty room with a high ceiling, corrugated-steel walls, and a concrete floor. It was pretty dark in there.

I couldn't tell what the building had once been. There was a pile of collapsed, badly rusted lockers in one corner, and some kind of concrete ring set into the floor that looked like a scale model of the sort of ruin druids might leave behind. There were no windows. The two doorways, one on each side, were nothing more than blown-out, yawning holes, through which the outside had begun to reclaim the inside, tendrils of ivy edging around the doorframes and racing up the walls. The roof was mostly still intact. In the couple of spots where it had fallen away, the green vines that cloaked the façade were creeping across the void above me, making a trellis of the roof beams.

Flimsy as the building's metal walls seemed, at least they broke the wind. When I went to the far doorway to look across the island's weed-choked interior at the main factory building, a hostile breath of air rushed up through the beach weeds and sent a chill through my whole damp body.

Still, I stood there in the cold, unable to take my eyes off that surviving main factory building. Colossal and well past its prime, it had a tumbledown industrial grandeur about it. At ground level, two square loading bays in the side wall were sealed off with a peculiar patchwork of colored rectangles. High up on the factory's flank, each of its several windows was covered with a corrugated plastic square the cloudy cataract green of an old man's eyes. As day yielded to night, I saw, or thought I saw, a thing that gave me both hope and pause. A weak light seemed to seep from the window square on the far right, high up near the roof.

That was enough for me. I jumped down from the doorway and hurried toward the factory. But I didn't get more than a few feet in the shadow-thick bracken before I was turned back by the sheer density of the overgrowth. I doubted it was possible to penetrate the interior of this island without a machete, even by day, but it certainly couldn't be done at night. The low moon gloomed behind a gravy of cloud, and I couldn't risk getting caught out in this wilderness in the dark. I had to get back inside and sit tight till morning.

44

I AWOKE AT DAWN to an insistent *flap-flap*ping from above, as of a broad-winged bird struggling to get in or out. Disoriented at first, I quickly recalled where I was: on the floor in the corner of that windowless building, my duffel as a pillow, hugging the blankets around me. I rolled onto my back. The anxious bird was no bird at all but a swatch of damaged roof. Invisible fingers of wind had gotten beneath a section of tar paper at the edge of a gash in the plywood and were trying their damnedest to pry it loose.

My jacket, which I had spread out overnight on a hanging vine to dry, was only a little damp. I pulled it on over the fisherman's sweater and went to the doorway to look across the overgrowth at the silver bulk of the factory and the glowering sky above it. The wind was fierce, hectoring the thousands of beach-weed stalks into neurotic, shushing waves of disorder. But I saw what to do next. Though the interior of the island looked every bit as impenetrable as it had last night, by the day's first light I could now make out a narrow cement footpath curling out from below the door toward the water's edge. I hopped down and followed it, leaning into the wind and hugging my jacket around me. The cement was a mess, with generations of plants, both dead and alive, poking through its cracks. But a path was a path. It led out to the waterfront, then followed the shore until it reached the front of the main factory building, where waves were crashing against the concrete landing, exploding into bouquets of white spray.

The gridwork structure on the landing had looked like a railway last night for good reason: it *was* a railway. Two ancient, not-quite-parallel tracks arced uneasily from the loading area in front of the factory way up to a broad rectangular opening, something like the door of a hayloft, set into the wide cupola at the factory's top. The mad crisscross of rusty beams supporting the tracks reminded me of the Statue of Liberty's tangled insides.

The factory's front wall here was made of ripply steel, blotched by salt and age. But there was no ground-level entrance, just that hayloft opening at the top of the rails. So I walked around the corner and followed the long corrugated-steel side wall, the one I'd seen in the fading light yesterday evening. The wall adjoined a wide concrete loading area on which increasingly aggressive waves kept smashing. Set into the wall's middle were those two square loading bays I'd also seen yesterday, both of them completely sealed from the inside by a colorful patchwork of wooden apartment doors, the sort you saw surrounding demolition sites all over Manhattan. Peculiar as this was, things only got stranger. The third side of the factory had no doorway at all. And access to the fourth side, which in any event had no doors, either, was blocked by the settling carcass of the adjacent, fire-ravaged building. There was no way in.

Covering my face against the wind and sea spray, I hurried back around the factory to the front wall and stared up at that hayloft opening at the top of the rails. I began to climb.

My progress was slowed by the wind. The higher I rose, the stronger and sneakier its gusts became, slipping between me and the creaking gridwork and trying to fling me down to the concrete. I found if I moved closer to the façade, the factory's bulk acted as something of a windbreak. I told myself this wasn't much tougher than climbing a jungle gym, so long as I took my time. The rusted metal was scrapy against my palms, staining them orange-brown, and I had to keep wiping them off on my jeans. But there were enough diagonal supports running between the crossbeams that I was rarely without a good hand- or foothold.

Near the top, I paused for breath. Directly over my head, above the cupola's wide hayloft door, a shiny black metal crane arm extended upward from the façade on a diagonal, the tallest thing on the island. A braided cable ran its length, over a pulley at its tip, and then down to a dangling ball and hook. It put me in mind of a giant fishing rod with its lure reeled in. Except for one detail: a thin copper wire, tarnished chalky green like the grounding wire connecting our bungalow's lightning rod to the earth, ran from the base of the crane arm down the front of the building. I guessed that it, too, was a grounding wire. And in all likelihood, it was this crane that I had seen get struck by lightning yesterday morning.

I climbed the last few feet to the top of the railway. The cupola opening was closed. Blocked from the inside by a wall of hard metal. I gave the metal a push, first with my hands and then with my shoulder, really putting my back into it. Nothing doing. It was completely immovable.

A small clanking metallic sound was coming from inside the factory. Something intermittent and unreliable. At least I thought so. It was hard to be sure above the creaking whine of the wind harassing the gridwork beneath me.

Before starting down, I made the mistake of allowing myself to take a look around. From down there on the water last night, motoring closer, this island had seemed at least somewhat substantial. But from up here, in the first grim light of day, there was no escaping how raw and exposed it was, how tiny in this vast bowl of angry water. Over my left shoulder, the mainland was nothing more than an unhelpful gesture on the horizon. On my right, coming this way, was some seriously pissed-off sky, chalkboard gray and seething. The storm was already turning the bay to ocean, all surge and roil. I got the hell down.

The collapsing carcass of the adjacent factory building had bulged out over the years to clutter the space between the two structures with rusty debris. I decided to go around, following the broken cement path that had brought me here. It continued along the water before cutting inland, hugging the far side of the wrecked building. Here, too, though, the great carcass had bulged out as it settled, blocking the path and forcing me to walk inside the destroyed structure.

It was a terrible feeling. The whole damn place was a hard-hat zone, a precarious rusty wilderness overhead. Steel ribs and pipes and catwalks haphazardly intertwined. Railings and ducts and machinery tumbling in slow motion across the decades.

The sky began throwing down rain, hard-dropped and insistent, straight through the open roof. I kept moving. At the far side, three blocky redbrick monoliths stood in a row. Furnaces or boilers, I guessed, at least fifteen feet high. Each was girdled with bands of rusted steel. Amid all the wreckage overhead and on all sides, these structures seemed unusually sturdy, the sort of things the most cautious of the three little pigs might've put up as matching beach houses for himself and his two less responsible siblings. I didn't really get how these furnaces worked—what exactly all the wheels and hatches and porthole-like doors set into their brick walls were for—but they seemed basically to be giant chimneys. On a low platform between two of the furnaces were the rusted remains of a bunch of horizontal cylinder-looking contraptions whose sides bore the words UNION STEAM PUMP COMPANY. There were weeds growing out of them.

I picked my way through the last piles of smashed machinery and emerged outside, where I rejoined the cracked cement path. Cutting through an otherwise impassable forest of wind-whipped stalks and vines, it traveled inland a bit before splitting in two, one branch continuing across the interior of the island, the other making a sharp left. I took the left turn, but the rustling tangle of vegetation pressing in on either side was no less wild here. Spiky vines grabbed at the arms of my jacket, and I couldn't see more than a few feet ahead of me.

I was thinking about turning back to find shelter when I began to feel a sense of space up ahead, of widening out. But it wasn't just that. There was an unsettling feeling of transgression, too—mine or another's—a sense of intruding upon something terribly, terribly private. I pushed on, beating back vines from my face, catching glimpses up ahead of something dark and delicate, foreign and yet familiar, until all at once the path opened up onto a broad clearing of bright white sand. At its center, resplendent in a fresh coat of green paint, stood an ornate, fully intact, glass-and-iron IRT subway kiosk.

I'd never seen one in person—they'd vanished from the city when I was small—but there was no mistaking it. A sturdy yet intricate confection, the kiosk wore a high, sloping four-sided iron cap decorated with a fish-scale pattern and a couple of finials on top. Its glass side was adorned with two gold-leafed words: ENTRANCE, and just below it, in smaller letters, DOWNTOWN.

The sand surrounding the kiosk was so unblemished—not a twig, not a strand of seaweed—that it looked as if it had recently been raked clean. Beyond it, though, the clearing was ringed round with the same unruly vegetation as the rest of the island. To my left, looming not far behind these weeds, was the back wall of the sealed silver factory.

Daylight was seeping more rapidly into the sky, even as the rain came down harder, stinging my face. I hurried across the clearing, my sneakers sinking into the sand, and entered the kiosk beneath its elegant glass canopy, which was supported by a pair of swirly cast-iron brackets. Up close, you could see the trauma the kiosk had suffered during demolition. Much of its surface beneath the green paint was marred with thick scars, welded seams where the wounds from sledgehammers and cutting torches had been healed over. All the glass here must be new, it occurred to me.

The crumbly stone stairs inside were much narrower than the kiosk, probably half the width of a subway staircase. I wondered what kind of structure had originally stood here above these steps, what sort of service building or factory office.

I followed the old stairs down toward the factory, taking care not to slip on the sand, loads of which had blown inside. There was no railing, just a rough stone wall. The steps led down into a dark, humid basement. Wooden pallets lined one of the walls, piled high with big empty paper sacks, their bottom edges stitched shut with heavy string. Something crunched beneath my sneakers. I kneeled down in the weak column of daylight at the foot of the stairs and discovered that the basement floor was covered, wall to wall, with thousands of the tiniest fish bones I'd ever seen.

It got tougher to breathe the farther into the basement I penetrated. There was a soggy thickness to the air that was hard to take into my lungs. It was a relief to see another stone staircase a ways down on my right. This one went up.

A thin wash of light spilled down the stairwell, but far too little for comfort. I climbed the steps cautiously, twisting up out of the darkness, not trusting the rotting wooden railing in my hand. After a time, this loose railing gave way to a sturdier metal one, which guided me up, up, and around, until at last I emerged through a lavishly ornamented wrought-iron gate into the cavernous, dimly lit factory building.

I had to step back. My hand on the railing once again for reassurance, I stood on the top stair and craned my neck to take in the full, jaw-dropping scale of the place. There were no interior walls. It was just a single, colossal room, with virtually nothing to interrupt the gulf of dark space between the cement floor and the pitched corrugated-steel roof that rose and rose and rose some more to a point more than fifty feet above my head. The sound of the rain pelting that huge roof was deafening.

Small pockets of light wavered throughout the factory just above the floor, given off by glass camping lanterns resting on wedge-shaped stone blocks. I kneeled down to inspect the block closest to me and was startled to discover it wasn't just any old stone block but a tenement keystone, and not just any old tenement keystone but the noseless, squirrel-cheeked lady with the crooked smile my father and I had dug out of the rubble down on Second Avenue. The one I thought looked like my Woolworth's waitress.

The next stone block, deeper into the factory, was carved with a face I didn't recognize, a mischief-eyed bon vivant with grapes for hair. Beneath the swaying flame of the camp lantern, his narrow nose cast a long shadow on his chin, flicking back and forth across his dimple like an unsteady metronome. The keystone after that, also topped with a lantern, was the toothless lion we'd unearthed near East Twenty-Seventh, and farther into the room still was the smirking bar-brawler with the bandaged head we'd pried from the wall and hugged onto that kid's bunk bed together in that West Eighty-Eighth Street brownstone. Every one of these stone carvings, all the familiar ones, I could've sworn I'd seen Dad or Zev boxing up to ship to clients.

There was a raised plywood platform in the middle of the factory, bounded by a fancy railing. On the side nearest me, I saw as I drew closer, the platform was held aloft by the three stone ladies I'd seen on their backs in Dad's studio, the ones he said were paying the brownstone mortgage. I could tell these were the same caryatids because the one in the middle was unmistakably the lady whose eye I'd seen Zev scrubbing with a toothbrush. Her face and left breast were still stained with that spill of acid rain.

My eyes were starting to adjust to the factory's murky light, which was growing slowly, almost imperceptibly, brighter. Through the space between two of the caryatids, I spotted a set of wooden stairs spiraling upward on the far side of the platform. I walked around and saw that this was the richly carved oak staircase from that Hell's Kitchen church, the one that led up to the pulpit I'd helped restore, the one Dad said he was fixing up to return to the archdiocese. I climbed up the creaking steps to the pulpit, where two stacked milk crates provided a final big step up to the plywood platform. I took that step.

There was nobody up here. Just a crappy sheetless mattress with a squiggle of sloughed-off sleeping bag and an embroidered souvenir pillow, ripped along one seam, depicting that famous Cloisters tapestry of a unicorn trapped inside a circular fence. Scattered around the mattress were wads of Kleenex, along with an open can of Carnation condensed milk and a bowl with a few dried Cheerios clinging to the inside. A year-old calendar from the Franklin Savings Bank hung, crookedly, from a protrusion in the railing's ornament.

Something about that railing looked familiar. I peered more closely at its curving, violin-patterned filigree until it dawned on me that this was the very bronzework rail I'd seen in the *Times*, the irreplaceable Carrère and Hastings design swiped from the bridge on Ninety-Sixth and Riverside.

I had to lean on it to catch my breath, and as I did so, a detail in the factory's unusual beige stone wall caught my eye: a large carved starburst, or a sunburst maybe, repeated in pairs at regular intervals, each time beneath an empty, window-size rectangle, all the way across the wall and all the way up to the roof. At the corner, the beige stone surface curved gently inward before continuing, more or less flat again, on the adjoining wall, the sunburst and empty-rectangle pattern repeating itself clear across that expanse as well until it disappeared behind a tall scaffold at the far corner. Now that the room was brightening, light leaking in at the edges of the roof, I started to make out other details in the walls, too: skinny, ridged columns flanking the open rectangles—and wasn't that a small face there on the horizontal strip just above that column? Yes, sure it was: a woman's face surrounded by a writhing tangle of hair, the image repeated again and again atop the columns.

Looking at this stone wall, just the act of trying to see what I was seeing, was so disorienting I almost felt dizzy. I gripped the railing with both hands now, gripped and stared and then finally understood what so confused me about this place: This was no interior wall I was looking at. This was an *exterior* wall, and it wasn't stone at all; it was cast iron. This was the lost Bogardus Building, the 150-ton city landmark we'd stolen from TriBeCa and delivered for its destruction to the Bronx scrap yard. This was New York's oldest cast-iron building, a one-of-a-kind architectural treasure floated here in pieces and reassembled inside-out, bolted together panel by panel within this island factory's steel walls. The outside walls of the Bogardus Building were now lining the inside walls of the factory, facing in.

For a moment, and only a moment, I think I grasped what all the fuss over the Bogardus was about. Its age and hard travels aside, there was something about the building's grand symmetry I liked, something about its magician's trick of convincing the eye it was seeing stone. It was a clever building, an exultation of fragments that played on the human penchant for self-deception, our will to see a soaring, unified whole where there is none.

But here in this factory, if you kept looking, what you mostly saw in that inside-out landmark was confinement. Here were tall columned windows opening onto closure. Vistas of corrugated steel. Here was a whole city, a whole world, looking inward.

A voice boomed down from somewhere high up on the scaffold

in the corner, startling me: "So it's *you*, is it?" Four stories up, a man stepped forward on the scaffold planking. "Thought it might be that bastard Zev, come back to steal from me. Hold on a sec."

A lantern flamed on, bigger than the others, dangling from a scaffold pipe near the roof. Dad leaned forward into its light. He looked a bit like a salvaged city artifact himself, ragged and dusty. He had grown shockingly thin.

"What good luck," he called down. "Just the fellow I need. You came all the way out here alone, with this ugly storm brewing?"

"Yeah," I said.

"Pretty peculiar thing to do, I'd say, but as long as you're here, I could use your help before things get too leaky up here. Come on up, will you?"

The scaffold was pretty flimsy, a lattice of thin silver pipes. Its built-in steps carried me in long zigzags up the textured surface of the Bogardus, swaying, the higher I climbed, in a way that made me hugely uncomfortable. But the shakiness of the scaffold was nothing compared with the noise. The closer I got to the factory's ceiling, the louder became the machine-gun patter of rain on roof, until I couldn't even hear my own breathing anymore.

"Not bad, eh?" Dad said as I pulled myself up beside him on the top level of planking. "I told you my Washington Market studio was remarkable." He gestured grandly at the sweep of repeated ornamentation on the Bogardus's iron façade. Its scale and rigorous beauty were impressive from this height. "This is your birthright, if you really think about it. You were made inside these walls."

I stared at him dumbly.

"And I don't mind telling you, son," he went on, "I'm pretty proud of this restoration job." He tapped a window column with some kind of cylindrical metal tool. "With all the work I put into this, you can bet the old place looks a hell of a lot better than it had for maybe the last eighty years back on Washington Street. After all this time, it finally has an owner who values it enough to take care of it."

I was really confused. "But I thought the Bogardus panels we brought to the scrap yard were found by the police all smashed to pieces," I said. "That's what it said in the paper, and I *saw* the men cutting them up myself."

Dad chuckled. "Yeah, we did cut up a handful of panels at the yard for the city to find, that's true. I hated to do it, but it was the only way I could figure to make them think most of the pieces had been destroyed during the couple weeks we'd been carting them out of the lot down on West Street. Best way to get someone not to look for something is to convince them it doesn't exist anymore."

My mind felt numb. I found myself staring down at the ten or twelve remaining cast-iron pieces piled up on the scaffold planking all around our feet. They were a jumble of different shapes, the last uninstalled sections of what must have been just about the biggest jigsaw puzzle in the world.

"What about the last third of the Bogardus they *did* recover?" I asked, raising my voice to be heard over the staccato drumming of rain. "All those panels we left in the lot downtown. And the ones Curtis helped the city get back from the scrap yard. You went and stole all of *those, too,* after they'd been moved again?"

"*Stole* is such a harsh word, don't you think?"

"You, um, *liberated* those panels, then?"

"That we did. It was an open secret that after Landmarks scooped them up from West Street, they stored them in an old Housing and Development warehouse over on West Fifty-Second. Pretty much all we had to do was grease a palm or two and go pick them up."

I scanned the great expanse of the reconstructed Bogardus, both the near wall and the adjoining one. Other than a small, incomplete section right where we were standing on the scaffold, the four-story cast-iron façade was fully intact, floor to roof.

"But I don't get it. If you guys destroyed some panels in the scrap yard, why aren't there gaps in this Bogardus façade where those missing pieces should be?"

Dad was enjoying this. "Because I replaced them with new castings," he said. "Why do you think I needed you to keep such careful track of the stenciled numbers on the pieces we took? I had to make sure at least one of each of the Bogardus's component parts made it into the barges we floated here. That was crucial, 'cause the window bays are different heights on different stories—it's not one-size-fits-all. But as long as you have one of each kind, it's relatively simple to cast replacement pieces off the originals."

"So all that stuff you—"

"Shit!" Dad cried, looking up. In the corner, not far above where we were standing, the wind was working loose a section of the ripply metal roof, worrying it up and down with a terrific clatter. Each time the panel lifted, it revealed a swatch of roiling gray sky.

I tried again. "All that stuff you told me about the stencils, how the numbers had to do with foundries' production records and the weight of the panels and—"

"Made it all up, I'm afraid."

"Then how did—"

"*Please,* Griffin. Enough with the questions already." He gripped my shoulders in his big palms and turned me to face him. "Here, let me look at you." I avoided his eyes. The flesh around his neck had grown loose and a little wrinkly. The hair sprouting from the open V at the top of his corduroy shirt was going gray. "You've gotten a lot taller, kiddo. What's your mother feeding you these days, anyway, Miracle-Gro?"

I didn't answer. I didn't like when he talked about my mother.

"Let me see your hand." I lifted my left one and he held it in front of him, palm up, squinting as if he were trying to divine my fortune. "Yeah, that oughta do the trick."

He took the cylindrical tool from his belt and put it in my palm. It was only eight or so inches long, but it was extremely heavy. It had a big wide flat-head bit on it.

"That's an impact driver," Dad said. Despite its industrial heft, he explained, it was basically just a big old screwdriver with a rotating inner core. You hit the bottom of the rugged steel handle with a two-pound sledgehammer and the impact driver's head rotated to turn a screw bolt with far more torque than you could ever generate using just your hand and wrist.

"Help me out with this spandrel, will you?" Dad said.

He squatted beside one of the double-sunburst panels lying flat

at our feet and nodded for me to do the same. We worked our fingers under it and tilted it up. Its front side was rough to the touch; it
seemed that Dad had put sand in the beige paint to give it the texture
of stone. With me following his lead, we gripped the top of the spandrel and shuffled over to the exposed factory wall together. Rain was
leaking in at the factory's seams, up where that wall and the others
met the metal roof.

From the looks of it, all that was left to install to complete the
Bogardus's resurrection were three window bays and the final section of cornice above them. The system for assembling this cast-
iron front, as Dad explained it, was ingeniously simple. Each bay had
a horizontal iron beam at the bottom, on which stood a pair of columns a window's space apart. Between the columns, and below the
window opening, went a double sunburst spandrel. Resting atop the
two columns was another horizontal beam, which in turn supported
the columns and spandrel for the window bay of the floor above. And
so on.

All of these pieces had small, strategically placed holes drilled in
them so they could be bolted together like a giant Erector set.

"Trouble is," Dad grumbled, "the goddamn steel wall bows inward
here on this whole section of the factory, so I can't fit my hand back
there behind the iron to get at the bolt holes on the column flange.
I was thinking you might have more luck with your smaller hand."

On the count of three, we lifted the spandrel again and Dad guided
it into place against the edge of the closest column. He walked carefully around me so we could switch places, then fished a screw bolt
out of a pouch on his tool belt. He handed it to me along with a small
sledgehammer.

"Just hand-twist the screw bolt into the hole on the back of the
spandrel there, then give the impact driver a few hits," he said. "The
bolt should screw itself right into the column."

But it didn't. Something kept blocking the bolt from going all
the way through the hole from the spandrel to the column.

"What's the *problem*?" Dad asked, irritated.

"It won't go." I removed the sharp-edged screw bolt. "I don't think
the holes are lined up right."

"Jesus *Christ!*"—he hurried over to see what stupid thing I was doing—"Are you *sure?*"

I closed my hand into a fist around the screw bolt.

He peered over my shoulder at the hole to make certain I wasn't being an idiot, then had a thought. He had me help him tip the spandrel back down flat on the planking again. He hurried over to a satchel on the other end of the scaffold and took out a sheaf of papers. "What's the number stenciled on the back of that spandrel again?"

I told him it was *327.*

"Shit. Three twenty-*five* is the one we want." He put the papers and the satchel down and came over to inspect the other two spandrels on the planking. I went over to take a look at the papers, my left hand still balled tightly into a fist.

The sheet on top was a line drawing of the Bogardus Building, labeled NORTHEAST ELEVATION. Each of the building's dozens of columns, spandrels, and beams had a line running to the edge of the drawing, where it was identified by a number. I flipped to the next page, marked ISOMETRIC OF FOURTH FLOOR DETAILS. It was one of those exploded diagrams showing a close-up of all the components of the very window bay we were working on, and how they fit together.

I was flabbergasted. "But I thought you told me none of Bogardus's construction drawings of whole buildings survive!" I could feel every muscle in my arms and fists tense up.

"These weren't made by Bogardus. These are measured drawings done by a bunch of grad students when the building was dismantled four years ago. Landmarks got the city to kick in preservation money to have architectural historians document every inch of it as it came down. How else would they have known how to reconstruct it at the new college?"

I flipped quickly through the drawings. At the bottom of one, marked TRANSVERSE SECTION A-A, were a lot of small handwritten words: DRAWN BY JAMES DALY TOBIN, 1971. HISTORIC AMERICAN BUILDINGS SURVEY, SHEET 13 OF 17."

"Let me guess," I said. "You liberated these drawings, too."

"Of course not."

"Then how'd you get your hands on them?"

Dad looked at me in surprise. "You really don't know?"

I shook my head.

"*You* got them for me."

"*Me?*" I was horrified.

"Sure. The Laing drawings. That's what you swiped from the Gardner girl's party. Her dad ran the historic preservation program at Columbia. He was in charge of the whole documentation project."

The Gardner girl. The one who *dumped* me for stealing those drawings. The one who wouldn't talk to me anymore.

I felt a pounding in my temples. In my hand, too, which was suddenly in horrible agony. I unballed my fist and was astonished to discover I had gripped the bolt so tightly that the sharp edges of its head had opened a gash in my palm. It was bleeding like a son of a bitch.

Dad didn't notice. "And I really owe you, Griff," he said. "I couldn't have done any of this without your help."

I closed my hand again to hide my wound. I couldn't stop thinking of Dani, how I had driven her away by stealing that folder. "Why are they called the Laing drawings, anyway?"

Dad took the sheaf of diagrams from me and showed me the cover page. THE EDGAR LAING STORES, it said. N.W. CORNER WASHINGTON & MURRAY STREETS, NEW YORK CITY, NEW YORK COUNTY, NY (1849).

"Laing was the fellow, a coal merchant, who hired Bogardus to put up this building on the site of his old coal yard," Dad said. "Bogardus designed it to read as a single façade, but it was really five contiguous storefronts wrapping around the corner. Laing rented them to fruit and flour wholesalers. The one I lived in in the sixties had been used for years before me by a butter-and-cheese guy."

Before I could even gather my thoughts, a wrenching, whining sound ripped through the factory. I looked up in time to see the corner roof panel lift right off the building and sail up into the sky and out of sight. Wind roared in at us through the new hole. The camp lantern swung anxiously on its pipe. Its flame darted and shuddered in its glass like a small trapped animal, then quickly died.

"We've gotta get down from here," Dad said. He brandished the drawings and tried to wave me down the scaffold with them.

"Never mind," he said when I stood there frozen. "Follow me!"

He grabbed a scaffold pipe and swung easily down to the next level, unconcerned by the way the whole thing was swaying. I followed carefully. Once on the ground, he ran around turning the gas off in the other lanterns, a couple of which had blown off their keystones and shattered.

The green plastic square sealing one of the high windows in the long corrugated-steel wall opposite the Bogardus façade tore away and blew off into the sky, end over end. Wind and light poured in.

"Come on, son! Hurry up," Dad called when he saw me standing terrified at the base of the scaffold, clutching one of its horizontal pipes for no good reason. When I still didn't move, he hurried over and unpeeled my fingers from the bar. My hand in his, he led me across the factory floor, past his plywood sleeping platform with the Carrère and Hastings railings and past the elaborate wrought-iron gate I'd stepped through when I came up from the basement. I now recognized that gate, I felt sure, from one of Dad's old postcards: it was not so much a gate, really, as a pair of tall iron doors, now absent their glass, that had once been set into the grand Fifth Avenue entrance of the Gould-Vanderbilt mansion on Sixty-Seventh Street.

But Dad had no patience for my sightseeing just now. He yanked me by the wrist to the far side of the factory, pausing just a moment to rummage around in a trunk beneath a makeshift kitchen counter—a marble slab resting across a pair of overturned, richly carved stone corbels. Lined up alongside the counter as stools were the matching stumps of three granite columns. On the counter's other side, extending at a right angle from its far end to create a defined kitchen space, was a jury-rigged stovetop of intricate open ironwork that I recognized—again from one of Dad's vintage postcards—as a section of balcony railing at the now-demolished Union League Club on Madison Square (right across the street from the building where I chipped off that carved nose and got my own nose busted). The balcony railing was laid flat now in Dad's kitchen, with two pots, a frying pan, and a coffeepot resting atop it and Coleman camping stoves positioned beneath the iron filigree to create four burners, as in any ordinary kitchen. For a double sink, a regular wood-panel door had also been laid flat, resting on a couple of sandstone stoop railing supports carved in the shape of dogs. Dad had sawed two holes in the door panels and set a cheap plastic basin into each one. I picked up a dishrag and balled it up in my left hand to stop the bleeding.

"Hold this, will you?"

Dad handed me a bunched-up blue tarp over his shoulder. He rummaged around in some big cardboard boxes, cursing.

My feet were suddenly freezing. I looked down to discover I was standing in three inches of water. And it wasn't coming from the sink. The floor of the entire factory had become a shallow pool.

"Jesus!" Dad said. "This is a lot worse than I expected." He handed me another tarp, this one black, and stood up.

"Let's *go!*" he barked, as if I'd been delaying him.

He led me out of the kitchen area and into the back of the factory, where dozens of tenement and row house doors were laid out flat on the floor in a vast grid, almost like a model of the city, and piled high with a displaced populace of New York architectural sculpture: huddled masses of gods, grotesques, and dragons; angels, admirals, and gryphons; bartenders, Vikings, and poets; schoolboys, queens, and cops; presidents, mailmen, and pelicans. They were keystones and friezes, medallions and plaques, spandrels and pediments. They were cornices. They were carved from sandstone, limestone, marble, and granite. They were cast in terra cotta. They were pressed into zinc and tin. And they were all New Yorkers.

We hunkered down among them, my father and I, and waited for what was to come, the tarps pulled over us for shelter. Rain was coursing down the walls of the factory, streaming through a hundred holes in the roof.

The water kept rising. It topped the first level of keystones, so we clambered up the highest pile we could find: the stacked sections of a monumental sculpture of a drowsing woman, sliced into ravishing fragments. She looked an awful lot like the nocturnal half of the missing Night and Day pairing that had stood above the old Penn Station entrance on one of Dad's antique postcards—"*Shushh!*" he hissed when I started to ask about that. "Can't you see I'm *thinking*?"

Emma wasn't messing around. I don't know how long we were under those tarps, but I know it was no fun. Every so often, I'd hazard a faceful of windblown rain to poke my head out. And every time, the destruction was more severe than I could have imagined. The wind made short work of the factory's roof, peeling it away section by section until there was nothing left up there but a dark striped cage, clouds racing past above it. The sea poured through the twin loading bays, knocking loose first the feeble patchwork of tenement doors and then the lower panels of that whole broad wall of corrugated steel. The oak pulpit tore loose from Dad's sleeping platform and washed into the caryatids, bringing the whole thing crashing down.

The waves rolling in at us from the Great Bay were as big as anything I'd ever seen in the *ocean*. Wind battered the factory, inside and out. The sheet-metal walls were shaking loose. But the worst part was the sound. A horrible shrieking of metal, a great twisting ache, as if the Bogardus were wrenching itself apart at the seams. It was hard to tell exactly what was happening, but the magnificent iron façade was unmistakably on the move, its wall above us leaning inward, its other wall outward, all of it placing impossible stress on the thousands of little bolts holding the antique structure together.

The wind plucked off my tarp, then Dad's, and hurled them, flapping manically, high across the factory, two mismatched wings of a single grounded moth. Dad's eyes grew wide.

"We can't stay here," he said, stating the obvious. He paused, just a moment, to gain his footing on a partly submerged terra-cotta grotesque, then stepped all the way down to the ground, into water that came up to his knees. He helped me down after him—my first steps so achingly cold it felt like I was barefoot—and helped me wade across the factory to the top of the basement stairwell, where water poured steadily over the edges and swirled down the steps as if into a big sink drain.

"We can't go down *there*!" I protested. "That's *crazy*!"

"I know. But I think it'll be okay. Trust me."

The water's chaotic circulation had pushed one of the iron Vanderbilt doors closed and the other open. Dad made his way carefully down a couple of steps and looked back at me. "Just take it one step at a time. Hold tight to the railing."

I watched as he eased himself down the twisting hole and out of sight. Unable to bear being alone in the storm up here for even a second, I quickly followed, though I was certain it meant I would be drowned within minutes. The moment my second foot hit the top step, the sloshing water knocked my legs out from under me and I slid down the staircase on my ass, my arm raised to protect my head from smashing into the wall. As I twisted down and around, I caught up with Dad and knocked him over, too. The two of us rode the sluicing waterfall the rest of the way down, banging into each other, until we were spit out into the dark enclosed pool of the basement.

Dad didn't even yell at me. We got up on our feet, and though the water came up to my thighs down here, it was quite a bit calmer once you got away from the stairwell. He led me over to some kind of tall cylindrical cistern built along a side wall and gave me a boost onto its lip. After a couple of failed attempts, he managed to haul himself up, too.

The water rose a bit more in the next hour, wooden pallets and empty fish-scrap bags floating around on its surface. But we rode out the storm okay in that spot, huddled together in the wet shadows. When Dad noticed me shivering, he laid a corduroy arm around my shoulder and pulled me into his big warm body, pretending it was he who needed the warmth.

There was a postapocalyptic feel to things when we climbed back up to the factory from the basement, overcoming the weakened current of seawater spilling down the stairs. The violence of the storm had given way to a dead calm, but the devastation was vast. The Bogardus, all 150 tons of it, was torqued almost beyond recognition, its heavy iron sections accordioning in on one another; it seemed it might collapse at any moment. Tenement doors and debris floated about. The architectural sculptures were scattered, many of them swallowed up by the bay. Outside was inside. Charred driftwood from the old dock was lodged in the decorative ironwork of a contorted Vanderbilt door.

Dad was frantic. He splashed this way and that in his big boots, unsure what to do, how to begin salvaging his salvage. An ornamental bronze lamppost, probably one of the pair stolen from the Riverside Drive Firemen's Memorial, lay athwart the steel doorframe of the nearest loading bay, its glass globes smashed. Dad stepped over it and stood on one of the slant slabs of the loading area out front, which had collapsed onto the beach, providing a ramp directly into the bay for countless of his prized possessions. I thought he might cry.

As he looked desperately this way and that, the realization dawning that much of the island lay underwater, something partway down the tilted slab caught his eye: the haughty head, hooked beak, and regal plumage of a spectacularly grumpy marble eagle. It was half-submerged in dark water, one of its wings caught beneath the shaft of an antique bishop's crook streetlamp. Dad hurried down to inspect the bird.

"This is good," he murmured, trying to reassure himself. "This is a good thing. We can do this." I didn't like the way his voice sounded. Or the word *we*.

Swinging into action, he splashed back inside and rummaged around in the soggy debris until he found a tangle of yellow nylon strapping that seemed to satisfy him.

"Go get the hook!" he called to me. "From the crane. Go get the hook!"

I hadn't seen him so agitated since the night he made me save the last Woolworth gargoyle.

Outside, he hurried back down the slab and trussed up the eagle, looping the nylon wildly all around its wings and across its breast. His hands were shaking. Only once did he pause, looking up from his knots just long enough to observe me standing in the doorway, spent and overwrought, making no move to help him. I couldn't stop shivering.

When he was done rigging, he gave me an irritated look and rushed over to the toppled crane arm, which lay at an angle on the smashed landing below the cupola it had fallen from. He picked up the heavy ball-and-hook assembly and tugged it along the edge of the factory, the cable unspooling behind him. For extra leverage, I guess, or to direct the eagle's return path up into the factory, he passed the hook around a vertical steel support in what was left of the factory wall, then walked it straight down the slab to the eagle. He hooked it into the bird's rigging.

"Come on, son!" he called up to me urgently. "Get over to that crane already! I need your help."

His desperation made me sorry for him, but I was tired and freezing and I just didn't have the energy for any more of this.

"Why?" I asked, almost in a whisper.

"*Why?*" Dad cried. "*WHY?* This is one of the lost eagles from McKim, Mead and White's Penn Station, for Chrissakes! I took my first steps into New York under it when I was a kid, on vacation with my parents. *Everyone* did! I passed under it as an adult every time I went to get a slice of pie at the Savarin coffee shop inside!"

I didn't know what to say to that.

"Now come on, son, *please*! Get over to the crane! This is a *two*-man job!"

I looked up at the destroyed, roofless factory, the buckling Bogardus, the whole crazy mess. I looked down at Dad on the tilted slab, kneeling alone in the water with his hands grasping the marble eagle's wings. If ever there were a *one*-man job, this was it.

"Dad," I said quietly. "This is crazy. I don't think I can do this anymore."

"Nonsense! All you need to do is get over to the crane and give the hoist a turn every time I count to three."

"But you're not thinking straight," I said to him. "Isn't this the eye of the storm? Aren't we just about to get walloped by the back end of the hurricane? We have to find somewhere safe!"

"It's your *mother*, isn't it? She told you not to help me!"

"No! She doesn't even know I'm here. She doesn't even know *you're* here."

"Well, you're doing her bidding anyhow!"

"I'm not doing anyone's bidding, Dad. I just missed you. I just needed to know where you were."

He seemed not to hear me. "She never supported me on any of this. She grew up in the city, always took it for granted." He was talking very fast, too fast. "Well, you tell her—you go home and you tell her—"

"*No*, Dad! Tell her yourself if you've got something to say to her. I'm tired of being in the middle."

I *was*, too. I was sick of being caught in between. I didn't want to be the bridge anymore: between one parent and the other, between a messy present and an irretrievable past, between my father and whatever part of him was missing, would always be missing.

"The middle?" Dad asked, genuinely taken aback. He let go of the eagle and stood up. "It's being in the *middle* that upsets you?"

"Yeah. Sometimes I'd just like to crawl to the side of things and be my own middle for a while, without having to worry all the time about where I fit in between you and Mom, whether I'm holding you guys together or pushing you apart. That shouldn't be my problem, but you've made it my problem. You both have."

Dad stood up and thought this over. He seemed to soften. He walked up the slab to where I stood just inside the loading bay.

"But you're missing the whole point, son," he said gently. "Don't you see that? The middle is where all the really *interesting* stuff happens."

"Oh, *please*."

"No, I'm serious. In architecture, the space *between* things is the point of greatest vulnerability but also of greatest possibility. An architect I once knew told me that 'the joint is the beginning of ornament,' and whatever *he* meant by that, I always took it to mean that the design challenges posed by the joint between two elements—the *middle*, as you call it—can force an architect into greater creativity."

I told him that all sounded way too abstract for me.

"No, it's the most concrete, practical thing in the world. C'mere."

Dad stepped back inside and led me to where one of the walls of the accordioned Bogardus loomed above us. The wind moving through its twisted members made a whining, screaking sound.

"You remember when I explained to you earlier how cast-iron buildings have a line of horizontal beams, one bolted to the next, resting on top of a row of columns? And how the next row of columns rests, in turn, atop those beams?"

"Yeah?"

He pointed up. "So what do you see above every column, laid right over the surface of those horizontal beams?"

I told him I saw *decoration:* a bunch of fancy leaves and stuff swirling all around, and at the center, the head of that beetle-browed lady with her roiling, snaky hair.

"Exactly. And what *don't* you see?"

"I dunno. I can't see it."

"The *joint!*" Dad said. "Where the two beams meet. That's where water can get in, rust away the bolts. So what did clever Mr. Bogardus do? He made that fiercely beautiful casting of the woman's head—the best thing on the whole façade, by the way—and he used it to cover the joint, to protect it from the rain. Simple as that: the scarring over, the concealment of separation, is where the most imaginative, marvelously surprising things happen."

Someone's apartment door had washed through a ground-floor window of the Bogardus and deposited a stone ornament between the iron front and the steel factory wall behind it. Dad wrapped his long arms around the snark-lipped gargoyle, trying to dislodge it, but it was wedged in too tightly back there. He let go and turned back to me.

"You know, even gargoyles evolved out of need, if you think about it," he said. "When you see a really quirky gargoyle leering down from above a brownstone doorway, it might look like it was put there just for decoration—but without that gargoyle keystone, the whole arch would collapse."

"I know. I know that. But what does any of this have to do with me?"

Dad sighed. "All I'm saying is that I know your mother and I have put you in a tough spot, but there's no point in regretting that.

Being stuck in the middle—negotiating the gap between us—is how you've become *you*. It's a big part of why you're such a terrifically peculiar kid."

I eyed him cautiously. "Peculiar is good?"

"Hell yeah. Do you aspire to be ordinary? Let someone else's kid do that."

This was the first moment I was ever sure he liked me. *Peculiar was good.*

I gave him a nod, a very faint one, but I know he understood his words had hit home, because he lost no time leaning hard on me again: "So you'll help me hoist my eagle back inside?"

The wind was picking up sharply. It sent a fresh shiver through my wet body, stirred up the water we were standing in.

"No, Dad. I think you should leave it and come with me, I really do. I know a safe place."

"But it's from *Penn Station*! Carved by Adolph Weinman!"

"Dad, please. You don't need all this *stuff*. I mean it. Can't just coming home with me, just being my dad, be enough?"

He turned and looked with longing at the stricken eagle, the broken beauty all around him. Then he turned back, arms at his sides, palms open, and gazed appraisingly down at himself: his thin, sodden legs submerged in water, his empty, flood-wrinkled hands. He shook his head, unable to conceal his disappointment at how little he saw. *"Enough?"*

"It is for me," I said.

He blinked at me a few moments—disbelieving, or maybe just uncomprehending—before raising a hand and swatting away all I had said.

"It's from *Penn Station*, don't you get it? The city's greatest civic masterwork!" His voice was breaking. "We *have* to put that eagle back in my collection! We *have* to put it back!"

I thought about telling him that maybe some things couldn't *be* put back. That maybe loss is the only thing no one can ever take away from you. But he wasn't a man you could talk to—not anymore, any-way—so instead I just looked down at the water, at the concentric rings rippling out from my legs as I jiggled them for warmth. I don't know what expression was playing across Dad's face while we stood there together, what he thought as he stared across the flooded factory floor and out across the Great Bay at the wall of weather bearing down on us. I never got a chance to find out. When I looked up again, to learn from his face how this would all turn out, I discovered something that I understood was permanent this time. My father was no longer beside me.

It's not a comfortable feeling, climbing into a furnace. No matter how much you reassure yourself that it's an antique, that nothing has been burned in here for decades, it's hard not to think of Hansel and Gretel when you willingly yank open a rectangular metal hatch and crawl inside.

As soon as I got in there, though, I was pretty sure it was the safest place to be. Those three furnaces were built like brick shithouses, *enormous* brick shithouses. I'd chosen the middle one, figuring that its neighbors on either side might protect it further. Just inside the hatchway, the bottom several feet of the furnace were cluttered with an apparatus of looping, element-like metal tubes, maybe to hold or distribute heat. I climbed up and through those tubes, then pulled myself up to an arched brick alcove with a metal hatch closed from the outside. There I holed up, hugging my legs to my chest and burying my face between my knees until I stopped shivering. Though it wasn't exactly cozy, it was much warmer in there, protected from the wind. The brick walls and the confined space of the alcove reminded me of my old hideout beneath Mom's window seat.

I think watching the storm hammer the island might have been less disturbing than drowning in its sound, as I did. The furnace was basically a big brick shaft, roofed over but with lots of square apertures near the top, through which the wind roared and echoed, a raging static without letup. The crashing of the surf was relentless, too, so *all-around-me* that it sounded not just like being near the waves but *inside* them. Seawater rushed in through the ground-level hatch, climbing the shaft below me. Most agonizing, though, was the piercing metallic shriek of convulsing iron, a lurching, derailing subway wreck of a sound.

Dad never gave up on that eagle. He'd left me standing alone in the flooded factory and had splashed down to wrangle with the great bird, his back hunched against the rising wind, the waves rolling in and exploding against the slab all around him. I shouted at him to leave the eagle behind, to hurry with me to the safety of the brick furnace. But he either didn't hear me or pretended not to, his every faculty bent to this one impossible task.

I reached the far corner of the factory and stood there watching longer than was safe, delaying my sprint to the furnace. With the help of the surging seawater, Dad managed to shove the streetlamp off the eagle's pinioned wing, and I watched as he heaved the stone creature up a few inches and raced to deny the bay his treasure, running back and forth, eagle to hoist, hoist to eagle, shoving impediments out of the way and laboriously winching the sculpture back up the slab. The winds were growing dangerous, battering the factory, stinging my face with raindrops and sea spray. The Bogardus swayed and groaned. But I'll be damned—and this was the last thing I saw before bolting for the furnace—if Dad didn't winch that unwieldy marble hunk of lost New York all the way up the slab and back inside to his collection. I never saw him again.

45

I MAY HAVE NODDED OFF in that brick alcove. Just to shut off my senses as the storm raged. Just to escape. When I opened my eyes again, all was still. Sunlight penetrated the furnace through the square holes up top, casting slant parallelograms on the dark bricks.

The water had retreated from the shaft as emphatically as it had surged in. I dropped down, climbed back out through the tubing and the hatch, and emerged into a dazzlingly bright seascape of blue sky and endless sand. The waters of the Great Bay had receded halfway to the horizon, leaving behind a beach seemingly without limit, glinting with a revealed treasury of shells and polished pebbles. The beauty of the sun-smashed morning mocked the violence that had preceded it.

There was wreckage, too, plenty of it. But nothing I wanted to look at for long. The Bogardus was unrecognizable, a contorted pileup of old iron driven out onto the seabed between the island and the mainland, where it was certain to be swallowed up when the waters flowed back. Little remained of the factory but its listing steel uprights and the collapsed cage of its roof beams.

I turned away to face the ocean. The revealed seabed there, the ephemeral expanse of new beach, held remnants of more pasts than my own. Out beyond the margin of yesterday's island, beyond where I'd come ashore and tied up my now-vanished boat, stood a crumbled colony of pink-brick chimneys, headstones of homes perhaps engulfed by a previous century's hurricane. Strewn among them, and in front of them, and beyond them as far as the eye could see, were the tumbled heads of hundreds of stone and terra-cotta New Yorkers.

I removed my sneakers and walked out barefoot over the crunching carpet of shells. With the carved and cast faces lying every which way, some nose-down, some half sunk in sand, this raw aftermath of a landscape had the feel of a Civil War battlefield. Some of the keystone portraits stared skyward with an empty, smooth-pupiled gaze; they looked dazed, as if wondering what had brought them to this place. But most of them simply looked like what they were: lifeless objects made of rock or fired mud. Wrested from the living city, deprived now even of the animating passion of their collector, all they were was dead.

When the tide began its return, I headed out to greet it, my sight blurred by what I suppose were tears. I wasn't in the mood to gather fragments, whether polished blue shards of sea glass or keystones from dismembered townhouses. I picked up no carvings, and left behind the terra cotta, too, all but a single oblong castoff, which fit surprisingly snugly under my arm.

The distant mosquito buzz of an engine came to my ears well before I saw its source. Visible at first only as a white speck sparking diagonally across the bay, the vessel turned out to be a Coast Guard powerboat with one red stripe and one blue stripe slanting across its bow. I made a move toward it as if stepping off a curb, and my arm shot up, two fingers raised, hailing a ride home.

46

THE FIFTY-THREE-STORY RIDE in the express elevator was exhilarating, like moving through time. Backward, to the Gothic tower's 1913 debut as the world's tallest building, but forward, too, for reasons only I knew. This was a city where you could inhabit multiple eras simultaneously.

The shoulder strap of my duffel was digging into my collarbone. When the doors chimed open, I humped the bag down the hall as briskly as I could, right past the clouded-glass door marked FULMER & ASSOCIATES, the name I'd given as my father's place of business for the second day in a row when I told the lobby guard I was visiting my dad. Unlike yesterday, when I'd headed back downstairs a short while after dropping my supplies in the gutter that ran around the outside of the building, this time I hid in the stairwell inside for a couple of hours. As soon as I was pretty sure everyone on the floor had gone home, I came out of hiding. I slid open one of the two tall windows on the building's western wall and climbed outside with my duffel.

I couldn't have chosen a better evening. It was one of those days when the moisture rolls in off New York Harbor and blankets Lower Manhattan in white fog. From up here, the whole city had vanished, all but the great twin rods of the World Trade Center, rising out of a puffy bed of cotton. From up here it was possible to imagine Dad was still down in the remembered streets somewhere, driving his phantom Good Humor truck up to the Carnegie Hall Cinema for a double feature, or over to his friend DeCarlo's to pick out a nice casket for himself. From up here I could get away, for a while anyway, from all of Quigley's tiresome crying about Dad's drowning, and from Mom's unconvincing pretense that she was perfectly happy in our cramped new apartment in an oppressively dreary redbrick urban renewal tower on West 100th.

Zev loved what I was up to today. He'd helped me out with tools and materials, told me the best way to go about it. He'd called his friend at D.D.&M. to confirm that the Woolworth's maintenance crew still kept a ladder and planking in the fifty-third-floor storeroom. He even offered to come along, but I told him a boy would attract less suspicion than a man. This was something I wanted to do on my own.

The Woolworth's "restoration" was complete. All four tourelles were now entirely faced in tacky beige-and-blue aluminum siding, with those cheapo giant toothpicks jutting out where the vivid terra-cotta gargoyles had once lived. A pair of two-foot-long steel supports ran horizontally from the building to the northwest tourelle. I slid the maintenance crew's planks across these supports to make a little bridge I could stand the ladder on. After leaning the ladder against a downtown flank of the tourelle, I ran an extension cord from an outlet in the darkened hallway and plugged in the Sawzall I'd brought up here yesterday. I carefully climbed the ladder and took great pleasure in using the saw's saber-toothed blade—*zhigga-zhigga-zhigga*—to amputate a southwest-facing aluminum toothpick. Then I used that same blade to enlarge the hole in the aluminum siding, revealing the original 1913 terra cotta behind it. You could see the jagged wound where a gargoyle had been lopped off.

I swapped the Sawzall for a power drill with a very long one-inch-diameter bit and climbed the ladder again. The rest of the work went smoothly: the drilling of the deep hole in the terra cotta, the splooging of the epoxy into that hole with the caulk gun, the slathering of the mortar on the terra cotta.

Quickly now, before the epoxy had time to dry up, I unzipped the duffel and removed the gargoyle I knew best, that sly-eyed, exiled sky-beast I had both severed from this building and rescued from the wet sand of the Great Bay's exposed seabed. He was already prepped for his return home. Zev, with a little kibitzing from me at the Green-point machine shop of a friend, had core-drilled a new hole in the gargoyle's neck and inserted a length of rebar rod swiped from a construction site.

I cradled the gargoyle against my chest with my left hand and carried him gently up the ladder to the hole I'd just drilled. But I didn't put him back. I put him *forward*. I thought maybe he'd gotten tired of looking at things that had already happened. I thought he might enjoy a change of scenery. So instead of returning him to his original spot on the northeast tourelle, where for sixty-one years he had gazed out over City Hall and the old New York Times Building and the Brooklyn Bridge, I had chosen to place him here on the northwest tourelle, facing slightly downtown, with a panoramic view of a neighborhood in the making: the still-new Twin Towers, with work under way on the complementary high-rises around them, and the sprawling, undeveloped landfill above Battery Park made from earth excavated for the towers' foundations.

At the top of the ladder, I slipped the rebar into the drill hole and tenderly lowered the peculiar terra-cotta creature until he came to rest. To set him securely in the mortar for the long haul—to make sure *he* wouldn't leave me, too—I put my arms around his neck and hugged him against the wall. For a long time we stayed like that, feeling each other breathe, listening to the fog-muffled sounds of the city. I probably could have let him go sooner than I did, but I hung on awhile for good measure. I needed him to stay put. I wanted him to get a good look, from his new perspective, at whatever might befall our shared hometown. He hadn't been situated in this spot in generations past to watch Washington Market and the Bogardus Building take form and thrive and then be swept away. But New York's story is always retelling itself. In years to come, from this new perch, he would see a neighborhood rise and fall and rise again.

47

A NY NEW YORKER WHO'S PAYING ATTENTION will tell
you that the city is a living, breathing organism at war with
itself. This is as true today as it was in 1975, or for that matter in 1856,
when that *Harper's Monthly* writer was grumbling about how New
York "is never the same city for a dozen years altogether."

I've made a bit of a study of the city's self-cannibalization for
"Ghosts of New York," my wistfully cranky *New Yorker* architecture
column. As part of the job (and for two decades before it, out of a personal compulsion I blame on my father), I've made a point of showing
up at the deathbed of pretty much every noteworthy city building or
storefront to meet its maker in the past thirty-six years. I stood outside Grand Central in 1981 and watched a teardrop-shaped wrecking
ball sail into the Palm Court of the Biltmore Hotel, beneath whose
clock generations of New Yorkers met their lovers (and where Zelda
and Scott Fitzgerald honeymooned so boisterously they were asked
to leave). The following year I was on hand the morning the Helen
Hayes Theatre's dazzling terra-cotta façade of gold, turquoise, and
ivory was massacred, joining four other destroyed early 1900s the-
aters to make way for the fifty-story Marriott Marquis hotel. And in
2005 I nipped inside the doomed Times Square Howard Johnson's to
drink, by myself, what I'm pretty sure was the last dreadful martini
ever served by that illustrious institution.

I'm not the only one who does this sort of thing, either. You probably wouldn't know, unless you're one of us, that whenever one of these storied city structures is shuttered or razed, a handful of mourners shows up to say goodbye. It's a wisecracking, heartsick crowd for the most part, but what's always interested me is how you tend to see the same people at these things over the years.

There's no single type of person in our crowd, though many of us are middle-aged or older. You get pink-faced codgers in stained Brooklyn Dodgers caps, designery-looking black guys in geek-chic eyeglasses, and dowdy old Village matrons who probably used to meet Jane Jacobs for coffee at the Figaro. New Yorkers, basically.

The one who repeatedly caught my eye, though, was a pigeon-toed, thirtyish woman with a long bronze braid down her back. She was a photographer—I rarely got a glimpse of her face because her Leica was so often in front of it—who started showing up in the early Bloomberg years, as the real estate developers were stampeding to the D.O.B. to grab demolition permits by the fistful. I think I fell for her way of seeing things before I fell for *her*. In fact, I know I did. While the rest of us bruised nostalgists were shaking our heads at the wreckers smashing the enormous plate-glass windows of the Beekman Theatre, she was the only one who noticed its salvaged popcorn machine tied to the roof of a BMW parked up the block. And the day the original H&H on Eightieth and Broadway was shut down after a tax fraud indictment, it was she who spotted an enterprising rat making off with the era's last, valedictory everything bagel.

It took me ages to work up the nerve to talk to her. Turns out that she is not so much a devotee of lost New York in particular as she is, more generally, an aficionado of derelict things, which is probably why she doesn't mind living with *me*. We've been married just under four years, and our son will turn three next month. He's an inquisitive little fellow, but my wife has made me promise to go easy on the pontification about Ye Olde New Yorke as he gets older, lest he be forced to pretend he's deaf. ("Griffin's Edifice Complex," she calls my obsession.)

Now that our schedules are largely ruled by babysitter availability, my wife and I can't get away as often for our morbid little dates to visit doomed city buildings and storefronts. But we'll always have Rizzoli. And the Moondance Diner. And the Ziegfeld. And the Original Ray's and Caffé Dante and the Cedar Tavern. And the Jackson Hole and Steinway Hall and O'Neals. We'll have Café Figaro and Pearl Paint and Kim's Video and Ratner's (with Lansky Lounge in the back). We'll have the Four Seasons. We'll have Cafe La Fortuna and CBGB and the Fulton Fish Market. And the Knitting Factory and Dojo and Guss' Pickles. We'll have the Second Avenue Deli, too, and La Lunchonette and J&R. And Endicott Booksellers and Mars Bar and Fez (downstairs from Time Café). We'll have Astroland, the Bottom Line, Café Edison, and the Complete Traveller Antiquarian Bookstore. And the P&G Bar and the Provincetown Playhouse and Around the Clock and Joe's Dairy. We'll have Elaine's and Luna Lounge and the New York Doll Hospital. We'll have Roseland and the Roxy and the Back Fence. We'll have Claremont Stables and Yaffa, the Liquor Store Bar and the Stoned Crow, Jefferson Market and the Drake Hotel. And Bleecker Bob's Records, the Donnell Library, and Pete's Waterfront Ale House. We'll have St. Vincent's Hospital and Sutton Clock Shop and Shea Stadium. And Café des Artistes and Kenny's Castaways and Gotham Book Mart ("Wise Men Fish Here"). We'll have Mimi's Pizza and Lascoff Drugs and Andy's Chee-Pees. We'll have Coliseum Books and Hogs & Heifers. We'll have El Teddy's. We'll have Florent.

Another thing we'll always have is the Woolworth Building, which was not destroyed but was merely eviscerated and expensively tarted up, shortly before having its private patch of sky invaded by 30 Park Place, the eighty-two-story monument to obscene wealth that Larry Silverstein built down the block. As you've surely heard by now, the top thirty stories of the Woolworth have been gutted and transformed into—what else?—yet another luxury condo for hedge-funders and Russian zillionaires (cost of the seven-level pinnacle penthouse: $110 million).

Not long ago I wangled my way into a press tour of the palatial new apartments, and while my fellow ink-stained wretches were admiring the finishes in the kitchen of a $27 million fifty-first-floor pied-à-terre, I slipped upstairs and poked my head out a west-facing fifty-third-floor window, the one through which my father and I climbed together that terrifying February night forty-three years ago. You'll understand why I didn't quite have the nerve to climb out there again, but I am happy to report that my gargoyle is alive and well, keeping watch over twenty-first-century Lower Manhattan from his private perch on that northwestern tourelle. I thought it best not to approach him. He is a timeless creature, whereas I, having crossed into my second half century a few years ago, am running out of a little more time each year. So it seemed preferable just to leave us both with our memories of each other.

I still love the Woolworth Building, no matter how crass its "superluxury" new residents may turn out to be. I think a building that beautiful can transcend the vulgarity of the humans rattling around its innards, and not long ago I wrote a column making that very argument. Working things out in my column is how I make sense of my hometown's relentless demolition and recomposition. Over the years I've written pieces—some rueful, some accepting—about most of the lost buildings and storefronts I listed above, and I've also written a number of architectural books about New York's ever-changing streetscape. All in all, I've come to know, and helped my readers to know, intimately, several hundred city buildings. But this is the first time I've ever been able to write a word about the brownstone where I grew up, or the Bogardus Building, or the demolished Kips Bay tenements whose rubble yielded up so much shattered treasure. It just wasn't something I could bring myself to do without also telling the story of my father's own demolition, and my attempts to salvage a sense of self, and a sense of my city, from what was left.

Last week, my wife, always the playful provocateur, gave me a set of four-inch-tall rubber erasers in the shapes of notable New York buildings. I left them on the kitchen table a minute to go bang out an e-mail to my editor, and by the time I came back, our household's smallest native New Yorker had already gotten his sneaky little fist around the American Folk Art Museum. He was lying on his belly on the linoleum floor, his face alight with the exuberance of the born troublemaker, feverishly rubbing away the last of the museum's distinctive textured façade. I shouldn't have been surprised, I guess, because that is New York as I know it: the city that sets about erasing itself the moment you take it out of the box.

But disappearance isn't the whole story, either, is it? Because however much we might mourn what the city is doing to itself, the damned place never fails to regenerate. It's a snake that grows by swallowing its own tail. It's a Möbius strip of self-annihilation and re-creation. And that's what my father was as well. In the end, he erased himself, and in so doing, he created me.

There are days, whole weeks sometimes, when I see myself as no more than the sum total of all those messy rubbery bits left over from the eraser after my father had completed his final vanishing act. But there's always a chance to cobble something together on the site of that absence, too, combining those scavenged scraps with whatever else comes to hand. It's worth a shot, anyway. We are all disposable, but with any luck, when the time comes for me to be rubbed away, there will be enough useful bits among the resulting debris to help my boy build something grandly peculiar of his own. What I'd give to see what it turns out to be.

ACKNOWLEDGMENTS

This book would not exist without the love and support of my wife, Julina Tatlock: first reader, first responder—first everything, really. The help of several other early readers was also indispensable in refining this story: Samantha Gillison, Hilary Reyl, Alex Coulter, and Sarah Burnes. The deft hand of my editor, Jordan Pavlin, was essential in the final sculpting of these gargoyles. My agent, Julia Kardon, provided valuable feedback and passionate representation.

I am grateful to my parents, Jill Gill and Ardian Gill, whose love of words and belief in the value of making things made me what I am and this book what it is. In addition, the passion for New York's streetscape that my mother instilled in me is evident on every page. I am also thankful for the love and invigorating silliness of my wondrous children, Arden, Cormac, and Declan. And I am grateful to my sisters, Tracy and Claudia, for their unflagging support and keen eyes for period detail.

Ivan C. Karp, the founder of the Anonymous Arts Recovery Society, and Marilynn Gelfman Karp were pivotal figures in the development of this book. At their home and at their jewel box of a museum in Charlotteville, New York, Ivan regaled me with tales of gargoyle hunting and introduced me to scores of the myriad gargoyles saved by him and his merry band of scavengers back in the day. Of all the 1960s and '70s rescuers of New York architectural sculpture I interviewed, he was the most influential. Marilynn, over dinner with Ivan and Julina on West Broadway and later at the Karps' SoHo loft, introduced me to her concept of Poignant Repairs and showed me her collection, several items of which appear in this novel, mingled with objects of my invention. (Interested readers should investigate the concept further in her wonderful book, *In Flagrante Collecto,* from which some details of Zev's collection are drawn.) Timothy Allanbrook, a preservation architect and gargoyle wrangler who spent several years restoring the façade of the Woolworth Building beginning in the 1970s, was extremely generous with his time and expertise, sharing unpublished information and photographs of that restoration and walking my characters step-by-step around the crown of that remarkable building. Katherine Allen of Allen Architectural Metals and her colleagues, led by Chris Lacey, were equally generous in allowing a stranger off the street to climb with them up the side of a TriBeCa landmark to inspect the piece-by-piece dismantling of a nineteenth-century cast-iron building. New York architectural history authority Christopher Gray generously vetted the manuscript. Susan Weber-Stoger, a demographic expert at Queens College, analyzed 1970s census data for me, providing me with a clearer understanding of the landscape of my youth. Avram Ludwig joined me on a sea voyage to scout a certain untamed island off the Atlantic Coast, where he gamely helped me bushwhack through the forest, braving an empire of mosquitoes and poison ivy, to explore the colossal rusted carcass of an abandoned factory devastated by fire.

Some of the research that went into this novel was conducted for a feature published in *The Atlantic* that was kindly underwritten by James Bennet and edited by Timothy Lavin. Additional research was performed in the course of roaming New York for the City section of *The New York Times,* under the leadership of Connie Rosenblum, who gave me the great gift of letting me go wherever my curiosity took me. I have generally taken pains to respect history in this book but have occasionally compressed time or adjusted other elements to serve my purposes as a novelist.

Cast-Iron Architecture in America, by Margot Gayle and Carol Gayle, and *The Skyscraper and the City,* by Gail Fenske, were important sources. The works of Andrew Scott Dolkart, Oliver E. Allen, and Susan Tunick were also very helpful, as were interviews with Margot, Andrew, Susan, and Roy Suskin, manager of the Woolworth Building, who provided me with unpublished restoration diagrams and photographs, and guided me and my characters around the upper reaches of the Gothic cloudscraper. I also relied upon conversations, in person and online, among fellow lamenters of New York's incessant self-demolition.

My gratitude goes out as well to Anne and Bill Tatlock, Desmond Heath, Simeon Lagodich, Anna Hannon, Annie Proulx, Eleanor Gill Milner, Colum McCann, Gretchen Rubin, Mary Morris, Ethan Crenson, Amanda Alic, Paul Minden, Sebastian Heath, Alex Wright, Doug Liman, Michael Feigin, Samuel Langhorne Clemens, Roger and Rose Marie Hawke, Eric Rayman, Mary Ann Blase Howard, Marika Brussel, Robert Balder, the Brooklyn Writers Space, Scott Adkins, Erin Courtney, Jennifer Cody Epstein, Bettina Schrewe, Paul Slovak, Joanna Hershon, Hal Bromm, Mary Evans, Mary Gaule, Carol Willis, the Gill & Lagodich Fine Period Frame Gallery, Sonny Mehta, Nicholas Thomson, Carol Devine Carson, Kristen Bearse, Paul Bogaards, Ellen Feldman, Christine Gillespie, Katie Schoder, Sara Eagle, Anne-Lise Spitzer, and *everyone* at Knopf.

It is important to me, too, to toast the inspiring English and writing teachers who nurtured my love of language and story from elementary school to graduate school: Peg Summers and Carole France, both of whom saw something in me when I was a child and graciously took me under their wings; Lucy Rosenthal; and Mary La Chapelle. Thanks are also due to John F. Kelly for lending Griffin his red Puma Clydes.

Lastly, I extend my deepest thanks to the anonymous artists who came over from Europe in the nineteenth and early twentieth centuries and incised their visions into New York, transforming the streetscape of my hometown into a marvelously quirky public art gallery. Their imaginations fired mine.